JAGGED THORNS

THORN TRILOGY
BOOK 1

JANUARY JAMES

Jagged Thorns (Thorn Trilogy Book 1)

Copyright © 2023 by January James

All rights reserved.

This is a work of fiction. Names, characters, businesses, places, events and incidents are either the products of the author's imagination, or used in a fictitious manner.

Edit by Susan Barnes
Proofread and cover design by The Word Tank
www.januaryjamesauthor.com

In memory of Leslie
A true Blackpool illumination

AUTHOR'S NOTE

No sex please, we're British...

Just kidding! Well, about the first bit, not the bit about being British.

While these pages contain a fair amount of steam, I should probably point out before you dive in, that I'm a British author, writing about British people, in British settings. I occasionally use universal terms for things like 'elevators' and 'panties', but sometimes regional variations do sneak through. 'Gob-smacked' for instance, is a Britishism meaning 'lost for words', and I use it sometimes because it carries a greater punch (pun totally intended). 'Sex-hausted' on the other hand, is not a Britishism; I just made it up. I probably wasn't the first.

Now onto the triggers...
This is book 1 of a **gothic romance trilogy**. There are elements of darkness and some potential triggers including

blackmail, references to murder, drug use, chronic pain.

And please note, this book ends with a **MAJOR CLIFFHANGER**. Read at your own risk. You have been warned...

On that note, enjoy!

Prologue

*R*upert

I STOOD with my feet braced on the sullied gravel and watched the trucks disappear over the horizon, taking the last of the moonlight with them. I sucked in one last stinging drag of nicotine, almost punishing my own throat for watching this continue. I rarely smoked, but the more I saw of those trucks, the more I felt the urge to draw my own demise closer.

I blew out a long stream of smoke and watched it rise bleakly into the thick stench before flicking the butt to the floor and grinding it beneath my shoe. What was one more piece of ash when this whole place would one day go up in flames?

I sensed someone behind me and the nasal tutting told me exactly who it was. "You just going to stand out here sulking like a salty bitch?"

. . .

I PLASTERED a fake smile to my mouth and spun around to face my older brother. "Just making sure they've gone."

He rolled his eyes hatefully. They were small and sat too close together, almost touching the bridge of his nose, just like Father's. "The ferry's waiting. They'll be gone in less than ten minutes. So, I suggest you wipe away those little girl tears and get your scrawny ass home. Big day tomorrow."

I steadied my breath even though it was racketing to burst out of my lungs in a scream. "What's so special about tomorrow?"

He huffed like he was all out of patience with me, as usual. "The big announcement. Don't tell me you've forgotten. Oh, wait a minute, you've had your head stuck in the sand ever since I suggested it to the partners. Who were in unanimous agreement with my proposal."

"The tours," I stated. "I had hoped you and Father would have come to your senses. Clearly not." I raised my arms in a helpless shrug. "How can you not see that giving the general public access to an island that hasn't allowed anyone in for over a century, and the labs where the drug *du jour* is produced, isn't going to satisfy their curiosity, it will only *increase* it. It won't end with one tour."

"And why would that be a bad thing?" Ossian asked, a nauseating picture of innocence.

"Oh, right." I laughed bitterly. "That's what you want? Notoriety? Fame? To be the subject of national envy? I should have known." I needed no further proof of the narcissist that lingered barely disguised in the inner sanctum of my brother.

"No," he bit out, his frown battening his eyes into slits. "To increase the buzz for when we launch Bas 2.0."

I gritted my teeth. I hated the way he referred to the next generation of the drug we'd been selling to city boys and seedy politicians like it was some sort of technological advancement. It was not. It would be the exact same drug we'd always developed but mixed with other dubious pharmaceuticals to create something we didn't even understand. It made my skin crawl. Even the chemists we employed looked frighteningly uncomfortable about it.

"That won't happen for months. Maybe years. Maybe ever," I stated with confidence. I knew Father had been blinded by the success of Basidiomine, but he still had enough of his faculties to know we couldn't put the product of what was essentially an experiment in Class A narcotics on the market. Bas was largely plant-based, whereas Ossian's recent concoctions included chemicals that had been banned in some parts of the world. Father wouldn't allow it, I was sure.

Ossian kicked his head back and laughed. A nasal, clawing cackle that rang through my head like a pneumatic drill. "You know, Rupert. That's the difference between you and me. When I want something done, I don't waste time fretting over rules and rights and wrongs. I just get it fucking done. If we all worried about consequences, nothing would happen."

I swallowed the realisation he had zero morals. Something I'd always known but rarely heard him voice so blatantly. "Rules exist so we can be sure the product is safe."

Ossian slithered towards me, stopping just far enough away that I could see the brown edges of his teeth when he bared them. "No one cares if it's safe, little bro'. They only care that it *works*."

I didn't back away. Nothing about my older brother's physical presence frightened me. At six-foot-five I towered over him, and the weights I lifted every day without fail ensured I could flatten him with one blow. But it was his mind and the blatant evil it was capable of that scared me half to death. "Works at *what*?"

His breath cut like a knife across my face. "At making people *lethal*, Rupert. That's what. They think they can bring home trillion-dollar deals now? They think they can screw over the lobbyists and socialist wankers already? They haven't seen anything yet. Bas 2.0 is going to give them even more energy, clarity, courage, speed. They'll be able to work for *days*. Their wives will forget who they are and they'll be free to screw that perky-titted secretary over their desks again, and again, *and again*. Think Viagra for the body *and* the brain, little bro'. That's what this is."

I resisted the urge to throw up in his face and looked past him to the reason we were standing there – the glowing red-topped mushrooms sprouting from the ground like eerily grinning soldiers waiting to spear their next victim. I hated them. Ever since we discovered them growing on our land, and learned their effects when eaten, or dried, ground and snorted, the dynamics of our family, and its role on the island, became unrecognisable.

My glare panned back to my brother, meeting his own. "I don't agree with the tours, Ossian."

"Just as well you don't get a say then, isn't it? If you were more involved in the expansion or, fucks' sake, even just the day-to-day running of this place, then maybe – *maybe* – your opinion would count for more than shit. Anyway, you're two weeks too late to do anything about it.

We've already got recruiters searching for the right person to manage the tours."

I turned away, the black of night feeling more claustrophobic than ever. Ossian lingered, his pupils firing into my cheek leaving shards of shrapnel in their wake. Then, he slid backwards, withdrawing his bullet-like stare. "I'm leaving. You coming?"

I shook my head. "Going to finish up a few things inside."

Back was the suspicious stare and biting tone. "Like what?"

I lied smoothly. "I left some plans for the distillery in the office. I want to go through them tonight. May as well do it here while it's quiet."

His gaze assessed me one last time before he turned his back and flung open the door to the lab. "Make sure you tell security when you're leaving."

I didn't dignify his instruction with a response. I wasn't his lackey; I was his brother. Not that he'd ever treated me like one. To him, I was a stone in his shoe. A thorn in his side. Someone he resented for not being wholeheartedly invested in what he considered to be *his* business. But that was the problem. It wasn't his business. Thorn Pharmaceuticals belonged to our father, and Ossian and I were joint heirs to his estate.

Just like my father, Sinclair Thorn, and his younger brother Aro, Ossian and I would one day be the Chair and Vice Chair of the Consortium, a conglomerate of all the wealthiest families on the Isle of Crow. It was our birth right, simply because we were privileged enough to be born into the Thorn family – the oldest, richest and most influential family on the island. That meant I was destined to play second fiddle to my older brother for the rest of my life. Not a job I had particularly bought into. But the alternative – leaving him to run the place all by himself – was too abominable to think about.

Ossian was a law unto himself. He not only had no moral compass, he had no respect for human life. At least if I aimed my gun at someone it was mostly to get a fucking response. If Ossian aimed a gun at someone, it would likely be the last thing they ever saw. He couldn't be allowed to run this place without someone like me limiting the extent to which his evil would permeate the island and the people who'd lived on it for generations. It had to be me. No one else was close enough to know what he was doing, yet far enough away that they could throw the occasional grenade into his plans without being the suspected source.

I continued to breathe in the rotten dust the trucks had kicked up until I heard the tyres of Ossian's McLaren burning through the barbed gates. Then, I bypassed the offices and made my way straight to the labs.

"Good evening, sir," came a voice that led with confidence but tailed off with fear. It was the sort of voice I heard a lot.

I glanced down at the night watchman sitting behind the security desk. I didn't recognise him. He must have been one of Ossian's recruits. If he worked the night shift, the only time we ever took deliveries, Ossian would have got something to pin on him stored in his back pocket. No one ever got this job unless they could be NDA'd to within an inch of their life, and as a bonus, had a family whose lives could be threatened should they ever leak a whisper about our business.

I came to a stop in front of him and noted, first, the bracing of his chest, and second, his name badge. "Evening, Wilson." His eyes widened and the whites glowed, even in the clinical brightness of the lobby.

"Anyone in the lab?"

He shook his head and swallowed. "No, sir. It's all locked up." He nodded to the security panel before him. We didn't use keys. We had all manner of fingerprint and retina scans to control who entered each area. And then we had the master control board. It didn't matter if you had the correct fingertip or eyeball. If the control board battened down the hatches, no one was getting in.

"Unlock Lab One," I ordered.

He swallowed again. "I'm sorry, sir. No. I work for Mr. Ossian Thorn and I'm under strict instructions…"

"Unlock it," I repeated. "Now." I needed to get inside, not to see whatever progress Ossian had made on his so-called Bas 2.0, but to check on the progress of my own project. Despite my father's orders to abandon it long ago, I hadn't. We needed an alternative means of cultivating this drug, not just for the future of my family, but the future of this island. So, I'd kept it up in secret. It wasn't bearing fruit yet, but I wasn't giving up. I couldn't.

The man looked back at me with misplaced arrogance. Clearly, he hadn't got the memo on who I was and just how closely related to Ossian Thorn I happened to be. Holding his gaze I reached into my jacket, the back of my hand brushing against the smooth lining of my tailored suit. Then, I pointed my gun at his skull.

"Don't make me repeat myself again."

His fingers drummed against the desk as he fumbled to bring the screen to life, then he tapped it a few times, gulped, and looked up, not at me but at the barrel of my gun. "It's open," he whimpered.

I lowered the gun, slowly. "Next time," I said, firmly. "Just fucking do it."

He nodded sullenly, his face turning a cool shade of alabaster despite his petulance. I turned down the corridor towards Lab One, the soles of my shoes ringing loudly against the surrounding silence. During the day, the labs were a hive of activity. People in white coats bustled around with their hands full and heads down. People in suits scattered about with phones clasped to their ears, laptops balancing on their forearms. Almost as many security guards roamed the halls silently, always watching with their shoulders braced. But, in the dead of night, it was empty.

I held my face up to the scanner by the side of the lab door and placed my fingers on the pad at waist height. Just as the locks clicked open, I heard a voice. The hair on the back of my neck stood fiercely as I realised what the night watchman was doing. Turning silently, I retraced my steps towards the lobby, and sure enough, there he was, muttering into his mouthpiece. *Pick up, Mr. Thorn, sir. Pick up.* I knew Ossian wouldn't hear the call. He would be blasting death metal from his car stereo like it hadn't already been out of fashion for two decades.

I appeared at the side of the security desk but didn't wait for him to turn his head towards me. I aimed the gun at his right thigh and shot a bullet straight through it. An open-mouthed scream tore through his throat as he collapsed to the floor. He dragged himself to the other side of the desk, the searing pain choking his pleas. I followed him, my gun aimed at his other leg. As I passed the desk I pressed a button on the screen, ending the unanswered call to my older brother.

"Please…" he gasped. "Please… don't shoot again. Please… I'll do anything."

"Just like you'd do anything for my brother?" I asked.

"He… he told me… to report anybody… entering the labs…" His stutters gained in pitch and my eyes narrowed with each of his attempts to speak. I bent at the knees to bring myself face-to-face with the terror behind his eyes.

"You don't report a Thorn to *anyone*," I growled at him. "Do you understand?"

"I… but…"

"DO YOU UNDERSTAND?" I thundered. *How many fucking times?*

"Yes, sir. Yes… I'm s-sorry."

I straightened, my eyes still pinning him to the floor. "You will get back on that chair and complete your shift. When you finish, get yourself to a hospital. Tell them I sent you, and nothing else."

He nodded, slower this time, his eyes glazing over.

"I'm going back to the lab, then I'll see myself out." I turned to walk away then stopped and threw one last threatening glare over my shoulder at the blood streaming from his leg. "And clean that shit up. It's a laboratory for fuck's sake."

Chapter 1

*V*ivian

I SAT UP IN BED, dread flooding my chest like seawater flowing into the hull of a sinking ship. It wasn't a dream. It was my daylight nightmare. The sound of my sister's agonised moans coming from the next room. A sign she was in the depths of yet another onslaught of chronic pain. I leapt out of bed, ran past her door knowing she would be too far embedded in the tomb of agony to know I was even there, and sprinted to the kitchen. I ran a flannel under the cold tap and filled a glass with fresh water. I rummaged in the medicine drawer for some painkillers. After discarding several empty packets, my fingers landed on some Codeine. That would be marginally more effective, but even the prescription painkillers seemed to have lost their potency.

I PAUSED at her door to slow my breathing. Seeing my sister writhing about in so much pain never failed to whip the air from my lungs and pierce the corners of my eyes with pins. I couldn't let on how disturbed I felt. It was just the two of us. I was the only surviving family member she had. I had to be strong for her, no matter how weak I felt in the face of her illness.

I braced myself and pushed open the door. Bedding was strewn about the floor of her room and her head hung over the side of her mattress. She'd once said that the feeling of blood rushing to her crown was the only thing that distracted her from the screaming clench of spasming muscles. I sat on the bed, pulling her head onto my lap. She groaned with the movement. A sound echoing with the pain of childbirth, of torture, of despair. I bit back a cry of my own and laid the damp, cold flannel across her forehead. She stilled briefly while I stroked the tips of my fingers down her cheeks to soothe her. After a few minutes, I placed the tablets onto her tongue and let her take a few sips of water. Then, I laid her back against her pillows and watched as her eyes fluttered through whatever dreamland her pain had transported her to.

I looked at my watch. It was three a.m. I doubted I would get back to sleep. This was a frequent enough occurrence that I knew the drill. If I went back to bed I would toss and turn, thinking through all the treatments we'd already tried, wondering if we'd given up on them too soon. Then I'd drag out my laptop and start researching again. Maybe there was something we'd missed, or a new invention, a wonder drug discovered overnight. I still had hope. It was the only thing that kept me afloat.

Months ago, there were still things we hadn't tried. Water therapy, talking therapy, exercise programmes, prescription drugs, non-prescription drugs, TENS machines, massage treatments. Not anymore. We'd tried them all. So, instead of reliving the aftermath of my sister's moonlit episodes, I stayed with her. I stroked her cheeks and wiped my own. Soon, morning would come, and I wouldn't have to suffer this helplessness alone.

THAT MOMENT CAME hours later when I opened the door to the two most important people in our life. "Richard," I gushed, flinging my arms around the sixty-year-old man standing on the doorstep. "Thanks for coming." I pulled away and delicately encircled my arms around his wife. "Anna," I said, almost a whisper. "It's so good to see you."

Richard edged around us into the kitchen and switched on the kettle. I took Anna's hand, noticing how much smaller and more fragile it seemed, and seated her at the pine table my mum had owned for as long as I could remember.

I took the chair opposite and peered into her lashless eyes. "Is it over now? The chemo?"

She nodded slowly, fatigue dimming her usual effervescence.

Richard dropped three teabags into mugs before facing us. "Had her last session yesterday, didn't you, love?"

Anna raised what used to be her eyebrows in agreement. "How's Pegs?" she said, quietly. Even her voice had been beaten to bits by the cancer treatment.

I took a deep breath and noticed Richard stiffen,

readying himself for the continued bad news. "The same," I breathed out. "She had another episode last night."

"Have you spoken to the doctor again?" he asked.

I shrugged. "I've tried but I think they're avoiding my calls now."

"What about the local hospital? Have you tried taking her to the A&E?"

Richard brought the mugs of tea over and sat next to his wife. "I took her last month but we had to sit in a stifling hot waiting area for five hours before anyone saw us, and even then, they shooed us away with some more painkillers. I don't think I can put her through that again."

"Maybe you should call an ambulance," Anna suggested.

I shrugged again. "Believe it or not, I've tried that too, but when they hear it's just cramps, or back spasms, or headaches, they tell me to visit the doctor instead. It's hopeless."

"Have you thought about going back to work?" Anna asked. "Maybe some normality is what you both need."

I blew at the tea before taking a sip, then looked up. "I don't know what I'd do if she had a really bad episode and I wasn't here."

Richard and Anna glanced at each other, then Richard reached across the table and placed his hand over mine. "She could stay with us," he said, softly. "We've already talked about it, Anna and I. We're both retired, and you know you and Pegs mean the world to us."

"And I could do with the distraction," Anna added. "You know, having someone to look after besides myself. And this one." She nudged Richard's elbow fondly, and not for the first time, my heart pulsed with yearning for what they had.

I remembered the exact moment Richard and Anna came into our lives. It was one year after our mum had passed, leaving me at the age of nineteen to be the sole guardian of my younger sister, then fourteen. They took us under their wing. Richard did DIY around the house, Anna cooked for us, even teaching me to make her signature dish, sausage and white bean casserole. I'd come to love them like they were grandparents, and whenever Peggy was conscious, she would say the same thing too.

Anna's cancer diagnosis broke all our hearts. Peggy had already been suffering from chronic pain but when Anna was diagnosed, the episodes simply got worse. We'd understandably seen less of them both, and when my temporary contract at the PR agency came to an end, I didn't look for another job. I couldn't bear to leave Peggy alone.

"You don't have to answer now," Richard smiled. "Think about it. You're too young to let your life pass you by while you care for your sister. Especially when we can do that for you." His eyes narrowed on me with intent. "You know I will guard her with my life, Viv, love. You *know* that."

"I know," I whispered, the two of us acknowledging a past we didn't like to talk about anymore.

Another knock at the door broke the subdued silence, and the person at the other side positively shattered it.

"Vivi!"

The second I opened the door, my best friend smothered me. All gangly arms, legs and emo-clothed enthusiasm. "It's been toooooo long!"

I shot an apologetic glance at Richard and Anna while peeling Emerie's arms from around my neck. "It's been two days."

"Well, it feels like… Ricardo and Annabaloo!"

More squeals escaped her lips as she dove round me to clasp both of their shoulders in a somewhat impractical group hug. "Oh my God! Now, it really *has* been ages since I last saw you two." She took Anna's face in her hands. "We have to go wig-shopping, Anna. You could really rock pink, you know…" Anna blushed that very colour as she allowed herself to be swept up in Emerie's enthusiasm. "Or, wait… *violet*. Yes! It would match your eyes. It would make you look even more beautiful, if that were possible."

"Tea, Em?" Richard asked, getting to his feet, possibly by means of escape. Emerie quickly took his seat.

"Would love one," she replied, then turned to me. "So, what's new? What's not? How's Pegs?" I would never get enough of my best friend. She never just walked into a room, she bounced. For all her dark clothes, thick eyeliner and skull tattoos, she was the brightest, happiest, most self-less human I'd ever met. The worst emo in the world.

"Not much change," I said, mustering a little bright-ness. I wanted to feast on her happiness, not bring it down. "She was up again last night."

"Ah, Vivi." She clasped a hand to my cheek with such kindness, the temptation to break down in tears was considerable. "I take it she's in bed now? Sleeping it off?"

I nodded and sipped my tea again in a bid to ward off an emotional breakdown.

"Wow, Vivi." She lowered her voice. "She's been in

bed the last few times I've seen you. In fact, I haven't seen her up and about for weeks."

I nodded again and fielded the same questions Richard and Anna had asked. Yes, I'd called the doctor. Yes, I'd tried A&E. Yes, I'd even called an ambulance.

Emerie persisted. "And there's really no other medication you can try?"

I shook my head. "I'm pretty sure I've researched it all."

Richard delivered another mug of tea for Emerie then pressed both his hands to the table, a serious expression settling on his face. "There *is* one we haven't considered…"

"What's that?" I asked, hopefully.

His eyes surveyed each of us before he shrugged and straightened. "Basidiomine."

Anna's brow reflected the same blank I had drawn, but Em's eyes widened, the way they did whenever she stumbled across an ingenious idea.

"Basidi-what?" I asked.

"The city boy drug," Em replied breathily, her voice filled with the implication she wished she'd thought of it first.

"The designer drug? The one bankers and politicians are all micro-dosing? Isn't it like some kind of psychedelic?"

"It's made from mushrooms," Em explained, "and in certain quantities it can be used as a stimulant, a confidence booster. But used in other ways there's speculation it can do all sorts of things. Help anxiety, depression… *pain*."

I glanced up at Richard who was nodding, seemingly deep in thought.

"Ok," I rushed out, looking between the two of them. "How do I get it?"

"Well, that's the tricky part," Richard replied. "It's in very short supply and even higher demand. According to the articles I've read, it goes to the highest bidders and the greatest influencers, which tend to be rich city boy bankers and politicians."

"And the landed gentry?" I asked with a snort.

"Well, they could have it if they wanted it," Richard replied. "They could certainly afford it. But they don't need to work, and that's where it seems to be in demand. It boosts peoples' confidence, makes them feel invincible. It gives them energy so they can work long hours and still think clearly. I read that the drug has even made its way to Silicon Valley where people work all hours trying to create the next Google, or Uber, or whatever."

My shoulders slumped. For a moment there, I thought perhaps there was another option. Hope had returned to my thrumming heart, only to evaporate upon hearing how impossible this drug was to get hold of. "Where does it come from?" I asked weakly.

Richard's reply was not what I was expecting. "Somewhere up in Scotland."

"Really? It's made in the U.K.?"

"As far north of the U.K. as you can possibly get. It comes from that island where all the big billionaires live." He squeezed his eyes closed and clipped the bridge of his nose between his fingers. "What's it called?"

"Oh, wait, I remember," Em cut in. "The Isle of Crow."

Richard pointed a quick finger at Emerie. "Yes! That's the place. Isle of Crow. God, my memory is getting worse."

I glanced back at Emerie whose face was scrunched up as if trying to recall something. "I only remember because I read something about it the other day at work."

"That doesn't sound good," I mumbled. Emerie worked as a lobbyist for a sea life charity. It was sort of how we'd met. We both studied public relations at university. She'd branched out into public affairs, while I'd splintered off into consumer PR. Despite my eventual 'selling-out', we'd bonded over our passion for the environment, our love of nature. Instead of spending our weekends getting shitfaced down the local students union bar, we went camping anywhere we could. Sure, there was still alcohol involved, and late night skinny dipping in freezing cold rivers with boys we met along the way, but our lives were spent outdoors in the lashing rain and beating sun, not teetering across the beer-soaked floors of sweaty nightclubs. Emerie now spent her days campaigning against organisations that threatened the health of our seas. If the Isle of Crow had passed across her desk, it probably wasn't for good reason.

She continued as if she was conversing with herself. "Something to do with the North Sea... We want access to the islands around Crow, but... that's it!" She looked up, her face alight. "They don't usually let anyone on to the island, but they've given some of our guys special dispensation to visit the south-westerly coastline. Apparently, they're being slightly less precious about it now because they're going to be opening up the island to visitors soon anyway..."

I held up a hand. "Wait a minute. Is this the same island where there are more billionaires per square mile than anywhere else in Europe?"

Em gulped down a mouthful of tea. "Yup."

"Isn't it notoriously private? Hasn't allowed anyone to visit for, well, ever?"

She nodded. "The very same. That's where this drug comes from. It's made from mushrooms that only grow there, apparently. And…" She paused dramatically and ran her eyes across each of us. "If I remember correctly, they're trying to hire someone on the downlow to lead tours on the island."

Richard drew another chair and sat down. "Are you sure?"

Em pulled out her phone and swiped the screen. "I'll check my emails, but I'm pretty sure that's what I read."

While Emerie scrolled, Richard and Anna turned to me. "If they are recruiting, Viv, you should go for it," Richard said, wide-eyed.

"Why?" I said in a half-laugh, half-cough. "So I can get the drug for Pegs?" The smile slid from my face the longer they stared at me. "*So I can get the drug for Pegs*," I repeated, slowly.

"Why are they opening their doors now?" Anna said, turning to Emerie.

"Well, it has to be because of the drug, right?" Em replied, without looking up from her scrolling. "Interest in it has skyrocketed. Everyone wants a piece of the island, and the whole operation has been so secretive up to now. Maybe they're bowing under pressure to let people see how it's made. Ah! Here it is."

We all leaned forward, holding our breath as she read

through the email. "We can permit up to two people... yada yada... no cameras... yada yada... going to be establishing some tours... there will be a significant cost attached. Ah, that's it. They're going to let our team visit but they'll be kept on a tight leash because tickets for these tours are going to go for a pretty penny. They need to maintain a sense of exclusivity."

She continued. "It says here they've hired a recruitment consultant to find the right person. Grimm, Burns and Mathers. Heard of them?"

We all shook our heads.

"Well," Em grabbed a notepad from the middle of the table and started scribbling. When she finished, she pushed it towards me. "Here's the number. I suggest you give them a call."

My eyebrows shot up. "You're serious?"

Emerie held my surprised stare as she slid her phone back into her pocket. "As serious as a precariously attached toenail."

"Remember what we said, Viv, love." Anna took my hand in hers. "If you need to go back to work, we'll look after Peggy. We would love to. You know we don't have children of our own. She's like a daughter to us. Both of you are."

I looked up at Richard, expecting to see the same reassuring gaze and sympathetic head nod, but what greeted me was something entirely different. His face was seared with determination, his pupils burning.

"Do it, Viv," he urged. "You've got nothing to lose."

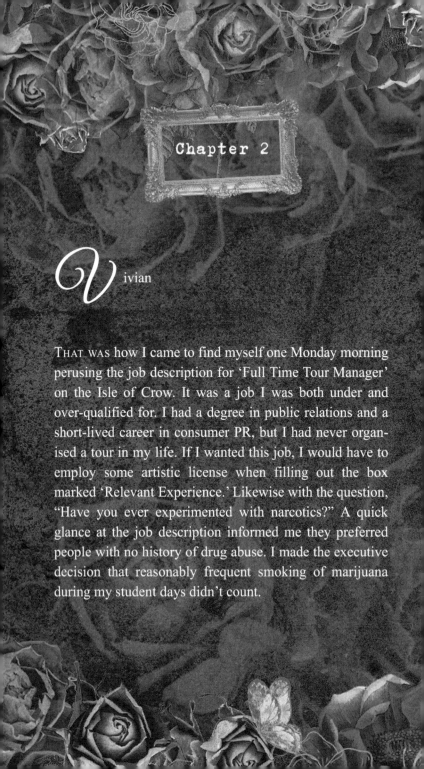

Chapter 2

*V*ivian

THAT WAS how I came to find myself one Monday morning perusing the job description for 'Full Time Tour Manager' on the Isle of Crow. It was a job I was both under and over-qualified for. I had a degree in public relations and a short-lived career in consumer PR, but I had never organised a tour in my life. If I wanted this job, I would have to employ some artistic license when filling out the box marked 'Relevant Experience.' Likewise with the question, "Have you ever experimented with narcotics?" A quick glance at the job description informed me they preferred people with no history of drug abuse. I made the executive decision that reasonably frequent smoking of marijuana during my student days didn't count.

As I RAN my eyes down the application form I spotted another question I would have to answer with an outright lie. 'Do you have any family responsibilities?' *Um, well, I am sole carer to a younger sister who currently can't get herself out of bed in the morning and has nothing at all to do with the fact I desperately want this drug.* Another glance at the description told me they preferred someone with no family responsibilities, who could dedicate themselves to the island for an entire twelve-month period. That was fine by me. So long as the postal system worked and I could get some of this wonder drug back home to my sister, they could have my dedication all they wanted.

I completed the form and emailed it back to *Mr. Jonathon Mathers, Esq.* then made my way up to Peggy's bedroom. She was sitting up, her back cushioned against heaps of soft downy pillows. I'd maxed out my credit card getting as much comfortable bedding as I could, hoping it might help her to sleep or relax, which might help with the pain. It hadn't shown any signs of helping, only a suggestion that I needed to get a job of some kind, sharpish, so I could pay for said bedding.

"How are you feeling?" I asked, tentatively. She smiled and the whole of my insides melted. That smile had become so rare I wanted to capture it in resin so I could hold onto it forever.

"Much better, Vivi. I'm coming out the other side. I feel almost normal again."

I climbed into bed next to her and squeezed my arm around her shoulders. "Is that how it feels?" I asked, quietly. "Like you're in a dark tunnel and you're travelling through it, then at some point you begin to see the light again?"

She rested her head against mine. "It's a bit like that. I don't picture it as a tunnel though. More like a mountain I have to climb over."

She dragged in a shaky breath.

"What is it?" I mouthed, my lips against her hair.

"That's what scares me the most, Vivi. The mountain."

Something inside me stilled, as though my body was trying to stop time so I wouldn't have to hear what scared my sister more than a debilitating back spasm. "What about it?"

"Each time I have an episode…" Her breath stuttered from her chest. "The mountain gets bigger." My blood froze at her words. "It gets harder to climb. I worry that one day… I won't have the strength to reach the top… to get to the other side."

I tugged her closer and kissed the top of her head. "You're stronger than you think, Pegs," I whispered. "You feel tired now because you've just battled through that pain. But just wait and see. You'll be back to full strength in no time."

She hugged me back but something about her embrace felt hollow. "Until the next episode comes along."

The lump in my throat expanded, making it hard to breathe, let alone speak. We sat in silence for a few minutes, clinging to each other. Then, eventually, Peggy spoke.

"Did you fill out the application form?"

I nodded. "M-hm."

"You think they'll buy your embellished tourism experience?" she chuckled.

"I hope so. I Googled tourism jargon and Em sent me a

tour strategy document she found somewhere. Hopefully, what I've written sounds authentic."

"What if they try to follow up with references?"

I took a sobering breath. "I guess I'll cross that bridge if it happens."

Peggy twisted herself around so she could shine her pale blue eyes into mine. "I'm so lucky to have a sister like you, Vivi."

I closed my eyes and kissed her forehead. I wasn't sure she'd say the same if she knew I'd just lied about having a sister at all. I didn't want to take any risks. Perhaps the fact I was an orphan (as far as *I* knew) and completely free of all family ties (as far as I wanted *them* to know) would make me stand out as a prime candidate. I could only hope. "Well, that's lucky, because you're stuck with me," I replied, pulling her back into my arm.

Before she had a chance to argue, my phone buzzed in my pocket. I swiped it open to look at the email that had just arrived.

From: Mr. Jonathon Mathers, Esq.
Subject:RE: Application for Job Ref 90119

Dear Ms. Gillespie,

Thank you for your recent application for the role of Tour Guide based on the Isle of Crow, Scotland. Your experience is exactly what the hiring manager is looking for and we would like to interview you on their behalf this week. Time is of the essence as they wish the position to be filled as soon as possible. Please let me know your availability.

Sincerely,
J. Mathers

"What is it?" Peggy asked.

"The recruiter," I replied, shockwaves fluttering through my veins. *That was fast.* "They want to meet me this week."

"That's amazing news!" To my further surprise, Peggy got to her knees and placed her hands on my shoulders, her wide smile making me feel optimistic for the first time in a long time. "Get back to them right away. See them as soon as possible. Don't wait, Vivi. This is the opportunity of a lifetime."

"I don't know about that…" I started, but her warning stare shut me up.

"It's the Isle of Crow, Viv." She paused to let her words sink in. "The most secretive and mysterious place on the planet. It *is* the opportunity of a lifetime."

———

LATER THAT WEEK I helped Peggy downstairs to sit on the sofa. Em was coming round and Pegs was desperate to see a face other than mine. Only minutes after I had her settled with a cup of tea and a blanket across her knees, a knock came at the door. Without waiting for me to open it, Em rushed in and made a beeline for the living room. She practically threw herself on my sister, hugging and kissing her like she might suddenly evaporate. In the midst of it all, Richard also appeared, having walked through the door Em had left wide open in her haste to see Peggy.

"It's a good thing the most valuable item in your

kitchen is your eight-year-old Kenwood toaster," he tutted. "Someone could've had a field day with all that free access to your house."

"Sorry Richard," Em squeaked. "My fault."

"She just got here," I shrugged, turning back to inhale more of my sister's beaming face. No one cheered her up quite like Emerie, which only made me love my best friend even harder.

Richard leaned in to peck Peggy on the cheek.

"How's Anna?" she asked.

"She's on the mend, Pegs, on the mend. How are you?"

Her face fluttered as she fixed a convincing expression to it. It would have been noticeable to no one but me. "I'm okay, thanks. The pain's not so bad today."

"Well, Vivi here might be the key to your cure," Emerie sang, elbowing me in the ribs with a grin.

"Let's not get our hopes up," I cautioned. "So, the interview went well. Doesn't mean I've got the job. I bet thousands applied for it."

Emerie sank onto the sofa next to Peggy. "I doubt it. They didn't advertise it much, just used that recruitment place. So, come on. What exactly did they say to you? I want every detail."

Richard perched on the arm of the sofa, so I sank onto the shag pile rug and crossed my legs.

"Ok, where do I start?" I mused, almost to myself.

"Who did you meet?" Em asked, wriggling impatiently. "Anyone from the island?"

A light frown descended on my brow as I recalled it. "No. I just met Mr. Mathers. He was nice, normal, bit salesy. It was all pretty standard as far as interviews go. Although, there were some questions I found quite odd."

Em jumped on this information. "Like what?"

"Well, for a start, they asked to see my medical records. They want evidence that all my vaccines are up to date."

Richard's nose wrinkled. "Which vaccines? Flu? Tetanus?"

"Everything. They threw a bunch of acronyms at me, which I wrote down. If I'm offered the job, I have to prove I've had all of them. They were weirdly adamant about it."

All three looked at me expectantly.

"Oh, right. Let me grab my notebook."

I returned from the kitchen to face their strangely unchanged bug-eyed expressions and read the notes I'd made. "MMR – that's Measles, Mumps, Rubella. I've had that. PCV – something I can't even pronounce…"

"Pneumococcal conjugate vaccine," Richard stated, quickly, while rotating his hand for me to move on.

"W—wait…" I questioned.

"I have a wife with stage three cancer. You learn these things. Carry on."

"And BCG," I concluded.

"What's that?" Em directed the question at Richard because I clearly had no idea.

"Tuberculosis," he replied.

"Wow, they really are particular about who travels there, aren't they?" Em asked. "Will paying visitors need the vaccines too?"

"They said no because the visitors wouldn't be in contact with many people and will be limited to a small number of sites during the tour."

"Do you think they bought your 'experience'?" Em smirked.

Nerves sparked in my chest as I recalled the blatant lies that came out of my mouth when recounting my work 'history.' "I think so. I guess time will tell if it was enough."

"What else did he say?" Richard asked.

"Well, they were very clear I would have to sign a complex non-disclosure agreement, and I had to be super transparent about my family and friends situation. I think they want to be sure I'm not going to get homesick halfway through the contract and leave them without a tour manager."

"Did they mention the drug at all?" Peggy asked, hopefully.

I sighed out a lungful of air. "Only that it was the reason why interest has been so piqued. I didn't press them too hard on its availability. I thought I better wait and see if I can get there first."

Silence descended as we each pondered the implications of my possibly getting the job, until I remembered the cake I'd bought earlier. I jumped to my feet. "Anyone for Death by Chocolate?"

Em tipped her head to one side. "Does a bear shit in the woods?"

"Well, that's kind of put me off chocolate," I muttered, leaving the room.

We were halfway through giant slices of cake when my phone buzzed. We all looked around at each other. "Well, Anna's asleep," Richard shrugged, then raised his eyebrows accusingly at me. "Do you have other friends?"

I shot him a glare as I picked up my phone and stared at the screen. "It's them," I whispered. "The recruiters."

"Answer it, Viv!" Em said, dropping her cake to the plate and slurping on her fingers.

I took a deep breath and put the phone to my ear. "Vivian Gillespie."

"Ah, Miss Gillespie. It's Jonathan Mathers here, from Grimm, Burns and Mathers."

I looked up at the three pairs of eyes staring at me, unblinking. "Yes, hello. How are you?"

"I'm very well, thank you. I have some wonderful news."

I gently laid my plate on the rug and took a deep, sobering breath.

"My client is delighted to offer you the role of Tour Manager for the Isle of Crow. Congratulations, Miss Gillespie."

I pressed a chocolatey hand to my chest and cleared my throat. "That's… um, that's fantastic. Thank you."

Through the haze I could just about make out Emerie nodding feverishly and Richard brandishing two big thumbs up. Peggy's face was unreadable.

"They would like you to start as soon as possible. That is, if you are happy to accept?"

"Yes!" I gasped. "Yes, of course, I accept. How soon are they talking?"

"Monday, if that works for you?"

My vision cleared as I stared in disbelief at my friends and sister. "That's in three days."

"Yes, Miss Gillespie. But the employers have assured me your transport and everything on the island will be taken care of. They will make sure you have everything you need to do the job. All you have to do is turn up." Mr. Mathers sounded very pleased with himself, no doubt visualising the commission coming his way.

My silence must have spoken volumes.

"You did say you had no other commitments, Miss Gillespie…"

I noted the biting edge to his tone.

"No professional or personal matters to attend to. So, other than the vaccinations you are required to have, we were led to believe you could commit fully and quickly."

"Um, yes…" I gushed, hurtling suddenly out of my shocked stupor. "That's right. You're absolutely right. Monday it is, then."

My eyes moved to Peggy's just before she covered up her fearful gaze with an optimistic smile. Despite her determination I try to get this job, I could tell the reality of me leaving was going to be hard on her. But she was the reason I was doing this. I wouldn't do it for anyone else, no matter how mysterious and alluring the island was made out to be.

I ended the call, dropped the phone to my lap and looked up at the faces eagerly awaiting confirmation. I took a deep breath and hardly believed the words as they left my mouth.

"Well, that's that, then. I'm off to the Isle of Crow."

Chapter 3

Vivian

I CLASPED the headphones to my ears and clutched my skirt tight to my knees. What was I thinking wearing a flippy-flappy dress to ride a helicopter across the North Sea? If the walk across the tarmac hadn't been perilous enough with the propeller wind gifting me with a tsunami of Marilyn moments in the space of sixty seconds, the breeze funnelling through the cabin ensured I wore a permanent blush. If only I'd worn a pair of inky dinky shorts instead of an even inkier-dinkier thong. And if only the entire crew on and off the ground was female, instead of red-blooded, hard-bodied male.

I'd done my research, or as much as I could considering there was very little record online of the people who lived on the Isle of Crow.

I'D READ the strict dress code outlined in the employment contract, and hastily pulled together a wardrobe I thought would be commensurate with the accepted fashions of the island. Which was why I was travelling in a dress and high-heeled, very expensive shoes. Indeed, wearing a dress for the first time since I was about seven, and high-heeled, very expensive shoes for the first time in my *life*. I considered myself fortunate to have made it across the tarmac without falling on my face.

I fished in my jacket pocket for a hairband and managed to scrape my hair back one-handed. Then, before I could relax into pre-flight excitement, we were in the air. The noise was deafening *with* the headphones, let alone without. There would be no talking during the flight – not that there was anyone to talk to. It was just me and the pilot. Apparently, I would be met on the island by a chaperone and taken directly to meet Mr. Sinclair Thorn.

The Isle of Crow had famously been a billionaire's playground for the better part of a century, so I imagined mansions and manor houses stretching for as far as the eye could see, and maybe some smaller housing for those people who kept the island's services running. I would be one of those people. The lesser species. I snorted at the thought.

As much as I was opposed to their drug distribution strategy, I was curious about the billionaires and the lives they led, and keen to see the paradise they'd created on this little island that had been cut off from the mainland for so long. I wanted to see the landscape, learn about its flora and fauna, observe the wildlife, meet the locals. I was excited to see how it had been nurtured and preserved. So much natural beauty was being eradicated in the United

Kingdom – the hedgerows, the parks, the woodlands – and
with eye-watering pace. I couldn't wait to see an island
unaffected by development and industry.

As we reached the edge of land and flew over the sea, I
leaned into the window, hungry to see the island I was
about to make my home for the next twelve months. But I
saw nothing except a vast expanse of water. I checked my
phone and brought up the last update. I'd had several from
Jonathon, all assuring me my belongings had landed, my
paperwork had been processed and my accommodation
and transport finalised. It was all disarmingly organised.

My mind wandered and before I knew it, a voice came
through my headset. The pilot was announcing our
descent. I looked down and focused on the land now
beneath us, and released a slow breath. I hadn't seen countryside that shade of green before. It was dark yet vivid,
humming with an understated vitality. The trees swayed
like lazy smiles in a soft breeze. The sea surrounding the
edges was a rich turquoise – not the murky, dirty grey-blue
I was used to seeing around our coasts. I saw the occasional building but we were still too high in the sky for me
to ascertain whether they were mansions or houses of
similar grandeur.

I swallowed as we descended, trying to maintain some
physical equilibrium. The closer we got to the ground, the
less I could see, but it didn't matter because I was blinded
by the excitement of being about to step foot on what may
as well as have been hallowed ground.

We landed slowly on a patch of tarmac surrounded by
harshly manicured lawns. I devoured as much as I could
while I waited for the propellers to slow down. Even with
the engine off and the headset removed, my ears continued

to ring and probably would for a few hours. The pilot made no move to exit the helicopter so I stayed put too. Then, a gentleman in a perfectly fitted midnight-coloured suit strode up to the helicopter door, opened it and held out a hand. I took it gratefully and stepped down to the tarmac, relieved the lack of breeze meant I didn't have to clutch my skirt as though it were a life raft. What I wouldn't have given for a pair of butter-soft leggings and my Doc Marten boots.

Another long, sleek black car waited across the tarmac. I nodded my thanks to the suited gentleman and slid, as delicately as I could, onto the soft leather seat, and folded my stocking-clad legs and stiletto heels inside the footwell. The door closed with a gentle *thunk* and the man climbed into the driver's seat. He turned and presented me with a wide, welcoming smile.

"Good morning, miss. My name's Archie McFadden. I'll be driving you to meet Mr. Thorn. Welcome to the island."

As tricky as the manoeuvre looked, he extended a hand between the front seats for me to shake, which I did with a giggle. I took in the lines around his eyes and brow, and the smattering of silver hair around his temples and hazarded a guess that he was in his late forties. His eyes sparkled and his smile seemed too generous to not be natural. If anyone could make me feel at home in a strange place, I decided, it would be him.

"Pleased to meet you, Mr. McFadden. I'm Vivian Gillespie. My friends call me Viv."

"Well, then, Viv, you must call me Archie. And I will be your tour guide for the next hour and a half."

"Hour and a half?" Stupidly, I had expected the island

to be so small that everything was situated within a half hour radius.

"That's right, miss. I mean, Viv…" He grinned into the rear view mirror. "Sir Thorn lives in the highlands, ninety minutes from the coastline. Up on a hill in his castle, like all great Scots."

"But, Sir Peregrine Thorn isn't Scottish, is he?" I asked, feeling proud to have done my research.

"You're correct there, miss. No, he isn't. He's a cockney lad, through and through. But his boys were all born here. Not that you'd know it. They speak like they're heirs to the English throne, you know?" I could tell by his tone his comment came from a place of pride.

"He has two sons, is that right?" I asked. "Sinclair and Aurelias?"

"That's correct, miss. Sinclair is the eldest. He runs Thorn Pharmaceuticals. Aurelias – or Aro as everyone calls him – has a number of travel businesses. He's away a lot. A boy done real good."

"I understand Mr. Sinclair Thorn is my new boss."

"That he is, miss. And a better boss you will never meet." I noticed his eyes flicked away from the mirror as he delivered that last line. It sounded rehearsed. Almost as though he was being watched.

"How long have you lived here, Archie?" I asked, as we pulled off the tarmac onto a narrow road flanked by herbaceous borders, I took deep breaths, inhaling the car's deep wood and rich leather fragrance, and watched as the scenery changed from heavily clipped vegetation to wild, unkempt forest. My heart pulsed at the welcome sight and I felt instantly privileged to be seeing this as-yet unaffected island in all its natural, unmanicured glory. It was early

March—almost Spring—and where I had expected an island bursting with colour, what I got was a rich darkness filled with raw, untouched, dew-drenched nature. It was nothing short of breath-taking.

"I've lived here all my life, just like my father, and his father, and his father before that. My family was here even before the rich arrived."

"That must have been quite a change," I said.

"It was. A welcome one too. Until then, we were just another Scottish island, getting by on agricultural exports. When the rich arrived, the roads were flattened, we got better jobs, better housing, better places to shop. Now, we're more than just farmers. I mean, you just have to look at me. I'm a special assistant to a Thorn, a *billionaire*. If I told that to someone on the mainland, if I were to ever go there, that would get me places, you know?"

I nodded. It absolutely would. Through all the research I'd carried out, the one unequivocal discovery I'd made was that the Thorn family was revered. Famous. For reasons good and bad. They may have generated the bulk of their recent fortune off the soil of the island, but their influence extended way beyond. Peregrine, in fact, had made his millions in banking. His father had set the stage building unprecedented wealth through the import and export industry. Success, it seemed, ran in their blood. But their notoriety also preceded them. While the right-wing press covered their endless gains, the left exposed dirty dealings, tax evasion and rumours of mafia-style threats and manipulation. How much of it was true was the question no one could answer. And it was that ambiguity that burdened my shoulders as we edged closer to the heart of the island.

"Do you go to the mainland often?" I asked.

Almost a minute and several tight, hairy clifftop turns passed before he answered. "Never, miss."

I swallowed my surprise and replied with as much nonchalance as I could muster. "Why's that?"

Another minute passed, despite the road ahead now being straight and open. "Never wanted to, miss."

That didn't make sense to me. If he was so sure he could have got pretty much anything he wanted on the mainland just by being a trusted servant to the Thorn family, why hadn't he tested the theory?

"It is a beautiful place, from what I've seen so far. I can understand why you wouldn't want to leave." I smiled, kindly, in a bid to ease his suddenly tense shoulders. I hadn't intended to make him uncomfortable.

Back on safer ground, he smiled up at the rear view mirror. "Precisely. My heart is on this island. My ancestors are buried here. This place is all my children know…"

"How many children do you have? I enquired, politely.

"Three, miss." He paused before continuing. "We were blessed with four, but we lost our son at five weeks."

I gulped back a gasp. "I'm so sorry."

"It's ok. It was a few years ago now, and we are so lucky to have our girls."

"What happened? If you don't mind me asking."

"No, not at all. He was born with severe respiratory problems. If he'd lived, he would have needed a lot of medical support his whole life." I watched his gaze lengthen down the road we were travelling. "Funny thing was, he was the third boy that year to be born with that condition."

"I can't imagine how that must have felt," I said. "I really am so sorry for your loss."

He held my eyes in the mirror for a few seconds. "Thank you, miss. Our girls keep us so busy it takes our mind off our loss."

I transferred my gaze out of the window. We were up high, affording us an almost panoramic view of the hilltops descending to the turquoise sea. "The coastline on our approach was stunning," I said. "I think it was the southern tip."

"Oh, yes. That will be the Sunken Glade. It's called that because it used to be much higher on the hill. If you follow the land to the bottom, there's a petrified forest at sea level."

"A what?"

"Forest fossils. Thousands of years old."

"Amazing," I breathed out in wonderment. "I can't wait to see."

"Ah, now that, you won't be able to do, miss."

"Oh. Why not?" I asked, not disguising my disappointment.

"Landslides have been reported in that area. It's not considered safe to go there anymore. It's Thorn soil so they've closed it off. A real shame, but it's for everyone's safety."

"Hmm," I mused. "That is a shame."

I resumed my gaze out at the dramatic landscape and allowed myself to become hypnotised by it until thirty minutes had passed and I realised we had yet to see an actual building. Just as the thought entered my head, a large stone wall appeared. Beyond it, I could just make out a majestic structure rising out of the grounds. A mansion.

The first I'd laid eyes on, and it didn't disappoint. Dark stone façade, hundreds of heavily-curtained windows, ball-shaped olive trees and entrance steps presided over by two enormous stone lions. Giant, ancient oak trees surrounded it, and from what I could see through the vast iron gate, preened gardens, voluptuous plants and reflective fish ponds decorated its circumference. I released a slow breath through pursed lips. It finally hit me where I was. I was in the richest part of the British Isles, home to the lauded one percent, ultimate playground of the billionaire. The house – or home – we just passed was the norm. I wasn't sure I would ever get used to seeing that.

Another half hour and a handful of imposing homes later, Archie turned off the main road and pulled up to an enormous gate. Bigger than those before it. It towered over the car, almost prison-like. "Here we are, miss," he announced proudly.

We waited an age for it to slowly creak open, then we ambled at a leisurely pace up a long winding driveway bordered by more ancient oaks and sycamore trees, their branches hanging lazily over the grey gravel.

The covered darkness felt starkly different to the light of the main road and I suddenly missed the illusion of warmth. Then, as the car finally slowed, I looked ahead through the windshield and felt my breath catch in my throat.

We reached the top of the half mile-long drive and swept around in a circle putting the passenger side in direct line to a giant black double door. Even as I craned my neck, my eye line still didn't reach the top of the building.

This stately home was more repellent than inviting, its once-pale yellow limestone walls now a soot-sodden grey.

The slate-tiled roof was dull like charcoal, absorbing whatever sunlight made it thus far through the canopy of leaves. Topping off the haunting view were actual turrets, black as night, and decaying window frames doing nothing to temper the overall sense of foreboding. It was the architectural equivalent of a sneer.

I was no expert but I knew enough about history to spot designs from certain periods, but this house didn't seem to fit anywhere. Like it was older than time itself. There was a grotesqueness about it, like it should have belonged in Gotham City.

The passenger door opened and I thanked McFadden for the informative ride. I stepped out in as ladylike a manner as I could, and tried not to shudder at the sound of blistering gravel beneath my feet. A doorman dressed in black wearing a top hat and tailcoat with gold trim materialised from the frontage's many shadows. He smiled and pulled one of the giant doors towards him. "Good morning, ma'am. Welcome to Blackcap Hall."

I forced a confident smile and stepped past him into an echoey entrance hall with unfathomably high ceilings. It was as dark as the womb of a cave, and my eyes took a few long seconds to adjust. At the far end of the hall was a wide staircase made of mahogany and lined with a crimson runner. At the foot of it were two polished black console tables, each topped with a glass vase overflowing with hothouse lilies. Despite their voluptuousness, and the splintering gleam that bounced off every object d'art in the hall, all I could smell was dust and decay.

"This way, ma'am," the doorman said, leading me towards a doorway to the right. I followed dutifully, gulping as we entered a long, thin, unlit corridor lined with oil paintings of men and women I didn't recognise. Our footsteps echoed eerily as we walked the length of it.

"Where are we going?" I asked, my eyes darting about, trying unsuccessfully to locate an escape route other than the main door.

"The east wing, ma'am. To Mr. Sinclair Thorn's office."

We turned into a room that, thanks to a few long, thin windows, was made fractionally lighter. It was sizable, absorbing the sounds of only a handful of men and one eccentric-looking woman sitting in wingback chairs discussing what appeared to be very serious business. The wood-panelled walls cast a darkness that made it feel more like evening, but the tinkling of a tea tray gave a classic reminder it was still very much morning.

I followed the sound to a corner of the room where a maid was pouring hot coffee from a metal decanter into a delicate china cup. She bent low to ensure she didn't spill a drop, and I caught her eyes blink up at the person she was serving. Whoever it was sat with their back to me as I approached. Her expression was timid as she carefully poured the coffee, but when her gaze was caught, it changed. She no longer looked timid; she looked *terrified*.

She placed the jug back down on the tray with a shaking hand. She looked up again and blinked submissively at the person she was serving. I narrowed my eyes, trying to understand the chemistry that surrounded her like an aura. As she stared straight ahead I noticed something else disguised among her features. Mingling with the shyness and the fear was an emotion I had never seen step forth so brazenly from someone's person.

Desire.

I glanced in the direction of her eye line only to be met with the back of a navy velvet armchair. Raven hair rose over the top and the sole of a man's shoe jutted to the side. The doorman continued to pace ahead but I slowed to catch a glimpse of whoever had caused this maid to feel so… *nervous*. She mouthed something to the man, then lifted a small jug. She poured a thick dribble of cream into the cup, replaced the jug, then went to pick up a teaspoon, but a large hand came down on hers. The maid's skin flushed instantly, but she made no move to pull away her hand. Instead, her eyes darted across to mine as I watched the scene unfold.

I was almost alongside them now. I knew it was rude to stare but I couldn't stop myself. There was something indescribably tense and delicious about the way this maid was practically bowing to the gentleman in the armchair, and the hold he seemed to have over her. My skin caught fire, sizzling up and down my nerve endings.

"This way," the doorman clipped, a slight bark in his tone.

I gave him an obedient nod, but I couldn't help looking back over my shoulder to catch a glimpse of the man in the armchair. Not only was the maid still staring after me, with a look of territorial smugness, but as my eyes glided to the right, they were pierced by a glare.

Eyes as sharp and black as stone stared back at me, pulling me up short. They secured me to the spot, pinning me to the ground like an earthquake. Despite their threatening undertone, I saw magic in them. Dark, dirty, beautiful magic. Time slowed as I skimmed over an angular jaw and watched it jut as his teeth ground. A long straight nose led to nostrils that flared, inhaling air that filled out his slick suit.

My heart had been slowly picking up speed with anticipation but now it slammed against my ribcage like I'd been identified as prey, ripe to be hunted, stripped bare and eaten alive. While I fluttered my eyelids in a bid to determine I wasn't having some gothic nightmare, he didn't blink once. And despite the pretty maid having resumed her full attention on his masterly presence, his focus was solely, unwaveringly on me.

I spun my head back around so fast I almost gave myself whiplash. My feet felt like they'd been superglued to the expensive carpet and it took an otherworldly amount of effort to move them in the direction of the doorman. The dark glare remained printed on my eyelids as I walked away, and a shiver zigzagged down my spine. *What the actual fuck?*

A burning heat scorched my back as I followed the doorman through to yet another dark, echoing corridor, then a violent shudder racked my whole body. There was something about the way the man had looked at me that rendered me naked and exposed. While his entire being danced in the shadows, it felt as though each of my secrets had been laid bare in stark sunlight, for everyone to see.

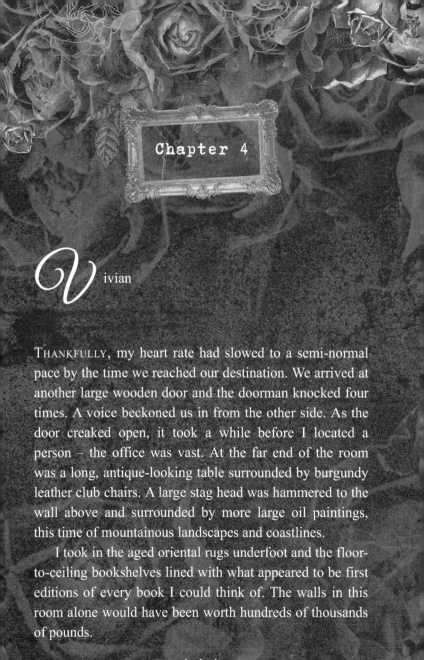

Chapter 4

_V_ ivian

THANKFULLY, my heart rate had slowed to a semi-normal pace by the time we reached our destination. We arrived at another large wooden door and the doorman knocked four times. A voice beckoned us in from the other side. As the door creaked open, it took a while before I located a person – the office was vast. At the far end of the room was a long, antique-looking table surrounded by burgundy leather club chairs. A large stag head was hammered to the wall above and surrounded by more large oil paintings, this time of mountainous landscapes and coastlines.

I took in the aged oriental rugs underfoot and the floor-to-ceiling bookshelves lined with what appeared to be first editions of every book I could think of. The walls in this room alone would have been worth hundreds of thousands of pounds.

· · ·

Eventually, my gaze landed on a solid wooden desk topped by a sleek, state of the art computer system and various other screens and pieces of digital equipment. And just behind that was a lean, middle-aged man with dark, silver-flecked hair, a weathered complexion and eyes like bullets.

He didn't stand as I approached. "Vivian Gillespie."

I nodded as his eyes drifted beyond me, and with the briefest of nods, the doorman was dismissed.

I lowered myself into the firm leather seat opposite him, trying to shake the black stare from the front of my mind. "It's an honour to meet you, Mr. Thorn. Thank you again for this opportunity."

He watched me steadily as I spoke, as if sizing me up. "Yes. It is a popular position. I hadn't wanted it to gain quite so much attention, but it is the first time we've created a role like this."

"The island is stunning," I said. "What I've seen of it so far, anyway. And your home…"

He raised a hand to cut me off and a cold shiver ran up my spine.

"I'm a busy man, Miss Gillespie. Allow me to get straight to the point." His acerbic tone cut like a sharp blade.

"Of course," I hurried out, reaching into my bag for a notebook and pen.

"As you know, we've valued our privacy on this island for many years. Since the nineteen thirties, when my great-grandfather and his acquaintances moved here, we've been able to live undisturbed. But, as you are no doubt aware, with unprecedented success comes heightened interest, and we've been under no small amount of pressure to reveal a little of how we produce our pharmaceutical product."

"Where is that pressure coming from?" I asked, with my pen poised.

He sighed heavily, tented his fingers under his chin and looked up at the ceiling. "Everywhere. Obviously, those who can't afford it are the most intrigued. They want access because they think they can get their hands on the product."

I tensed away a shiver. I was one of those very people.

"Then, there are people who don't give a monkeys about the drug but want to see the island, and our homes…" His lip curled in disgust. "Like the voyeurs they are. And then there are our partners, the people we work with to cultivate the product and the clients we sell it to. Their view is the more we can satisfy the curiosity of the masses, the more likely it is they will leave us alone. And, I have to say, I agree with them."

My spine straightened. "How are they not leaving you alone now?"

"We are under constant pressure by tourist boards and the media to allow people onto the island. It isn't privately owned so, in effect, anyone could come here if they so wanted, but we own all transportation to the island and the seas around it. We have the right to refuse anyone entry if they don't have the requisite paperwork. But, the more we refuse to play ball, the more suspicious people will become, and that is precisely what we *don't* want."

"Why is that?" I probed.

He dropped his loaded eyes back to mine and ground his teeth together as if contemplating how much to tell me. "Because if people want so desperately to find something, they will. Even though we have *nothing* to hide." That sounded like an ambiguous and contradictory comment to me, but his impatient expression deterred me from prying further.

He sighed again, his advancing years showing in the creases along his forehead. "In an ideal world, we would prefer to keep the gates closed, as it were, and our lives private. It is valuable to us." His eyes dragged over me and even a person without the power of sight wouldn't have missed the patronising tone of his glare. "Very few people have the sort of wealth we have on this island, therefore I don't expect you to imagine even a fraction of what we are going through."

I was thankful I hadn't been offered so much as a glass of water because I was pretty sure I'd have spat it out all over his eighteenth century desk.

"The discovery, and subsequent commercialisation, of Basidiomine – or *Bas*, as we call it here – has been both a blessing and a curse. It has enabled our prestigious clients to achieve great things. They can work longer without tiring, think with exceptional clarity, and many have reported a difference in their resilience." A faraway look appeared on his face as he looked beyond me to the door. "Some of our clients have tripled their income, be it through trading, sales or campaigning. We could probably influence election votes if we were so inclined."

I made a conscious effort to keep my mouth shut, as tempting as it was to let my jaw plummet to the floor. I knew the drug was powerful, but only in regard to people's health and abilities. I hadn't stopped to think it might be so powerful it could influence democracy.

"As you can imagine," he continued, "given the positive impact the drug has on its users, many people who are unable to purchase it have grown bitter." He said this with another curled lip. "They are, frankly, desperate to uncover something sinister about the drug and, it seems, the lives we live here on the island. Many people don't like the idea of a single island being inhabited by the very rich, even though every penny of those riches has been earned through hard, honest work. They feel as though they deserve some of that, despite having never lifted a finger themselves."

He transferred his gaze to the window, giving me a crystal clear view of the chip on his shoulder.

"And, to add further insult to injury, not everyone on the island is entirely on board with this *strategy*. So, before we begin, I need to be sure you can advocate for opening up the island to the…" he closed his eyes and winced, "*general public*. I need to be convinced you can stand up to the few naysayers among us who would prefer that no one outside our families ever stepped foot on our soil."

I inhaled a deep breath and leaned forward, summoning as much conviction as I could. "I promise you, Mr. Thorn, you have no stronger believer than me that this is the right thing to do."

He sat back, his chair giving a mild groan, and exhaled slowly. "Good. Now, you will work here, in Blackcap Hall, but you will be staying in Sandpiper Cottage overlooking Mossy Crag in the north. A car will be delivered to you for personal use. Sandpiper Cottage isn't far from here, but I expect you will need to explore the island."

"Yes, of course," I said, working overtime to contain the thrill that just wound through my body. I was being given a whole cottage? I swallowed before venturing the one question I came here to ask. "I'm assuming the tour will pass through the site where Basidiomine is produced? If that is the main reason interest has spiked so dramatically?"

He ground his teeth as he considered me, his gaze roaming shamelessly over every part of my face, my outfit, my body.

"The labs, yes. It will pass through some parts, but not all. It will be explained to you when you have settled."

I tried hard to contain my excitement. I was going to be so close to the drug. I was already so close I could almost smell it.

The door behind me opened and footsteps walked briskly across the floor. Sinclair looked up, his intense expression relaxing only a little.

"Ah, Ossian. Meet Vivian Gillespie, our new tour manager."

I looked to my right to see a tall, wiry figure with a face much like his father's – thin, weathered and harshly angled. But where Sinclair's face was slightly softer, his eldest son's was hard, pointed and unhappy. It almost repelled me, but the moment – and year to come – called for utmost professionalism, so I stood to shake his hand.

"It's a pleasure to meet you," I said. His response was to simply stare at me as though I was some shit he'd brought in off the street.

"I was about to have someone escort her to the offices," Sinclair stated. "I don't want to waste any more time."

"I can take her," Ossian said. His voice was as wiry as his figure. Nasal and inexplicably tense. "But I need to talk to you about the deliveries."

Sinclair's seemingly permanent frown intensified. "What about them?"

Ossian sat in the chair beside me, so I settled back down too.

"A windfall is coming our way."

My ears pricked up.

"When?"

"Over the next few weeks. I'm going to need more ferries."

"You need money."

"Yes, but we'll make it back, three-fold."

"Fine. Speak to Reese. Tell him I okay'd it."

"Of course. When will the tours start?" Ossian turned his fox-like face to me, but thankfully, Sinclair stepped in with the answer.

"In exactly four weeks. Vivian here will get started on the preparations right away but we will need to produce promotional materials, finalise logistics, complete our investigations into those who've purchased tickets. The last thing we want is to be hosting rogue reporters or people looking to get their hands dirty while they're here. We'll keep numbers low but do several tours per week. That way we keep our partners appeased but we get to monitor every single visitor closely."

Ossian looked at me and raked his steel gaze down my face and chest. "Think you can manage all that?" he sneered, in a patronising voice.

I nodded, an obliging smile fixed to my face.

"Four weeks," Ossian mused. "I can get two deliveries in before the tour starts. Maybe three."

"And…" Sinclair cleared his throat, ominously. "Where will they be dropped off?"

"I have a few sites in mind," Ossian replied. "I'll have the guys start preparing for—"

Ossian was interrupted by the sound of the door to Sinclair's office being flung open with a loud bang. I felt almost afraid to see who was behind the dramatic entrance so I kept my eyes on Sinclair. His jaw sharpened but his eyes lit up.

"What the hell is this?" a terrifying voice boomed behind me.

Sinclair leaned forward and rested his scrawny forearms on the desk, while Ossian dramatically rolled his eyes.

"Rupert, we discussed this." Sinclair spoke to the voice behind me as though it belonged to a toddler he was trying to placate during a particularly embarrassing tantrum.

"No. *You* discussed it. I just listened and told you it was a crazy, stupid idea. But you've gone ahead with it anyway. What happened to this being a *family* business? I don't mean to disrespect you, Father, but this is possibly the worst decision you've ever made and we're all going to pay for it."

"Watch your manners, Rupert," Sinclair hissed through gritted teeth. "Our new tour manager is sitting right here."

I felt the presence behind me still. Something felt oddly familiar about it but I fought every impulse to turn and look at his face. The voice was loud, booming and pissed off, and of course I wouldn't recognise it – I knew no one here. But the heat... the *heat*. It radiated from wherever he was standing, which may as well have been flush against me because it leached into my bones.

"It's a mistake," the voice continued. "We should wait. We're so close."

So close? To what?

"It's only twelve months, Rupert," his father said, as though he was trying to placate the man behind me. "And we'll be in full control of exactly who visits and exactly where they go. We have to do it, you know we do. Otherwise the hacks and the baying crowds will never leave us alone. Just twelve months. That's all the price we'll pay for getting our goddamn privacy back."

The atmosphere in the room crackled with tension. Sinclair stared at the person behind me, barely blinking, and Ossian's frown obliterated his small, narrow-set eyes. I snuck a glance at Ossian's profile, and pushed away the instinctive urge to recoil. There was nothing warm about him, or his father. While Sinclair was intimidating for sure, his eldest son had sinister tentacles reaching out of him at every angle. Both were cold, harsh businessmen through and through, and something told me I was going to have to dedicate everything to keeping them happy.

"We may be ready before the twelve months are up. This is what I've been telling you. We don't have to do this."

"Rupert!" Sinclair's face reddened in an instant and his growl passed from his throat, through his thinly veined arms to the desk, which rumbled under the vibration. "Now is not the time. It is happening. The plan is underway."

I looked down at the floor, feigning interest in the artfully worn rug, but as my gaze slid outwards, my throat constricted. I recognised that shoe. As my eyes travelled upwards, I recognised more. The navy blue suit that had blended so beautifully with the velvet armchair, and the thick fingers that had rested on the maid's, that now clenched and unclenched about a foot from where I sat. My eyes continued to travel upwards until they reached a sharp jaw and black eyes that now bore into mine. They were narrowed in recognition, and disapproval.

His father's threat broke through the fragile thread of connection that stretched between us. "If I hear of you doing anything to derail it, there will be hell to pay. Do you understand?"

Rupert turned his attention back to Sinclair and laughed. A hollow, bitter sound that made both Sinclair and Ossian stiffen. "Are you threatening me, Father?"

Sinclair watched him carefully, while my gaze flitted between the two of them. Sinclair looked sharp, angular and on edge, whereas Rupert towered over the desk, his wide shoulders blocking out any light from behind.

"Everyone whose opinion matters thinks this is important. If you attempt to sabotage it in any way, I won't be able to protect you, son." The last word was spoken as though it were an afterthought. "Do you understand?"

"You're mistaken. Aro is not on board with this." Rupert bit out between clenched teeth.

Sinclair let out a hollow laugh and smiled, venomously. "Aro's opinion on this matter is irrelevant. This is *our* family business, not his."

"Aro *is* family," Rupert ground out. "He's your brother. And in case you'd forgotten, he's also the Vice Chair. I would have thought his opinion would be *very* important."

I scrambled to remember what I could about Aro, but nothing about him being a Vice Chair of anything came to mind. All I knew was he ran several successful travel businesses.

"You have a lot to learn, Rupert," Sinclair said, in a

low vibrating voice. "When I decide something, that is what we do. That is the power of being head of the premier family. This responsibility will one day be yours and Ossian's."

Sinclair glanced at his eldest son. I sensed Ossian turn to face Rupert, finally. There was very little family resemblance between the two of them, but clearly a lot of bad blood. "Just get the fuck on board, Rupert," he sneered.

I heard a tight intake of breath behind me.

"If I can't talk you out of it, fine," he said, slowly. Then, those black eyes consumed my face whole as he concluded, "But I want nothing to do with this."

Sinclair's shoulders slumped slightly. "As you wish."

Out of the corner of my eye, I saw Rupert's fingers flex again like he was ready for a fight, then he spun on his heel and stalked out of the room, slamming the door behind him.

Rupert's departure did nothing to ease the tension in the room. Sinclair's half-rigid, half-deflated posture didn't change as he rotated his head to face me square. "My son is one of the naysayers," he said, in a resigned tone. "Just make sure he doesn't try to sabotage this operation. In fact, I want you to convince him these tours are the right thing to. Do I make myself clear?"

How the hell did he expect me to do that?

"Um, yes, sir. I will try my best," I said, tipping my chin in what was hopefully a show of confidence.

"No, Vivian," Sinclair replied. "Trying creates the option for failure. You have no option here. Just do it."

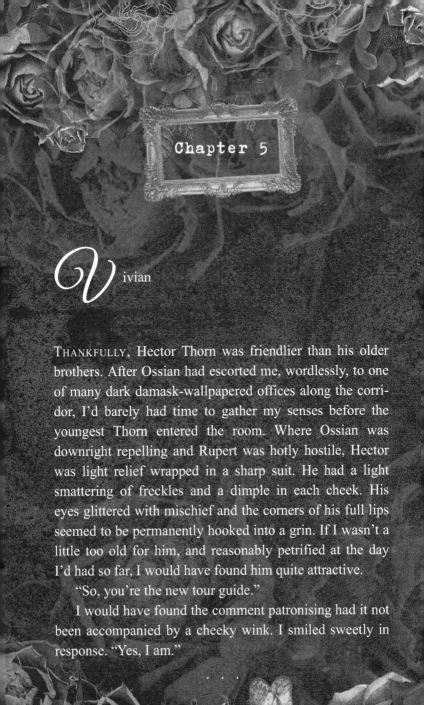

Chapter 5

Vivian

THANKFULLY, Hector Thorn was friendlier than his older brothers. After Ossian had escorted me, wordlessly, to one of many dark damask-wallpapered offices along the corridor, I'd barely had time to gather my senses before the youngest Thorn entered the room. Where Ossian was downright repelling and Rupert was hotly hostile, Hector was light relief wrapped in a sharp suit. He had a light smattering of freckles and a dimple in each cheek. His eyes glittered with mischief and the corners of his full lips seemed to be permanently hooked into a grin. If I wasn't a little too old for him, and reasonably petrified at the day I'd had so far, I would have found him quite attractive.

"So, you're the new tour guide."

I would have found the comment patronising had it not been accompanied by a cheeky wink. I smiled sweetly in response. "Yes, I am."

. . .

"WELCOME TO THE ISLAND. I gather you've met with my father?"

My smile remained fixed. "Yes, I have."

"And you're still here. That bodes well." He pushed himself off the doorframe and sauntered into the office, lifting up various papers on the desk and scanning his eyes over them, nosily. My gaze followed.

"What do you mean?"

"We don't hire many outsiders here," he explained, furrowing his brow in thought. "But when we do, it doesn't seem to take much for them to run a mile shortly after their first meeting with Father."

"He was direct and to the point," I said. "I admire that in a boss."

"Well, then. You're going to have a grand time here!"

I continued to follow his movements as he roamed the room as though he'd never stepped foot in it before. Chances were he hadn't. The Hall was so enormous, I'm not sure I'd have explored it all during his reported twenty-two years. "I don't mean to be rude, but you are Hector Thorn, yes?"

He spun round like a circus master, his arms outstretched. "Correct! How did you guess?" He turned to the side, angling his head in various ways. "Is it my uncanny likeness to Ossian?"

"No, actually. I don't think you look very much like him at all."

"Rupert, then?"

I swallowed, recalling those rock hard eyes that seemed to hammer right through to my soul.

"Maybe a little. Look, I only just met them both. It's hard to say."

He seemed content with that response and rubbed his hands together as though he'd just stumbled across Christmas. "So, Vivian Gillespie. I've been summoned to give you the grand tour."

"Of what?" The tendrils of excitement in my stomach were a welcome alternative to the sinister moths that had fluttered there since my encounter with Sinclair.

"Blackcap Hall, of course. Your home away from home." He looped his arm and glanced over his shoulder at me. "Shall we?"

I rose and smoothed down my pencil skirt, feeling his eyes on the movement. It didn't feel lecherous though, as it would have if it had been Ossian or his father. I wondered for a brief moment how to describe Rupert's gaze. That wasn't lecherous either. It was menacing and hateful. And overwhelming.

I looked up and slipped my arm through Hector's. I had to not think about his brother's black accusing eyes, or the way his glare burned a hole in my back. Fortunately, the promising glint in Hector's expression told me he was going to provide a suitable distraction.

We walked out into the echoey windowless corridor. My eyes had finally adjusted to the darkness of the house, so I was able to see more of the detail, like the wall sconces, the gigantic crystal chandeliers that outnumbered people by around ten to one. When they drew my eyes upwards I noticed the elaborate mouldings on the ceilings. The chalky slate effect absorbed all the light from the chandeliers rendering them rather pointless.

Hector showed me around several offices that were mostly occupied by elegantly coiffed women sitting with ramrod spines, tapping ferociously at computer keyboards.

"Who lives here, at Blackcap Hall?" I asked, as he swept me up a flight of stairs. They were low, wide and elegant. We reached the top and walked out onto a corridor. A bannister overlooked the entrance hall below and I noticed the same doorman who'd led me inside, waiting for more visitors, his top hat in perfect place.

"Well, Father, of course, and Mother. Grandfather, Uncle Aro and Aunt Isobel, Rupert, and me."

"Not Ossian?"

"No, he moved out after he got married."

Ossian, married? The thought that someone would want to lay next to a man like that every night made me shudder.

We reached a set of double doors that must have stood around fifteen feet tall. Hector placed a hand on each handle, pressed down and pushed forward. The wider the doors opened, the more breath was dragged from my lungs.

"This is the Great Hall," he said, with the slightly bored tone of a waiter outlining the specials to the hundredth party that evening. I stood with my toes halfway over the threshold. "You can come inside, you know. You won't go up in flames."

Hector walked into the room, his hands stuffed casually in his pockets, while I gawped around at the incomprehensible splendour. The walls were a chalky grey with silver and gold accents. Black polished floorboards gleamed underfoot, and a black crystal chandelier the size of our whole house back in London, hung in the centre.

"How... um, how often is this used?"

"Few times a year," Hector said, shrugging his shoulders.

"For what?"

"Balls and banquets mainly. Most of the houses have a space like this so the families take it in turns to host the larger gatherings."

My eyes widened. Most of the houses had ballrooms?

"You could probably fit my entire street in this room," I muttered.

"Yeah, I guess it's big," he replied, with another shrug. I followed him out and waited while he pulled the heavy doors closed. He guided me through the lounge where I'd first seen Rupert – which was actually the breakfast room – a drawing room, a maid's parlour, the kitchens and the chapel. Everywhere but the living quarters.

"Where do you actually sleep?" I asked, perplexed that we hadn't seen any accommodation yet.

"In the towers."

I swallowed back a snort and ended up almost choking. "Where are we? Corona?"

He frowned in confusion. "Sorry?"

"It's where Rapunzel lives."

"Oh right. In that case, *yes*." He shook his head and continued walking.

"So, where are these towers?" I asked, looking around for hidden doors and more shadowy corridors.

"They're attached to the four corners of the house," he replied. "They're almost separate buildings, but not, if that makes any sense?"

"Not really."

"It doesn't matter anyway. You're not permitted to enter any of them. But, if you must know, Mother and Father live in the South Tower; Grandfather, Aro and Isobel in the East; me and Rupert in the West."

"And the North Tower?"

He paused to open a door to the gardens. His eyes followed me as I walked through, and I thought I detected a note of wariness in them.

"That's where Dax lived before he got married. My cousin. It's empty now."

I silently grieved for my Doc Marten boots as Hector led me out onto an ancient cobbled path leading to acres of trimmed grass and wild borders. "Do you all work for Thorn Pharmaceuticals?"

"No. That's mainly Father and Oz, and Rupert to some extent."

"Why only to some extent?" I asked, suddenly ravenous for information about the man who, with just one look, had made me feel things I couldn't begin to explain.

He began walking, oblivious to the fact I was teetering precariously behind him. "You do ask a lot of questions."

"Well, it will help me to answer other peoples'," I replied, arching an eyebrow he couldn't see.

"Fine." He pushed his hands into his pockets again with the nonchalance of a fifteen-year-old. "Father and Oz want Rupert to be more involved in the pharmaceuticals business but he doesn't want to be. It's not his bag. He's happy enough working with me to manage the distillery."

"Is that Blackcap Whiskey Distillery?

"Och aye," Hector replied in a terrible Scottish accent, turning around just as I almost levitated off a cobble, head-on into a herbaceous shrub. "Are you ok walking in those?"

"Yes," I lied, grabbing the arm he held out. "I'm fine."

"Few more steps and we'll be on the gravel."

I held onto him until we reached my equivalent of dry

land, then I metaphorically brushed myself down and tilted my chin up.

"So, is that your business? The distillery?"

"It's Rupert's really, but the more he gets pulled into Bas business, the more I take on."

"Don't take this the wrong way but... you're only twenty-two, right?"

"You are absolutely right," he grinned. "But the distillery has been in our family for years, so I practically grew up there."

"Can I ask you a personal question?" I asked after we'd walked a few more paces.

"Another one? I'm surprised you're asking my permission."

I ignored his jibe. "How do you feel about opening up the island to visitors? Are you Team Tour, or Team No Thanks?"

He chewed his lip as he contemplated his response. "Officially, I'm on board," he said, side-eyeing me. "Unofficially, I'd prefer we didn't have to do this. No offence to you."

"None taken." We walked through a criss-cross pattern of grass borders and around the edge of pond filled with enormous multi-coloured Koi. "Why are you against it?"

He sighed, lazily. "Many of us are against it, but I can only speak for myself. I just have a bad feeling about it. Letting people on the island who are desperate for a drug they can't have... I think it could backfire on us."

"Why is it in such short supply?"

He rubbed his jaw and avoided my eyes. "I think Rupert is the better person to answer that question."

"Ok. When you say many people are against it, who, exactly?"

"Well, Rupert. *Everyone* knows how dead against it he is. I know Uncle Aro would prefer it didn't go ahead, which is probably one of the reasons it will."

I stood for a moment watching the mesmerising creatures swim back and forth – a rainbow in motion. "What do you mean by that?"

He groaned as if battling with himself. "Hell, I'm not telling you anything you won't pick up on yourself. Aro and my father don't get along."

"Aro is Sinclair's younger brother, right?"

"Correct. They've had a few major disagreements in the last few years, and they seem to have grown further and further apart. I could speculate on specific reasons, but the truth is, they've never really seen eye-to-eye."

"That must be difficult for you, with Aro being family and all."

"Sometimes. Aro is a good man. You'll meet him soon, I'm sure."

I didn't ask about his inference that in comparison, perhaps his father wasn't a good man. Hector moved away from the pond and I followed him along another path towards what looked like another property on the estate.

Hector continued, for once without me having to poke him for information. "He's been like a second father to Rupert and I."

"Not Ossian?" I blurted out, then immediately regretted it. *What the fuck, Vivian?* Fortunately, Hector didn't seem perturbed by my brazen nosiness.

"Ossian has always been Father's favourite. No one even tried to hide that fact from us. I think Aro took it upon himself to make Rupert and me feel as though we mattered." He laughed. A hollow laugh, the bitterness of which lingered on its surface.

The air around us suddenly felt thick, so I changed the subject. "Where are you taking me now?"

"Caspian House." Hector pointed to a small road leading through a gap in the perimeter wall. "It's through there."

"What is it?"

"It's a member's club. A place where anyone from the island can go and relax, have a drink, grab a bite to eat. We have leisure facilities – a golf course, as you can see, a gym, swimming pool, tennis courts – and meeting rooms, event spaces, that kind of thing. We own it, but anyone can use it." His jovial smile tapered off. "Well, most anyone."

"What do you mean?"

He clicked his tongue. "Not everyone can get into the club, that's all. I suppose it wouldn't be a club if it were open to everyone."

"Who isn't allowed then?"

"People who aren't members," he clipped. "Now, tell me. What do you make of the family so far?"

"Well, it's only been a couple of hours…"

"First impression. One word."

"Formidable."

His feet crunched lightly along the gravel. Even the soles of his shoes sounded expensive. "Interesting. Another."

"Intimidating."

He laughed, a tinkling sound that I could easily imagine would have all the island girls positively dribbling. "You find me intimidating?"

I smiled, timidly. "Not as much as your father and brothers. But I expect you can hold your own."

"Not a bad answer. Another."

"Hmm." I made a show of giving it deep thought as we walked through the gateway. A brick building, painted the same chalky grey as the Thorns' ballroom, rose out of the ground. Blinds covered every window, banishing what little daylight snuck through the trees. A black gravel car park extended in front, and every sports car and menacing four-by-four imaginable was lined up along the edge with its nose pointed at us.

"Mysterious."

We reached a set of steps presided over by two enormous stone gulls, and Hector turned, blocking my path. "Mysterious?" An arched brow told me he was enjoying this game as much as I secretly was.

"Of course. Everyone who lives on this island is a mystery."

He huffed and made his way up the steps, leaving me to titter after him in my increasingly painful heels. "The question wasn't about everyone else on the island. It was about us – the Thorns."

I followed him through double doors and what appeared to be a sizeable boot room lined with rows upon rows of shining golf shoes.

"Fine," I muttered, looking around at the lounge we'd walked into. Like every other room I'd seen since my arrival, it was dark and it took my eyes a while to adjust. Shadows covered every corner and matte velvet furniture disappeared into them. The only light came from recessed bulbs in the ceiling and floor, and cabinets lining the walls, illuminating abundant cut crystal glassware. The effect was hypnotic. Hector walked across to a pair of sofas facing each other in the centre and gestured for me to sit.

"One more," he commanded. "Last one."

"Ok. Charismatic."

He side-eyed me. "Did it pain you to say that?"

"No it didn't."

"You think we're charismatic?"

"Yes, I do."

"So, what do you make of the idea that charisma will ultimately be the undoing of great leaders? I think it was Peter Drucker who once said charisma convinces people of their infallibility, and makes it impossible for them to change. Does that describe us?"

Way to put me on the spot. "I wouldn't say you were resistant to change. The plan to open up the island is proof of that, isn't it? But as to whether you're infallible, it's too soon for me to judge, but looking at the riches you've amassed as a family, I would say failure is not a regular feature in your lives."

As my eyesight adjusted, I noticed the dimples had disappeared from Hector's cheeks. "Not failure in the material sense, I suppose."

"What do you mean?"

"Oh, nothing."

"No, come on. You started this game."

He shifted uncomfortably on what looked like an exquisitely comfortable sofa. "Isn't it often the case that what you see on the outside is not necessarily reflective of what's going on inside?"

"Is that a rhetorical question?"

"Maybe."

His watched me steadily as if putting me through some

kind of test. The prickling sensation along the tops of my shoulders was not a welcome one so I attempted to lighten the mood.

"Anyway, if we're quoting great thinkers, wasn't it Freddie Mercury who said, 'The reason we're successful, darling? My overall charisma, of course'?"

A beat passed, then Hector burst into raucous laughter, which turned the head of every person in the room. It was infectious, and before I knew it, I was laughing too.

"You're comparing us to a deceased showman?" he spluttered.

"Hey!" I cried, genuinely offended. "Freddie Mercury was an absolute genius. And yes, he was charismatic too."

Hector continued to laugh.

"Anyway," I frowned. "I can think of worse things to be compared to."

"And I can think of more accurate things too," Hector chuckled.

"What's so funny?" A now-familiar voice vibrated behind me and my heart literally shot into my throat.

Hector looked up and almost doubled over with a fresh round of laughter.

"Nothing," I rushed out. "Nothing at all." For some reason, I didn't want Rupert to know I thought his family – and by extension, he – was mysterious and charismatic.

"It doesn't sound like nothing," Rupert grunted. "Aren't you supposed to be at the bank?" he said to Hector, accusingly.

"I was showing Vivian round the estate," Hector said, wiping his eyes. "I can head over there now, if you can give her a ride back to the Hall?" He glanced down at my brand new stiletto courts. "I don't think those

Manolos would appreciate another walk across the gravel."

Manolos? He knows Manolos? If he hadn't already won the heart of every teenage girl on the island, it wouldn't be long.

Rupert had shifted to my left, giving me a front row seat to glimpse his fisted hands. "I don't have time. I have to go to the distillery."

"Then take Vivian with you," Hector replied, jovially. "I'm sure she'd love to see the site. Maybe try some of the latest batch…"

Rupert's teeth ground together. I couldn't see them but I could hear them.

"It's okay," I said. "I can walk back to the Hall. My shoes will be fine."

"No, Vivian. Rupert would love to take you." Hector smiled sweetly at his older brother and I could tell that outside of this uncomfortable standoff, they were possibly quite close.

"Fine. I'll be back in thirty minutes," Rupert snapped.

"That okay with you, Vivian?" Hector asked.

"It's fine," I smiled thinly. "Thank you."

"Great. Better get to that bank," he said, rolling his eyes. He pushed himself off the sofa and gave me a shit-eating grin before walking ahead of his brother to the door. Rupert glanced once over his shoulder, pausing mid-stride, then stalked after Hector, flexing his fingers.

I watched them leave, my eyes traitorously glued to Rupert, feeling his angry aura bounce off the walls. His shoulders were broad which helped to balance out his towering height. His suit jacket narrowed slightly at the waist, giving a small hint at the definition beneath. The suit pants positively hugged his backside and my mouth almost watered watching his thighs thicken as he walked.

"He's a doll, isn't he?"

A voice at my side made me gasp. I spun around to see a woman with bright blonde hair dyed turquoise at the tips leaning over the table with a cloth, wiping away non-existent dust. "I'm sorry?"

"Rupert Thorn, whose ass you were just admiring. He's one of the nicer ones." She straightened and gave me a warm, completely non-judgemental smile. *Nicer?* That hadn't been my experience so far.

I laughed, nervously. "I wasn't. And what do you mean by nicer ones?"

"It's perfectly fine, honey. We all do it. Personally, I think you'd be damn strange if you didn't think Rupert Thorn was damn fine."

She must have seen the shock on my face, because she shoved the cloth into her back pocket and sank onto the sofa Hector had just left an ass print on. "Enough about him. I'm guessing you're Vivian Gillespie, right?"

I would have gasped in surprise again, had I not been all out of gasps for the day. "How do you know?"

"Oh honey," she drawled. "*Everyone* knows who you are. You're the first proper stranger to step foot on the Isle of Crow since 1902. Your picture was even circulated in the *Crow Courier*."

"The what?"

"The local paper."

"You have a local paper?"

"Sure we do," she grinned. "Where do you think we all get our island gossip?"

I stared at her, my brain scrambling to comprehend the

fact I'd been featured in the local paper. I'd only accepted the job three days ago.

"Oh my gosh, where's my manners?" she said, her voice high-pitched. "I'm Minty. Minty Greenwood. I work here."

"Vi—" I began. "Well, apparently, you know who I am. It's nice to meet you, Minty. You can call me Viv."

She beamed and shook my hand. "Where they got you living?"

"Sandpiper Cottage, somewhere near to some north cragg."

Her eyes widened. "Really? My, they do want to impress you. We all thought they'd put you in municipal housing with us. Maybe they figured since you'll be selling our island to tourists, they would want you to be immersed in it. That would make sense."

"I hadn't thought of it like that."

"Hey, listen…" She spun her whole body to face me. "I'm guessing you don't know anyone else here yet. How would you like to come to the night market with me a week Saturday?"

"That's very kind of you. It sounds fun," I said. "What kind of market is it?"

"Local goods," she said, holding out a hand and ticking off each finger. "Seafood, cheeses, fresh juices, crafts… island-distilled gin. And there's usually a band or two playing and food stalls where we can grab a bite to eat. I could pick you up from the cottage around seven p.m.?"

"Sure, that sounds great! Do the Thorns go?" I figured it would be nice to enjoy myself somewhere my bosses weren't looking over my shoulder.

"No. The families don't really go to the markets.

They're too busy dining on caviar and veal, or, if you're the Cartwright sisters, bird seed." I had no idea who the Cartwrights were and it still felt a little early to be gossiping, but I couldn't help but chuckle at Minty's sarcasm. She reminded me of Em and I realised then just how much I was going to miss her. I also realised I was an absolutely terrible friend for not having contacted her since I arrived. I'd told her I would the second I landed. "No, the markets are more for the common folk, like us. Ah shit," Minty muttered under her breath. "Gotta go."

I followed her gaze to the door where Ossian Thorn was standing talking to a small, eccentric-looking man in a beige three-piece suit and bowler hat.

"See you a week Saturday," she winked at me. "Wear something warm."

And with that parting advice, she sprung up from the sofa and trotted back to the bar. I looked over to Ossian who was making his way towards Minty, then I watched her plaster a smile to her face. I'd only known her a few minutes but it was long enough to know she was faking the pleasantries; she found nothing enjoyable in the interaction with Ossian at all, and I didn't blame her. She nodded and set to work pouring him a drink, while his head rotated, taking in the room with a narrow glare. I quickly looked away, hoping Rupert would show up soon to take me back to the Hall before Ossian realised I was alone.

I felt his cold, piercing gaze land on me and I physically shivered. To my relief, Rupert chose that moment to walk back into the lounge. I could have hugged him for saving me from the possibility I might have to speak to his even more terrifying-looking older brother.

Rupert walked towards me and stood square in front of

my table, blocking out the already limited light. I could barely make out his features amid his silhouetted form. "Are you ready?"

I nodded and was about to stand when someone called Rupert's name. It was a woman's voice. An alluring one. A possessive one. I watched his expression change rapidly from one of annoyed obligation to one of dark detachment. His gaze dropped as the object of his attention reached his side and I found myself staring at a fucking supermodel. A tall, willowy woman with a small, perky cleavage and even smaller waist, topped with copper hair artfully curled to complement her heart-shaped face and enormous green eyes. As if that didn't make her alluring enough, her voice ramped up the lust factor a million times. She looked the picture of perfect health but sounded as if she smoked two hundred cigarettes a day.

"Rupert, darling," she drawled, sex dripping off the end of her tongue. "Will I see you at the Carmichaels' on Friday?" She prodded his chest with a long, impossibly pristine fingernail. "You promised me another dance and…" she winked, long and slow, "a private game of poker."

My eyes flitted to Rupert and I almost collapsed back into the sofa at the sight of the sheer boredom on his face. Maybe that look is what these women go for, I thought. There must be slim pickings on the island.

It was the first time I heard him speak at a normal decibel. "I'm sorry, Sienna. I have other plans. Maybe next time."

I looked back at the woman, marvelling at how undeterred she was by the obvious brush-off. "Absolutely. I've been practising you know. Training with the best. You're not going to win next time, and you know what that means…"

Rupert inhaled deeply and released a slow breath. "Remind me, Sienna." His voice was deep, dark and promising, and if I had been Sienna-whoever-she-was, I would quite possibly have fainted.

She ran a finger slowly from the collar of her blouse to the hem of her skirt, then licked it upwards. "Strrrrrrippp," she replied, popping the 'p.'

I refrained from shaking my head. *Girl, hold something back*, I advised her silently.

She turned, slowly and dramatically, before walking away. My guess was she was positive his eyes were on her bottom. In reality, they'd flicked back to me, as if to gauge my reaction. When I gave him none, his eyes panned the room. Small talk and conversation seemed to quiet and the walls of the lounge closed in exposing its darkness and dubious depth. The atmosphere tightened and I noticed some clientele draining their glasses and leaving the room. It struck me then, you can tell how dangerous a person is by the way their eyes absorb all the light leaving everyone else in the shadows. The saliva left my mouth as I realised that every other person in the room receded into the background when Rupert's attention landed on me.

"Well?" he barked.

Only then, I remembered I was about to go somewhere with him. I couldn't for the life of me remember where, but I knew I had to show some physical intent. I stood on shaky legs, and for the first time realised how tall he was. His head and shoulders towered above me, my head only reaching as far as his broad chest. I muttered my thanks as I walked past him, out of the lounge and away from the fermenting presence of the older Thorn who had watched the whole exchange with Sienna, closely. I felt Rupert walking behind me, then he overtook to hold the main door open so I could step outside into the late afternoon chill. I hugged my coat around myself and looked to him for direction.

"You'll warm up in the car," he said, jerking his head to the left. "It's over here."

I kept pace with him as we approached an absolutely stunning black Ferrari parked on the gravel at the side of the building. The car park was littered with supercars, but the black Ferrari stood out for its understated prowess. It was like a vehicle version of its owner: dark, terrifying and elusive. He clicked a button in his hand and the car lit up like a damn Ferris wheel. *Not so understated after all.*

"Nice car," I said, as I slid into the passenger seat. I snuck a glimpse of him; his expression was dead straight. He didn't care whether I liked the car or not. He started the engine and pulled gracefully out of the car park. I always had a thing for the way men drove cars. For some illogical reason, two-hands-on-the-wheel, sensor-aided reverse parking did absolutely nothing for me. But give me a one-hand-on-the-gearstick guy who turned corners using the heel of his palm to rotate the wheel, who rested his arm across the back of the passenger seat and breathed hot air in my ear as he reversed into seemingly impossible spaces, then I was all there for it. Every single bit of me. And of course, Rupert was that guy.

He drove almost lazily, resting one hand on the stick, despite the car being automatic, and he used that damn palm to turn the car around blind corners. I almost prayed for a tight parking spot at the distillery. Five minutes of dead silence later we pulled, disappointingly, into a wide open space.

"Wait here," he commanded. I watched him step effortlessly out of the car and take long, muscular strides into the rustic building. While he was gone, I took the opportunity to scribble down in my notepad everything I'd heard and seen. Not only might it help me do a job I was barely qualified for, it might give me clues as to where I could find the drug itself. People could say things in passing that turn out to be meaningful later.

I was still scribbling when Rupert returned to the car. He didn't say a word as he slid in beside me, filling the vehicle with the scent of cinnamon, tobacco and leather. We drove silently, again, back to the Hall.

When we arrived ten minutes later, I climbed out of the car – uneasily, given the floor of it was so low it almost grazed the gravel – and looked to Rupert for direction. Despite having been there only that morning, I wasn't sure where to go, how to get there, or what to do. He was apparently thinking the same thing.

"We'll go to reception first. Hopefully, they'll have a desk set up somewhere for you. Then we'll check on the delivery of your car."

I couldn't help making a joke. "Same brand as yours, I hope?" He blinked, his swirling eyes lacerating mine. "I'd prefer mine to be red though, if at all possible." I dipped my head towards his fierce monstrosity, then he caught on and tutted loudly, unimpressed.

We walked into the entrance hall and I followed Rupert to a small office. The sign on the door said, "Thorn Enterprises Administration".

We walked in without knocking and three secretaries

looked up, immediately straightening, the result being a small sea of breast unfolding before our eyes. Rupert paid no attention.

"Where is Vivian Gillespie's new office?" he said, in a voice somewhat softer than the one he adopted when addressing me directly.

A secretary with deep red bouffant hair and dark-rimmed glasses resting a third of the way down her nose, cleared her throat. "I'll find out for you right away, sir."

She tapped a few keys on her keyboard, her fingers flying over them so speedily they probably caused a breeze. She paused and peered at the screen, then narrowed her eyes and swallowed. "Um, sir. She's been allocated a desk in…" she blinked back at him nervously. "In… your office."

"Pardon?" He baulked as though it was the worst news he'd heard all day. "That can't be right. Let me see."

Rupert walked around to the side of her desk and closed in on the screen. The secretary pointed to something in front of him. "Look, see? Mr. Sinclair Thorn requested it."

My eyes rolled back in my head. Of course this was Sinclair's idea. He knew Rupert was fundamentally opposed to the tours and he wanted me to get him more involved. What better a way to help me do that than to sit me in the exact same office.

Rupert straightened, his jaw rigid. For a few seconds he was motionless. The room was deathly silent, everyone frozen in anticipation of his next move. His shoulders rose and fell as heavy breaths left his lungs.

Without warning, he stormed past me and flung open the door. "Vivian," he barked. I assumed it was a request for me to follow him, which I dutifully, if a little reluctantly, did. I didn't particularly appreciate being ordered about, but it was still my first day and I had friends to make.

I jogged to catch up as he thundered down the corridor, round a corner, down another corridor, across the entrance hall to the east wing, along another corridor. My heels skittered across the wooden floors as I followed. When he stopped outside another forebodingly dark door, I almost crashed into his back. I caught myself just in time. He unlocked it and stomped inside, throwing his car keys onto a large, solid wooden desk. He did it with such force, they clattered and slid right off the other end. I stayed in the doorway, unsure of my next move. Another desk sat adjacent to the one Rupert had attempted to throw his keys onto. It didn't match any of the décor in the room, so I assumed it had only recently been erected.

Rupert spun around quickly, despite his hulking form almost filling the now-small space. "Welcome," he almost growled. "There's your desk. Make yourself at home." The sarcasm dripped from his lips.

"I... erm... I'm sorry. I don't know what to say." I metaphorically kicked myself. Why was I apologising? This wasn't my doing. But Rupert seemed to be in such acute discomfort over the situation, I felt compelled to ease it somehow by accepting some of the responsibility, as nonsensical as that was.

Rupert's phone buzzed and he whipped it out of his pocket, angrily, and stared at the screen. "Great," he muttered under this breath. "There's been a delay on the water. Your car won't arrive until next Monday."

My chest tightened. Did that mean he was driving me back to the cottage?

His deep purple eyes flickered up to me as a thought flashed across them, then he stiffened. "I'll call you a driver."

———

TEN MINUTES LATER, I was sitting in a sleek black Bentley, rolling along a pretty country road lined with narcissus buds eager to bloom. We rolled along slowly, until the road began to dip in a slight incline. I looked ahead through the windscreen and saw the ocean laid out below. My breath caught in my throat at the picture postcard view. I was still breathing abnormally when the car pulled onto a small lane. We continued further until we stopped, then I positively swooned. Right at the end of the lane stood a house that looked like something out of a fairytale. It had a smaller-than-average front door, painted sage green, and nine sash windows to the front. A hedge ran along the front and a small gate wedged in the middle displayed a sign carved into a piece of wood: Sandpiper Cottage. *Cottage*? This was like no cottage I'd ever seen. It was *huge*. A giant oak tree stood majestically to the side, swaying its branches above as if to say 'ta da, you like?'

"Wow." I couldn't remember getting out of the car; I was transfixed and suddenly standing in front of the studded door.

"Here's your key, ma'am."

I tore my eyes from the door to the large, brass key being held out to me. The driver gave me a stiff smile, as if he saw this kind of beauty every day. "This is pretty," I said, curious to get some sort of reaction from him.

"You have Rose Thorn to thank for that," he said, plainly.

"Rose Thorn," I grinned. "How about that."

The man's expression didn't change. I wanted to ask who exactly Rose Thorn was – she hadn't appeared on any of the Thorn family trees I'd tracked down – and if that was indeed her real name. It seemed beautifully serendipitous.

The man nodded. "Go ahead."

I fed the key into the door and turned it. The lock clunked and I pushed the door inwards, then gasped. The interior of the cottage was just as lovely as the outside, if not more so. The flagstone floors were dotted with rugs, and painted French dressers lined the spacious hallway. To the left, a large kitchen rimmed with shaker units, deep sage to match the front door, and to the right, a living room filled with damask print sofas, bubbly armchairs and Moroccan pouffes, all in opulent jewel colours. The whole place looked and felt like a glass of mulled wine. Whoever Rose Thorn was, she had genius running through her veins.

I thanked the driver and cast an eye over the bags he'd placed by the door. The second it closed, I kicked off my shoes and ran through the house, squealing. While I wasn't yet convinced I had the job everyone dreamed about, I was pretty certain I had the home.

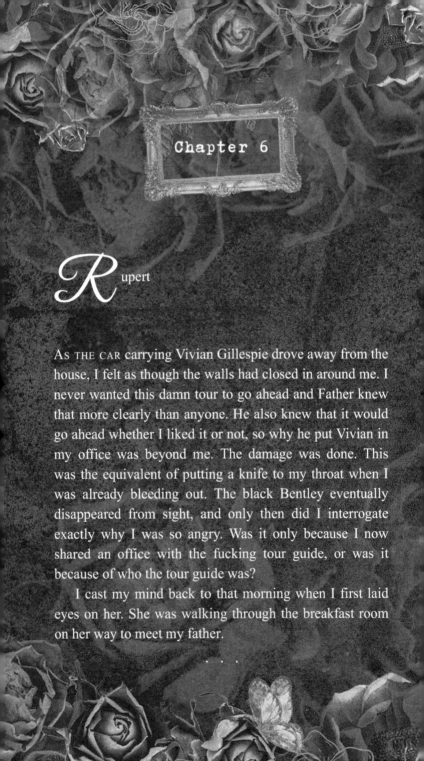

Chapter 6

*R*upert

AS THE CAR carrying Vivian Gillespie drove away from the house, I felt as though the walls had closed in around me. I never wanted this damn tour to go ahead and Father knew that more clearly than anyone. He also knew that it would go ahead whether I liked it or not, so why he put Vivian in my office was beyond me. The damage was done. This was the equivalent of putting a knife to my throat when I was already bleeding out. The black Bentley eventually disappeared from sight, and only then did I interrogate exactly why I was so angry. Was it only because I now shared an office with the fucking tour guide, or was it because of who the tour guide was?

I cast my mind back to that morning when I first laid eyes on her. She was walking through the breakfast room on her way to meet my father.

. . .

MY FIRST THOUGHT was that Father had hired yet another beautiful personal assistant to add to the growing pool of assistants he didn't need but liked to look at. She had the requisite looks. The hourglass figure of a fifties siren, and a sense of style that did nothing to conceal it. There was one difference though. Father tended to prefer flaxen blondes whereas this girl had dark, unruly curls that fought to escape the ponytail she'd wrestled them into.

When she turned to face me, I lost all track of thought and all trace of saliva. Like most people who meet me for the first time, she looked fearful. I was born with obsidian hair and unnaturally dark eyes, and I cultivated a presence that communicated my mood and intentions before I stepped foot in a room. It made life more efficient. But, something else lurked behind the fear. It was less than desire – a look I knew well – but more than curiosity. It was recognition. I got the impression, in the space of what couldn't have been more than six seconds, she saw something in me that made her want to either run in my direction, or run a fucking mile. It made my stomach tighten in a way I hadn't felt before. I needed the freshly poured coffee to give me something to swallow.

Anger at my father and hatred for everything Vivian Gillespie now stood for crawled through my muscles and I tensed involuntarily. I walked back inside the house and stalked along the corridors, hammering my feet against the hardwood floors in a bid to drown out my simmering rage.

I threw open the door to Uncle Aro's office without knocking, and didn't flinch when it slammed against the wall of the empty room.

"Can I help you, sir?"

I turned to see one of the housekeepers jogging towards me.

"Where's my uncle?" I demanded.

"Mr. Aurelias is with Sir Peregrine, sir," she answered.

"Thank you," I bit out, then I slammed the door and stomped to the East Tower, to my grandfather's living quarters.

I heard their voices as I knocked on the door.

"Yes?" came a grizzly voice.

"Grandfather, it's me, Rupert."

"Come in, my boy, come in."

I pushed the door, more softly this time, and entered the room. My mood instantly lightened the second I laid eyes on my uncle and grandfather. They each had a way of soothing my anger that my father instead seemed to stoke.

"Rupert." Uncle Aro enveloped me in a giant hug. "I haven't seen you for a while. You've got taller."

"No, Aro. I stopped growing when I hit eighteen. Nearly eight years ago." I gave him a crooked grin when he rubbed his knuckles in my hair as if I were five years old. "And you're the one who's been away. How was New York?"

"Good," Aro said, returning to my grandfather's bedside. "I've confirmed three new routes around Bermuda and the Caribbean."

"Which ships?"

"Thorn Duchess and Peregrine Steed. And we've secured a new caterer for Duke."

"Sounds productive," I replied as I walked to the other side of my grandfather's bed and leaned over to kiss the top of his head. "And how are you, Grandfather?"

"Same as ever," he rumbled. "The doc ordered more bed rest until I can shift this chest infection."

"You got another one?" I frowned, my eyes darting to Aro.

"Mild," Aro said. "The doctor's being cautious."

"Let me know if I can bring you anything," I said, sitting in the chair opposite Aro.

"I will," Grandfather smiled. "Now, what brings you here?"

"I think you know," I looked pointedly at them both.

"The tours," Aro confirmed, his voice bleak.

"I've made it abundantly clear how I feel. It's a huge risk, for everyone on the island, not least our family. I know Father feels certain it will help with our reputation and relationships, but Ossian… he's revelling in it. And that worries me."

I thought I saw Grandfather's eyes flick to Aro but it happened so fast I questioned whether they'd moved at all.

"He's even viewing it as an opportunity to create buzz about the next generation of Bas. A drug we haven't even made yet, and that, quite frankly, with Ossian leading it, may end up killing people."

Aro sighed as though he'd had this conversation a thousand times and no longer saw the point in it.

"Rupert…" Grandfather placed his hand over mine. "I admire your tenacity, boy. You have a good head on your shoulders. You're certainly the smartest of all of Sinclair's boys. But you're a Thorn. You have to know when to toe the party line. The tours are happening, whether you like it or not. It's for the greater good of the business, and our family."

"So, you're in favour?" I asked with a frown.

His back steeled. "I have faith in whatever Sinclair chooses to do." Aro began to roll his eyes but stopped when I transferred my gaze to him.

"And what about you?" I asked my uncle.

"I'm with you Rupert. I don't agree, but you know as well as anyone, Sinclair doesn't listen to a word I say." He leaned forward placing his elbows on his knees. "Listen, it may feel like a risk but I'm sure that Miss Gillespie, with her credentials and our support, will ensure it runs smoothly. Have you made her acquaintance yet?"

I ground my jaw at the recollection. "Yes. And we are to become exceptionally more acquainted in the coming weeks because Father has put her in *my office*."

Aro bit back a laugh. "Well, as much as I disagree with most of what my brother does, even I have to admit that was sharp of him."

The dormant anger resurfaced, curling my fingers. "You think this is funny?"

"Well, yes," Aro smiled. "Look, I know it isn't what you wanted, but think of it this way. You'll have company. You're too much of a recluse Rupert, and that's going to end this year. You may as well enjoy a bit of female companionship in your last few months as a bachelor."

Grandfather cleared his throat, also amused. "What's she like?"

I let out an irritable sigh. "She's like every other woman my father hires."

"Oh, so she's pretty?" Grandfather goaded.

I didn't respond. Weirdly, I couldn't force a lie out of my mouth but neither could I admit to finding her attractive.

"Well, enjoy the view, Rupert," Aro said, sitting back

in his chair. "But make sure that's all you enjoy. You know how the Consortium will frown on you getting involved with someone other than an islander."

Yes, I knew that. It had been drilled into my brain from birth.

"There's no chance of that happening," I forced out. "I resent this situation, and by extension, her. I won't be making my office particularly hospitable. If she's still around in two months, I'll be surprised."

Aro walked me out, closing the door once we were safely out of Grandfather's suite. "I'm as worried about these tours as you, Rupert," he said, quietly. "But if there's one thing I've learned about my brother over the years, it's that there will always be something. Sinclair will never be satisfied. He wants more of everything. More land, more money, more power. And he'll stop at nothing to get it. It's why we continue to live in such luxury."

"That's not true," I snapped. "You make a lot of money. Hector and I hold our own. So does Dax."

"Not the kind of money Bas makes for us though, and you know that. What I'm trying to say is, Sinclair has few morals when it comes to *how* he acquires all those things he wants. There will be many battles the two of you will fight in your lifetime. I suggest you pick them wisely." Aro narrowed his eyes, as if to ensure I got the message.

I breathed out a resigned sigh. "I understand."

"In the meantime, Rupert. Just keep your head down and… keep doing what you're doing."

I did a double take. Aro knew. And this was his way of telling me I had his support. Ever since we learned how to grow more of the Bas mushrooms, I'd been trying to throw grenades into different parts of the production. I couldn't stop it from happening, but I could slow things down, make things difficult. I'd intercepted supplies, anonymously cancelled orders, orchestrated broken machinery, even broken the locks on the labs so no one could enter. These were all small acts of defiance, but they added up.

The plans to expand were now at least a year behind schedule, and no one suspected the delays were down to me. The only problem was, Father and Ossian responded by limiting their circle of confidence, only sharing information with a select few. And recently, because of my obvious opposition to 'progress', that stopped including me. Father still wanted me to be involved. It was his dream. His two eldest boys working together to build the world's biggest pharmaceutical business. What a legacy to behold. But Ossian resented my disapproval. Apparently it wasn't disloyal enough that I outperformed him a million to one in school. Now, I had to look down on his business. He hated that Father wasn't giving up. But Ossian needn't have worried, because neither was I.

I ARRIVED in the office three hours earlier than usual. Something told me I wasn't going to get much work done with someone whose presence I vehemently disagreed with sitting in front of me all day. Besides, I'd hardly had an ounce of sleep.

As soon as the grandfather clock in the hall chimed eight, I couldn't stop my eyes flicking to the door every few seconds. She wasn't even due in the office until nine. At eight-thirty, the door opened. I looked up and immediately wished I hadn't. What the hell was she wearing?

Something inappropriate for where Father had instructed I take her today.

"Good morning," she trilled. Her tone was overly bright, as if to compensate for my dark mood. I watched out of the corner of my eye as she hung her jacket on the coat stand and smoothed her hands down a snug navy dress. The long sleeves tapered to her wrists, the boat cut neckline covered all but her collarbone, and the skirt fell to below her knees. Hosiery covered her legs, and black heels lifted her up so she would stand less than one foot shorter than my six-foot-five inches height. It was an impressive look but, sorry Father, it did nothing to dissuade me from thinking this was a very bad idea.

"Morning," I forced out.

She slid into the seat at the desk opposite. "You're an early riser too," she commented.

"Sometimes," I said, monotone.

"I'm usually in the office way before now, but I slept so well in the cottage. I think it must be the sound of the waves. It's just so soothing. I went for a walk along the coastline before dark and I think the sea air wiped me out. Is this computer for me?" She looked down at the brand new, state of the art Apple set-up glaring at me from across the room.

"You mean the computer that's been put on your desk? With your name on a post-it note stuck to the screen? You know, I think it might be."

I transferred my gaze away but I could tell she was staring at me while chewing the inside of her cheek.

"Great, thanks."

She pulled out the chair and sat down, then began rummaging around in her bag, pulling out all manner of paraphernalia. Pencils, pens, a calculator, a diary, note-books, paperclips, folders. I watched out of the corner of my eye as it all piled up, then felt a tickle of irritation crawl up my spine. I'd never had to share an office before, and I prided myself on keeping everything in its place. It had always been neat and tidy, and now my view of every-thing was being obscured with office *crap*.

She noticed me watching and smiled, timidly. "I didn't know if you'd have a stationery cupboard, and I like to have everything to hand, even if I end up not using it. I'd rather have it than not need it."

I hoped my lack of reply reiterated my lack of desire to converse.

"And I like to catalogue everything I do, so I never forget a thing, which is why I have all these notebooks. They each serve a purpose…"

I stopped grinding my teeth and cut her off. "Do you always talk this much?"

Her cheeks flushed a deep pink that was almost endearing.

"Oh. I'm sorry, I was just making conversation."

I ran my eyes down my inbox, filing away emails that needed my urgent attention. "Neither of us are here for conversation, Vivian. If you have to sit in my office, you'll respect my desire for silence."

"Oh, right. Of course. I'll let you get on."

Silence did indeed fall as we both focused on our computer screens. After a few minutes I snuck a glance at her. She was already engrossed in whatever she was read-ing, chewing her lip and twirling a strand of hair around her finger. I forced my eyes back to my computer. I read the same line over and over until it made no sense at all, then when the tension in the room got the better of me, I stood up, the sound of the chair bumping across the floor making her jump.

"I'm going to get a coffee. Would you like anything?"

Her expression was one of confusion, then a secretarial type of efficiency took over. "Oh, no. Please, let me get it." She went to stand up.

What the fuck?

"Sit your ass down," I commanded. "I asked *you* if you wanted anything. You're not my fucking assistant."

Her eyes widened in shock. "I… um…"

"How do you take it?"

"Um… I…"

"*Coffee*, Vivian," I boomed. "How do you take it?"

"Black," she rushed out. "Black's fine."

"Coming up." I stormed out of my office and down the hall, my pulse hammering in my ears. I rounded the corner to the kitchen. I normally had Amie, my secretary, get my coffee, but I'd dismissed her for the day. I was on edge enough with Little Miss Tour Guide sitting in my office for the foreseeable future.

I made two black coffees in large mugs, grabbed a small plate of shortbread, and walked back to my office. I had marginally calmed down by the time I placed a mug in front of her. She pulled her hand back from the keyboard in surprise, the back of it brushing against mine. Heat radiated from it, rendering my hand cold as I drew it back.

"Thanks," she said, in a quiet voice.

I sat back down to re-read the same line, secretly watching her out of the corner of my eye. She cupped the mug with her palms as if to warm them and nibbled on a biscuit. After several minutes she took a few sips of the coffee, then proceeded to type like a crazy person with a sugar rush. It gave me the impetus to actually do some work. Thirty minutes later, I shut off my computer.

"I'm going to the labs," I announced. "And you're coming with me."

She looked up as if she'd forgotten where she was. "Really? Now?"

"Yes. I have to meet some of our partners there. They want to see some of the production so I may as well show you at the same time."

"Right. Fantastic," she gushed, scrambling to her feet.

I pulled my coat off the stand as I thundered out of the room, hearing her heels skitter along the corridor after me.

"Am I dressed appropriately for the labs?" she asked as we came within a mile of the site.

"No," I replied.

She clicked her tongue. "That's helpful. Any suggestions?"

I trained my eyes on the road. "I have overalls you can change into."

"And shoes?"

"I have work boots you can wear."

"Not yours, surely. What size shoe are you?"

I narrowed my eyes. "You want to know my shoe size?"

Fresh blood flooded her face. "No! I mean, yes? I mean, not like that... oh God."

I anchored a palm to the wheel and spun us smoothly

round a sharp corner. "If you're genuinely interested, I'm a size twelve."

I didn't miss the way she swallowed hard as she turned to look out of the window. After a few more minutes of silence, her phone pinged and she looked at the screen. She sighed and slid her phone into her bag. Her demeanour changed in an instant. The bubbliness evaporated and a heaviness filled it's place.

"Everything ok?" I asked.

She looked out of the window again, avoiding my gaze. "M-hm."

A few more minutes and she asked the question everyone asked as soon as they summoned the courage. "Will I get a sample of Basidiomine?"

"I'm afraid not," I replied. "Demand is too high and it's costly to produce. We simply can't give it away."

"Uh huh. I suppose that makes sense," she muttered quietly.

"Here we are," I confirmed as we pulled up to a set of iron gates. The security guard nodded to me and the gates opened. We drove through and began the long drive up to the labs.

"It's not what I was expecting," she said.

"What were you expecting?"

"More greenery, more flowers, more undulating landscapes. In comparison to what I've seen of the rest of the island, this seems a little... subdued."

I steadied my breath before I spoke. "Just how the mushrooms like it. Shade, darkness, moisture. Between all of these trees is a sea of red. Thousands upon thousands of agarics – or red tops as we call them – clustered together, nurtured by the undergrowth."

The labs were housed in a concrete block, which was pretty soulless compared to the rest of the island. I swung the car around, depositing us at the reception door. Vivian climbed out before I had a chance to open her door. I grunted in annoyance and sensed her smiling behind my back. At the door, I entered a code and stepped forward for a routine retina scan. The metal door clunked open. We entered the dimly lit foyer and I nodded to the guy behind the desk. "How are you doing, Jasper?"

"Very well thank you, sir."

"I have a guest," I said, putting a hand on the small of Vivian's back. "This is Miss Gillespie… She's going to join me on a quick tour with the partners. We'll go to my office first so she can change."

"Ok, Mr. Thorn. They've arrived and are waiting for you in meeting room four."

I guided Vivian through another set of doors and down a corridor, then I stopped at my office and unlocked it, holding the door for Vivian to walk through. She rolled her eyes, presumably at my chivalry. As soon as she was inside, I let the door close heavily. "I'm going to give you a small piece of advice, Vivian," I said, bearing down on her. "I don't know what kind of men you encounter on the mainland but I am a gentleman. I fetch coffee, I hold doors open, I let ladies walk ahead. If you have an issue with that, I suggest you keep it to yourself."

She stared at me, at a loss for words.

"Do I make myself clear?"

My eyes dropped from her eyes to her lips and my jaw clenched without instruction. Her eyes did the same but she physically shuddered. "Fine," she pouted.

I stalked across to a locker on the wall and pulled out a

standard issue set of yellow overalls. They were a size XS but would still engulf her.

"These will have to do," I said, passing her a pair of size eight work boots.

She immediately tipped them up and looked at the soles. "These are three and half sizes too big," she stated. "You want me to look like a clown?"

"Nothing you wear will make you look like a clown," I replied, without thinking.

"If I trip up and fall on my ass..." she warned.

"I will pick you up and we'll keep walking," I said, changing into my own work boots.

"No overalls for you?"

"I don't care if I get my outfit dirty."

"Well, I don't care if I get mine dirty either."

"I do," I snapped. I shoved a lab hat into her hands and held the door open wide. "Ladies first."

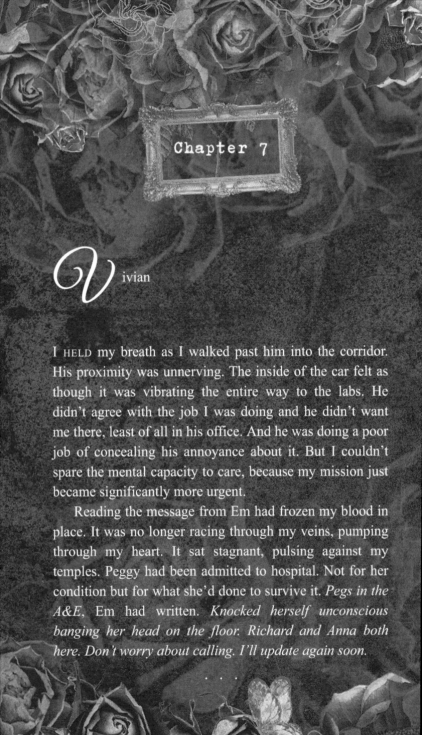

Chapter 7

*V*ivian

I HELD my breath as I walked past him into the corridor. His proximity was unnerving. The inside of the car felt as though it was vibrating the entire way to the labs. He didn't agree with the job I was doing and he didn't want me there, least of all in his office. And he was doing a poor job of concealing his annoyance about it. But I couldn't spare the mental capacity to care, because my mission just became significantly more urgent.

Reading the message from Em had frozen my blood in place. It was no longer racing through my veins, pumping through my heart. It sat stagnant, pulsing against my temples. Peggy had been admitted to hospital. Not for her condition but for what she'd done to survive it. *Pegs in the A&E,* Em had written. *Knocked herself unconscious banging her head on the floor. Richard and Anna both here. Don't worry about calling. I'll update again soon.*

. . .

THE ACT THAT FOLLOWED, to not give away any suggestion I was upset about something, felt, frankly, Oscar-worthy. The unexpected banter with Rupert certainly helped. Despite how much he seemed to despise me, he managed to make it feel light-hearted somehow.

I followed Rupert through a complex network of corridors. On each door was a retina scanner and some had fingerprint scanners too. Security was tight and there was no way I would have been able to come this far without him. We reached the meeting room and Rupert held the door open for me, to my slight annoyance, but mostly amusement – again.

After some pleasantries, he introduced me to the small party. There were too many names to remember but the group included three government officials, two CEOs of leading banks, a representative of some Silicon Valley business I'd never heard of but would probably be a household name before the year was out, and, to my surprise, a journalist. They each carried copies of non-disclosure agreements and were accompanied by what was clearly security personnel.

We followed Rupert out of the room like eager ducklings getting ready for our first swim. I noticed how he commanded the group with professional ease. They hung onto his every word, mirrored his hand gestures. They seemed to idolise him.

The first room we came to was a large industrial-looking storage space.

"This is the first stage of the process," Rupert explained.

At the back of the large room was a machine clanging noisily, spewing out a conveyor belt. In front of them were large vats, some overflowing with the flesh of blood-red mushrooms. "This is where we remove the caps from the stems. Both are used in the final product, but are processed differently. Here, the red tops are washed and separated, ready for the next stage."

I gestured to the vats. "Can I?"

He nodded but followed me closely. I had already decided that if I couldn't get a sample of the drug, the mushrooms would be the next best thing until I could locate where the actual tablets were kept. Then, if I was brave enough, I could steal some. But, as I looked at the gleaming caps, then around at the influential people in the room, I knew I had to bide my time. There was no way I could sneak anything into the pocket of my overalls here without anyone noticing. I picked a large red cap out of one of the vats and turned it over in my fingers. "It's so soft," I whispered, my words almost lost in the sound of the machine.

"I know." Rupert moved towards me, his proximity raising the hairs on every inch of my body. He took my hand in his and turned my palm upwards, exposing the mushroom's upper flesh to the light. "See how it shines here? The surface is completely blemish-free, unlike with other agarics that tend to be vulnerable to even the mildest conditions."

He continued to hold my hand as I ran a thumb over the cap of the mushroom. Any sensation I should have felt though was obliterated by the heat that overtook my whole arm. I told myself it was nerves. I was in the middle of the labs, surrounded by VIPs and the very things I wanted to get my hands on. Millions of them.

"And here," he continued, pointing to the delicate gills,

"these are softer than other fungus of this type, but they're hardy, which is useful when we go on to the next stage of processing."

His hand slipped away from mine before he tapped my elbow sending the red top hurtling back into the vat. *Damnit.* I looked up, but he was already walking towards the conveyor belt with two of the government officials. I caught up quickly. "Is it used for anything other than a stimulant?" I asked, following close behind. "It's something the visitors will ask, I'm sure."

Rupert nodded to three workers who disappeared quickly after one of them hurriedly switched off the machine. Little red tops rolled across the surface at the loss of momentum. "Well, as some of our clients will testify…" he gestured to the group, everyone except the journalist, "it is used mainly as a stimulant. But it can be used to treat neurological conditions like anxiety and depression."

"And pain?" I couldn't help myself.

"That too."

I looked down at the stalk-less caps below us. "How does this one fungus do all of that?"

"It's the psilocybin, the extract. It can be used as a psychedelic agent…"

That was the part I was most nervous about. "For hallucinations and stuff?"

"It was historically used for that, yes. But how severe the impact is depends on how much is consumed and the type of mushroom used. Magic mushrooms are most likely to give you those kinds of experiences. This fungus is unique to the Isle of Crow. We've tested it extensively and it doesn't seem to promote the psychedelic effects of other mushrooms. Instead, it stimulates the brain in such a way that it can sharpen your thinking or it can inhibit serotonin receptors – the part of our brain that controls mood and emotion."

"So, that's why people want it to be distributed more widely? Because it could be a natural remedy for depression and anxiety?"

"Exactly. But, it's impossible to produce the quantity people want. You'd need a heck of a lot of these things to create mass medication which, unfortunately, is what the western world seems to need. We're working on ways to increase the yield without…" His pause drew my eyes to his face. It looked pained. "…taking over the entire island. The conditions need to be just right for this fungi to flourish, and that's… *difficult* to scale."

He continued to discuss business with two other men while the journalist approached me.

"So, you're Vivian Gillespie, the new tour manager?" He smiled and held out a hand. "I'm Cash. I write for the *Herald*. Been trying to get into this bloody place for years."

I shook his hand. "Good to meet you. Congratulations for getting this far."

"This your first glimpse behind the scenes?" he asked.

"Yes," I nodded. "I only started yesterday."

"And what do you make of it so far?"

I narrowed my eyes at him. My limited career in PR had taught me to be wary of the press. Nothing was ever off the record.

"It's a beautiful island," I said. "The Thorns are generous and eager to make the tours as interesting and worthwhile for visitors as possible."

It was Cash's turn to narrow his eyes. "Hmm. That's

good. I think it's great that they're opening the place up. But, what I cannot get my head around is why? And why now? I know people are curious about the place and the people who live here, but no one's forcing them to do these tours. I don't buy that there isn't some sort of ulterior motive, you know?"

I cocked my head to one side and smiled thinly. "Like I said. This is only my second day. I know as much as you."

He reached into his pocket, pulled out a card and handed it to me. "Take this. When you learn more, and you don't like what you learn, you call me."

I took the card warily. He seemed sure there was something untoward going on that we weren't being told about. But, right then, I couldn't find it in myself to care. All I cared about was getting my hands on the drug, or some part of it, for my sister. My heart squeezed. The thought that she was in hospital, without me by her side, suffering through another episode almost killed me. It was small consolation that at least she'd get some decent painkillers while she was there.

Cash nodded knowingly at me then walked back to Rupert. With everyone's backs turned I seized my chance. Without giving it a second thought, I reached into one of the vats, pulled out a handful of red tops and pushed them as gently as I could into the pocket of my overalls.

I avoided eye contact with everyone as we made our way to another room, this one sparkling white, immaculate, with not a speck of dust on any surface. About ten people dressed in white overcoats, latex gloves and protective goggles moved around silently and efficiently, transporting test tubes of clear liquid from one table to another. If that didn't give away the fact we were now standing in a science lab, the scenes to our left would have left no doubt. A large clear container boiled liquid, while an umbrella top caught the steam and channelled it into a separate container. Next to it, two more men in lab coats were prodding the gills of mushrooms with a syringe.

Behind them, what looked like a sealed pizza oven burned orange while more scientists looked on with timers and thermometers in their hands.

"We're experimenting with different methods of extraction," Rupert explained. "At the moment we extract psilocybin manually, which is hugely time-consuming, so we're trying different processes like steam distillation, drying out, and baking at high temperatures. Then over there…" I followed his gaze to the back of the room. "We're experimenting with different quantities and combinations of other plant extracts." I noticed Cash dictating into his phone.

"So, how is it grown?" one of the CEOs asked.

Rupert straightened and delivered what sounded like a much-rehearsed line. "In the same way all mushrooms are grown. With highly nourishing soil, moist conditions, shade."

"So, why do you think this mushroom only grows on the Isle of Crow?" Cash asked.

"Because the soil here has an unusually low pH value," he replied smoothly.

"What pH value is it?" I chipped in.

He turned his stare on me. "What do you know about pH values?" The aggression in his tone made me rigid and I was sure the other members of the group heard it too.

"I know it's an acidity measurement. I learned it in

Physics. Doesn't everyone?" I all but held up my hands in surrender.

"Well," he said, his face softening as he turned it to the others. "It's five."

I whistled through pursed lips. "Wow, that is low."

"There's one more room we can take a look at," he said, changing the subject. We followed him out and down another corridor.

"This is where we keep spores and spawn in case we have to fulfil an emergency order, or the crops suffer some sort of damage," he explained as we all stood in a small storage area. "The red tops are exceptional at colonising so we don't often need to step in, but if we do, this is where we come."

My heart thumped. Forget the red tops in my pocket... *this* was what I needed. The source – the seed. With this, I could grow the mushrooms myself. I waited until Rupert led the group around the various glass cabinets lining the walls. When I was sure no one would suddenly turn around, I reached out and gently picked up a cellophane bag containing a good amount of spawn. I went to drop the bag into my pocket, but missed. Rupert turned as I placed my boot over the bag on the floor.

"What was that?"

"What was what?" I looked back at him, innocently.

"That sound."

"Oh, I adjusted my bra," I replied, regretting the words the second they left my mouth. What was wrong with me?

His eyes dropped to my breasts even though they were covered in bright yellow overalls, then just as fleetingly, he turned back to the group. I bent as quietly as I could, snuck the bag inside my overalls and shoved it down into my pants. There was no way I was going to risk those falling to the floor again.

A few minutes later, a lab employee came to escort the partners to another building where they were to meet with Ossian to discuss opportunities. I then followed Rupert down the corridor to his office. He beckoned the guy from the front desk to join us.

"Jasper, can you see Miss Gillespie back to my car? I need to attend to a few things before I leave."

"Of course, Mr. Thorn."

The door closed and I was left alone in Rupert's stark office wearing his overalls, the pockets stuffed full of mushrooms. I carefully peeled them out and placed them inside my bag, taking care to not pack them in so much they might be crushed. Then I placed the boots and over-alls by his locker and stepped outside.

"This way, ma'am," Jasper smiled, and I followed him back to the main entrance. I held my breath as we waited for the mechanical doors to rotate. Any second now, I would be home safe and dry, or at least, outside of this iron-clad building, clutching the very things I came here for. I couldn't believe I'd done it. I'd got what I came for, in less than two days!

The doors opened and I stepped into the rotating disc, then suddenly, my ears rang so hard I had to clamp my hands over them. A voice shouted behind me to step back-wards out of the doors. My heart sped up again and beat unevenly against the wall of my chest. Jasper was gesturing wildly to no one in particular, but the sound continued. I stood still, my hands clasped to each side of my head, and waited. A minute later, three security men came sprinting down the corridor towards us. One of them yanked my hands from my ears, forcing me to close my eyes against the piercing squeal. I felt them tear my bag from my shoulder and start patting my body from my neck to my feet. Shit. I knew without opening my eyes I was busted.

Several more minutes passed, then finally, the squealing stopped, but the ringing went on. One of men spoke in a voice that sounded fuzzy and distant. I shook my head – my way of saying I couldn't understand him. Then a second man held the handful of mushrooms up to my face. I dropped my eyelids shamefully. I couldn't believe my bad luck. How could I have been so stupid?

"What's going on?"

Rupert's voice boomed down the corridor.

"This young lady activated the alarm, sir. We've disabled it temporarily."

"Vivian?"

I reluctantly opened my eyes only to close them again to avoid witnessing the hatred in Rupert's.

"What the hell were you thinking? What did you take them for?" There was a note of desperation in his voice, like he was shattered on my behalf. *That* made me look up.

"I… I don't know. I guess I wanted to try them for myself."

"What were you going to do? Make yourself a fucking omelette?"

I would have laughed had I not been so terrified.

"I don't know. I wasn't thinking. God, I'm so sorry… It was a stupid thing to do."

"You're damn right it was," Rupert snapped.

A small flicker of defiance lit up inside me, and I squared my shoulders. "Is it so bad that I want to know what all the fuss is about? I have to be knowledgeable about it if I'm to appear at all credible. Do you want me to do a good job or not?"

"You don't need to sample the fucking drug to do a good job as a *tour manager*," he snarled. "Don't you realise what's just happened? You've just been caught stealing. From *my* family. On *my* watch."

A low growl erupted from his throat like he was trying to hold something back. I stared back at him, scared half to death but defiant. They'd brought me here and they were denying me the one thing the job existed for. To my horror, Rupert's fingers leapt out, gripped my jaw and squeezed until my eyes smarted. Through unfallen tears I glanced about for a witness, but the security guards and Jasper seemed to have melted away as soon as Rupert arrived on the scene.

"You won't pull that shit again." His voice was low, his face menacing.

I tried to shake my head but he stilled it in his grip.

"It wasn't a fucking question."

I tried to swallow but the whole bottom half of my face was constricted. "You're hurting me," I whimpered.

He ignored me and continued. "You want to know why you won't pull that shit again?"

I blinked seeing as I couldn't nod.

"Because you'll be thrown off this island with a metaphorical rock tied to your leg. You forget we have influence *everywhere*. Those city boys and politicians you just met? They know we can cut them off and fuel their enemies. They might collectively want this damn tour, but we selectively have their balls in the gap of a car door. They will spin whatever favour we ask them for. If my father ever finds out about this, he will ruin your life. That's a guarantee. But if you do as I say from here on in, he doesn't have to know. Do you understand?"

I paused before blinking. What did he mean by doing as he said?

"Do you?" he growled, his grip tightening around my jaw.

I blinked rapidly and he released me. My hand immediately flew to my face and rubbed at the skin to try and soothe the soreness.

"Now get your ass in my car," he snapped, walking towards the door.

I stood my ground, fear freezing the blood in my veins. "What did you mean?"

He stopped but didn't turn around. "What do you need clarity on, Vivian?"

"Doing as you say? What does that mean?"

He shoved his hands in the pockets of his sleekly tailored suit and gritted out a breath. "You'll know soon enough. Now, get in my car before I throw you in it."

We drove in silence all the way back to Blackcap Hall, him grinding his jaw as he steered one-handed again, forcing me to stare out of the window for most of the journey. I'd never felt more confused in all my life. His hand around my jaw really fucking hurt, but the heat from his touch lit me up. What the hell? I should have hated him with every fibre of my being, but instead, embers burned in my stomach, making me sweat feverishly.

We pulled up at the Hall to find a gorgeous, brand new, duck egg blue baby Aston Martin parked out front. Rupert scowled as I climbed out of the car without waiting for him to hold the door, then stormed into the house, disappearing into its shadows. The doorman grinned and threw me a set of keys which I only just caught because I was gazing adoringly at the stunning vehicle.

"Here's your car, miss."

"Wow," I said, breathless. "This is beautiful."

"That it is, ma'am."

"This is the car that was delayed on the water?" I asked, tearing my eyes from the vehicle.

"No, miss. That one was turned back around. This is a gift from Mr. Rupert, miss. It's a beauty. Enjoy it."

What? Rupert just gave me a car? Ok, I take back what I thought earlier. Now I'm more confused than I've ever felt in my life.

I slid into the seat and started the engine. My head was spinning. In the space of an hour I'd felt the softness of Rupert's hand as I held the mushroom, and the steel of his conviction when he gripped my jaw. And now he'd given me a car worth two-hundred-thousand pounds, despite seemingly hating my guts.

Guilt, shame and confusion continued to prick at me the entire drive back to the cottage, and I could hardly wait to curl up in bed and sleep the day away. It wasn't until I'd run a hot bath and peeled down my pants that I realised I still had the mushroom spawn. The security guards assumed the mushrooms were all I'd taken, and they'd disabled the alarm. In the midst of all the chaos, I'd clean forgotten the small bag secured in my underwear.

I carefully wrapped the bag in tissue paper and placed it in my bedside drawer. Then, I fell uneasily into a restless sleep, dragging my feet through dreams of shadows, red tops, and venomous, beautiful, jagged thorns.

Chapter 8

*R*upert

Uncle Aro, Dax and Hector were already standing around Grandpa's bed when I arrived. Father and Oz had their heads bowed together in one corner, a sight that was becoming more familiar each day. Everyone – including Grandpa – warmed a lowball of copper-coloured whiskey in their fists. Our Friday evening soirees moved from the cigar room to Grandpa's sleeping quarters shortly after he became immobile. We were Thorns, Grandpa always said, and the show must go on. So the show did go on; we simply moved the stage.

"Rupert's here now. He'll vouch for me," Hector said, beckoning me to the head of the bed where Grandpa sat rolling his eyes.

"Like I'll believe anything that comes out of Rupert's mouth when it comes to your mischief, boy. You two have always been thick as thieves."

I BENT down and kissed Grandpa's forehead as he continued. "Nothing is stronger in this world than family, and don't you forget it. Blood is thicker than water, isn't that right, Aro?"

I glanced up at Aro, knowing full well his blood connection to my father was not one he relished. He deflected the question instead of answering it. "He used to get all sentimental after five whiskeys. Now it's two. Just saying."

While Hector pushed a lowball into one of my hands, Grandpa took my other hand in his. "How did your meeting with the partners go?"

"Fine, Grandpa. I just showed them around. Ossian met them afterwards."

At the sound of his name, Ossian's ears pricked up. "What are you talking about?"

Grandpa cleared his throat. "Your meeting with the partners. Did it go well?"

Ossian slithered up to us, shooting me a death glare before quirking his lips up at Grandpa. Dax stalked out of the way. It was common knowledge he and Ossian were not on speaking terms. I often wondered why Grandpa insisted on these weekly drinks when most of us couldn't bear to be in each other's company. "It couldn't have gone better," he said in his nasal voice. "I did have to throw one of them off the island."

"Not literally, I hope," Grandpa replied, with not a joke in sight.

"He was held at the port then put on a separate boat back to the mainland."

"Who was it?" I asked.

"The journalist. He asked far too many questions."

"Well, that is his job," I said.

Ossian continued, ignoring me. "He was far too prob-ing. Disrespectful. And the CEO of Hailthorpe told me he saw the guy slip Rupert's girl his card."

"My girl?" I asked.

"Vivian," Ossian hissed, spitting saliva over my brand new suit.

"She's *not* my girl," I snapped. "You're the one who hired her. I never wanted her here."

"Anyway," Ossian continued. "He won't be coming back."

"Then we can probably expect some shitty press, Oz. Nice."

Ossian's small, beady eyes panned to me. "That won't happen," he said with a sadistic grin. "I took care of that."

I rolled my eyes blatantly. "Please tell me he's still alive."

"Oh, he is. For now."

Ossian sidled back to Father and they resumed their clandestine discussion. It made my skin itch with irritation. Did they have to be so obvious about the fact they were keeping secrets from this supposed 'blood thicker than water' family? I detested the way my father and Ossian had become single-minded about the pharmaceutical company. I knew as well as they did, the only way we could grow more would be to take over the entire island, and that, in my mind at least, was not an option. I hated that they now kept me in the dark.

But now I had a way in. A living breathing listening device, in the shape of one Vivian Gillespie. I had a hold over her now; she would do whatever I asked, otherwise she could say goodbye to this island. And something told me she desperately needed to stay.

Task number one would include relaying any conversations Ossian and Father had without me present. She wouldn't be privy to the raw truth, but a coded version of it, which would be plenty enough. I looked forward to giving her the brief and watching her squirm. Despite the fact she had sticky fingers, she was a tight-assed professional who would hate every second of spying on her employer for me. And that, I was going to relish. If I had to sit and look at that annoyingly attractive face, whose very presence was essentially fucking up our family, for the next twelve months, I was going to make it, at the very least, fun.

"Earth to Rupert..." Hector's voice cut into my thoughts.

"What?"

"You were miles away. Aro asked how you were getting on sharing an office with Vivian."

"Fine," I clipped. "It's a squeeze in there now, and I'm not sure how either of us benefit from the arrangement, but..." I glared at my father, "it's fine."

Father grunted. "She needs guidance and supervision. I don't have the time and Ossian is too involved in the production. Hector is capable of running the distillery and you are being stubborn about your role in the pharmaceutical company, so this is what you get."

"Well, the girl is trouble, if you ask me." And now I'd heard she'd taken that journalist's card, she was going to be in even more shit.

Ossian snorted from across the room. "She's the kind of trouble you could take home and handcuff to the bed."

I spun around so fast the lowball flew out of my hand and smashed into a wall, small shards of glass tinkering tunefully across the floor. My top lip curled under as the words seeped out like poison. "You say any such thing about her again, I will kill you."

The whole room fell silent, the only sound being my heaving breaths.

Hector laughed, nervously. "You're not soft on her are you?"

"Don't be ridiculous," I barked.

"That's just as well," Father stated. "You know what your future holds."

I took another glass from Dax. "Oh don't worry, Father. I know exactly what's expected of me."

"How is Elspeth Cartwright these days?" Grandpa asked, brightly.

"I have no idea," I replied.

"Sienna St. John?"

"No idea about her either," I clipped, impatiently.

"You saw her only this week at the Club," Ossian sneered.

I shot him another glare. "She's fine, Grandpa."

As conversation thankfully turned to other things, Aro moved up to my side.

"Now, tell me," he said, with a wicked glint in his eye. "Is it really so bad sharing an office with Vivian Gillespie?"

I loved Aro like a brother, or even a father, but I was already sick of talking about the unwelcome addition to my life. Vivian Gillespie was a thieving little upstart with a propensity to run her mouth off when I was trying to work. Unlike the other male members of my family, I didn't see a plethora of curves only to be gawped at. I saw a tool to be used, a brain to be wary of, and someone who, if not kept at several arms' length from my person, could become a problem. Her blatant disrespect for my chivalry, and insistence on parading in front of me wearing outfits that, frankly, should be outlawed were already pushing my patience to its limits.

My eyes narrowed on one of the few men in my family I actually admired. "Yes, Aro. It is."

Chapter 9

𝒱ivian

I STOOD on the steps to Caspian House, holding my phone to my ear as if it were a lifeline.

"She's been discharged?" I asked Richard. "Well, that's good news. Is she back home with you?"

"She is, love. They gave her some decent painkillers so she's having a good long sleep now. One of the nurses told us about a support group for people who suffer from chronic pain. She's going to give it a go."

I clasped a hand to my chest. "Oh, that's great news. It sounds really positive."

"It could be, love. Now, how about you? How's it going there?"

I looked around to check the coast was clear before recounting my disastrous attempt to steal mushrooms and my successful attempt to steal spawn. To my disappointment, he was more worried than impressed.

"PLEASE BE CAREFUL, love. I know this is the whole reason you've gone, but don't get yourself into a dangerous position just to get your hands on this stuff. We'd rather you came home empty-handed than not at all."

"I know," I groaned. "I'll be careful."

We said our goodbyes and I ran up the steps to Caspian House, hoping to God there were no Thorns inside. I'd had enough of them for one week.

I settled onto a stool by the bar and ordered a red wine. Alarmingly, I was presented with an actual brochure of red wines to choose from. How big was their damn cellar? I looked up at the bartender, apologetically. "Do you have any recommendations?"

His expression remained fixed as he sighed a breath that reeked of disappointment. "Usually, I would pair a red wine with food," he began, in a patronising tone. "But in the absence of that, may I suggest something light and fruity... Perhaps this New Zealand Pinot Noir?"

I faked a smile in return. "Thank you."

He made an elaborate show of removing the cork and splashing a drop into a large bulbous stem glass, before passing it to me. "Taste," he hissed when I looked at him bewildered. I took a sip and nodded, even though it wasn't the thick, delicious full-bodied merlot I would normally have selected. He filled the glass a quarter way and placed it on a black napkin, along with the bill. "That will be thirty-six pounds when you're ready."

I gulped down the mouthful I'd just taken and forced back a splutter. "How much?"

"It's on the house," came a familiar voice making the barman snap his head up, poised to argue. But the second his eyes landed on Minty making her way over, his expression twisted into one of confusion.

"Don't you know who this is?" She stared at him pointedly. "It's Vivian Gillespie, the new tour manager, working directly for the *Thorns*." She drew out the last word, narrowing her glare.

The barman's demeanour flipped instantly. "My manners. I'm so sorry." He held a hand over the bar, which I took, slightly bemused. "Michael. It's a pleasure."

"Vivian," I replied, then added in a doubtful tone, "Likewise."

"Time for your break, Michael," Minty smiled. "I've got this."

He shot her a look of gratitude and scurried away.

"Well, you got him all of a fluster," she giggled, picking up a polishing cloth and rubbing it over an already spotless champagne flute.

"Not in the way a girl tends to enjoy," I replied, taking another sip. "Does this really cost thirty-six pounds?"

She shrugged. "It sure does. I'm surprised you chose that one. It's a bit lacklustre in my opinion."

I curled my lips. "You're right there, but I was under pressure."

"What would you really like?" She slipped the glass from my hands and tipped the thirty-six pounds-worth of wine down the sink, to my horror.

"Um, a merlot? And really, it doesn't have to be an expensive one," I added, the red puddle in the sink gleaming up at me, accusingly.

She replaced the glass with another, this time filled with something much darker, slightly thicker, with legs that stuck to the side of the glass, which I loved. I took a grateful sip. "Mmm, much better."

"You're welcome. So, how's your first week been?"

God, where do I start, and what can I tell? After Rupert caught me stealing the red tops three days earlier, I'd hardly seen him. He spent about ten minutes in his office each morning then disappeared for the rest of the day.

"It's been… interesting," I started.

"Ha! Say no more. Have you been taken to the labs yet?"

"Yes. Rupert took me on Tuesday."

Her eyebrows lifted. "Rupert himself?"

"Yes. I share an office with him."

"You do? In Blackcap Hall? My word, you are privileged."

"I don't think it's on account of who I am. It's more that Rupert needs to be more, shall we say, *immersed* in the tour, that's all."

"Yeah, it's fairly common knowledge he's not a fan of the idea. I feel for Rupert, you know. This ain't going to be the best year for him."

My senses heightened. "Why's that?"

"Well, first Peregrine's health has got so much worse. Rupert's close to his grandfather, so that can't be easy. Then the tour which, as we know, he's not on board with. And after that, in just a few months, he'll become engaged to one of the daughters on the island. I know for sure he isn't seeing anyone, so whoever the lucky lady is, there's a fair chance he won't be on board with that either. It certainly won't be a love marriage."

I felt as though all the blood had run from my head

down to my toes, and I had to focus on the glass between my fingers to stop the bar from spinning. Rupert was getting married? My head filled with a tsunami of questions. First and foremost, why did I care? And why the hell did the thought rack me physically?

I stilled each of them while I asked the most logical. "Why does he have to marry?"

She looked at me like I'd grown three heads. "Did you do any research before you came here? The marriage law is tradition on the Isle of Crow. It only applies to the Consortium families but it's as old as time and one of the pillars of our community."

"Consortium families?"

"Yeah, all the big billionaire families are a part of the Consortium. The marriage thing is how we keep all the wealth on the island, to be owned and shared by all the families. If the heirs to all these fortunes were to marry outside the Isle of Crow, the families could say goodbye to that wealth. Even with the tightest prenup in place, there would be children who'd inherit the estates. It's for everyone's good that the money stays here."

"So, why does Rupert have to marry now? Why this year? Why the rush?"

"The male members of Consortium families have to be married before they turn twenty-seven. And Rupert turns twenty-seven in December."

My chest tightened. "Why twenty-seven?"

Minty shrugged. "Who knows? It's like the 27 Club right? Except, instead of dying, they're signing their life away to another person."

"That's optimistic," I murmured.

"Ha! It's not all bad. The arranged marriage thing only

happens if they haven't found anyone by then. If they do find someone, they can marry for love. That's what usually happens, but not in Rupert's case."

"So, he turns twenty-seven in December? That's only nine months away."

"Right? And the engagement has to be at least six months in advance of that, so…"

My heart hammered. "He needs to be engaged in the next three months? And he doesn't know who he's marrying?"

"Well, he knows who all the candidates are, not that he's shown interest in *any* of them for as long as I can remember. There'll be a banquet held in his honour at Blackcap Hall in the summer. All the eligible women will be there and he'll select a fiancée shortly after. Then there'll be an elaborate celebration. And with Rupert being a Thorn – the richest family on the island – you can bet the celebrations will be epic. And that's before we even get to the wedding."

I almost asked what happened at the wedding but I didn't want to know. I would find out first hand in good time. But that wasn't the reason I didn't ask. The reason was a piercing pain that had taken up in my abdomen. It must have been the stress of my first week coming to a head. I clasped a hand over my heart as it beat erratically.

"Wow, that is… quite a year," I muttered.

"Yeah. He can handle it though. Of all the Thorns, he's the brightest and most resilient."

"What makes you say that?"

"Straight A student, IQ of a hundred and forty. He's grown up in Ossian's shadow and he's no weaker for it. In fact, I suspect he's grown even stronger than his older brother, and not just physically." She changed the subject suddenly. "Are you still on for next weekend?"

"What?" I looked up at her, dazed.

"The night market?"

"Oh right, yes. Yes, I'm looking forward to it."

"Excellent. You're going to love it."

And with that, she turned to serve another sharply dressed customer, leaving me to battle a bundle of nerves and emotions. I was starting to think I'd made the worst decision of my life, even if it was with the best of intentions. My thoughts strayed back to my sister, and I remembered why I'd risked so much to be here. I drained the last of my wine, waved goodbye to Minty and left the lounge with a sense of purpose weighing heavy on my shoulders.

I WOKE up early from another fitful sleep, threw on a pair of leggings and a t-shirt, downed a strong coffee and set to work. First, a short trip to the potting shed at the end of the garden. I filled three small pots with compost and carried them back into the cottage. I'd already selected the perfect windowsill – in the parlour off the side of the kitchen. It was out of the way, so it wouldn't be spotted if any visitors arrived unannounced, and the room was warm and the light scarce. That seemed to be how the red tops thrived – in warm, damp soil under the cover of branches. I carefully potted some of the spawn and drizzled a little fertiliser onto the soil before placing them in their warm, shaded spot.

I took a step back to admire my handiwork, before reaching for my phone to call Emerie with the good news.

"You're still alive then?" No pleasantries, nothing.

"Nice to hear from you too," I grinned.

"I'm being serious," Emerie said. "Richard told me what happened. You got caught stealing?! Are you crazy?"

"Hey! I did what I came here to do. I've planted up the spawn, so hopefully it won't be long until it bears fruit."

"You really don't think you can get the drug itself, instead of going to all the trouble of growing it? I mean, do you even know what to do once you have an actual mushroom?"

"I asked if I could try a sample of the drug and they said no. It's in such high demand they keep it under lock and key."

"So, find the lock and the key."

"Yeah, it's not that easy, Em. The whole place is secured by eyeball and finger scans. I can't even go into the labs without an escort. Especially now. After my little stunt the other day, they likely won't take their eyes off me."

I cast one more motherly glance at the little pots then closed the door to the parlour. "I've only been here a week and I've made some progress. Don't lose hope yet, Em."

"This is what I love about you, Vivi."

"What is?" I smiled before collapsing onto the sofa.

"When something really gets under your skin, you cling on with both hands until you've done whatever it is you need to do."

"Wow. I didn't know that about myself."

"Sure you did." Her voice lowered until I had to concentrate to hear her. "Take your sister and everything that happened four years ago."

I stiffened instinctively. "What about it?"

"Well, as soon as you knew something wasn't right, you didn't stop until you got to the bottom of it. I mean, can you imagine what would've happened if you hadn—"

"Stop," I said, quickly. "Don't. I don't want to think about what could've happened. It's hard enough coming to terms with what did happen."

"What do you mean?"

I sighed and blew the steam from my cup. "Well, look at where we are. She's plagued with chronic pain now, isn't she? It's no coincidence. It might even all be my fault."

"What? Don't be ridiculous, Vivi. How would it be your fault?"

"Maybe…" I took a deep breath. I'd never said the words aloud before, and they immobilised me. "Maybe I didn't find her soon enough."

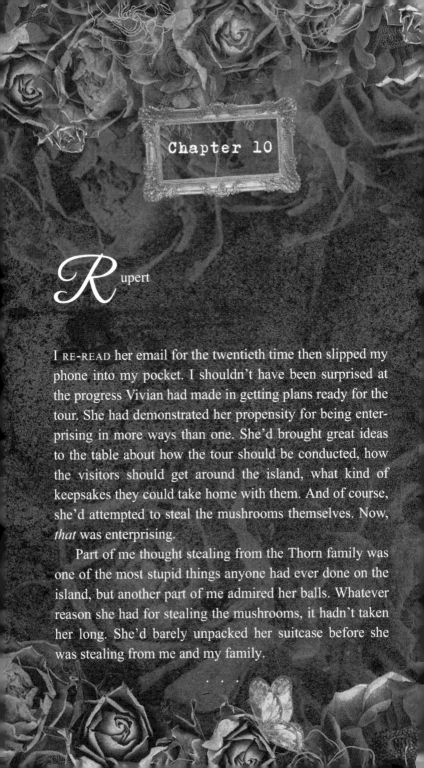

$\mathcal{R}$upert

I RE-READ her email for the twentieth time then slipped my phone into my pocket. I shouldn't have been surprised at the progress Vivian had made in getting plans ready for the tour. She had demonstrated her propensity for being enterprising in more ways than one. She'd brought great ideas to the table about how the tour should be conducted, how the visitors should get around the island, what kind of keepsakes they could take home with them. And of course, she'd attempted to steal the mushrooms themselves. Now, *that* was enterprising.

Part of me thought stealing from the Thorn family was one of the most stupid things anyone had ever done on the island, but another part of me admired her balls. Whatever reason she had for stealing the mushrooms, it hadn't taken her long. She'd barely unpacked her suitcase before she was stealing from me and my family.

. . .

B<small>UT</small>, far from feeling angry, I felt intrigued. There was clearly more to Vivian Gillespie than met the eye.

Fighting this battle against my father and Ossian was a lonely and boring business. At least I would have the pleasure of manipulating my new office imposter in the process. Starting now.

The email I just read was one Vivian had copied me into. She was asking my father and Ossian if she could discuss tour logistics. What days the tour would take place, what parts of the production plant visitors could see, which members of staff would need to be involved.

I knew this was where they'd need to tread carefully to keep our secret sauce from prying eyes. Deliveries and supply dictated when the tours could take place, and this was precisely the area in which my father and brother now ceased to keep me informed. They might disclose something to her that could be useful to me. So, this was where Vivian would begin to atone for her actions.

When she walked into my office that Monday morning, I was ready for her. She was humming to herself, but stopped abruptly when she saw me sitting at my desk.

"Oh! Hello… I didn't expect to see you."

"Why not?" I grunted. "This is my office."

Her eyes glinted from across the room. "I know that. But you weren't here for most of last week."

"I was busy."

She removed her coat, revealing another snug pencil dress. This one emerald green with shorter sleeves and a thick black belt, with no room to spare over the round of her curves. Didn't she have any other damn style of outfit in her wardrobe? We had a professional dress code, sure, but I didn't recall any part of our contracts stating that figure-hugging, Miss Moneypenny style dresses were mandatory at all times.

She pulled out her chair but before she sat down, she glared at me. "Are you this friendly to everyone?"

"No," I replied, narrowing my eyes. "You're special."

"Lucky me," she muttered, sitting down. My chest hummed with relief and disappointment. I could no longer see that ridiculous waist to hip ratio that usually made my mouth water. Which was good. I couldn't be distracted. I had another twelve months of this shit. "Thank you for my car, by the way. That was awfully generous of you."

I brushed off her gratitude like the gesture meant nothing. "You are working for the Thorns now. I would like you to look as though you are."

She tipped her head to one side and shone large baby blue eyes at me. "What car was I supposed to have?"

I focused on the more comfortable view of my computer. "A Mini Cooper."

"I might have liked a Mini Cooper," she challenged.

"Sure you might," I clipped. "But it was no Aston Martin."

I detected a small smile without looking up. It curled something in my chest.

"What's on your agenda today?" I asked.

"I have a visit to—"

"Cancel it."

"I'm sorry?"

"Cancel all your plans, Vivian."

"Why?"

I dragged my face back to hers. Those fucking eyes seemed larger every time I glanced at them, and they were always filled with challenge, despite who I was. "Because there's something I need you to do."

"Oh." Her shoulders sank.

"Yes. *Oh*," I repeated, with a small smile. "You don't have to crap your pants just yet. It's something you've been planning anyway; I just want you to expedite it."

She looked up, warily. "What is it?"

"The meeting you've asked to have with Ossian and my father."

A frown ghosted her brow. "What about it?"

"I want it to happen today, and I want you to take note of every single thing that is discussed."

Her frown deepened. "Why? I don't understand."

I ground my teeth and bit my tongue. "You don't need to understand it, Vivian," I hissed. "You just have to *do* it."

She stared at me as though I'd gone mad, and why wouldn't she? I was asking her to relay back to me a conversation she was about to have with my own family. Why couldn't I have that conversation myself? Because I knew they would let things slip that they knew she wouldn't pick up on.

"Do I need to remind you *why* you have to do it?" I asked in a low voice.

She shook her head once. "No."

"Good." I returned to my screen but I could still feel the heat of her stare. "What?" I demanded without looking up.

"How do I get them to agree to a meeting today?"

I straightened and forced a smile. "You found a way to get this job, Vivian. You can find a way to secure this meeting."

Her face flushed as she blinked away. I stood and

buttoned my jacket. Part of me wished she would squirm more, but there was a defiance about her I surprisingly liked. I felt her gaze on me again as I walked to the door. I turned to catch it before she could look away.

"Meet me here at the end of the day. I want to know everything they say, Vivian." I placed my hands on the desk and brought my face to hers. The last time she was this close was when I gripped her jaw between my fingers, digging them into the soft warm flesh of her face. The one memory of the moment that overrode all others was the change in her expression. Before I gripped her, it was one of fear, guilt and shame. But when I dug my fingers into her skin, titling her face up to mine, her eyes brightened and her lips parted. Breathy gasps left her mouth as I threatened her. It was almost as though she *enjoyed* it.

As I leaned into her, those very same eyes dropped to my lips just as she licked her own. It heated everything south of my belt, making the fuse I had when it came to Vivian Gillespie even shorter. My parting word came out like a bark. "*Everything.*"

I stood and watched the flush in her cheeks deepen shamelessly, then I flung open the door and walked out.

Chapter 11

*V*ivian

"THANK you for meeting me so soon," I said, forcing the apology out of my voice.

Sinclair sat behind his desk steepling his fingers and glaring curiously at me through narrowed eyes. Ossian was pacing at the back of the room talking quietly into his phone.

"Hmph. Out with it, Vivian. What's the rush?"

I told him the lie I'd been rehearsing in the ladies' bathroom for the last half an hour. "I'm afraid my transport supplier has fallen through. I've narrowed down alternative options and have found one with the perfect luxury ferry, but I need you to sign it off before someone else snaps it up."

I pushed the papers across the desk for him to sign. I was not looking forward to firing my original supplier for no reason at all.

"I've also had some thoughts about the tour itself," I began as he scratched his fountain pen across the pages. "Given the few parts of the production plant you've agreed to let visitors see, I'm slightly concerned the tour will be over in a matter of hours. I thought, perhaps to extend it and give our guests something else to talk about on their return to the mainland, we could have them visit the distillery and then host them at Caspian House…"

Sinclair's head shot up and Ossian lowered his phone to face me.

"You don't think we're showing them enough?" he said with a throaty rumble.

"Don't misunderstand me," I rushed out. "I think what we're showing them is incredibly interesting, but that part of the tour will be over quickly. The visitors will be curious about how the islanders live. And showing them more of the island might make them more sympathetic towards the work you do, and less focused on the drug. I know you wanted the tour to ultimately satisfy peoples' hunger for information. Expanding the tour to other places could help."

I felt Ossian's stare boring into the side of my head as Sinclair pondered my suggestion. "I suppose it wouldn't hurt to take them to Caspian House…"

"And you could sell special edition whiskey sets at the distillery," I suggested. "That would make a great souvenir."

"That's not a bad idea." Somehow, even when Ossian said a positive thing, it still sounded like a biting criticism.

"Fine," Sinclair sighed. "Re-work the schedule and email it to me."

"Great!" Despite their woeful lack of enthusiasm, I felt

as though I'd won a small victory. I was still shit-scared about organising a tour for the first time in my life, but maybe I could do it after all. "There's just one other thing…"

Sinclair's eyes narrowed again and Ossian suddenly – silently – appeared at his side.

"For the big VIP visit, how about we host a cocktail party at Blackcap Hall?"

Ossian's head tipped back and a nasal cackle slid up and out of his windpipe. "You're crazy if you think we're letting those cretins into our home."

I turned my attention to him. "We need to make that particular tour more special than the rest. What better a way to make our visitors feel special than to give them the pleasure of your company in your own home? Seriously, they will forget all about the drug. And the famous Thorn charisma will have them gushing about you for days." I didn't mention the fact it would likely be Hector and Rupert visitors would gush about. The brand of charisma exhibited by Sinclair and Ossian was slightly less appealing.

"Fine," Sinclair replied, earning a glare from his son. "Add it to the plans."

I LEFT Sinclair's office with the buzz of someone who'd just landed a multi-million-pound deal. The bubble promptly burst when I pushed open the door and found Rupert staring intensely at me.

"Well?"

"Can you wait until I've taken my coat off?"

"Can you pack your bags in sixty seconds or less?"

I huffed. He might have been the one with the upper hand but that didn't mean I had to play along exactly as he wanted.

"Fine. I updated them on the plans…"

"I need details."

"Here…" I passed him a copy of my notes. "I talked through this. I asked for sign-off on a new transport supplier and proposed new sites to visit during the tour. The distillery was one," I added with a nonchalant brow. "They liked that idea."

"What?" He glared at me. "You're taking the tour through my distillery?"

"Well, technically, it's not yours. It's your father's. But, yes, he agreed to that. It could make some good money if you sell limited edition sets for visitors to take back to the mainland."

His nostrils flared as he seethed breaths in and out. "What else?"

"I talked through the tour of the labs—"

"Did they ask any questions?"

"No. But they did discuss between themselves which rooms in the site we should cover in the tour. They were in agreement with you," I nodded. "They thought the view of the red tops growing in the wooded areas on the drive in, and the cleansing in the labs were all that needed to be revealed. They talked about who from the labs might conduct a talk—"

"And who did they agree on?"

"McFadden."

Rupert's cheek tensed. "What else?"

"Just everything in those notes," I sighed.

When he looked again, his eyes were black. "Nothing about timings? Dates?"

"Oh, well, yes. But, nothing out of the ordinary."

"What did they say, *Vivian*?" He drew my name out on his tongue like he was feasting on it.

"They confirmed the date of the first tour – three days later than I'd proposed. They need to clean up part of the site." I shrugged. "Then, I think it was Sinclair who asked Ossian about a delivery…"

Rupert's jaw sharpened, a crisp line appearing along the edge of his face.

I looked away as I delivered the rest, not bothering to disguise the boredom in my voice. "Ossian said one delivery will arrive later this week, then another a few days before the tour begins. There…" I turned back and glared at him, unfazed by the dark mood that had draped over him like a blanket. "That was seriously everything. Now, can I get on with my job?"

In a flash that had me questioning whether we'd had a different conversation altogether, Rupert's features rearranged. He sat back, a thin smile on his face, and the bitter glare gone. "Well done, Vivian. You've excelled yourself."

"Right," I muttered, the thrill of his praise blossoming in my belly as I wrenched off my coat and hung it over the back of my chair.

He placed his elbows on the desk and rested his chin on clasped hands. He'd rolled back his shirt sleeves so I could make out, in the corner of my eye, strong forearms, threaded with pulsing veins and lightly covered with soft, dark hairs. A band of gold and silver glinted around his wrist where his Rolex ticked silently. "You're not just a pretty face after all."

My eyes darted back to him. "Is that all you thought I was?" I tried not to let the fact he thought I was pretty override my annoyance. His eyes burrowed beneath my skin, making it tingle like a hot current was running along the surface. "What's wrong with being just a pretty face, anyway?"

He stood up slowly and pulled his own jacket on. The disappointment that I could no longer see the taut pectoral muscles beneath his white shirt was visceral. He walked around the desk towards me, then to my shock reached out and placed his hands on my hips. Electricity sizzled across my whole body and my lips parted without instruction. His dark eyes bore down on me, turning the whole room black. He gently shifted me to the side and I realised I'd been standing in front of the door. His hot fingers left my hips and they froze in objection. And his lips barely moved when he whispered his answer. "Nothing. There's nothing wrong with pretty faces. It's just…" He clicked his tongue bitterly and opened the door. "This island is full of them."

I WALKED into Caspian House and made my way to the lounge where Minty was clearing a recently emptied table.

"Hey, Viv," she said, looking up as she lifted the tray of empty glasses. "What brings you here this evening?"

I followed her back to the bar. "I was hoping to use the pool," I replied. "Will that be ok?"

"Sure you can. The salons are right down the corridor. There are fresh towels and slippers in each one."

I blinked. "Slippers? Towels?" My bag suddenly felt heavy with the potentially unnecessary beach towel I'd brought from home, but I silently thanked the member's club gods I wouldn't need to expose anyone to a neon parasol print and the words, 'I heart Ibiza'.

"Oh, you are in for a treat," Minty grinned. "Go and indulge yourself right now." She shooed me away with her hand. As I walked back out of the lounge, she called after me. "And make sure you try the sauna. It's the best you'll ever use."

I wasn't really a sauna person, but I planned on trying *everything*.

I walked through what looked like a posh hotel corridor, then opened one of the salon doors, revealing a spacious changing room complete with a shower, shelves laden with very expensive toiletries and a vanity table with Dyson hairdryer, straighteners and curlers, and an array of brushes, combs, lotions and sprays.

I changed quickly and hung my clothes up in the small closet provided, then I padded out in the perfectly fitting slippers with a towel over my arm. I felt like I'd slipped into a dream, every new scene being more beautiful and indulgent than the last. The pool was not so much of a pool as an oasis. Palm trees and bright foliage lined the outer edges and cut across the sections, giving each pool a suggestion of privacy. A small tiki bar stood at one end of the space surrounded by voluptuous chairs and loungers.

I walked across to the main pool, hung my towel on some discreet hooks lining a dry grass wall, then lowered myself into the water. Not another soul was in the place apart from a lone bartender reading a well-thumbed copy of *The Shining*. I let out a long sigh before submerging myself completely in the warm water.

I swam a few lengths, trying not to feel self-conscious, like I didn't belong. When my muscles began to protest, I climbed out, wrapped the towel around myself and went in search of showers. I eventually found them, hidden among more palms and succulents. I dropped the towel and slipped under a giant waterfall shower head, bracing myself for the downpour.

The temperature was perfect, the drops light and feathery. I closed my eyes and held my face to the falling water, letting it run down my throat, my hair, my back. I wasn't sure how long I'd stood there for, but I had to blink a few times when I opened my eyes. My mind had wandered back to three days earlier when I stood in Rupert's office obeying his demands to recount everything his brother and father had discussed. Heat built in my lower body just feeling his penetrating glare on my skin. A part of me wanted to feel his fingers digging craters into the skin of my jaw, just like when he caught me stealing. It had hurt, but the pain felt exquisite – like nothing I'd ever felt before. It made me want to do something bad again.

I shook the water from my hair and towel dried it, trying not to focus on the growing heaviness between my legs. Then I stepped into the sauna.

Unlike other saunas I'd sat in, and not particularly enjoyed, this one felt fresher. There was a definite humidity, and the wooden benches were roasting, but I could breathe easily. I sat on a bench, closed my eyes again and let my thoughts drift.

Only seconds passed and he filled my vision again. The heaviness between my legs persisted. It had only become needier. I opened one eye and peered through the glass door. I was still the only person in the place. It was cocktail hour and the lounge would now be full of members rushing to start their first socially acceptable drink of the day. I doubted swimming made a superior rival to a Tom Collins.

As the heat between my legs grew needier, I tried to think of something else, something that wasn't Rupert Thorn. But it was impossible. No matter how I tried to think of the tour, or the gorgeous cottage, or even my sister's deteriorating health, Rupert's dark stare and demanding words filtered straight back through my consciousness. I decided to give up and just go with it, and the relief that issued from my lungs was immense, like I'd been holding back the walls of a dam.

I focused on his face. The fine jaw and sharp cheek, strong nose and shadowy brow. He had rock and roll eyes and an asphalt soul, darker than the shadiest tragedy. His hair gleamed black beneath the dimmed light of his office chandelier, but I'd noticed flecks of brown under the harsh glare of the fluorescents in the lab. His suits were immaculate and filled to perfection. His stature tall and darkly foreboding. The heaviness between my thighs turned to a yearning throb. I could feel the blood pulsing through me like a drum, aching for release.

I was too immersed in the vision to give heed to thought, and my fingers found their way beneath the material of my bikini. The instant flesh met flesh, I shuddered. I couldn't remember the last time I had done this. It had been a long, long time. I also couldn't remember ever feeling this desperate for it.

As I pressed a forefinger into my folds, I let out a soft

gasp. I was soaking wet and not from pool water. It was like I'd coated myself in a fine, silky lotion that helped my finger slip back and forth over my clit easily, setting the nerve endings alight. I parted my legs and slipped a second finger beneath the fabric to join the first. A small hum danced from my lips when his face dipped closer to mine. I stared at the mouth I wanted to taste so badly. His deep, punishing frown warmed me inside and made my sex grow heavier still. I slid one finger inside myself, stilling at the rare invasion. As I relaxed, I pushed it deeper, then withdrew it, circled the rim, and pushed back inside.

I imagined him grinding his jaw and sinking his own hand into my heat. I held his wrist as he stroked my clit and fucked me with his fingers, his focus growing in intensity. Would he grunt? Moan? Curse? In my head, he did all three and my need grew suddenly impatient. Holy fuck, I was going to make myself come in record time. Withdrawing my fingers, I rubbed my clit back and forth, increasing the pressure, bucking my hips for greater friction. God, I wished it were his hand. He stared down at me, rubbing me roughly, demanding that I come for him, otherwise he would tell his father what I did. I came, hard, pressing my sex into my hand, desperate for more of the release. A curse was choked out from the depths of my throat, along with his name. Not loud, just enough to expel the demons from my sex-starved body.

My head slammed back against the wall and I withdrew my hand, panting for breath. I sat for a few minutes both revelling in what I'd just done and cursing myself for giving in to thoughts of a man who'd made it clear he only found me useful for one thing: spying on his own family.

When I finally opened my eyes, my heart stopped and my entire body froze.

A man stood about twenty feet from the sauna, his back to me as he walked away. My breath held taut at the base of my throat as I squinted to focus. There was a large tattoo covering most of his right shoulder blade. A climbing rose, entangled in sweeping vines and distorted with sharp specks. Even at a distance, it looked beautiful. I squinted until more of the tattoo came into view and it became clear what the specks were.

Thorns.

Hundreds of them.

And when I took in the whole of his naked back, the way he held himself, the inky black hair flecked with burning chestnut, I knew it was him. And from the beads of sweat still oozing from his pores, my guess was he'd been in the steam room all along. Right next door. With only a thin wall between us.

He'd heard.

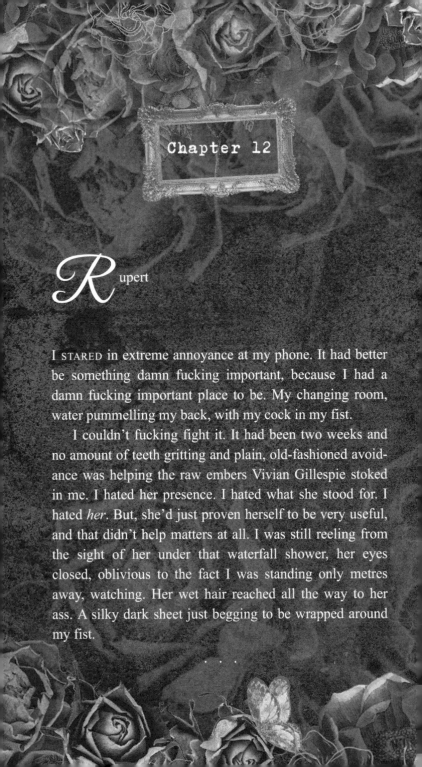

Chapter 12

*R*upert

I STARED in extreme annoyance at my phone. It had better be something damn fucking important, because I had a damn fucking important place to be. My changing room, water pummelling my back, with my cock in my fist.

I couldn't fucking fight it. It had been two weeks and no amount of teeth gritting and plain, old-fashioned avoidance was helping the raw embers Vivian Gillespie stoked in me. I hated her presence. I hated what she stood for. I hated *her*. But, she'd just proven herself to be very useful, and that didn't help matters at all. I was still reeling from the sight of her under that waterfall shower, her eyes closed, oblivious to the fact I was standing only metres away, watching. Her wet hair reached all the way to her ass. A silky dark sheet just begging to be wrapped around my fist.

. . .

As she moved her head, the sheet glided from left to right revealing a tattoo of a butterfly in the small of her back. The bikini she wore should have been outlawed, if it could even be called a bikini. It was essentially three small triangles of virginal white fabric, covering her pussy and her nipples. The rounds of her breasts and ass were ripe for biting into and my mouth actually watered at the sight. *Fuck.* Self-control was the only asset I solely owned – everything else could be attributed to the simple fact I was a fucking Thorn – but even that was being threatened.

I'd slipped into the steam room, partly hoping she'd walk in there, where I could torment her more with demands. The way she sounded downright bored as she recounted Father and Ossian's conversation both pissed me off and heated me up. No woman had ever been so brazenly disrespectful towards me, and it lit a fire in my chest. I wanted to punish her. Make her do more bad things. But make her do them *to me*.

When she didn't enter the steam room, I blamed the deflated feeling in my chest on hunger. I'd spent the previous three mornings doing punishing workouts in the gym and hadn't upped my nutrition. For some reason, I felt the need to work off steam, but I hadn't planned any further than that.

I'd heard the door to the sauna close and I slid up to the adjoining wall and pressed my ear against it. I couldn't hear much. In fact, I couldn't hear anything for the first few minutes, but then, the sounds were unmistakable. She began panting and whimpering, releasing little breathless gasps and quiet melodic moans. My cock stiffened instantly. I removed the tented towel and stared at it. I'd never seen it so big. The veins bulged out of it, the skin shining with tautness. As her moans increased, I heard the tell-tale sound of slickened pussy. She was fingering herself. My cock pulsed and I ran my hand down it, fighting the fierce urge to get myself off.

I picked up my phone and hit record – this could give me further ammunition for blackmail – and returned to stroking myself lightly as her gasps shortened and grew in frequency. Then she swore. It was only the word *fuck* but it sounded like a goddamn prayer. I held back a moan of my own, then I heard my name.

I sat bolt upright, my cock throbbing for attention in my hand, and listened as the two syllables rolled off her tongue. Twice. "Ru—pert… Ru—pert."

I held my breath so as not to pollute the air with the unnecessary proof I was alive, but no more sounds came from the room at the other side. I sat back again and stared at the wall opposite. *Did I just hear what I think I heard?*

Then I remembered my phone. I stopped the recording, lowered the volume right down and held it to my ear. It was faint, but unmistakeable. Vivian Gillespie, one of many women I couldn't lay my hands on, and now one of the few I realised I quite wanted to, had just made herself come thinking of me.

I smiled to myself. Ammunition indeed.

———

JASPER WAS SITTING at the front desk when I walked into the lab building. "Ossian here?" I asked, without pleasantries.

"No, sir. Mr. Thorn is on the mainland meeting with a new supplier."

Is he now? More fucking secrets. "That's a shame. I hoped to talk to him about a few things," I lied. I knew that despite my threats, the workers here were so terrified of Ossian they would incriminate me if they knew it would save their asses and the asses of their families. "Never mind. I just have to do a couple of things in the office." Once out of Jasper's sight, I walked straight past my office and into Ossian's.

Once inside, I let the door lock, then went straight to the computer Ossian used to control all staff movements. I knew that if I logged a change, the worker in question would be automatically sent a text message to notify them of the update. I removed McFadden from the rota and added Burns. The latter wasn't part of Ossian's inner team, as far as I was aware. I closed down the computer and erased my presence from the office access log. Then, I left, giving Jasper a brief nod on my way out.

I'D ONLY BEEN in my rooms five minutes when the doors opened and the overpowering smell of Black Opium perfume wafted through.

"There you are, dear." Dressed head to toe in classic Chanel with her silver hair coiled elegantly into a chignon, and walking purposefully towards me, was Mother.

"Thanks for knocking," I said, kissing her on both cheeks.

"I've seen you naked more times than I could care to count, my darling. Nothing I might see on arrival is going to surprise me."

I turned away so she couldn't see my exasperated eyeroll. "What brings you all this way? I thought you came out in hives if you had to venture too far from the South Tower."

She lowered herself uninvited into a wingback chair by the fireplace. "I haven't seen you in weeks. What other excuse do I need? It's not like you ever visit me."

"I do, Mother," I protested. "But, you're never there. You're always in town, shopping, or at the Bridge Club, or on the mainland."

"Nonsense," she pouted. "I'm here at least one day a week."

"Maybe we should align diaries," I said, forcing a smile. "How have you been?"

"Frankly, Rupert, I've been better."

I hid another eyeroll. There was always some sort of drama where my mother was concerned. Rarely did those dramas involve me, but I had a feeling this one did.

"What's the matter, Mother?"

She lifted her chin, defiantly. "Your father tells me you are still refusing to support these tours."

"That's why you're here? Did he send you?"

"No, he did not. He mentioned you were still refusing to cooperate and frankly, Rupert, I'm disappointed in you."

I forced back a choke. "Excuse me?"

"The pharmaceutical business is the *future* of our family and yet, you're refusing to be involved."

"I met with the partners two weeks ago," I argued. "That is not a refusal to be involved."

"And one meeting with the partners does not a commitment make."

"What do you want from me, Mother?" I sighed.

"I want you to support Ossian more. Work on site with him, take on some of the supplier relationships…"

"No," I bit out with more venom that I'd intended.

"Then help him with the partners. Just *do something*, Rupert. Earn your place in this family."

I baulked at her words. I didn't ask to be born into this family, but I was doing my duty by running the distillery and treating everyone on the island with more respect than Ossian and my father were capable of.

"Aren't I going to be doing enough for the family this year?"

She sighed and chewed her words before spitting them out. "You always knew you would have to marry sooner or later. It's not like you only have to perform one duty a year. You've let this one run to the wire, Rupert. That's on you, not me."

I shoved my hands in my pockets and walked to the window. Looking out at the copper-drenched gardens as the sun set made me feel a little as though I wasn't wholly in the room.

"Look," she sighed. "I know you and Ossian don't always see eye-to-eye…"

I almost snorted at the understatement.

"But one day, he will be Chairman of the Consortium, just like your father. And you will be Vice-Chair, just like Aurelias. You have to get used to working together so you can carry on the family legacy. It's a position of power, a privileged one, and…" I turned to see her lean forward and purse her lips over clenched teeth. "It stays in this family. Do you hear?"

I turned back to the window feeling the dread of imposed obligation wrap around me like a burning sheet. "Yes, Mother. I hear you perfectly."

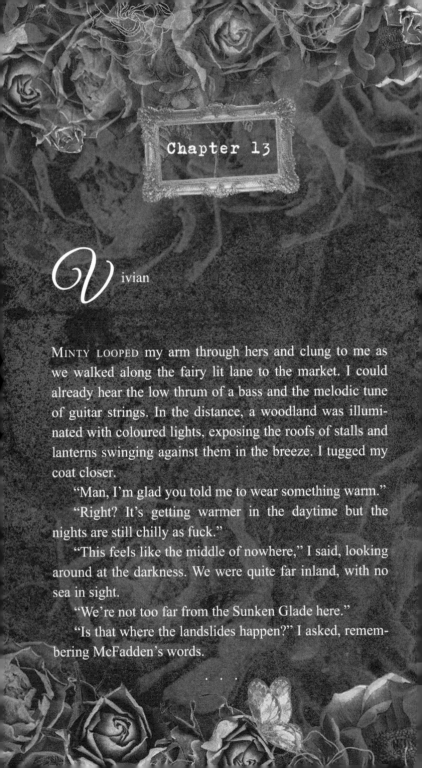

Chapter 13

*V*ivian

Minty looped my arm through hers and clung to me as we walked along the fairy lit lane to the market. I could already hear the low thrum of a bass and the melodic tune of guitar strings. In the distance, a woodland was illuminated with coloured lights, exposing the roofs of stalls and lanterns swinging against them in the breeze. I tugged my coat closer.

"Man, I'm glad you told me to wear something warm."

"Right? It's getting warmer in the daytime but the nights are still chilly as fuck."

"This feels like the middle of nowhere," I said, looking around at the darkness. We were quite far inland, with no sea in sight.

"We're not too far from the Sunken Glade here."

"Is that where the landslides happen?" I asked, remembering McFadden's words.

. . .

"THAT'S RIGHT. It's become almost mythical. It can only be seen from the sea but some of the fisherman paint the most beautiful landscapes of it. It's a shame we can't go there anymore."

I made a mental note to ask Rupert about it. The eco-geek inside me wanted to devour the whole island. I was no stranger to tricky terrain. Perhaps he would let me visit, especially if I continued to impress him with my reportage skills.

We followed the lane round a slight bend, the crunch of our shoes disappearing into the music. "So, how are the plans for the tour coming along?" Minty asked, looking straight ahead.

"They're going well," I replied. "It will start at the port, obviously, then take a scenic route through wood-lands to the distillery. Then up to Caspian House for lunch. Then up to the labs via the coastal road."

"What are the labs like inside? None of us have ever been allowed in. I'm envious of the visitors."

"It's exactly what you would expect a lab to look like. White, sterile, a bit too quiet for comfort."

"Lots of red tops?"

"Millions. The tour won't go through the whole place though. Sinclair has been very clear about the areas he wants to keep closed off. I can understand it. There are some trade secrets the company wants to keep."

We turned a dark corner and suddenly the view before us was awash with coloured lights swaying gently in the evening breeze.

"Come on," she said loudly, pulling me towards the nearest stall. "The best crab fritters you'll ever taste."

I laughed and let her drag me to a crowd huddled

around a vibrant stall. The smell of fresh crabmeat made my mouth water. Through the throng, I could see a man with a round face and red cheeks slotting crispy yellow cakes into paper cones and handing them to hungry punters. Minty wrestled her way to the front, tugging me beside her. I felt several pairs of eyes land on me and I heated beneath the weight. Perhaps naively, I hadn't expected such notoriety when accepting this job, and I found no comfort or joy in the attention.

"Two fritters please, Albie," Minty called out to the round-faced man.

He turned to us, his red cheeks puckering with a smile. "Anything for my favourite waitress." He lifted a fritter out of a pan of hot oil and slotted it into a paper cone and then reached for another, handing them both to Minty. "On the house," he winked.

She grinned then handed me a cone before ushering us out of the crowd. "I give him free drinks," she explained. "But please don't tell the Thorns."

I nodded. "This smells amazing."

"It tastes amazing too. Let's sit." She led us to a cluster of straw bales scattered about in front of a makeshift stage. A break between songs gave us a brief chance to talk.

"You come here every week?" I asked, before biting into my fritter. It was heavenly. A mix of crispy sea-salted batter and soft, sweet crabmeat that melted in my mouth.

"Most weeks. Although I've been working a lot of Saturdays lately, so I missed the last few. Good, right?" She nodded to my fritter.

"Mm-mm," I managed through a full mouth. I was going to devour this thing in seconds.

"This is kind of where the 'little people' catch up.

We're all too exhausted during the week. The families work us hard. But, Saturdays, we can come here, let our hair down without worrying about our drunken behaviour getting back to our bosses," she laughed.

"So, it goes on all night?" It felt reasonably quiet but more people were arriving in groups. The place was going to fill up pretty fast.

"Oh yeah, into the early hours."

"And you said none of the Consortium families come here?"

"Yup. Maybe Adele Lamont, but she doesn't count."

"Who's Adele Lamont?" I asked, before shovelling the last of the fritter into my mouth.

"She's the only daughter of Dexter Lamont, one of the most expensive lawyers in Europe. She hates living the Consortium life. Would rather spend her time with us, doing normal things like having barbecues on the beach and house parties. Hates all the pomp that comes with being from a Consortium family – the balls, the dinners, the gatherings. We get to go to the Summer Ball, but there are many more events we don't get invited to. Adele usually reports back to us what heinous things the elders get up to, like feeling up the butts of the younger girls and placing bets on which wife would pass out first from too much champagne. I wouldn't like to be a part of that either."

"It sounds totally backwards," I said. "Like there's been very little progress here."

"Don't think that shit only happens here," she said, finishing her fritter. "Wherever there's money, there's exploitation. And unfortunately, people who will exploit themselves for that money."

I grimaced at her words, recognising the truth of them.

"Dan!" Minty called out. "Over here!"

A young, freckled guy dressed in waders made his way over to us.

"Dan, this is Viv. She's going to be running the new island tours." He held a hand out to me and I shook it. "Dan works in the fishery by the port. That fritter you just inhaled? Dan here probably caught the crabs."

I smiled at him. "It was delicious, Dan."

"Thanks," he shrugged, bashfully.

I placed a hand on Minty's sleeve. "I'm going to take a walk."

She smiled. "Sure thing. I'll be around here somewhere."

"I won't be long. It was nice to meet you," I nodded to Dan.

"You too," he replied.

I decided to walk around the outer perimeter of the market, away from the guitar music that seemed to be getting louder, and away from the crowds of people whose eyes seemed to fall on me wherever I stepped. I felt relief as I moved into the shadows, my path lit only by the occasional lantern swinging gently at the back of a stall. As my eyes became accustomed to the darkness, I walked a little further into the woodland. The relative peace combined with the smells of venison charring on the open air grill was comforting and I let my feet wander.

After a few minutes, the music became a mere hum, the lights small and far. I placed my palms against a smooth tree trunk and inhaled deeply. I expected the air to be clean, crisp and smooth, especially out here in the untouched woodland, but it wasn't. There was a thickness to it I couldn't put my finger on. I must have been so wound up with tension, from the taut relationship with Rupert, to the weird curiosity of the other islanders, and the demands of the Thorn family, that I was struggling to breathe.

As I felt the bark beneath my palms, the hairs on my neck bristled. It felt as though someone was watching me. My chest filled with the urge to run, but the ground was too dark to see. I was being ridiculous. I clung to the tree as I tried to calm my racing heart. I released my grip and took some steps away from the tree, back towards the market. The hairs on my neck softened slightly. I'd imagined it. But still, it wouldn't hurt to get back to the safety of a crowd.

After a few more paces, goosebumps erupted all over my skin, despite the fact I had done as Minty advised and wrapped up in my thickest winter coat. My steps slowed to a standstill, my blood solidifying me to the spot.

Then I heard it.

The crunch of twigs underfoot made me spin around in a three-sixty circle, coming back to the tree. I held my breath as every hair on my skin bristled. There was someone close by, but all I could see was shadows. "H— hello?" I said, my voice cracking.

There was silence apart from the echoing throb of blood through my eardrums. With one eye on the market lights in the distance, and one on my blackened surroundings, I took a tentative step away from the tree, then it came again. *Crunch, snap. Crunch.*

"Who's there?" I said, my voice shrill but firm.

My heart shot up into my throat as the air around me grew warm with the presence of another breathing body. A body that wasn't saying a word. I had no idea how close the person was, but they were clearly not interested in communicating. The seconds passed slowly but I didn't have time to think. I drove my feet into the woodland bed and pushed off into a run, but a thick hand wrapped around my face, crushing my mouth and hauling me backwards into a solid, angular body. "Don't make a sound," a male voice rumbled, low and threatening.

I panted against his palm, my wrists bruising under the pressure of his other hand clasping them behind my back. I felt his eyes hot on my scalp while mine were stretched so wide they stung. "Mmm," was the only sound I could make as his fingers muffled my lips.

"There, there, Miss Gillespie," the voice said. "Keep still now, and you won't be hurt."

I steadied myself in his grip, afraid of what would happen if I didn't.

"This is what we're going to do. You're going to *listen* to everything I say, and then you're going to *do* everything I say, ok?"

I nodded frantically.

"We had a little trouble this past week at Thorn Laboratories…"

My mind raced. Who the fuck was this? It definitely wasn't Rupert. I'd felt his fingers and they weren't bony like this. They were softer, gentler, and… *Fuck. Focus.*

"We had some plans go, shall we say, *awry*. Which was strange really, because no one else knew about them. But, I'm told you have been privy to certain conversations, Miss Gillespie. I hope you are not repeating any of those conversations. To *anyone*. Not even someone you think you can trust."

I gave a small shake of my head knowing it was a lie.

"Now…" the gravelly drawl continued, "I could ask you nicely to not repeat anything else in future, but I don't think that would truly make you appreciate who you are fucking with."

My breath stuttered and his grip tightened until my mouth was pried open. My teeth grazed along muddy fingers but I didn't dare bite down.

"So, here it is. If you repeat *anything* that is discussed with any member of the Thorn family, to anyone, you won't make it off this island alive. Is that clear?"

I choked against his fingers, bile rising up my throat. The sinister tone of the man's voice left no question that whoever he was, he meant every word.

"Is that clear, Miss Gillespie?" he repeated, loudly. "You are to talk about the tour plans to no one. Not a soul. Otherwise, we will damn yours to hell, and that's a promise."

I choked back a sob and nodded weakly.

"Good." He released his grip with a hollow laugh. "Now, run, little rabbit."

I didn't wait to be told twice. I heaved in a gulp of air and ran as fast as I could through the cloaked woodland, grasping wildly for tree trunks and stray branches. Had I really walked this far? What the hell was I thinking? I didn't slow for fear the man was close behind, but as I reached the edge of the market, my breath was short and my legs burned with the release of lactic acid. Before I had a chance to stop, a giant boulder shifted in front of me and I slammed into it, almost knocking myself out.

"What the f—? Vivian?"

Warm, stabilising arms wrapped around me, pinning

me to a thick but soft winter coat. I gasped for breath and tried to push myself out of the arms. I didn't know anyone here, and after that encounter in the woodland, I didn't trust a damn soul.

"Wait, stop. Vivian, it's me, Rupert. What just happened? Are you ok?"

Rupert? I placed my palms on the chest of his coat and held myself as far from his beating heart as I could while his arms continued to hold me. "I—I didn't think you ever came to the market," I stammered. "Why are you here?"

In the dim light I could've sworn his Adam's apple moved in a swallow. "Of course I come here. Just not often. What happened? Why were you running? And why were you in the wood?"

"When did you get here?" I said, unable to hide the accusation in my voice. Was it him who just threatened me? No, the body I was pulled into was wiry, not broad like Rupert's. It was cold and sharp, not warm and firm. The arms were bone-dense and piercing, not thick with muscle and comforting. *Stop it, Vivian,* my head screamed.

"I got here half an hour ago. Why? What just happened to you? Tell me."

I gave one final shove, releasing myself from his grip. "Nothing," I said, with a gasp. "Nothing, it's fine. I wandered too far, I freaked myself out, then I ran into you. End of story."

"Vivian, you're white as a sheet. You look like you've seen a ghost. Now, I'm going to ask you again," he said, his voice unnervingly low and solemn. "And you know what will happen if you don't give me the truth. What *the fuck* just happened?"

I looked up into his now-black eyes. His jaw was set

hard and his shoulders stood rigid, his whole being on edge. I wanted to trust him, but after that threat, I couldn't afford to. I couldn't afford to trust anyone.

"Vivian..." his voice softened and he placed a gentle hand against my cheek in a move so nurturing, I couldn't help the sensation of conflict raging around my chest.

"I—I can't," I whispered.

Two hands gripped my shoulders as I confirmed something had happened. "Yes, Vivian. You can. You're safe with me, ok? This island practically belongs to my family – if someone has hurt you, or threatened you, I will *deal* with them, do you understand? I will do whatever I can to protect you, but only if you tell me what happened."

I wilted as the last defiant breath left my lungs. "I didn't see who it was," I said, bringing my hands up to my face as though covering my eyes might make the whole thing go away.

"What the fuck is *that*?" Rupert growled.

I pressed my hands to my chest. He looked like he might be about to kill someone. "What?" I whispered, alarmed.

He reached out, as fast as lightning and took both my hands, turning them over in the dim moonlight. Then I saw what he'd zeroed in on. Ugly black bruises were rapidly appearing around my wrists.

"Who did this to you?"

I stared at them in disbelief. No one had ever hurt me this badly.

My voice sounded like it belonged to someone else. "A man threatened me."

He shifted on his feet as though readying himself to spring. "What exactly did he say?"

I took a breath of syrupy air. "He said that I'm not to discuss the tour with anyone on the island except your family. That if I repeat anything, I won't..." I choked back another disbelieving sob.

Rupert stepped forward so his chest met mine, and his strong fingers gripped my jaw, angling my face towards his. "You won't... *what*?"

"I won't get off this island alive."

Rupert's fingers tightened around my jaw melting prints into my cold skin. The flame it had ignited in my belly the first time began to flicker again, even through the fear. His chest heaved against mine. "Did you recognise the voice?"

I shook my head before answering. "No."

He couldn't truly care, could he? He didn't want me there; he'd made that abundantly clear. So, wouldn't someone putting an end to me be a blessing?

Rupert's eyes glided over my head into the woodland. They searched the trees with intense focus, his jaw hardening further by the second.

"How did you get here?" he demanded.

"Minty brought me."

"Well, I'm taking you home."

"Now? But, I haven't seen—"

"Yes, now." He released my jaw and reached down for my hand, securing it in his. For a second, I froze. Another bolt of electricity jolted through my arm, ricocheting into my chest, and I wondered if he felt it too. I didn't have a chance to question it further before I was tugged along in a brisk walk around the perimeter of the market.

"I... I need to tell Minty," I said, hurriedly. "She was planning to take me home."

"Where is she?" he replied, still pulling me.

"In the middle somewhere," I phrased it like a question because I had no idea where she would be now. It was a whole hour ago that I'd left her.

Rupert didn't answer but instead he tugged me through a gap between two stalls and into the throng of people, which had thickened substantially while I'd been gone. My eyes skated around the crowd, trying to seek out a head of pale turquoise hair. It seemed Rupert had already spotted her, standing at least a foot taller than everyone else, because he suddenly switched direction and tugged me towards a different seating area to the one I'd sat in earlier. When he came to an abrupt halt, I narrowly avoided smacking into him. I stepped to his side and saw her, sitting with Dan, the two of them deep in conversation, oblivious to the hundreds of people surrounding them.

"Minty," I started. When she looked up, her jaw dropped. I don't know what she saw in the expressions of me or Rupert, but it made her stand so quickly she slopped cider all over Dan's foot.

"Is everything ok?" she rushed out, her eyes flitting rapidly from me to Rupert and back.

"Everything's fine," I assured her.

"We're leaving," Rupert said. "I'm taking her home."

Minty's eyes continued to dart from Rupert back to me. She stepped towards me and wrapped her arms around my neck. We hardly knew each other so I guessed this was a ruse to understand what the hell was going on.

"Are you sure?" she whispered in my ear. "You have my number, right?"

I nodded against her hair and pulled back to look her in the eye. I wasn't fine, but that wasn't Rupert's fault; he was the one apparently trying to make things better. "I'll see you tomorrow?"

"Yeah, drop by Caspian House. I'll be there until ten p.m."

I nodded once then felt my hand slip into Rupert's again. "Let's go," he barked.

He held on to me as we walked right through the middle of the market, and didn't let go even when we were out of sight and heading back down the lane. I could still feel the curious stares of onlookers as we sliced the throng of visitors down the centre. I guessed it wasn't every day one of the Thorn family waltzed into the night market and dragged away the one person everyone seemed to want a piece of.

"You don't have to keep hold of me, you know. I'm not going to run away."

"It's not you I'm worried about," he said. His gait had slowed but his voice still carried a sense of urgency.

"Aren't you worried what people will think? You just swept me out of that place like I belonged to you."

He snorted. "No, I don't care one fucking ounce."

We reached the patch of land used as a car park and he clicked his key fob. There it was: Blackpool Bloody Illuminations. He held onto me as he opened the passenger door and maintained contact until I'd sat and buckled my seatbelt. Then he closed the door and stalked round to the driver's side. Within seconds, his tyres were burning a crater in the sand and blowing a storm behind us as we flew back to the main road.

After several minutes of silence, Rupert spoke. "You're not to go there again. Do you understand?"

My mouth fell open as I stared at him. "You can't be serious."

"Oh, I am," he bit out. "Deadly serious."

"But that guy could be anywhere. What do you expect me to do? Stay indoors for a whole year? I refuse to live like that."

"Vivian," he warned, spinning the wheel round a corner with his palm, making my stomach flip on its side. "I'm not suggesting you become a recluse, just that you are extra vigilant about where you spend your time and... with whom."

"I am vigilant," I said, my teeth gritted.

Rupert yanked the wheel to the left and screeched the car to a halt before leaning one arm across the back of my seat and bringing his face close to mine. His angry voice filled the car. "You walked fifteen minutes into dense woodland, on your own, in the dark. You call that being vigilant?"

I backed into the passenger window, alarmed by his intensity.

"I need you to hear me, Vivian. This job you've been given. It's a political fucking hotcake. You know we don't want to open the island. For fuck's sake, even I'm opposed to it. But the simple fact is, we have to... And I'm not the only person opposed. Some people on the island are dead against it and we don't know what they're capable of. They see this move of ours to open up the island as a weakness, a treachery, and you..." He stared through my eyes as he breathed hard. "You as the face of it."

I was so rigid with fright, I sucked in a breath and felt my teeth tremble as I held it.

His voice softened and he pulled his arm back to press

a hot palm against my cheek. "I don't mean to scare you…"

"Ha…" I retorted in a gush of air.

"I don't. But I don't think my father has explained things clearly enough to you. This is by far the most polarising thing we've ever done on the island. For each person in favour of showboating our home, there's another two who think we need our heads examined. You need to be more careful about where you go. You need to be more aware of your surroundings, more cautious, ok?"

I nodded meekly, although my head was reeling with his warnings. When I accepted this job, sure, I never expected it to be easy. But, I *really* never expected it to be dangerous.

"Come on," he said, putting a hand back on the wheel. "Let me take you home."

I watched him steadily as he drove the rest of the way through dark, canopied woodlands, across barren open farmlands and along chalky clifftops until we reached Sandpiper Cottage sheltered on the hillside sloping down to the sea. He pulled into the parking space and turned off the engine. Before I could so much as thank him for the ride, he was round my side of the car, opening the door for me. I took his proffered hand and let him guide me out as though I was a baby bird learning how to fly, then he followed me closely to the entrance. I felt self-conscious as I turned the key and pushed the door. I switched on the hall light and turned back to face him. I wasn't sure whether I should invite him in, or say goodnight.

Luckily, my rambling thoughts were put out of their misery. "Get some sleep," he said, firmly. "And double lock this door."

I nodded and watched him spin on his heel and walk
swiftly back to his car. Just before he slid into the driver's
seat he held my gaze for an agonisingly long second, then
he disappeared from view. The car door slammed, the
engine roared and the car backed out of its space and thundered out onto the road, the growling noise symbolising
everything I'd seen in Rupert that night. I closed the door,
bolted every lock I could find then dragged my feet
upstairs and collapsed into bed, fully clothed, confused and
utterly exhausted.

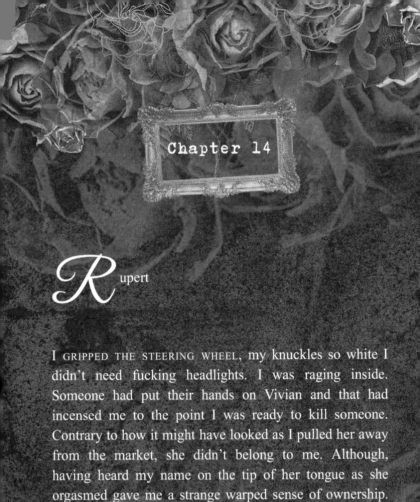

Chapter 14

*R*upert

I GRIPPED THE STEERING WHEEL, my knuckles so white I didn't need fucking headlights. I was raging inside. Someone had put their hands on Vivian and that had incensed me to the point I was ready to kill someone. Contrary to how it might have looked as I pulled her away from the market, she didn't belong to me. Although, having heard my name on the tip of her tongue as she orgasmed gave me a strange warped sense of ownership. But that was beside the point. Who had threatened her in the woods, and why?

It shouldn't have been clear to anyone that Vivian had done anything wrong. Yes, she relayed a conversation to me, but it was so heavily coded there was no way she would have suspected what was actually being said.

I BYPASSED Blackcap Hall completely and skirted around the perimeter to Woodcock Manor, where Ossian lived with his wife, Marcia. It was nearly midnight, but I didn't care. I nodded grimly at the security camera then accelerated through the black iron gates and up the long drive. I had barely swung the car around the island in the centre of the turning bay before I leapt out and stormed up to the door. It was too late for the doorman so I rang the bell and hammered on the door with my fists. I was ready to crucify someone.

I heard small footsteps at the other side of the door hurrying along the tiled hall. Several bolts unlocked and the handle turned. Through a small crack in the doorway, Marcia's thin, pale face peeked through. It flooded with relief when she saw it was me, before turning slightly ashen at the rage visible in each of my features.

"Rupert, is everything alright?"

My breath came out ragged. "Is Ossian home?"

She shook her head. "No. He must still be at the labs. He hasn't been home all day. I had his dinner specially prepared…"

"Are you absolutely certain he's at the labs?"

"Well, yes. Where else would he be? Rupert, is everything alright?"

"He didn't mention anything about going to the night market?" I leaned forward so she could see the deadly serious look on my face.

"No," she half-gasped. "Why would he go there?" The surprise in her tone wasn't a surprise to me. The Consortium families wouldn't ordinarily dream of stepping foot in that place. Far too rustic and rough around the edges. Marcia and Ossian included. I, on the other hand, would have visited more if it didn't reflect badly on my father. The only reason I'd gone there tonight was because Vivian had. She didn't know the island. She didn't know the night market really was in the middle of nowhere. Those were the reasons I went along to the night market this evening. Not because ever since that day in the steam room I'd felt a wholly unwelcome primal, instinctive need to know every move she made.

I was about to open my mouth when the sound of wheels tearing up the driveway and skidding to a stop behind me, drew my head around.

"Rupert," Ossian barked, in his usual abrasive manner. "What brings you here at this time of night?"

Marcia opened the door wide as I faced him fully.

"You, as a matter of fact."

"Wonderful," he said, his eyes squinted, his tone nasal. I often wondered if it was normal to dislike a sibling quite so much. "Well, don't just stand on the damn doorstep." He nodded past Marcia as though he hadn't even seen her.

I followed his nod and smiled at Marcia as I walked past her into the hallway. "Cigar room," he stated, simply.

I followed him through a dimly lit sitting room to a snug off to the side. I'd been in this room before when the house stood empty. Father only saw fit to gift us our own houses once we'd married, but that didn't stop us squatting in various halls and manors when we were growing up. During our teens we spent most weekends hopping from house to house. These days we were too busy and the novelty had worn off. Looking around at the sparse walls and threadbare carpet, I could tell very little had been done to update the house, despite Ossian and Marcia having lived in it for four years now. And it wasn't like they didn't have money to spend.

"No plans to start on the renovations?" I asked as he sat opposite me and dangled a large whiskey in my face.

"What renovations?" he sneered.

"You're going to keep the house the way it is?" I took the whiskey. I didn't particularly want to drink anything my older brother offered me right now, but I'd had one hell of a night.

Ossian popped open a small wooden chest and took out a fat Cuban cigar. He offered the box to me but I declined with a brief shake of the head. "If it's not broke, why fix it?"

I feigned nonchalance. "Fair enough. I just thought perhaps Marcia might want to put her stamp on the pl—"

"It's not her house," he snapped before I'd even finished my sentence.

I ran my tongue along my top teeth as we sank into awkward silence. "Right."

"Why are you here, Rupert?"

The suddenness of his question jarred me. There we were making small talk when the elephant in the room— the fact we never spent time together outside work and family obligations—loomed large.

"Were you at the night market this evening?"

His face contorted in an ugly grimace. "What?"

"The night market in the woodlands, Ossian. Were you there?"

He swallowed a mouthful of whiskey and took a long drag of the dull, musky cigar. Then he settled back in his torn leather club chair, crossed an ankle over a knee and allowed his dark gaze to hover over me like a rain cloud threatening to erupt.

"Why? he asked, finally.

"Don't toy with me, Ossian. Just tell me. Were you there? Was it you?"

Like a jack-in-a-box, he bolted upright. "Was *what* me?"

I ground my jaw while contemplating my next question. He was cornering me and I couldn't tell if he was guilty or if he was being a sly-assed jerk. He wasn't going to admit anything if it was him so I had nothing to lose. "A man threatened Vivian in the woods earlier tonight."

"Whatever was she doing in the woods?" he asked with an air of pure innocence.

"I don't know," I replied, trying my hardest to conceal my exasperation. "She went for a walk, to get some fresh air, it doesn't matter. What matters is the fact a man grabbed her, wrapped a hand around her throat and threatened her."

Ossian sat back again with an eerie look of satisfaction on his face. "And you think that person was me?"

"Whoever it was threatened her for supposedly leaking information about our family, which is ridiculous. She doesn't know anything."

"If they wanted to get rid of her, why did they let her go? Why did they merely threaten her with death, instead of actually killing her? No one would have known, would they? It's not like anyone goes out there other than for the night market."

He leaned forward, his sour breath reaching out to caress my face.

"It would have been so easy. She was caught off guard,

she was frozen to the spot. It wouldn't have taken much to pull out a sharp blade and slice it across her throat, would it?"

His daggered eyes drove into mine as I watched him play this little scene out in his mind. "And think of how vast the woodland is. There are literally thousands of places a body could be buried, not to be found for centuries. As for whether her absence would be noted, I'm not surprised to learn that one person in particular might object."

He sat back and raised his glass, then flicked his fore-finger towards me in a harsh line. My skin crawled beneath his words and the sinister tone with which he spoke. I hadn't mentioned that Vivian had been threatened specifically *with death*. There was only one way Ossian could have known that.

He eyed me steadily and my palms began to sweat. I wasn't afraid of my brother. I was absolutely certain that if it came down to it, I would crucify him in a physical fight, but mentally, I had to hold back. If I was to continue throwing grenades in his path, I had to keep him as close as I could.

"Anyway," he mused, his features softening as far as they physically could, which wasn't far at all. "I don't know who that would have been. But... I suppose I can ask around, see if anyone knows who might be so inclined as to threaten your new *friend*."

"She's hardly a friend," I scoffed. "She works for us. And in case you'd forgotten, she's responsible for a tour that I don't want, and that a lot of people are interested in, for better or worse. She's a target for blackmail." I conveniently stashed away the fact I myself was blackmailing her.

"Only if she knows things. If she doesn't, well…" He flicked his wrist as if that eventuality was none of his concern. I watched the ash tumble onto the floor and wondered briefly if he'd even bother to have it cleaned.

"She knows nothing," I stated, firmly.

He smiled thinly but his eyes remained taut and steady. "So, you have nothing to worry about."

I watched him for a second or two, then tipped the rest of the whiskey into my mouth, swallowing back a wince.

"Have you given much thought to what Mother said?" he sneered.

"About what?"

"Helping me with our partners. As much as it pains me to say so, you do have a knack for flattering and impressing people. You would probably do a reasonable job with partner relations."

Reasonable? I seethed inside. I would rather have vomited all over myself than have more to do with those arrogant city boys and corrupt politicians than I had to. "I'm too busy with the distillery."

"Liar," he spat.

I glared at him. I didn't care what the hell he thought of me but I didn't like the way he spoke. I embedded my clenched fists in the seat of the chair.

"You're entitled to your opinion."

"You know it will have to happen sooner or later, Rupert," he said, before taking a long drag of his cigar. The smoke curled up into the shadows as he exhaled through pursed lips. "You may as well just get the fuck on board."

I ground my teeth silently, then stood from the chair. "I don't want to keep you," I said.

"Hardly." He looked up at me with a cocky smile. "You only just got here."

I shrugged. "I have a busy day tomorrow. So, you'll ask around about who might've threatened Vivian?"

"Sure."

"Night, then." I turned towards the door as he made no move to walk me out.

"Night little bro'." I partially froze at his words. They were said with such insincerity a small part of me wished it weren't true, that despite the fact each of us had our right shoulder blades imprinted with the emblem of our family's name before the age of ten, there'd been some sort of mix-up at birth. But that wasn't likely. Ossian was such a ringer for our thin, wiry father, while I carried our grandfather's more sturdy build and warmer features.

We were both Thorns through and through.

There was no escaping it.

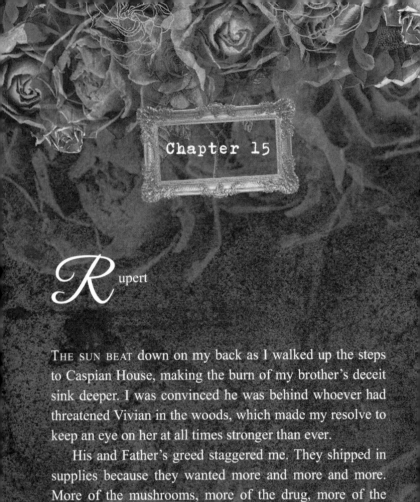

Chapter 15

*R*upert

THE SUN BEAT down on my back as I walked up the steps to Caspian House, making the burn of my brother's deceit sink deeper. I was convinced he was behind whoever had threatened Vivian in the woods, which made my resolve to keep an eye on her at all times stronger than ever.

His and Father's greed staggered me. They shipped in supplies because they wanted more and more and more. More of the mushrooms, more of the drug, more of the money. And screw the land it consumed. I knew what I had to do. It was ridiculous, unnecessary and downright annoying. It would mean I'd have to keep an even closer eye on Vivian, provided she did as I instructed. Which she would, because I had more ammunition she wasn't even aware of.

My dark mood preceded me and the bar area thinned the second I entered.

. . .

"MALBEC, SIR?" Minty's warm smile was replaced with an efficient show of professionalism.

"No. Whiskey. Blackcap. With ice."

Seconds later, a crystal tumbler appeared in front of me. "Thanks," I mumbled, before drinking the lot down in one. I relished the burn. It fuelled the fire of resentment in my chest for all things Thorn.

"Are you here to see Viv?" Minty asked. "She's upstairs in the library, finishing up a new batch of brochures."

"Give me another one of those and make it a double," I said, tipping my tumbler towards her. "Then I'll head upstairs."

Minty glanced at me warily, a look I chose to ignore. The fire was in my bloodstream now and it was only thing that talked over the burn in my chest. A minute later, a refill was placed on the black coaster beside me. "Put it on my tab," I said, swigging down the double and banging the glass back down on the bar. I slid off the stool, loosened my tie, and stalked out of the lounge and up the stairs.

The library was at the top of the building so I took two more flights of stairs, two steps at a time. The door was ajar and when I peered through the crack, I saw her. A mustard yellow dress clung to her curves, accentuating her waspish waist and full hips. It even revealed a hint of two rounded cheeks beneath and the slight imprint of a lace thong. My mouth watered, my voyeuristic tendencies getting the better of me. She was moving swiftly and gracefully from the printer to a table where the pamphlets were being laid out, and the smell of printer ink suddenly took on a new life in my nostrils. I pushed the door and entered, watching her as she continued oblivious to my presence.

"Here you are," I said, quietly.

"Christ!" she squealed and spun around, her hand fisted over her heart. "What are you doing creeping up like that? You scared the crap out of me!"

I couldn't help a wry smile forming at the sight of her so flustered. "I didn't creep up. You were engrossed. And the door was open."

She blinked past me to the door, then back to my face. A sheen of sweat glazed her brow. "What have you come here for?"

My eyes dragged shamelessly over her body and she shivered, her lips parted and glistening. Her eyes were as defiant as her hair was wild, tamed only by the punishing knot she'd wound it into. God, she could drive a man mad. I mentally shook my head. Not this man. For me, she had other uses.

"For the next instalment of your debt."

She swallowed and backed up against the table. Her eyes narrowed. "Have you been drinking?"

"I had a whiskey before I came up." It wasn't a lie.

"Just one?"

"Yes." Ok, that was a lie.

"Hmm," she surprised me with a smile. "I like the smell."

Do you like the taste too? I found myself thinking. "Remind me to treat you one day."

She tugged her bottom lip between her teeth and rested her hands on the table behind her.

"I need you to distract Archie McFadden on the night of the delivery."

"What? That's tomorrow."

I nodded. Exactly. If the supplies didn't get on to the island tomorrow, they would have to wait until there was a break in the tour, which wouldn't happen for at least two months.

She folded her arms and glared at me. "You can't be serious, Rupert. The last time I did something like this for you, a man threatened me in the woods. And you yourself told me I had to be more careful. This is not 'being careful.'"

I shrugged in agreement. "You will just have to make sure you do it *carefully*, then, won't you?"

"And how do you suggest I do that?"

"You're inventive, Vivian. Think of something."

"This is ridiculous. I don't even have clearance to enter the labs alone. How can I get to him?"

I handed her a piece of paper. She unfolded it, read it, then looked up at me, exasperated. "And this is…?"

"McFadden's home address. He will be there until five p.m. Then he'll leave for his night shift.

"And that's when I have to distract him?"

I tilted my head back in response. She was a bright girl; she could figure it out. Then she surprised me. "No."

My eyebrows shot up. "I'm sorry?"

"No. I'm not doing it." She screwed up the paper into a ball and threw it into the waste paper basket with absolute precision. "I already paid my dues. I reported back to you about the conversation between Ossian and Sinclair, and look where that got me. Threatened by someone with *my life*. I am not a pawn in your game. You are man enough to take this up with your family yourself."

A spontaneous and uncontrolled anger coursed through

me and I was suddenly standing chest to chest with her. When I looked down, her eyes blazed, like she was daring me to do something. I gripped her chin again, fixing her eyes on me. "You will do it, Vivian. Do you want to know why?"

She rolled her eyes which only fuelled my irritation further. I slipped my phone out of my pocket, held it up to her ear and pressed play. Her eyes darted to the side, craning to see, but I held her fast. At first, the only sound was the quiet bubbling of the water in the steam room. She flicked her eyes back to mine in a challenge.

"Oh, don't you worry, butterfly. It's coming."

She sucked in a breath, her frown questioning why, of all the names I could have called her, I chose that one.

The next sound was indecipherable unless you knew what was coming down the line. It was slick and sloppy, faint but distinguishable from the bubbling water. Her eyes narrowed as she strained to make out what the sound was. Then we both heard her voice. "*Fuck—*"

She slapped a hand over her mouth and squeezed her eyes closed. Her face flushed red and I smiled as my name rolled off her lips in the heat of her climax. I let the recording run to the end, then I released her jaw and took two steps back, reaching behind me to flick the lock on the door.

Her eyes remained closed, her hand still covering her mouth, and her shoulders heaved from the exertion of being humiliated.

"That's why you will do as I say," I said, calmly. "Because I can play this back to club management, who have every right to suspend you from this place due to inappropriate conduct, and believe me, the island gossip machine is rife. And remember, you have to live here for another eleven months."

She opened her eyes, blistering me with a glare of pure hatred. I smiled and lightly rubbed my jaw. "I'm quite flattered, by the way."

"I know more than one Rupert," she snapped.

"Oh?" I pushed my hands and phone into my pockets and regarded her. "Like who?"

She ground her teeth and blinked rapidly while failing to think of another Rupert she might have come all over her fingers for.

A part of me despised myself for treating her like a toy, but another part of me – the part that was positively Thorn – relished her discomfort. And it was that part of me that spoke up next, leaving the other part reeling. "I'll tell you what. We'll play a little game. Let's call it 'Dare or dare.'"

She tightened her folded arms and looked back at me warily.

"Seeing as you have already made it clear you are attracted to me, enough to get yourself off in a public place, which suggests you are not averse to a little exhibitionism, I have an alternative suggestion for how you can atone for your actions."

Her features hardened and I was almost pleased the humiliation had worn off quickly, because I was going to delight in seeing it come hurtling back.

"You can either do as I originally asked and distract McFadden – via whatever means you choose – tomorrow evening, or…" I paused for dramatic effect. "You can show me what you did to yourself that day in the sauna."

She sucked in a loud breath and clenched a fist over her heart. "You can't be fucking serious."

"I am *deadly* serious. Make yourself come while I watch, or go and be a good little butterfly and stop McFadden from starting his shift."

I watched the debate taking place behind her eyes. McFadden was popular on the island. He didn't have much but he was generous to a fault. He was also stupidly loyal to my family and he lived and breathed the lab like it was his own. It wouldn't be an easy task and she would hate herself for doing it. And as for the other option? Well, she wouldn't be doing something she hadn't done before. She found me attractive, that much was clear. What could be more pleasurable than doing it all again having the subject of her fantasy watch it play out?

She gritted her teeth and slowly unfolded her arms.

"What's it to be, *Vivian*?" I rolled out her name slowly, because I liked the way her eyes sparkled when I did that. Although, when I called her butterfly, her eyes lit up like fireworks. She pressed her palms to her dress and slid her hands down the front of her thighs. I swallowed back my surprise. When I delivered that ultimatum, I was toying with her. I never expected she would take *this* way out. When her fingers curled around the hem of her dress, the Thorn part of me spoke again.

"One more thing." I slipped my phone out of my pocket again. "I get to film it this time."

Her fingers froze. "No."

I tipped my chin up. "No?"

"Why would I let you do that? You could just use it to blackmail me even more."

The thought curled a corner of my mouth. "Yes, I could. Clever girl. But I believe I have enough ammunition already. This…" I clicked on the camera app, "is for my later viewing pleasure."

I held the phone up to her and pressed record. She glared at me with wild eyes, like she couldn't believe I had the nerve.

"Well, go on then," I nodded.

She swallowed and renewed her grip on the hem of her dress. I watched, passively, as the fabric rose fraction by fraction. Her jaw was solid, the exact opposite of how I guessed it was when she did the same thing in the sauna. Her fingers paused as the edge of the dress hovered just below the apex of her thighs and my eyes dropped from her face to her fingers. Her forefinger curled beneath the fabric as if to swipe against her clit. My breath caught in my throat and I stepped forward without thinking.

The tension in her hands fell away and ever so slowly, she lifted the dress high enough that I could see a slip of her underwear. I couldn't tear my eyes away. It was perfect. A dark, indigo thong made of sheer fabric, completely see-through to the hairless pussy beneath. My lips had dried out like the Sahara desert and I licked them, again without thinking. But while I was watching her fingers, she was watching my face, and I knew without glancing up, she was getting as much out of this now as I was.

She slowly slipped a finger beneath the fabric and found her clit. Oh so slowly and gently, she circled it, letting me see everything in high definition detail, and a soft sigh rang around my ears. I dragged my bottom lip through my teeth as I watched.

Then, she removed her finger and let the dress fall to her knees. I glanced up at her face, about to go ballistic, when she turned her back to me and looked over her shoulder.

"Zip," she pouted.

Holding the phone steady, I moved up to her. She scooped a few errant strands of hair out of the way while I felt for the zip pull. When I found it and tugged it down, it cut through the dress like butter, revealing soft, milky, unblemished skin, the thin strap of a bra in matching indigo, and the small butterfly tattoo in the small of her back. By the time I had pulled the zip all the way over her bottom, to the backs of her thighs, my cock was so hard it hurt.

She looked over her shoulder again at me, her eyes glinting wickedly, and pushed the sleeves over her shoulders, letting the dress fall to the floor in a pool around her feet.

Now it was my turn to curse.

A smile ghosted her features before she turned fully around and fixed a serious, sultry expression to her face. When I demanded she do this, I didn't think it would be quite so intoxicating. I didn't think at all, to be fair. Her tits jutted out beneath the bra, just large enough, nipples peaked to perfection. My eyes glided back down to the thong.

"Now do it, Vivian," I said. Sternly, in an attempt to cover up the break in my voice.

"Yes, Rupert," she purred, playing with me like a feral cat might toy with a baby mouse.

Her fingers slid beneath the fabric again, returning to her heat.

"Spread your legs," I ordered. She rested her weight on

the table behind and inched her legs outwards. I couldn't help but lick my lips again.

"You look like you might be hungry," she said in a low, sexy voice.

"I just ate." I bit out the lie. It was unethical enough that I was making her do this when I was set to become engaged within a matter of weeks. I couldn't touch her, let alone eat her out. Even though, right now, her observation was spot on. I was starving for it.

"Fuck yourself with your fingers," I growled, not recognising the heat in my own voice.

She did as she was told and slid two fingers into her pussy while I watched, glued to the movement.

"Now, let me see."

She pulled her fingers free and held them up so I could see the moisture stretch between them. *Jesus.* I closed the gap between us and let her feed her fingers between my lips. I closed my eyes to savour her taste, and murmured my approval. Without further instruction, she pulled her fingers free and slipped them back inside her pants.

"Rupert…" her voice broke as she continued to rub her clit. "Tell me what to do."

I didn't need to think. "Play with your tits while you finger yourself."

She obliged instantly, pulling the cup of her bra over one breast and tweaking the nipple between her fingers. Her eyes closed and her head dropped back slightly. She was mesmerising, and my cock was on another planet, but there was something missing. I turned the phone around so it was filming in selfie mode, then placed it on the table behind her. She opened her eyes and watched curiously, then I turned her to face the screen so she could watch as she got herself off.

While she continued to play with herself, I took her bun in both hands and removed the pins one by one. The room was deathly quiet other than for the sound of fingers against wet flesh and the metallic ting of hair pins landing on the table. When all the pins had been released, I let her hair uncurl and removed the band holding it up. I held my breath as her hair spilled in a riotous wave down her back. Errant strands fell over her face, only moving when she puffed air through pursed lips so as to not let them obstruct her view. God, maybe she was the real puppet master in the room. I curled one hand around the hair on her left and pushed it behind her shoulder blade, exposing her neck. I suddenly wanted to kiss the nape, the arch of her throat, feel the hot pulse beating away beneath the thin covering of skin, but I couldn't do it.

When I looked back at the screen, our eyes locked. Hers were as dark as mine felt.

"Keep playing with yourself, Vivian," I instructed.

Her fingers slid effortlessly from her clit to her pussy and back again, her breath becoming shallow and rasping.

"How does it feel, Vivian, to have me watch you while you pleasure yourself?"

She gasped, her shoulders arching forward. "God, Rupert. It feels so good, but it's so bad."

"You're right, butterfly. This is bad." I straightened and walked around her, slowly, watching her fingers work herself from every angle. "You are bad. And this is your punishment. Does it feel like punishment, Vivian?"

Another gasp. "Yes."

I leapt on it. "Why?"

Her panting breaths rivalled the wet suckling sounds coming from her fingers. "Because I want my fingers to be yours."

I stepped up to her ear and dragged my lips across it with a decadent whisper. "I think you know that can never happen." I walked around her front, holding her hazy eyes as I passed. "Because I have to marry someone else," I continued. Then I stopped at her other ear and grazed it with my tongue. "But when I fuck her, I'll think of you."

A choke erupted from her throat.

"Rupert, I'm so close…" she gasped, her hair falling in front of her face, obscuring the view of herself in my phone.

I moved until I was standing behind her, the stiffness in my pants pressed up against the crack of her ass. "I've got you, baby," I whispered, pulling her hair out of her face. I stood over her shoulder holding her eyes in the screen.

"Oh God…" A garbled sound came from her mouth.

"Let it go, Vivian." My words were drowned out by a cry so unkempt, I worried someone would have heard it two floors down. She almost buckled over so I wrapped an arm around her front. "Who are you coming for, butterfly?" My chest swelled as I watched her rub her clit frantically, drawing out the longest orgasm I'd seen a woman have.

"You," she choked.

"Who?" I demanded. "Say it."

Her efforts rubbed against my cock, taking me right to the edge of my own orgasm. I gritted my teeth to stop myself from coming.

"Rupert," she cried out. "*God*, Rupert."

Her entire body tensed and shook in my arm and I panted along with her, then held her as she softened again.

After a minute or two had passed, I took her hands and placed them on the table before releasing her boneless body, then I bent down and pulled the dress back up her never-ending legs, over the curve of her perfect ass and up over her arms, then I slowly and carefully zipped it all the way back to the top. She watched me in the screen of the phone as I scooped up her hair, tied the band around it, and fastened it back into a bun using each of the pins.

Then I reached forward, hit stop, and shoved the phone back in my pocket before turning her to face me. Her cheeks were flushed and glistening, her lips wet and loose.

"Now what?" she whispered.

"Now," I said, straightening up and thinning my glare. "Go and stop McFadden."

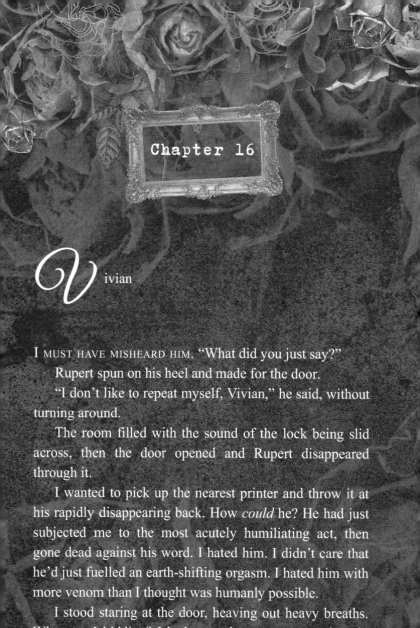

Chapter 16

*V*ivian

I MUST HAVE MISHEARD HIM. "What did you just say?"

Rupert spun on his heel and made for the door.

"I don't like to repeat myself, Vivian," he said, without turning around.

The room filled with the sound of the lock being slid across, then the door opened and Rupert disappeared through it.

I wanted to pick up the nearest printer and throw it at his rapidly disappearing back. How *could* he? He had just subjected me to the most acutely humiliating act, then gone dead against his word. I hated him. I didn't care that he'd just fuelled an earth-shifting orgasm. I hated him with more venom than I thought was humanly possible.

I stood staring at the door, heaving out heavy breaths. Who was I kidding? I had never been more turned on in my life.

I STILL WEIGHED HEAVY POST-ORGASM, as though no
amount of foreplay with Rupert Thorn would ever be
enough. The way he gripped my jaw, again. The way his
Adam's apple bobbed as he watch my fingers slide into my
pants. And the way he called me butterfly. It was such a
beautiful, innocent word, but he made it sound both dirty
and decadent as it dripped from his lips. I didn't think I
could get any wetter between my thighs, but when he
brushed his treasonous mouth against my ear and whispered into it, I nearly came right then.

His words were fire and dirt. *When I fuck her, I'll think
of you.* The thought of Rupert Thorn thinking of me while
fucking another woman made me wet all over again. Not
because of the obvious betrayal but because I wanted him
to *only* think of me. As much as I wanted him, I hated it
all. Because he was right.

I was his butterfly.

Too bad that Rupert Thorn was my flame.

I took myself to the bathroom to clean up, all the
while holding back vicious, angry tears. He had so much
material now with which to screw me over if he wanted.
I was literally at his mercy. My job hung in a balance
that was lorded over by him and there was nothing I
could do about it. I could have confessed to Sinclair that
I'd tried to steal the red tops, but Rupert was right,
Sinclair would fire me on the spot. Perhaps if I waited a
few weeks, until I'd proven I could create and run the
perfect tour, maybe then he might forgive my actions. I
could tell Sinclair that Rupert asked me to relay our
conversation, but I still had no idea what I repeated that
Rupert could have found so insightful. I was certain the
information I'd passed on was worse than useless. I

couldn't be certain that was why I was accosted in the woods.

I could lie and say the voice on Rupert's recording wasn't mine, but now he had the video footage which proved that voice was indeed mine. But then, the video footage featured him too. He was as complicit in the act as I was. I sighed out a fractured breath. He could edit himself out. He wasn't stupid. If he really wanted to bury me in deep shit, he could manipulate that video whichever way he wanted to. It was so easy nowadays to manipulate images, and the Thorns were one of the richest families in Britain. If it were a simple question of getting hold of the right technology, they had the money to pay for it.

I hit the heel of my palm against the wall. "*Fuck!*" How stupid had I been? I washed my hands and fixed my hair. Rupert had done an annoyingly good job but I didn't want him to have the last say when it came to my hair. He was about to have the last say in everything I did on this island.

I stared at myself in the mirror. "What have you turned into, Vivian? Allowing one of your bosses to film you doing *that*?" I shook my head. I couldn't believe I'd let it happen. Then a darker thought eclipsed that one. I hadn't let that happen. I was blackmailed. And now I was being blackmailed again. I closed my lids, unable to look my own reflection in the eye, and inhaled a shattered breath. Then I went back to the library, reached into the waste paper basket, put the crumpled up slip in my pocket, and left.

Halfway down the stairs I remembered leaving my bag behind the bar in the lounge. A ball of anxiety formed in the pit of my stomach. *Please God, don't let any of the*

Thorns be there. I couldn't face any of them. I turned the corner and all my nightmares erupted at once. Hector's face beamed at me from across the room where he stood with a tall slender girl with a sleek black bob, and someone taller still, with his back facing the door. But I knew that damned back. Rupert turned and stroked his gaze over me while I froze in the doorway. My heart was in my throat. He wouldn't have told them, would he?

As though he could read my mind, he slipped his phone out of his pocket and swiped the screen. Only then did he look away to type something out. My death sentence probably. Death by humiliation.

"Hey, Viv." Hector lifted his glass, beckoning me over. "Come meet Adele."

No! My head screamed. *Run rabbit run.*

I forced a smile and made my way over, training my eyes on anyone but Rupert. I knew if I caught his gaze I would blush a hideous shade of crimson. I was still hot all over from the way his eyes had devoured me upstairs. He'd barely touched me but all of my skin burned. Then, the way he demanded I do his bidding regardless of what I'd just done had frozen the blood in my veins. Something in me was going to melt and I couldn't be certain it wouldn't be my sanity.

I walked to the small group and let Hector introduce us. "Adele, this is Viv, the tour guide." I rolled my eyes at him. "Viv, this is Adele Lamont. She and Rupert went to school together."

"Hi." She extended an unfeasibly long, slim arm and lazily shook my hand. I wondered if she was in the pool of potential wives Rupert would have to choose from. "Rupert is working you hard, I hear?"

I felt his gaze on me and amusement dancing behind it. I couldn't look at him. "You might say that," I murmured.

A warmth closed in my shoulder. "Nonsense. I'm a *pussy* cat," he said, in a low voice that would have stroked me to another orgasm if it had fingers.

"Speaking of working *hard*," I said, finally flicking my eyes to Rupert – two could play at that game – "I must get going. It's a pleasure to meet you, Adele. Hopefully, I'll see you around."

"Definitely," she smiled.

"Great. Well, night everyone." I ducked away from the group and flew to the bar. Minty was already there, my bag hooked over an outstretched arm.

"Thought you might be needing this. Everything ok? You looked a little uncomfortable."

I shook off her comment and took my bag. "I'm fine. It's fine. Everything's fine. I'll see you tomorrow."

I walked out of Caspian House with my head down and my walls up. Absolutely *nothing* was fine.

I sat in the driver's seat of my car, watching the rain lash down on the bonnet. It made the dim evening light even darker. Twenty-four hours had passed in a heartbeat. No matter how much I wished for five o'clock to not come around, it rapidly did, and now it was only thirty minutes away.

I was half a mile from McFadden's house, and the time was ten minutes to five when I finally figured out what I could do to keep him from making his way to the labs in time for his shift. It was the location of his small house that gave me the idea. It sat solitarily on a sloping hill cut into one of the coastal mountains. There seemed to be nothing else around for miles.

I pulled over and tugged my coat around me, then jumped out and popped open the boot. Holding the torch from my phone in front of me, I searched for something sharp. The car jack was no good, nor was the complementary umbrella fixed to the inside edge. My gaze landed on a green and white package, which, on closer inspection, was a first aid kit. Propping up the phone, I pulled the zip, opening the bag, and rummaged through gauze, surgical tape and painkillers. Then... bingo. A small pair of scissors glinted up at me. I grabbed them and slammed the door of the boot, then without further thought, jumped back in the car and drove to McFadden's.

I parked only metres away and looked up at the house. It was small, its windows glowing orange from the light of life behind. In the brief moments when the raindrops softened, I could hear voices inside the house. Children racing around, the occasional movement against a curtain. The house held a lot of life. Was I about to bring that crashing down? I had no idea. All I knew was I needed this job. I needed to stay on the island. Because I needed to get a fruiting red top I could actually do something with. I couldn't go home empty-handed, or with a reputation tarnished by failure from one of the most coveted jobs in the country.

I checked my watch. I only had ten minutes before McFadden would be due to leave for his night shift. Before I could dwell any further on what I was about to do, I slipped out of the car, letting the door rest partially open. I ran to the car parked in McFadden's drive and crouched down by the back wheel. Just as I did so, the heavens opened and a loud downpour rained onto my head. I raised my arm back above my head, gripped the scissors and rammed the sharp end into the tyre. I imagined a small hissing sound would have started up but I couldn't hear anything for the lashing rain. I raised my arm again, and again, and stabbed the scissors into the tyre maybe ten more times. Then I moved on to the next. Five minutes later, every tyre had multiple punctures.

I glanced around, wiping the rain out of my eyes. It wasn't enough that I stop him from getting to the labs, I had to prevent him being able to tell anyone. My eyes landed on the telephone wire. I'd noticed that only the rich on the island seemed to carry mobile phones, so the chances were McFadden was reliant on his landline. I spotted the wire running into the side of the house and launched myself towards it. I sliced the sharp end of the scissors through the wire, severing it in two.

I jumped back into my car, kept the headlights off and rolled backwards down the road. As soon as I was out of sight, I spun the car around, flicked on the lights and sped back to the cottage as fast as the hammering rain would allow.

I pulled into the space beside the cottage, turned off the engine and stared at the rivulets running down the windscreen. For the first time in my life, I hated myself. I was playing a part in ruining someone's life. I hadn't even questioned what would happen to McFadden when he didn't show at the labs, and now I was too afraid to think about it. I might have put an innocent person in serious danger, and all the while lusting over an orchestrator of hell, and doing the devil's dirty work. It had been three weeks since I arrived on the island and I was no closer to finding help for my sister. Instead, I was allowing my boss's son to film me getting myself off to the sight of his face and the sound of his voice. It was fucked up.

My phone buzzed and my heart immediately stuttered. I looked at the latest message from Richard. *"Hey Viv. Quick update. Good news first. We finally got a diagnosis for Peggy."* My pulse quickened. This was huge. Maybe now her pain would be taken seriously at long last. Maybe I wouldn't need to get my hands on Bas after all. Maybe I could go home and be with my sister instead of out here getting deeper and deeper into sinister shit while she continued to suffer without me. *"She has something called fibromyalgia."*

I released a long breath and felt my shoulders lighten instantly. Finally, something we could talk to a registered doctor about and not be dismissed with a bunch of ibuprofen tablets. Then I scrolled further and the sadness re-emerged. *"The bad news, I'm afraid, is there's no cure."*

I dropped the phone to my lap, covered my face with my hands and wept, loudly and uncontrollably. Sobs racked my throat and chest, and tears flowed through my fingers. All the tension that had mounted over the last few years was coming out of my eyeballs. *There's no cure.* I moaned the words aloud like I was a wounded animal. *No cure.*

When I eventually ran out of tears, about an hour later, I renewed my gaze out of the window. Now, I really had no other choice. I had to get my hands on that drug. Whether I stole it or grew it, I had to get it, and I would die trying.

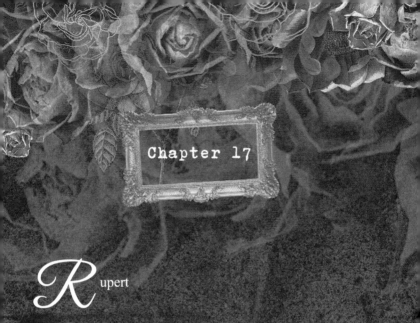

Chapter 17

*R*upert

I PRESSED the barbell into the air and held it while the cells in my muscles screamed with agony. It was the only thing that stopped me from re-watching the video I took of Vivian the day before. I'd got myself off to it five times and watched it probably ten times more than that. I told myself it was the visual, and the fact I played a part in it too, even if all I did was untie her hair and hold her up.

I now realised why people liked to film themselves. It was like turbo-powered porn. I could have watched myself command her for hours, and listened to the cute, desperate moans escape those ripened lips for just as long. Each time I watched, I braced myself for the novelty to wear off, but it didn't. Instead, with each viewing, I noticed another tantalising detail, like the shiver she made the second her fingers touched her clit, like the way she closed her eyes when I whispered into her ear.

THERE WAS NO QUESTION, she'd wanted it. Needed it, even. Enough to let me film it.

I toyed with the idea of showing someone, maybe Hector, to let her know I wasn't precious about using it, but a strange *un-Thorn* part of me wanted to keep it to myself, like a possession I didn't ever want to share.

My phone lit up again and I glanced down at the caller ID. Ossian again. I smiled to myself. I knew exactly why he was calling, but I let him stew. I held the weight above my head for a couple more minutes, until I could barely feel my arms, then dropped it to the mat, heaving air in and out of my lungs as I regained some composure.

When my phone lit up a third time, I answered it. "Ossian."

"Rupert, where are you?" He sounded out of breath, like he was running. But I knew where he was, and I knew there wouldn't be many places he could run to. He was panicking.

"I'm at the gym, bro'," I replied. "Where are you?"

"At home." I knew that was a lie.

"Everything ok?"

"I'm trying to get hold of McFadden. You seen him?"

"No. Why? Should I have?" My chest swelled with pride. She'd done it. My delicious little butterfly had fucking done it. I almost wanted to bend her over the bonnet of her brand new Aston and ease myself inside her as a reward for both of us.

"Forget it," Ossian snapped.

"No, come on. What is it? How can I help?"

"He was due on shift an hour ago. He should have started at five-thirty, and it's getting on for seven now."

"What's the urgency? It's not like anything needs to be

done at the labs, is there?" I ground my teeth as I awaited the next lie.

"I'm worried about trespassers. We've had a few sightings in the last week. I don't want to take any chances."

"Really? I've been keeping an eye on the CCTV and haven't noticed anything." I knew I was being facetious.

"You know what, Rupert? Fuck you. You're not taking this seriously."

"Oh wait, hang on, you're worried about him? That something might have happened to McFadden?" That would have been the obvious concern for a normal person. But my brother was the furthest from 'normal' a human being could ever get.

"Yes," he said. Another lie.

"Look, I'm sure there will be a perfectly innocent explanation. I'll make a few calls, see if anyone's seen him."

"Fine," Ossian hissed. "Thanks"

"No problem," I said, brightly, before hanging up.

Then I switched off my phone.

I KNOCKED on the door to Grandpa's suite, and entered. There was tension in the air so thick I could have sliced through it with my diamond cufflink.

"Evening Father," I said, his being the first face I saw as I stepped into the room.

"Rupert," he replied curtly. My blood ran several degrees cooler as I wondered how my orchestration of McFadden's late arrival had impacted the deliveries that evening.

"Oz not here yet?" I asked innocently.

"Working late," Father clipped. "Some issues at the site."

"I'm sorry to hear that," I said, taking the lowball Hector held out to me. "Anything I can do?"

I watched Father's face for any suggestion that was the last thing he wanted, because after all, no one was to know what the 'issues' were, including me.

He surprised me. "Thanks for offering, Rupert. I'll let you know."

Aro wandered over to me from Grandpa's bedside. "How are you doing Rupert?"

"Great," I replied, noting the concern in his tone. "Why?"

Aro took a deep breath and let it out slowly, while surveying my face. "Your mother talked to me about your impending engagement. How are you feeling about it?"

I looked back at my glass then threw the entire double measure down my throat.

"Easy tiger," Hector heckled. "Need a refill?"

I nodded and held out my glass. I looked back at Aro. "I haven't given it much thought, to be honest." That was the truth. The most I'd thought about it was when I whispered into Vivian's ear that I would think about her when I fucked said fiancée.

"You know your father will have to hold a banquet in your honour, like he did for Ossian. You remember?"

"How could I forget?" I mumbled, taking a swig from the topped up glass. Ossian's banquet was the most uncomfortable thing I'd ever attended. The banquets only happened if a love match hadn't been made first. In most cases, people found partners before they reached the age of twenty-seven, but not Ossian. He was widely regarded among the girls on the island as a leering snake, and most were dragged to the banquet by their social-climbing parents and forced to behave amorously towards a fox-faced man who was becoming more and more intoxicated with every passing minute. He grabbed the girls by their asses, he pulled them down onto his lap when they least expected it. He prised their mouths into a kiss, so he could "test the merchandise," and even ripped one girl's dress because he clung on when she couldn't get away fast enough. He loved every minute. Everyone else… didn't.

"Well, hopefully yours won't be quite so *uncomfortable*," Aro noted, diplomatically.

"Not for anyone but me," I said, without thinking.

"You'll find a good woman, Rupert," Aro said. "You have a good reputation on the island. You're the furthest thing from a player we have. You haven't let riches go to your head, you conduct your business professionally and clean. You're devoted to family." He swallowed then added, "And you're a good-looking boy, Rupert. You won't be short of decent girls who will do a great job of making you happy."

"Make me happy, how?" I asked, genuinely curious. How could a woman I didn't love make me happy?

"They'll keep a good house, lend an ear when you need to talk, keep you healthy with good food. If you choose well, they may have useful intelligence to offer. And, of course, there is the matter of sexual need…"

I almost winced. I could fuck a woman I didn't love as much as the next man, but for how long? And to what end? I wouldn't be able to make her happy; my heart wouldn't be in it. What kind of a life was that for anyone?

"What about you?" I realised I had no idea how Aro had met and married his wife, my Aunt Isobel. I only ever saw her at official family gatherings, never informally. She'd always seemed shy and rarely made eye contact with me. I couldn't remember ever having spoken to her. Which was strange because whenever I turned my back, I always had the curious feeling I was being watched. "How did you and Isobel meet?"

Aro looked momentarily surprised, then his features relaxed.

"We were childhood sweethearts," Aro said, tilting his eyes to gaze over my head. "Met at school. We were lucky. Her father was good friends with your grandfather. It was a match that everyone was happy with. No banquet was needed and we married in our twenties."

"It sounds perfect," I said, without emotion.

"Yeah." Aro's smile dropped. "Not always."

"What do you mean?"

He avoided my gaze and instead swirled his own drink watching the warm liquid flicker under the opulent chandeliers. "You know how it is. We're Thorns. Things aren't always easy. But, believe me…" he finally looked up, this time his eyes piercing mine with a warning. "Having someone by your side who you love and who loves you, makes it all a lot easier to bear."

Chapter 18

*V*ivian

THE HALLS DARKENED the closer I got to Sinclair's office,
and the noise of the main admin offices slowly fell away
into eerie silence. I peered up at the useless chandeliers,
wondering why they burned so dimly. It was as though the
entire hall had been designed to feel foreboding. It wasn't
as if the Thorns couldn't afford lightbulbs, or the electricity to power them.

"Come in," his voice barked.

I bit back nerves as I pushed open the solid wood door
and let it close heavily behind me.

"Sit," he commanded, as though I were a pet dog, not a
somewhat valued employee.

"I've brought my latest update with m—" I began as I
lowered into the chair opposite.

His snarl cut me off. "I'm not interested in that right
now."

"Oʜ?" I steadied my breathing. Was this about McFadden? Did Sinclair suspect it was me? I hadn't seen Rupert for a week so I'd had no idea whether or not my plan had worked. What if it had? What if someone had seen me?

"Where were you last Friday afternoon?" he said, narrowing his eyes.

I swallowed as discreetly as I could. "I was at the cottage," I lied.

"No you weren't. We have CCTV covering the entire area around Sandpiper Cottage. You were seen leaving around four p.m."

Panic threaded its way through my veins. "Right," I muttered.

"I'll repeat my question, shall I? Where were you – specifically at five p.m. – on Friday afternoon?"

I stuttered out a breath. My bones felt as though they were melting under the scrutiny. "I was... Um, I was at the edge of the Sunken Glade," I replied, dropping my eyes and hoping he didn't see the untruths in them.

It seemed to take him by surprise. "Why did you go there?" A note of tension appeared in his voice.

"I'm curious about the place," I said, quietly. "I've been told there is a petrified forest at sea level. I've never seen one before. I was hoping to get down there."

"It's off limits," Sinclair snapped. "If you'd been caught trespassing, you would have been thr—, *removed* from the island."

"I didn't get very far," I said. "I knew it would have been wrong to enter. I hoped I might see something from the roadside."

He shook his head, slowly. "The land dips dramatically. You'd have seen nothing."

I shrugged my shoulders. "You're right."

"So, that's where you were Friday afternoon?"

I sighed, feigning guilt. "Yes, sir. My apologies."

"Fine." He leaned back in his chair and rested his hands behind his head. "Thank you for your honesty, Miss Gillespie. You may leave."

I rose unsteadily and picked up my bag. With nothing further to be said, I walked self-consciously to the door and let myself out. Once back in the corridor and safely out of earshot, I let out a shaky, audible breath. I leaned a hand against a wall to calm my dizzying pulse. Whichever way I looked at the situation, I was in deep shit. Deep, deep shit.

I hated Rupert for putting me in this situation.

Hated him with every cell in my body.

I hated every devilish, destructive... *delicious*... cell in his.

And I hated myself all the more for it.

I OPENED the boot and pulled out the lambswool blankets I'd found in one of the cupboards, and a basket I'd filled with ham sandwiches, crisps, pork pies and pickles, a bottle of Prosecco and two glasses. I'd hoped for plastic ones but the only vessels on offer at the cottage were these plain flutes or cut crystal coupes. As I looped the basket onto my arm, I noticed the first aid bag partially unzipped and froze.

My one saving grace through the execution of my clandestine mission, was I'd had way too much on my mind to think about what Rupert had done to me in the library. Now my dark deed was done, I'd be able to let my mind wander back to the feel of his gaze as I played with myself, and the brush of his words against my ear as he told me to let go. They were the words of a man who cared how I felt, which went against everything I knew about Rupert Thorn. He didn't care about anything except money. He simply wanted to record himself watching me orgasm, so he could puff out his chest and congratulate himself on how accomplished and irresistible he was if he needed a boost. Though I doubted he would ever need a boost. His ego was so big it needed its own yacht.

"Over here!" My head turned to follow the squeal and I saw Minty jumping up and down at the far side of the parking area. I locked the car and made my way to where she laid out her own blanket and had already started on the white wine.

She apologised for the choice of location. "It's a bit blustery, but at least it's not raining."

"It's fine," I smiled. "I'm just glad to see beyond the walls of Blackcap Hall." I sank to the ground, pulled out the bottle and popped the cork. When in Rome...

"I would give my right arm to see inside that place," Minty sighed, wistfully. "I used to cycle past it after school and stand outside staring up at the windows."

"Really?" I poured some bubbles into a flute. "Why?"

Minty shrugged. "I don't know. Maybe I thought I'd see something in the windows. Something that gave me a clue as to how we could have that kind of life, you know? It sounds stupid now."

"The place is really not that interesting," I reassured

her. "It's dark, eerie, echoey and, if you're unfortunate to still be in the office after most other people have left, downright scary. But no one else seems to feel that way," I shrugged. "Maybe it's just me."

"Hmm," Minty took a long sip of her wine and quirked a brow. "I wouldn't be so sure. There have been enough rumours about that place over the years, I'd be surprised if anyone found it a 'comfortable' place to work."

"What do you mean?" I asked, slurping the rapidly ascending bubbles from the top of my glass.

"Some people have gone into Blackcap Hall and supposedly never come out. Some people came out but were never seen going in. Old architectural plans surfaced not long ago that showed what appeared to be dungeons beneath the hall and attics in each of the towers."

"Are attics so unusual?" I asked, sceptically.

"Does that place *need* any more storage?" Minty fired back at me.

"Fair point." I popped a couple of crisps into my mouth and thought as I chewed. "So, these people who disappeared or suddenly appeared. Who were they?"

"I don't remember all their names," Minty said, ripping open a packet of cold meats. "But the most recent case was Rose Thorn. Have you met her?"

My head cocked to one side. "No, I haven't, but I've heard of her. I was told she decorated the cottage I'm staying in."

"Oh yeah," Minty said through a mouthful of salami. "She's brilliant with interiors. She helped design Caspian House too."

"What's the deal with her name? Is it a total coincidence? Happy serendipity?"

Minty narrowed her eyes in thought. "No one really knows. Some say it's not her real name—that she was forced to take it when she came here."

"Wait… she's not from the Isle of Crow?"

"No," Minty confirmed. "She's from somewhere near London, I'd say."

"How is that possible?" I said, suddenly desperate to know. "Dax is a Thorn. How was he allowed to marry a non-islander?"

"Have you seen him?" Minty asked, gently.

"No. Why?"

"He's very badly disfigured," Minty said. "His face and allegedly half his body is scarred as a result of an acid attack that happened when he was younger."

"Seriously? Who would do something like that?"

"Some people say it was Ossian."

"What? His own cousin?" Even as I voiced my surprise, I realised I wasn't that surprised at all. After personally witnessing his bitter and intimidating presence, I could picture him committing such a horrific act of violence.

"Whoever it was or however it happened," Minty continued, with a shrug, "it really changed the way Dax looked. He used to be seriously gorgeous, but after the attack, none of the girls on the island were interested, so he had to go shopping. He might not have had the looks but he had the money."

"How did he find Rose?"

Minty shrugged again. "No one knows exactly, but I guess there are dating agencies, match-making services, that sort of thing. Some islanders think he bought her. Others think she was trafficked. Like I said, no one really knows the truth. Only the Thorn family. One thing I do know though is, regardless of how she got here, they are more in love than any couple I've ever seen. They seem to be completely consumed by each other. It's a bit weird."

"I'm pretty sure Dax is coming to the VIP tour party in a couple of weeks," I said, trying to recall the guest list.

"Then you can be certain Rose will be there too. He doesn't seem to go anywhere without her. So, you'll see for yourself."

"I'm intrigued. I like a bit of mystery."

I laid out the pork pie I'd sliced into portions, and two forks I was pretty sure were made of solid silver.

"Well, there's no greater mystery than the TB crisis," Minty said, casually, as she took a piece of the pie.

My hand froze, holding my slice in mid-air. "What?"

She stared at me as though I'd gone mad. "The TB crisis."

"TB? As in Tuberculosis?"

Her eyes narrowed. "Yes." There may as well have been a 'duh' at the end of that word.

"There's been an outbreak of TB?"

She was about to put the pork pie in her mouth but stopped. "You really didn't know?"

"No!" I gasped. "Are you being serious? You've had tuberculosis here? On the island?"

"Yes. We thought it was common knowledge, but apparently not. Didn't they ask you to get the vaccination?"

"Well, yes, but…" I recalled how odd I'd found the request, but hadn't given it much thought since dutifully getting the vaccine before I left for the island.

Her voice softened. "It's been here a while, but it

seems to be slowing down now. The Consortium insisted we all have the vaccine last year. Turned out some of us had already contracted the illness, to varying extents. But now everyone had has the jabs, the cases have dropped a lot.

I stared at her in disbelief. It couldn't be right. "Isn't TB rare around here? I thought it was at its lowest levels ever in the U.K. How on earth would we not know about it?"

"The Consortium has every damn politician and jour-nalist in their pockets. They would have strangled the story before it even took a breath. They clamped down on people leaving and coming onto the island, not that many made it here to begin with. Which is what makes it all the weirder that they're opening it up now to visitors. I guess they must feel so confident we're over the worst that chances are very low no one visiting will contract it."

"They have a duty to declare it," I said, my voice grave.

"Like I said, the government knows," Minty shrugged.

I shook my head. "How on earth did it get here?"

"It must have been one of the families," Minty shrugged. "They're the only ones who travel anywhere. They probably brought it back here."

We both fell silent as we ate. I watched the dark, threatening sea rolling large frothy waves up the coastline, and the enormous-winged gulls dipping and diving with deafening squawks.

"How are you getting on with Rupert?" Minty asked, changing the subject.

I was shocked at the fireball that suddenly came to light in my stomach. "Um, fine," I replied.

"I never asked you. What happened at the night market? He dragged you out of that place like you were about to be killed."

It's entirely possible I was. "I don't know. I'd walked pretty far into the woods. I think he was annoyed at me about that."

"I was surprised to see him there. Like I said, the families don't really go to the market." Minty said, raising both brows. "But, I suppose some sort of treatment by Rupert Thorn is better than no treatment at all. I can't believe none of the girls here have snapped him up yet. He's a catch and a half. I mean, have you ever looked at a man's hands and thought, 'woah'? His are huge, and they were wrapped around you like leather straps. I watched him bundle you into his Ferrari. That was the closest I've ever seen him get to an actual woman."

I swallowed trying to ease my dried throat. I felt as though my skin was burning up and I could hardly sit still. I had to change the subject.

"Can I tell you a secret?"

"Yes, please do," she gushed. "I'm going to feel guilty about bursting your Isle of Crow bubble with the whole TB thing."

That ship had already sailed but I couldn't burden her with that now. "I'm not a tour guide."

She frowned, her blue eyes darkening. "What?"

"I don't know shit about arranging tours," I said, throwing my arms up. It felt so freeing speaking the truth to someone other than Em and Richard.

Minty gasped, then chuckled, then burst into a rip-roaring laugh. When she finally caught her breath, she repeated, "What? Then... how?"

"I faked my CV," I shrugged.

"You didn't! Oh my God. Does anyone else know?"

I sipped some more Prosecco and shook my head. "Only you. And you have to promise me you won't breathe a word."

"Are you kidding? On my life, Viv. I won't tell a soul. But… why?"

I stared down at my glass, fingering the icy cold stem and felt the shiver tip-tap across my shoulders. "I need to get the drug somehow. Basidiomine. So, I faked my CV so they'd hire me. I feel bad about lying but I need that drug."

Minty placed her hand over mine. "You and the rest of the world," she said, quietly. "Why do you need it so badly?"

"It's not for me," I whispered, looking up into her pale, trusting eyes. "It's for my sister. She suffers from chronic pain and we've tried everything. We've run out of options. This is my last hope."

"Does Rupert know?"

"No." I hung my head shamefully. "I lied about having a sister too. They wanted someone who had no close ties to home. I feel terrible about it."

"Oh, Viv." She squeezed my hand before sitting back. "I'm so sorry to hear that. Do you really think they'll give it to you?"

I sighed. "I already asked Rupert. He said no…"

Minty shook her head, slowly. "That doesn't surprise me."

"So I need to get it another way." I was tempted to tell her about the stolen spawn but I figured one secret for today was probably enough.

"Jeez," she said on a long breath. "You know most

people on this island have been trying to get it too. No one has had any luck."

"Do you know anything about where it's kept? Is it all in the lab? The security is ridiculous in that place."

"Oh yeah, you won't get your hands on anything in there. But there is a rumour…"

I was about to say 'another one'? but I was eager to hear anything. "Go on."

"There's a room in Blackcap Hall."

"Are you serious?" Had I been sitting in the vicinity of the drug this whole time?

"There's some on the second floor of the north tower. A small supply of the drug is kept in a safe there."

Butterflies careened around my chest. "How do you know this?"

"Well, like I said, it's a rumour, but most people on the island suspect there's a great deal of truth behind it. The guy who leaked it died the next day. Shot between the eyes."

A sharp intake of air stung the sides of my throat. "What?" I whispered. "By who?"

"No one knows for sure but most people suspect Ossian."

Ossian, again? The thought slipped out of my mouth before I could stop it. "My bosses are murderers," I said with a shaky voice.

"Technically, there's no proof," Minty said, before emptying her glass. "So, don't go repeating that."

"The supply has probably been moved by now," I sighed.

"Maybe not. He was shot for leaking something else –

papers relating to the sale of Bas. He'd told a friend about the drug storage on the down low."

"Ah, right," I said, hope returning to my bones.

"But don't even think about being able to find it. The Thorns will end you, Viv. But, I think you already know that."

I wrapped up the remaining food and packed it away. "Well, in that case, I have one last favour to ask."

She side-eyed me warily. "Uh huh?"

I'd done a good job getting everything ready for the first set of visitors, but I could always use more expertise. "Do you know *anything* about hosting a tour?"

An hour later, after I'd drained Minty of as much information about hospitality as I could, I gave her a big, grateful hug, packed everything back into my car and drove out of the gravelly car park.

It was a short drive back to the cottage but I took my time, taking in the astounding views of a clear blue ocean, dramatic drops and cliff faces, and small sightings of blue-bells and primroses peeking through the heather.

I thought more about the tuberculosis. No one outside the island knew anything about an outbreak, and the island wasn't a million miles off the shore of mainland Scotland. It only added to my determination to find a way to grow the spawn so I would be free to leave if I wanted to. The mushroom spawn I'd planted had so far given zero indication it was going to grow into anything. I had to come up with another plan. Perhaps Emerie could post me a growing kit or something. Maybe the compost I'd used was old, or only worked well with roses... I had to keep trying. If nothing else worked, there was always the north tower...

I was deep in thought when a movement to my right caught my eye and something large, black and beastly, its engine roaring like Satan, smashed into the side of my car. The breath left my lungs in a gush and my attempts to claw it back failed as the car spun out of control. I clung to the steering wheel. The world twisted around me and became a blur of green, blue and demonic black. I was flung sideways into the window, my shoulder bruising in an instant, and I felt the pork pie and half a glass of Prosecco I'd drunk come crawling back up my oesophagus.

It didn't stop. The car continued to spin, but the direction, or rather, the terrain, changed. I was no longer on the road. I felt the wheels crash against a rock, then another bang rendered me blind. I was upside down, then the right way up, then upside down, then I lost all sense of where the hell I was.

And then there was nothing.

Chapter 19

*R*upert

I PACED the length and breadth of my office, checking my watch every two seconds like it held the secret to the meaning of life. *Where the fuck is she?* I had my back turned to the door when I heard her enter. With my hands pressed angrily into my pockets I stared at the framed picture of the port where exactly twenty VIPs were due to arrive in less than an hour for the first tour this island had conducted in the whole of its history.

"What time do you call this?" I growled, low. "You don't need me to tell you it's quite an important day, *Vivian*. Do you?"

When she didn't answer, no doubt out of the stubborn defiance I'd come to know – and almost like – her for, I turned slowly, fixing a menacing scowl to my face. The second I saw her, it fell and my heart turned to solid fucking stone.

. . .

HER OUTFIT WAS as knockout as I'd come to expect – dark red, the colour of dried blood, a high neckline and a fitted tweed jacket, perfectly befitting of a rural professional. But her face…

"What the hell happened?"

In a second, I was standing over her, lifting her chin as gently as I could, and moving it from side to side to get a closer look at the damage. Both her eyes were black and a long cut sliced down the side of her face. Her bottom lip had swollen to almost twice its size, and when she rolled up one sleeve of her dress, her shoulder and arm were mottled deep black and ghoulish green.

"Who did this to you?" I asked in an angry whisper.

She swallowed and took her time answering, clearly because it pained her. "Someone in a black car," she replied, slowly.

Black car. My blood boiled. "When?"

"Saturday."

"Why didn't anyone tell me?" Anger coursed through my veins at warp speed and my vision bled.

"I told the doctors not to. I wanted to rest and then tell you myself today."

"You were at the hospital," I stated, my mind racing.

She nodded and my brain scrambled. A black car. It could have been anyone. It didn't actually matter what type of car it was. If someone wanted her badly hurt, they could have paid any person on this island to do the deed. They were all as desperate as the next to make a fast buck. Yes, it could have been anyone, but one person in particular crept into my head and wouldn't fucking leave. *Ossian.*

The thought felt like a dagger to the heart. He was

pissed about the deliveries not reaching the island, but he couldn't have known it was Vivian who'd delayed McFadden that night. He must have had spies. Or taken a wild guess. Or maybe... maybe he'd done this to get to me.

I cradled her face in my palm with one hand and picked up my phone with the other. I pressed a button then, without taking my eyes off of her, I said, "Send Michelle to my office. Now." Then, I hung up and studied Vivian's face like it was a work of art.

"You were in the Aston?"

She nodded, her eyes glistening.

"It's a write-off?"

Another nod, then an attempt to speak. "I'm sorry."

Burning blood bubbled beneath my skin, threatening to erupt at any second. I couldn't afford to let it do that while she was standing in such close proximity. Who knew who I was capable of hurting? I'd never felt so angry in all my life. "You have nothing to be sorry for. I don't give a shit about the car. Where did it happen?"

"The coastal road, about five minutes from Gull Bay."

"Who found you?"

"Minty."

I'd always liked Minty. Now I owed her. Big time. She would get a raise the size of a fucking house.

"This is going to sound like a stupid question, but, how do you feel? You don't have to do the tour today if you don't feel up to it."

"I feel fine and I would hate to miss it, but how can I face people looking like this?" A fat tear finally rolled down her cheek and I wiped it away with my thumb. "I've worked so hard..." she hiccupped, unable to finish.

"Stop," I whispered. "It's going to be fine. If you really want to do it, you can do it. Michelle will fix you up."

Right as I said the name, a knock came at the door. "Sir, it's Michelle."

"Come in," I bit out.

She stepped into the room, took one look at Vivian and turned as white as a ghost. Her eyes flicked from Vivian's face to mine.

"She's been in a car accident," I explained. Michelle nodded. "I need you to make her look as though she hasn't."

She studied Vivian's face.

"You think you can do that?" I pressed. "Because if you can't, you're fired."

I didn't think Michelle's cheeks could pale any further, but they did. It was less of a threat and more of an assertion that only the best of the best would be able to fix Vivian's face. And I only hired the best. Now, Michelle had to prove it.

"I can do it," she said.

"What do you need?"

"My kit. And a nurse. We'll need to prescribe some serious painkillers to enable her to speak through that fat lip. No offence, miss," Michelle said.

"None taken," Vivian managed.

"Fine," I barked. "You have fifteen minutes." I took one last look at Vivian, then tore myself out of the room before I could wrap her in a fucking cashmere blanket and stow her away somewhere no one could reach her again.

I KICKED open the door to Ossian's office without knocking and found him in a compromised position, screwing one of the secretaries over his desk. She was face down, his fist pressing her cheek against the leather top as he leisurely stroked himself in and out of her. He looked up as I entered, then continued his lazy fuck as I walked around the desk towards him. He smiled doe-eyed at me, even as my chest pressed against his shoulder. The woman's eyes widened the second she realised another Thorn was witnessing her active participation in an extra-marital affair. I stretched out my fingers and bit back a threat. Marcia didn't deserve this.

"Get your dick out of this woman and ask her to leave," I growled into Ossian's ear.

He closed his eyes, glided them towards me, then opened them. He was fucked on something. "No."

The fury I'd been holding in since I saw Vivian's face surged forth and I saw blistering red. With both hands I pushed him backwards, his cock falling out and hanging limp between his skinny legs.

"Leave," I barked at the woman. She didn't need to be told twice. She pulled her pants up, pushed down her skirt and ran for the door.

"What the fuck, Rupert?" Ossian's jaded eyes tried to spear me but he was too far gone.

"What have you taken?" I demanded.

"Fuck you," Ossian drawled, then attempted to spit at me but it didn't get far and instead hung from his bottom lip. I couldn't talk to him about Vivian when he was like this.

"Is it coke? Have you taken cocaine?" I knew as soon as I said that, he likely hadn't. He seemed *too* out of it.

"Heroine? Crack? I wouldn't put either of them past you."

Ossian grinned like a maniac and held up a small bottle of Basidiomine. That didn't seem right. Bas didn't make people like this. Then he pulled another bottle out of his other pocket. It was an opioid he'd planned on experimenting with. Hadn't been tested.

"What the hell are you playing at, Oz? Do you have a death wish?"

"Just testing the merchandise," he slurred. His favourite saying. "Did you come here to talk about your precious Vivian?"

Every nerve-ending in me fired up. "Why would you think that?"

"Because you stormed in on your brother like you were about to kill someone. Guys don't do that unless there's a piece of pussy involved. And the only girl I've heard you talk about, ever, is the fucking tour guide."

Fury filled my chest and I couldn't stop it. I slapped him so hard he fell to the floor. He looked up at me, dazed, before dragging the back of his hand across his cut lip.

"What is it about her, Rupert?" he jeered. "You've never given a toss about any woman as long as I've lived. Why now? Why her?"

"Why do you think I'm here because of her?"

"Because... you've always been a miserable fucker, but ever since she arrived, you've gotten worse. Don't think I don't notice the way your face changes when someone mentions her name. You can pull the wool over Father's eyes but not mine."

"Was it you?" I growled between gritted teeth.

Ossian didn't bother getting back to his feet and

instead sat on the floor with his knees bent and rested his elbows on them. "Was *what* me?" he sighed, inspecting the blood on his hand.

"Did you have her run off the road?"

He looked sideways up at me. "*What* road? What are you talking about?"

"The coastal road, Saturday. Was it you?"

"I was with Father, going through the books. So, no."

"You could have hired someone."

He slowly got back to his feet and looked at me with a confused frown. "Why would I do that? What do I have against the tour guide? Other than the fact she's got you pussy-whipped. And distracted." He lifted his t-shirt and wiped it across his forehead. "You were the one who didn't want her here. Maybe I should be asking you these questions."

I sobered slightly. Either he was a far better actor than I'd given him credit for, or he genuinely didn't know what I was talking about.

"Fine," I said, holding my hands up. "But you are wrong about me being pussy-whipped. I couldn't give two shits about Vivian Gillespie."

He turned to face me as though he expected more. An apology.

"I'm not sorry I stormed in here without knocking. You shouldn't be screwing another woman behind Marcia's back."

"Oh yeah?" he said, rubbing the back of his neck with a dirty palm. "I'll ask for your opinion on that after you've been married to Elspeth Cartwright for four years."

I stared at him, horrified.

"That's right, little brother. If your heart's not in it to

begin with, it never will be. And a man's gotta get his thrills somehow."

I almost vomited on his desk, unsure which reason sat most prominent in my throat – was it the fact he was in a far better place than I to judge? Or was it because the thought of marrying someone I didn't love suddenly made me sick to the stomach.

"Just… use a condom," I said, as I walked back to the door.

"Why?" His words followed. "I've got to get my heir from somewhere."

I LEFT Ossian's office and kept going until I was standing on the gravel outside the hall, then I whipped out my phone. As soon as Kyra picked up, I got straight to the point.

"It's me. Any news?"

A sigh rang through the phone and I closed my eyes. I was getting used to this sound of defeat, and that was what pissed me off the most.

"Nothing, Rupert. We've tried organic matter – the leaves and grass clippings. That didn't seem to work. We've tried food waste, all different types. Nothing."

"What about the waste from the abattoir?"

"We've started on that. Nothing yet, but I'll keep you posted."

"I want daily updates," I said, unable to hide my impatience.

"Ok, fine," Kyra sighed again. "These things move

slowly, though. You know that. It may be weeks before I have something positive to report."

"I don't care," I snapped. "Keep testing."

I hung up and stared back at the hall. I hated it. The only thing good about this place was the one person sitting in my office with a black eye and a busted lip.

Chapter 20

V ivian

I watched Michelle's face as Rupert stormed out of the room. She followed him, if discreetly, with her eyes, then flicked them back to me with renewed compassion.

""I won't be a moment," she said, quietly. She picked up her phone, called someone and asked for her kit to be delivered "as fast as humanly possible".

She hung up and surveyed my face like a builder might survey a wall that was crumbling from damp.

"I'm sorry you got roped into this," I whispered.

"I'm not," she said, without hesitation. "I'm the best, Vivian. If anyone can make you look like you, sans the car accident, it's me."

I chose not to say anything else. I was surrounded by people who believed in themselves, backed themselves, while I was there with two giant black eyes and a busted-up lip, all because I hadn't stood up to my boss.

MY HEART REACHED out to Rupert when he stormed out, but my head was now screaming, 'Are you happy? Now leave me the fuck alone.' But, I knew in my heart of hearts, that wasn't what I wanted at all. I didn't want him to leave me alone. I wanted him to be all over me like a rash, and I hated myself for it.

I tried to relax as Michelle set to work making me look like a normal human being. I took the pills she offered and kept my face as still I possibly could. When she finally held the mirror in front of my face, I couldn't believe it.

I reached out to touch the glass. "How did you do that?" I whispered.

Michelle simply smiled and packed away her makeup tools.

"No, seriously. You are an absolute genius."

She stopped and looked me in the eye. "Thank you. I appreciate that more than being threatened with losing my job."

"I'm sorry about that," I said, looking down at my hands.

"Don't be. It's the first time I've seen any kind of passion in that man, and I've worked for him for eight years."

I looked up at her, prepared to see a sarcastic smirk on her face, because there was no way that was true. I saw none.

"You must mean something to him," she said. I didn't miss the warning tone in her voice.

"It wouldn't matter if I did," I said, as breezily as I could. The painkillers had helped. At least I could pronounce words with some measure of accuracy.

Suddenly, I felt her warm hands eclipse my cool ones. I

looked up and her eyes beat down on me. A warm glow in an otherwise frozen horizon. "Be careful, Vivian," she whispered. "Nothing good can come of you getting close to a Thorn, even if your feelings are reciprocated."

I went to stop her but she held up a hand and continued. "The Thorns are dangerous, pet. They will go to any lengths to keep their money on this island. If they see you and Rupert looking even remotely close, you'll be marked as a threat. And then… not even Rupert will be able to protect you."

I let out a breath and smiled. It was nervous and unconvincing. "Do I look like I have a death wish?"

"Honey," Michelle smiled back, her face a picture of sympathy. "Someone just drove you off the top of a cliff. What do you think?"

I WOULD BE FOREVER in debt to Minty. Reportedly, as finished the last of her wine she heard a dull crash, which turned her attention to the coastline where a plume of smoke had risen up into the air and hovered above the coastal road.

The second she saw it, Minty jumped in the car and followed the road to where they thought the plume originated from. That was when she found me.

I'd spent all day Sunday laid in bed staring at the walls and jumping fully out of my skin at every sound that passed the window. I always thought I was resilient until I was spun a hundred and eighty degrees several times, then rolled down the side of a cliff in a brand new Aston Martin. The black eyes were the result of one of the best inventions of the modern day: the air bag. The shoulder flush was a result of being flung into the window at approximately sixty miles per hour, and the cut on my face and the split lip came from the gear stick and my own arm as I tried to maintain some equilibrium as the car tumbled over and over.

Seeing Rupert's face as he studied mine made my heart swim. I'd never felt so cherished. Despite how damaged I was, he still looked at me as though I was a piece of treasure he'd just pulled out of the ocean. The shadow of anger only grew as we waited for Michelle to arrive, and peaked as he left. I wouldn't have been surprised if he'd killed the first person to cross his path, such was the venom in his eyes.

As I watched Michelle pack away her things, and heeded her warning, I couldn't help but feel devastatingly hollow. My relationship with Rupert was nothing short of complicated. He knew I was sexually attracted to him. He had two orgasms with his name on them as proof. I knew he was attracted to me because I felt his steel cock like a baton against my back. Despite the fact he had an agenda of his own and was using me to further it, I trusted him. I believed he wanted to protect me, in his strange fucked-up way. And in my strange, fucked-up way, that made me feel like the luckiest girl in the world.

THE TOUR BEGAN the second the very first group of visitors disembarked from the luxury ferry. I'd laid on a champagne breakfast with fresh strawberries, smoked salmon, poached eggs and asparagus. Many of them were already slurring their words. Those were my instructions. *Make them so woozy they forget where they are*, were Sinclair's words. *Make the first few bottles the best, then top them up with cheap fizz. I don't want to waste any more of my fortune on these greedy, nosey bastards.*

Once they were all safely on board the coach, we set off on a tour of the island. After a brief stop at the Blackcap distillery, where they loaded up on more alcohol, we journeyed to Caspian House.

"Are they drunk?" Minty whispered in my ear as I nipped out to visit the ladies'.

"Yeah," I shrugged. "Most of them are."

"Isn't that a risk? When they get to the labs I mean. They could wander off."

"That will never happen," I replied. "Sinclair has installed eyes everywhere. If a visitor so much as trips, they'll be hauled out and held by security until the tour has ended."

The supposed 'tour' of the labs, which in effect was a tightly controlled, highly restricted view of some rooms that actually had very little to do with production, went well. I answered all the questions I could, with the help of two of the scientists, and got everyone back on the coach in good time. The only thing that struck me as unexpected was the absence of McFadden. I'd been told he would be at the front desk, but instead, it was a guy called Wilson. And come to think of it, I hadn't seen or heard of McFadden since Sinclair had hauled me into his office. A uneasy feeling settled in my stomach as I climbed back on board the coach.

With this being the first tour, every single guest was a VIP. That meant they were friends, relatives or colleagues of key connections. Wives of politicians, top-rated sales-people, influential land owners. Each one had buckets of money and bags of arrogance. At first glance I was worried someone might interrogate me ruthlessly, just to make a point. But, in actual fact, they were each more interested in the free booze than the lab itself. As we disembarked outside Blackcap Hall, one of the friendlier guests, a Mrs. Antonia Lonsdale, pulled me aside to ask if I would fix a small tear in her skirt. I asked one of the doormen to escort the guests to the drawing room, where a small cocktail party was to be held, while I fixed Mrs. Lonsdale's dress. Then, we walked back to join the rest of the party.

I felt his gaze on me without looking up. It was hot, like his touch, and searing, like his temper. It was as though no time at all had passed since he stormed out of his office leaving Michelle to fix my face. The heat of his focus only intensified the closer his steps became.

"Where have you been?" he rumbled, in a low, agitated voice.

I turned and held my breath, knowing if I didn't, it would be ripped from me by the intensity in his eyes.

I tipped my chin, defiantly. "I had to help one of the guests with a wardrobe malfunction."

His gaze darkened. "Which guest?"

I arched an eyebrow. "Mrs. Lonsdale. The seam tore on her skirt. I sewed it back together for her."

"Why you? We have other people who can do that."

"It was nothing. It only took a minute and she made it quite clear she didn't want to make a fuss."

"You were late joining the party."

"Barely," I replied, bending to flick a damp leaf off the tip of my shoe.

"I didn't know where you were." He enunciated each word with irritated precision.

"I was fine," I said, through gritted teeth.

"You are not to leave my sight, Vivian," he said, looking at everything around us, but not me.

I straightened and glared at him. He thought it was fine to blackmail me to do his dirty work, then acceptable to become all protective of me when others chose to seek revenge.

"I've been out of your sight all day."

"That's what you think. I've had eyes on you throughout the tour. Trust me."

"Why, Rupert? Because you don't trust one of your darling relatives isn't going to try to end me with a blunt machete?"

"Vivian," he growled low into my ear. "I don't know what happened to you on that clifftop. I don't know who was to blame. All I know is I'm not letting you out of my sight. I will drive you home. I will collect you every morning. I will take you to wherever you need to go. I will make sure nothing else happens that puts you in danger. But..." his voice softened. "I can't protect you if I don't know where you are."

His words would have infuriated me if it weren't for the hand he placed on my arm. The heat of it seared through my skin and lit my core on fire.

"I don't need your protection." Even as I said the words I knew it was a lie.

He pulled back and daggered me with his eyes. "I don't care what you *think* you need or don't need, Vivian. I'm telling you I am not letting you out of my sight from this point on."

"That's impossible," I hissed at him, closing the space. "You can't be with me when I'm in meetings…"

"Try me."

"…when I'm doing the tours."

"I'm here, aren't I?"

"…when I'm lying in my bed, asleep."

His eyes dropped to my lips and he swallowed. "I can put someone outside your house."

I stepped back and lifted my arms in defeat. "Fine. Do whatever you *think* you have to do. Just remember, it's your fault I'm in this mess."

In the beat of a second, his face was up against mine again. My head flipped to the side as his hot breath grazed my cheek. "Do you see me trying to steal red tops from my boss?"

Now it was my turn to swallow. It was his fault I was being targeting by someone who didn't want me around, that was obvious. But I wasn't entirely blameless. The chance to dwell on it passed quickly as my feelings were overridden by his imposing proximity. Heat blossomed between my legs and a gasp left my lips.

"You might *think* you don't need my protection," he said, flames licking from each word. "But, answer this. Do you want it?"

Time slowed as I contemplated how to answer his question without putting us both in deeper shit. His eyes burned a hole in the side of my face, his hot breath fuelling the flame.

"Yes," I whispered.

Before I knew what he was doing, I found myself

being pushed backwards, forcefully, into an alcove I hadn't even noticed was there. I was suddenly surrounded by darkness, the sounds of the drawing room muted by the thick walls shielding us from view.

"Rupert," I whispered, conscious that although we were out of sight, we were still standing in a room half full of VIP guests who'd be noticing our absence before long. "What are you doing?"

He straightened and stared at me with eyes that would have eaten me alive if they had teeth. He reached out and stroked his fingers down the side of my face, so gently I barely felt them. "I know I haven't done right by you, Vivian."

My name rolled off the tip of his tongue like dripping silver, and my knees almost buckled.

"I've used you to get information from my family. I've forced you to do things against your will, without any concern for your safety."

I swallowed, watching every inch of his face move as he spoke, devouring it all, knowing I wouldn't be able to hold onto it forever.

"Vivian…" he swallowed too, his Adam's apple prominent, like he had a lump in his throat. "I can't protect you forever. But I can protect you while you're on this island. Even when I can't be with you in person, I will make sure someone reliable is. But I will be that person… for as long as I can be."

I knew what that meant. Until he took a fiancée. I read the pain in his eyes. "I understand."

"Do you?" His voice sounded thin, desperate, like it had run out of oxygen.

Did I understand what it meant to only be able to give

so much of myself, that I would always be obligated to something else? Of course I did. "Yes, Rupert. I understand more than you know."

Several seconds passed before he released me, leaving cold air to flood into the space where his warm body had been. "I'll be waiting for you at the dock after the guests have gone," he said, stepping back into the light of the drawing room.

I nodded curtly and stepped past him, fixing a professional smile to my face. His determination to protect me was everything, but knowing it would only be for so long wrenched my gut.

I made a beeline for a cluster of guests and tried to focus on something that wasn't Rupert or the throbbing sensation between my legs.

I feigned interest in our visitors for a painfully long hour before my arm was tugged by a longer, slender one. I looked up, strangely relieved to see someone I recognised on the other end of it. "Adele."

"Hello, Viv. Finally, I get to speak with the woman of the moment," she smiled.

I waved off her comment. "I don't know about that."

"Nonsense." She sipped at her whiskey. Did these people drink anything else? "You're the word on everyone's lips right now." She looked out at the small gathering of visitors being regaled by Hector and Aurelias with stories of life as a Thorn. "Looks like your first tour has been a roaring success."

I scratched the side of my face. My skin still burned from where Rupert had breathed hot words onto my cheek. "I'd prefer to wait until they're safely back on British soil before I congratulate myself on a successful day."

She let out a dark, breathy laugh. "What do you think is going to happen between now and then? Of course it's already a success darling."

I inwardly arched a brow and muttered under my breath. "Knowing this island, anything could happen between now and then."

"I'm sorry, what?" Adele's glass had been halfway to her lips but she paused and directed her eyes at me.

"Nothing," I shrugged. "I'm just mumbling."

"About what?"

"I don't completely trust that nothing will happen to our visitors before they get home. I know how stupid that sounds."

She looked around, and seeing that no one else was in the slightest bit interested in our conversation, she bent slightly towards my ear. "It doesn't sound stupid at all. It sounds astute."

I glanced up at her in surprise. Was she actually admitting I was right to worry about our visitors' safety?

"Nothing will happen to them," she reassured me. "But you… I can't be as sure."

My head rotated like an owl's. "What?"

She brought her glass to her lips, just close enough to hide the movement as she spoke. "It's hearsay at the moment, but there are rumours in the camp that Rupert might be enjoying your company a little too much. That's not a good rumour to be a part of."

My heart racketed in my chest and I turned my body to face her, shielding my own face from the rest of the room. "I know nothing can come of it," I said, in a low, shaky voice.

"Does it matter?"

Her question stunned me. "What do you mean?"

"What I mean is, is that going to stop either of you?"

A blush rose up my throat, threatening to choke me with its heat. "Nothing is going to happen."

Her voice lowered even further. "Are you sure it hasn't already?"

That made me look up sharply into her kohl-lined feline eyes. "No!" I hissed. What did she know? Had Rupert shown her the video? "What would make you say that?"

"It's just…" she looked over my head and quirked a small smile at someone across the room. "You two seem… *familiar*. The kind of familiar you only get from seeing someone stripped bare."

I gulped a breath of air and felt the walls closing in.

She leaned into me again. "Metaphorically," she clarified.

The air gushed from my lungs. "Well, we haven't," I confirmed. Neither of us had bared our souls, yet. And that was the truth.

"You seem like a nice girl, Viv," she continued. "Here's some advice. It will be easier to keep away from Rupert once he's engaged. In the meantime, do yourself a favour. Work from Caspian House, get yourself a driver, only visit Blackcap Hall when you absolutely have to. Get over him. You might think it's hard now, but trust me, once you've fallen, it'll be harder than hell."

She stepped back to welcome a couple into our small circle, oblivious to the fact I was gasping for breath.

"Rosie, my love. Darling Dalziel. Have you met Vivian Gillespie?"

I looked up and froze to the spot. Standing before me

was a tall man, broad-shouldered, dark-haired. I would have been confident he was a Thorn had half of his face not been covered in hideous patchwork scars. I quickly corrected my expression from one of shock to one of warmth. Not that it mattered. He seemed to be so absorbed in the woman at his side, he barely noticed me, let alone the expression I wore on my face.

"It's a pleasure," he said, staring adoringly at her. My eyes glided to the left and froze again. The woman looking back at me was incredibly pretty, with strawberry blonde hair curled like tendrils around her face. Her eyes were large, wide and bright blue, almost mesmerising. And for a fleeting second, they were familiar.

"Do I know you?" I asked, without thinking.

"I doubt it," she smiled. "I'm Rose. It's good to meet you Vivian." She held out a hand and I shook it, growing more convinced I'd seen her before. "This is my husband, Dax."

Dalziel – Dax – gave me a courteous nod before returning his eyes to feast on his wife. "You will perhaps have seen paintings of my dear Rose hanging around the Hall," he explained, his eyes remaining on her. "She's too exquisite not to have in every room."

My heart swelled. I'd only heard lines like that in fairy tales. And I no longer believed in those. I cleared my throat.

"It's a pleasure to meet you both. Thank you for coming."

To my relief, Adele cut through the strange atmosphere. "We were all given our orders. Sinclair would have had our guts for garters if we hadn't shown our faces. The only person I can't see here is Oz." She glanced at

Rose and Dax and snickered. "I daresay the party is better off without him."

I noticed Dax's features harden beneath the skin grafts and Rose stiffened too. Clearly, not a lot of love had been lost between those members of the family. It amazed me how comfortable they all seemed existing in a bubble of apparent *dis*comfort. I, however, couldn't bear it any longer. The party had to end shortly if our guests were going to make their ferry. "I'm sorry to leave you so soon," I said, looking at all three of them. "I have to wind things up here. Get these guests back to the mainland before the ferry turns into a pumpkin."

"Of course," Dax said, finally turning his attention to me. "We certainly wouldn't want that, would we? Pumpkins, after all, sink."

I searched his face for a suggestion of humour but there was none. Nothing of the sort registered in the faces of Adele and Rose either. I gulped my second mouthful of air that evening and turned away. I couldn't remove myself from their macabre gazes fast enough.

Chapter 21

R upert

I LEANED against the bonnet of my car as I waited for her to wave off the first group of visitors. My jacket had been flung onto the passenger seat, the top buttons of my shirt opened and my sleeves rolled up. I'd noticed the way she lapped up my forearms a few weeks ago, so I was going to make a point of bearing them as often as I could. That would be the price she paid for making it so hard for me to drag *my* eyes away from *her*. Plus, seeing Vivian flushed and tongue-tied was my new favourite thing.

When she walked towards me, her hips swaying deca-dently, the light from the ferry illuminated the swell of her lip and fresh anger coursed through me. I grunted and opened the car door. "Get in."

"Spoken like a true gentleman," she sassed, slipping into the seat like she belonged there.

. . . .

I SLID IN BESIDE HER, just as she laid my jacket over her knees. I suddenly envied it. "Are you cold?"

"A little. This will help." She smiled up at me and I didn't miss the way she stroked the fabric of my tailored jacket against her thighs. I swallowed and forced myself to look ahead as I started the engine. I leaned an arm across the back of her seat and looked behind as I backed out of the space. My breath grazed her ear and a small flush of air left her lips. I swallowed again, then rested my hand about two inches from her leg as I spun the car out of the car park and down the drive.

I glanced down at her fingers and saw them fisting the fabric. "Are you ok?"

She stopped abruptly and smoothed down the fabric again. "Oh, um, yeah, fine."

I cleared my throat. "You pleased with how the tour went today?"

"Yes, I am. Everything went to plan and I think the visitors really enjoyed it."

"Good. I agree."

"Do you think your father was happy?" I felt her gaze transfer from the road to me and it made my stomach clench.

As ever, Father's face gave very little away, but I knew better than most that if he wasn't happy about something, everyone in a twenty metre radius would be well aware, and probably splattered with spit. "I think so. He would have said something if he wasn't."

A sigh of relief escaped her chest. "That's good."

"How's your lip?" I asked, after we'd driven for a few minutes in comfortable silence.

"It feels much better, thanks. Whatever pills Michelle gave me worked a treat."

A few more minutes of silence passed before she inhaled a shaky breath. "Who do you think crashed into the car?" she asked in a trembling whisper.

My nostrils flared as I turned a corner and channelled my aggression into the accelerator pedal. "I don't know. But I will find out, I promise."

"First, the threat in the woods, then the car accident. Someone doesn't want me on the island."

I sighed. "I hate to break it to you but I'm not the only one who doesn't approve of these tours. There are others too. Maybe they think that if you weren't here, the tours wouldn't go ahead."

She shook her head and let out a bitter laugh. "That's not true. Sinclair would simply replace me."

I hitched my eyebrows in agreement.

I felt her gaze hot on my cheek. "He asked me where I was the day I stopped McFadden from getting to the labs."

I curled my fingers tightly around the steering wheel and steeled my shoulders. "When?"

"Friday."

The day before she was driven off the cliff. If Father had suspected her, Ossian would know. Father wouldn't want to rock the tour boat, but my brother had no such scruples. I knew in my bones it was him, despite his Oscar-worthy argument to the contrary. Even if it wasn't Ossian who personally crashed into her, he was behind it.

"I'll talk to him."

"Are you going to tell him the truth? That you put me up to it?"

My foot pressed down harder. "No. The last thing I

want is for them to know I actively tried to sabotage their plans."

"Why do you do it?" she asked, suddenly. "Why do you try to make things difficult for them? Is it simply because you don't approve of the tours?"

I ran my tongue across my teeth. I knew she'd ask that question at some point. I could only ask so much of her before she demanded answers. And I owed them to her. But not all of them.

"I don't like the way my brother does business," I said, finally. "He's experimenting recklessly with different drug concoctions and all he sees is pound signs. He doesn't care if there are side effects either to people or the environment…"

"The environment?"

I clenched my jaw. "The red tops need a certain type of environment in order to propagate. The island is small and I can't stand back and watch my brother plunder it all for his own selfish ends."

"So, it's safe to say you don't get along?"

"We don't always, no."

"Why don't you leave?" she asked, like it was that simple.

"I have a duty to my family," I sighed. "But more than that, I have a duty to the island. If I stay and keep doing what I'm doing, slowing Ossian's progress, I'm keeping the other islanders in their homes for one more day."

"Why do the islanders stay?"

I shifted in my seat as we glided through more dark woodland. "This is their home. They don't want to leave. Their ancestors are buried in their back gardens. They know the lay of this island like the backs of their hands.

Many of them simply wouldn't make it on the mainland." I glared at her, pointedly. "And they shouldn't have to."

"And that's all you can do? Slow Ossian's progress?"

I huffed out a heavy exhale. "Mostly. Although I mentor some of the kids at the Academy. I want to help them build enough confidence that they can survive somewhere else. Their parents might be stuck here of their own volition, but the kids don't have to be."

She fell quiet – uncharacteristically. So quiet I had to turn to check she was still there. "What it is?"

She stared out of the windscreen and lightly shook her head. "You disappoint me, Rupert," she said, with a small smile. "There I was thinking you were a treacherous demon who got off on exploiting others' attraction and forcing them to do bad deeds against their will. When, in actual fact, you're just a normal human who is trying to protect people who can't always protect themselves."

Something bloomed in my belly and my hands tightened around the wheel again. "I can go back to being a demon if you want me to?"

She turned her mischievous smile in my direction. "You would do that for me?"

I met her eyes and noticed her pupils swell in the moonlight. "Just say the word, butterfly."

My heart rammed hard inside my ribcage as I resumed my focus on the road. We passed a signpost to the north cliffs and I realised I was driving so fast we'd be at Sandpiper Cottage within minutes. I pressed the brake.

"What's that?" she asked suddenly. I followed her eye line to the horizon and everything in me froze. "Are they trucks?"

"I doubt it at this time of night," I lied. I knew exactly

what they were and they shouldn't have been there. Not then. Not the very same day we hosted the VIPs.

"Then, what are they? They look pretty big. And there's several of them. How did they get here?"

"They'll be site trucks preparing the ground," I said, smoothly.

Her head panned towards me. "At night?"

"We work all hours here, you know that," I clipped.

She turned to stare out of the window so I took a right so she could no longer see them. "Are you coming to the Summer Ball?" I asked, changing the subject.

"I don't know. I haven't been invited—"

"I'm inviting you."

She fisted my jacket again.

"It's a week Saturday, at Blackcap Hall."

"Who else will be there?"

"Everyone. Me, Hector, Dax and Rose…"

"Minty?" she asked, shyly.

"Sure. The whole island is invited. Whether they choose to come or not is another matter. Minty usually attends these things."

In the corner of my eye I noticed a few delicate lines appear on her forehead. "I don't have anything appropriate to wear to a ball."

I nodded to my jacket resting on her legs. "Look in the left inside pocket." She looked up at me, nervously. "Go on," I urged. "It's not going to bite you."

She tentatively slipped her hand inside the pocket and pulled out a business card. She held it up. "This?"

"I was going to give it to you earlier."

She squinted in the darkness and read the words. "Madame Gallette, Couturière."

"She's our resident dressmaker. All the ladies use her but she's retained by my family." With reluctance, I turned onto the road that led to Sandpiper. "Tell her I sent you."

I didn't need to look at her to know a blush had blossomed across her cheeks. "You don't need to do this. I'm sure I can find something."

"I'm sure you can, too. But, you're busy and you have better things to worry about than where to find a ball dress on a small island in the middle of the north sea."

"Oh, okay." She gulped. "Thanks."

I pulled the car into the space beside the cottage and let the engine run as I faced her. "Besides, I know Madame Gallette's work. So, believe me," I said, unable to stop my eyes from gliding over her flushed cheeks, parted lips and delicate collarbone as her shallow, ragged breaths pushed her chest towards me. "The pleasure will be all mine."

Chapter 22

*R*upert

A SQUAWKING SOUND rudely awoke me from my desk-bound slumber. I looked at my phone and groaned. I was too tired to have this conversation today. Too tired after sitting in my car outside Sandpiper Cottage until four in the morning – the soonest I could hand over security duty to one of my men. I made a mental note to hire more people.

"Hello Mother." I leaned back in my chair and rubbed my eyes.

"Darling. You've been avoiding me, I can tell."

I yawned, audibly. "Whatever makes you think that?"

"You haven't been returning my calls, you haven't joined me for afternoon tea for weeks, and you haven't so much as checked in. I know what you're trying to avoid, Rupert, but your time is up. We have to discuss your engagement."

. . .

My chest suddenly felt like a lead weight. "Why do we need to discuss it?" I replied, monotone. "It's not like I have any say in the arrangements." I was aware I sounded like a petulant child but there was no way I was going to make this easy on her.

"Of course you do, darling. You will have a say in who you marry, for a start."

"Barely," I argued. "I will be able to choose from a pool of pre-approved young women, each of whom is likely to be as vapid and uninteresting as the next."

"That's unfair, Rupert," she snapped. "The young women you will get to choose from are each educated and accomplished, not to mention beautiful…"

"Expensively-manicured, you mean…"

"Rupert." I could tell she was losing her patience. "What's got into you? You've never had such an issue with this before. And it's not like you didn't know it was coming. You've had twenty-six years to get used to the idea. Why you didn't make life easier on yourself and select someone for love before now, I've no idea, but here we are. You have a limited window now in which to choose someone to spend the rest of your life with. You've taken it up to the wire. Now, I don't have time to dither on this, Rupert. I have a date for the banquet."

"Already?" My chest ached with the sudden onset of panic. "What's the rush?"

"The rush, Rupert, is that the longer we leave this, the higher the chance you will have of your head being turned by someone we do not deem appropriate for you."

I scrubbed a hand over my face. "Like who?"

"Don't think it's gone unnoticed, your *closeness* to a certain tour guide."

"Vivian?" Was she kidding? I'd been barely civil to her in public. What had there been to see?

"You were seen speaking intimately with her yesterday evening at the cocktail party."

I laughed bitterly.

"And you were seen driving her home—"

"She doesn't have a car, Mother. *Someone* drove her off a cliff."

She ignored the blatant jibe that our family might have had something to do with it.

"And you were seen sitting outside her cottage until the early hours," she finished, with the flourish of a hand I couldn't see but knew was there.

"Someone is trying to hurt her," I replied, exasperated.

"So, have one of your men look out for her. Why does it have to be you?"

Because it's my family's fault she's in this mess? Because I owe it to her to keep her safe? Because I can't get the sound or image of her orgasm out of my goddamned head?

I squeezed my eyes shut to stop the vision of Vivian coming for me creeping across my eyeballs. "You have nothing to worry about, Mother. I haven't laid a finger on her."

"Good," she clipped. "Make sure it stays that way. Now, do you want to hear the date I've set, or not?"

I clipped the bridge of my nose. "Go on."

"June twentieth. Block out your diary, and the three days leading up to it."

My eyes shot open and my temples burned. "June twentieth? That's in just five weeks!"

"Exactly. And don't you dare be angry at me, Rupert.

If this has come as a surprise, you only have yourself to blame."

I huffed a breath from my tightened chest. "What do you need me to do?"

"A week from today, you will have a suit fitting…"

"I have plenty of suits…"

"Not like this, you don't," she snapped. "I appreciate your schedule is tight, so I will arrange to have someone take you through the guest list at the same time. Both the general guests and the girls."

"Girls?"

"Yes, Rupert," she replied, in a tight, exasperated tone. "The girls you select to attend. A shortlist, if you will, for your potential fiancée."

"How romantic." I didn't bother disguising the sarcasm and let it positively drip from my tongue.

"Indeed," she replied, matching my tone. "In three weeks, there will be a menu tasting. I will be there. If you would like to attend, you are welcome, but it is not mandatory."

"I'll leave it in your capable hands. I doubt you'll wish to poison anyone."

"In the two days prior," she continued, ignoring my comment. "You will be required to attend a last fitting, a final run-through of the guest list, and a family day. But, what is of most urgency is a gentleman's drinks, tomorrow evening at Blackcap Hall."

"A gentleman's drinks?" My voice rose an octave. "Who are the gentlemen?" I asked, thankful she couldn't see me putting the term in air quotes.

"The fathers of all the girls. The Consortium members. No one you haven't met before. But remember, Rupert," she warned, "as revered as our family name is on the island, this isn't all about you. These people are protective of their daughters. While they want them to marry well, they are not interested in feeding the poor girls to the lions. Regardless of who you are, son, you still have a good impression to make."

I remained silent.

"I will have Madame Gallette prepare your outfit for the gentleman's drinks. There are certain rules we need to follow, but I'm sure you own clothing that is perfectly appropriate for such an event."

I crossed a foot over my knee and coiled the shoelace around my finger. I apparently wasn't an active participant in this conversation, so I just let her run on.

"During the banquet, there will be an order of events. You will be taken through this by a member of the Consortium and expected to adhere to the schedule for the evening. Typically, there are drinks on arrival and mingling. You will be expected to converse – pleasantly – with each of the girls and their parents, before sitting down for dinner. You will be seated at the head of the table, with your father and I either side of you. Ossian to your father's right and Hector to my left. The eligible girls will be positioned in your eye line so you will have plenty of opportunity to observe them in a dinner setting."

"Don't you mean 'cattle market' setting?"

She paused and I could hear her losing even more patience on the other end of the line. "For each quip like that, Rupert," she resumed, her voice reflecting a new glimmer of steel, "I will bring the banquet forward by one week."

I almost laughed until she caught it. "Don't test me on

this, Rupert. I am tired to the back teeth of waiting for this day to arrive. As keen as the rest of the island is to see you choose a wife, no one is as eager as I am. And your father backs me one hundred percent. So, if you value the short amount of supposed freedom you have left, I suggest you cut the sarcastic comments and show a little cooperation."

I swallowed, but there was no way I was going to apologise for hating every second of this. "Go on."

"After dinner, you will be allotted a short amount of time with each girl, then you will be permitted to enjoy the rest of the evening with a girl of your choosing, or you can retire, if you must. You will then have exactly twenty-four hours in which to make your decision. If…" she added, reluctantly," you do *not* make a decision in that time, a decision will be made for you, by the Consortium. And I shouldn't need to tell you, but your tone implies I ought to reiterate the consequences, if you refuse to marry you will be removed from the island, from the family and from all beneficiaries to which you are currently entitled."

I could practically hear her spine straightening with resolve. "And trust me, Rupert. I won't be able to save you. Once you resist abiding by the oldest rule we have on this island, the one condition that has assured the retention of great wealth within the four corners of the Isle of Crow, any decision to keep you within our broader family will be determined by the Consortium, whether I oppose it or not."

She waited a moment for the final blow to sink in, then said, in a far softer voice – the voice I associated with the mother I knew growing up, "Do what you've always known you would have to do, Rupert. Don't make this harder for yourself or your family. You're my son, and I love you. Don't make me disown you."

"How are you holding up, cuz?"

I opened the door allowing Dax to walk into my suite. For once, I envied him. He'd never had to go through this ridiculous charade. But, while he ended up marrying for love, he had to search the four corners of the world to find it. He had the ultimate disadvantage: a face that seemed to repel most women, through no fault of his own.

"Ok," I lied. "It's only the fathers tonight. At least I don't have to flirt."

"I don't know about that," he chuckled darkly. "Have you met Horatio Grant?"

Horatio was from one of the oldest families on the Isle of Crow, and although married to a beautiful woman he'd known since school, he failed miserably to hide the fact he couldn't resist checking out most male inhabitants of the island.

"Fair point. He isn't coming though. His immaculately conceived daughter is four years too young."

"Ah," Dax said, pouring us each a large whiskey, "Lucky Hector."

We snickered and touched glasses before both downing the lot in one.

"Eeesh," I said, wiping my mouth. "I hate to say it but I needed that."

"There's more where that came from," Dax said, taking my glass. "Hector going to be there?"

"No. Older brothers only, apparently."

Dax's features could barely move but he still managed to look sympathetic.

"If I had any say, I'd scrap the whole damn thing."

"Interesting," Dax mused.

I took the refilled glass from him and settled into a leather armchair. "What does that mean?"

"Well, someday you may well be in charge of that rule. You're Sinclair's son. The Thorns are the oldest family on the island, and Sinclair is Peregrine's eldest son. Not to sound morbid, but when they both die, this place will look to you, Ossian and Hector. There may a world in which you *could* scrap this whole thing."

I shook my head. "No. Ossian isn't going anywhere, and the arranged marriage worked out for him. He got to screw a few girls who wanted his money, then choose one who would manage his affairs so that he wouldn't have to. It's all worked out just fine for him. He will be in no rush to scrap it."

"What about other stuff?" Dax said, avoiding my gaze. "Like the way he runs that pharma business like he's discovered the secret to everlasting life? Don't think I haven't noticed the way he and Uncle Sinclair have become obsessed with trying to expand it. Do you trust Ossian to do a damn thing for any reason other than profit and exploitation?"

Dax had fired an arrow right into the heart of my reason for existing. The simple and immediate answer was 'no.' I didn't trust Ossian as far as I could spit.

"I don't know what Ossian's plans are," I replied, truthfully. "I can hazard a few guesses, but he doesn't share a great deal with me anymore."

"But, you will get closer to him when he inherits your father's position in the Consortium, won't you?"

Dax didn't use to be such a compassionate person and I was still getting used to the side of him that materialised after Rose came on the scene, which is why it was all the more disconcerting that he was sharing any concern about my father's succession.

"Not if I can help it," I said, casually.

In a beat, Dax leaned over my chair bringing his face up close. I could see the indentations of his scars, the actual outline of the splashes of acid that had burned into his skin. He'd had multiple surgeries to reconfigure his face but he put a stop to them when he realised that, if anything, they were making him look less like who he was and more like someone who'd spent millions trying to look like anyone but themselves.

"Rupert. You have to stay close to him." His voice lowered to a threatening rumble. "I don't trust Ossian. No one trusts Ossian. The whole fucking Consortium is nervous about what will happen when he inherits it all. He's a loose cannon with even looser morals. He can't be allowed to lead this island alone. You have to stay close, Rupert." He straightened and looked me dead in the eye. "You inherited this responsibility too. If he's left to his own devices, Ossian will destroy this island and you know it. He almost…" Dax turned away and wiped a palm down the damaged side of his face. "He almost destroyed me."

His eyes switched to mine with a pointed glare. We'd always suspected Ossian had a part to play in Dax's acid attack but no one had ever confirmed it and no one had dared to ask. "I mean it, Rupert. You are the only person who can stop him from destroying *everything*."

I tipped back my glass before realising it was empty. I knew Dax was right, but I didn't give birth to Ossian; he wasn't my responsibility. But when I looked into the faces of Dax, Hector, Aro, Adele – the people close to me who I actually cared about – I knew with true clarity I couldn't leave them to manage Ossian on their own. He was my older brother after all. I'd known him all my life, and when the time came, I would be in a better position than anyone to support or destroy his reign.

I nodded at Dax and let him refill my glass one more time. I still wasn't looking forward to playing the perfect husband-to-be in a room full of potential fathers-in-law, but I felt a renewed sense of purpose. If I was going to do this, it wouldn't be for me, or my parents, or the Consortium. It would be for everyone else who suffered at the hands of this island. With that thought in mind, I downed the whiskey Dax had freshly poured and got to my feet.

I nodded to my cousin. "Thanks for the pep talk."

"Any time," he replied. "And I mean that."

I hesitated, considering his words, then turned and walked out of the suite, towards a future I was no longer able to deny.

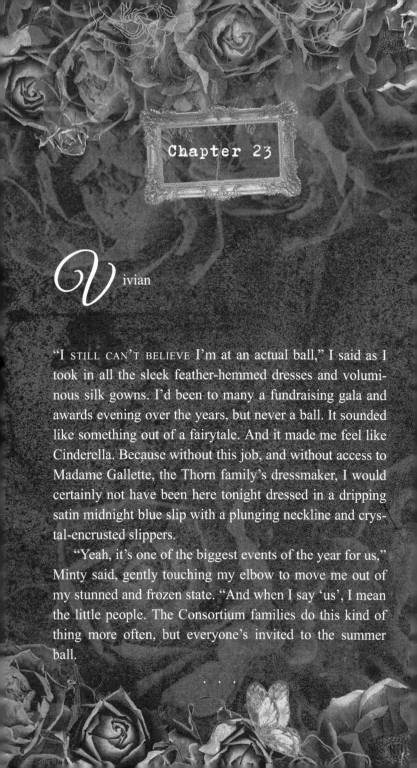

Chapter 23

*V*ivian

"I STILL CAN'T BELIEVE I'm at an actual ball," I said as I took in all the sleek feather-hemmed dresses and voluminous silk gowns. I'd been to many a fundraising gala and awards evening over the years, but never a ball. It sounded like something out of a fairytale. And it made me feel like Cinderella. Because without this job, and without access to Madame Gallette, the Thorn family's dressmaker, I would certainly not have been here tonight dressed in a dripping satin midnight blue slip with a plunging neckline and crystal-encrusted slippers.

"Yeah, it's one of the biggest events of the year for us," Minty said, gently touching my elbow to move me out of my stunned and frozen state. "And when I say 'us', I mean the little people. The Consortium families do this kind of thing more often, but everyone's invited to the summer ball.

. . .

THE YOUNGER KIDS, those fresh out of college, use it as an excuse to get hammered drunk and then make out with each other in the gardens. It's the only time you'll openly see a Consortium guy hitting on a girl from the other side of the track, so to speak. Other than that, its supposed aim is to bring together everyone on the island, but just you watch – the rich stick with the rich and the poor stick with the poor. You just stick with me, girl... We'll form our own clique."

I laughed and followed her through highly polished glass doors into the main ballroom. "It's usually held on the summer solstice but it was brought forward this year because of the other main event happening."

"What event is that?" I asked, too busy people-watching to engage my brain.

"The Great Matchmaking," Minty snorted. "Rupert Thorn's banquet."

I suddenly became aware of my pulse thudding loudly at the side of my neck. I hadn't forgotten. I had completely failed to forget. I was surprised I didn't get whiplash the night of the VIP tour. One minute he was hissing at me for being late to the party, the next he was promising to protect me, the next he was demanding I get in his car and the next telling me how he mentored young kids. Everything about his actions that night screamed contradiction. His eyes were warm yet his anger was chilling. And then there was his presence outside the cottage while I undressed, show-ered and got into bed. I laid there for what felt like an hour, wondering if he'd dare to come inside. Every fibre of my being hoped he would. But when I awoke the next morning and ran to the window, he'd gone, and in his place was a steel grey Range Rover with a man I didn't recognise sitting in the driver's seat.

Rupert had driven me to the hall or the port whenever he could, but more often than not, I was met at the door by tall burly men I didn't know who nodded darkly and drove me silently to wherever I needed to go.

"Will all the Consortium families be here?" I asked, changing the subject.

"Oh yes. I'll point out some of them if you like?"

"Yes please," I replied gleefully. I'd seen many of the island's rich while wandering the corridors of Blackcap Hall and perching at the bar of Caspian House, but those at the very top? I wouldn't have known who they were if they'd come and slapped me around the head with a diamond-encrusted fish.

"You can probably pick them out already, to be honest. They're all weirdly tall and skinny with suspiciously straight noses that point up to the ceiling. If you're lucky enough to get a smile out of them, beware of the blinding gleam of their porcelain teeth. And they all, for some reason, seem to be allergic to colour. I swear I've only ever seen them dressed in black, grey or very, very dull beige. Although they probably have far fancier names for it, like pebble, or pine nut."

I hid a smirk behind my hand. Come to think of it, Madame Gallette did seem surprisingly hyped when I told her I fancied wearing blue.

"First though, let me fuel up on the free bubbles. Care to join me?"

"Absolutely." I threaded my arm through Minty's and we made our way along the polished floor to a room where a small army of wait staff glided about holding aloft trays of champagne and canapes. As I waited for Minty to fetch two glasses, something caught my attention from above. When I looked up, I let out a small gasp. Circus performers were dangling from ropes and hoops, contorting elegantly into shapes, making patterns through the air. They were beautiful. My eyes were glued to them even as Minty pushed a flute into my hand.

"Fucking idiots," she muttered, following my gaze. "You wouldn't catch me hanging by a piece of string above all these antique tables and sharp knives and expensive cut crystal."

I delicately spat my bubbles back into my glass and composed myself. "I'm sure they know what they're doing."

"Hmm, even so, let's get out from under them, shall we?"

She tugged me to the outer edge of the room and touched my hand. "Ok, so, to your right, about four o'clock, that's Oscar Dimitri. He owns a bunch of tech companies in Silicon Valley. Does some work for the British government too, I think. Old money. Way, way old. The couple over there – ten o'clock, they're the Barringtons. Made their money in offshore banking. Retired now. The younger guy behind them, that's their son, George. He has two sisters, May and Sage. They'll be here somewhere."

And, Elspeth? All I could think about was the woman everyone supposedly had their sights on Rupert marrying. And even though I wouldn't ever be in the running, it didn't stop me feeling as jealous as hell of someone I hadn't even met.

"The Cartwrights?" I asked, as innocently as I could.

"Oh, Andrew will be in some dark corner somewhere discussing business – or whatever it is these billionaires discuss with each other. That's his wife over there – Eleanor."

I followed Minty's eye line to a tall, willowy blonde woman gliding across the floor to a small group. She was beaming with a smile like sunshine and my heart plummeted into my borrowed slippers. If Elspeth looked anything like her mother, I felt like even more of a fool.

"There's one of her daughters," Minty added, and my eyes skated around manically for another tall blonde. "Nine o'clock. Moody face. Pink hair. That's Summer, the youngest." Shamefully, I sighed out a long relieved breath. While still pretty, Summer wasn't anywhere near as arresting as her mother. Hopefully, Elspeth wouldn't be either. "That's Priscilla, the middle sister." Minty discreetly pointed out another girl, around seventeen. She was almost as tall as her mother but with mousy brown lacklustre hair and a permanently grim look on her face. Not the happiest set of daughters I'd seen.

"Oh, and that's Elspeth."

I followed Minty's gaze and my partially-recovered heart thudded to the floor again. If ever there was a dead ringer for her supermodel-esque mother, it was Elspeth. A tall, blonde replica of Mrs. Cartwright shimmered in silver sequins across the dance floor, drawing admiring eyes with every step. I felt like an instant idiot, and even more nauseous.

"I might go outside for some air," I said, my voice sounding far away.

"I'll come with you. It's this way." Minty led us both to the other end of the room and just as we reached the doorway, someone called my name. I knew who it was because every hair on the back of my neck stood tall and a shiver rippled down my spine.

I turned slowly and one glance at him took my breath away. He was dressed in a pure black tuxedo, which matched his close-cropped hair. His hands rested in his pockets, the tension in his arms forcing his jacket sleeves to fill out and his shoulders to broaden even more than usual. His flawless skin was freshly shaven, his heavy-lashed eyes searingly dark. And his scent drew my feet towards him until he was all I could see.

"You look…" he started, his gaze travelling the length of my gown before resting back on my face. He didn't finish.

"Madame Gallette is a genius," I smiled.

Rupert's eyes roamed me as though he wanted to imprint every ripple and gleam of fabric on his memory. His Adam's apple bobbed as he swallowed and his eyes slowly grazed my face. "She's going to get a fucking big tip," he murmured.

I felt myself flush from the hair follicles on my head to the tips of my toes. "We were about to go outside for some air," I said, suddenly feeling torn. Part of me wanted to stay there sheltering under his shadowy canopy, while the other part of me needed to run into the cool night air and rid myself of the hot desire that was creeping across my skin.

Rupert nodded and cleared his throat. "Tell me when you want to leave and I'll drive you home."

"You don't have to do th—" I started, but his intense stare stopped me.

"I *want* to."

It was my turn to swallow. I felt as though Rupert and I were on the cusp of committing a heinous crime, becoming closer when we should have been pulling away, fast, in the opposite direction. "If you're sure," I whispered.

"I'm not letting anyone else take you home when you're dressed like that."

I did a double-take. Did he think I looked… promiscuous? My voice stuttered. "What do you mean?"

He leaned into me, his gaze stroking the top of my crown, his heated chest warming my face. His voice was deep, dark and full of promise. "What I mean is, you look fucking *lethal* in that dress… butterfly."

He stepped back again suddenly, leaving the air surrounding me to drop a couple of degrees in temperature.

"Elspeth," I heard him say, a bland, unimpressed edge to his voice.

I spun around and almost collided with the face of a freaking angel. Elspeth Cartwright herself. She looked like Rosamund Pike. Nose perfectly straight and just pointed enough. Face sublimely symmetrical. Eyebrows impeccably arched and groomed. Neck slim and long like a swan's. And hair fine and flaxen, just like a damn baby's.

My heart racketed around my chest, not knowing whether it was coming or going. Rupert had just fired an arrow of desire into it, which reached down to my very core. And now I was standing face-to-face with the person with whom he might spend the rest of his days. I felt both sopping wet and sick to the stomach.

"Well, well, if it isn't the tour guide," she said, with a thin smile that went nowhere near her eyes. "How are you enjoying your first ball? These things are rather extravagant aren't they? Not something you are likely to have seen in London, am I right?" She let out an open-mouthed laugh and batted her eyelids at Rupert, who stood as still and unimpressed as a stone.

"I've been to my fair share of dinners and galas," I replied. "But this one is certainly unique."

She blinked at me. "Yes. No one holds a better ball than Myrtle Thorn." Her eyes glided back to Rupert but the compliment intended for his mother did nothing to soften him. "Anyway," she flicked them back to me. "Don't let us keep you. I'm sure you want to get your fill of all the delicacies on offer before retiring. I imagine that doing all these tours is *thoroughly* exhausting. It's such a privilege to not have to work; I do so appreciate it."

I wasn't reluctant to take the hint. I couldn't stand to be in her presence a second longer. "Excuse me," I muttered, sneaking between the two of them to join Minty who'd been looking on curiously.

"That was awkward," she snickered as we stepped out onto a veranda.

"Yeah, I was kind of stuck between them—"

"No, I mean the death stare Rupert gave Elspeth. He looked like he wanted to shove her body into one of those tanks filled with solvent and watch her slowly disintegrate."

"Minty!" I almost gagged at the vision. "What the hell? He did not look at her like that."

"Then you didn't see what I saw."

"I saw exactly the same thing you saw."

"Ok then. Did you see how his eyes lit up when he spoke to you? And did you notice the dark cloud that descended over him when Elspeth showed up? Did you see any of that? Now look. He's back to being the straight, miserable, aloof Thorn, just like his dad and older asscrack of a brother." She took a long sip of her champagne. "I'm excluding Hector from this discussion. He's nothing like any of them if you ask me."

I recalled the image of Rupert's face. I didn't see light in his eyes, only demons. And I didn't see a dark cloud descend over him and Elspeth; just an inevitability so blinding it would forever be imprinted on my eyelids.

"Be careful, Vivian." Minty's words dragged me back with a bang. "His family will make your life hell, believe me."

I couldn't meet her gaze. Instead I inspected an imaginary crease in my dress. "I don't know what you mean."

"You're blushing," she said, quietly. "And that confirms my fear. Extract yourself, Viv. I mean it."

I looked up at her, finally, and nodded sheepishly. "If it's any consolation," I sighed, "he hasn't laid a finger on me."

It was the truth.

THANKFULLY, dinner was an elaborate buffet which meant I could eat well out of sight of Rupert. I managed only a few bites before giving in to my lack of appetite.

"Now I know why you're so slim," Minty said, nodding at the plate of food I'd hardly touched.

"I ate before I came here," I lied. "I didn't think."

At that moment, a waiter passed with a tray of champagne. I took two glasses and promptly drank one of them. I knew it wasn't the best idea, drinking so much alcohol on an empty stomach, but I had to get through the evening somehow, especially having seen Rupert with one of the prospects for his future wife.

"Everything ok? You've gone quiet."

"Mm-hm. I'm fine." I avoided Minty's enquiring face, and spotted Hector making his way towards us.

"Well, if it isn't my two favourite ladies," he grinned, before bowing his head as though we were royalty.

"Yeah, you say that to all the girls," Minty joked, but a blush still crept up her throat.

"Would either of you care for a dance?" He looked between us both. "I'm not picky."

I cocked my head to one side. "Which charm school did you go to, Hector?"

"The charm school of life, my dear. School taught me everything *but* how to be charming." His eye roll implied he was not a fan of his former school.

"I think Minty would like to dance," I offered, but, when I looked at her, the blush had crept up her throat and now covered her entire face.

She shook her head and stared wide-eyed at me. I turned back to Hector with a broad smile. "But, I would *love* to."

"Perfect." He held out an arm. "Miss Gillespie, shall we?"

I allowed Hector to lead me to the dance floor, feeling the eyes of every young girl in the place follow us, jealousy tinging them green. He took my left hand in his right, slipped an arm around my waist, then led me through a slow waltz. I hadn't been officially taught to dance, so it was fortunate that Hector was a strong partner, taking full command of where on the dance floor we moved, in what direction, and at what speed. Soon, our moves were flowing so easily, I didn't need to think about the steps at all.

"How are you finding the Isle of Crow, Viv?"

I looked up to see him smiling easily. Hector wasn't simply youthful in age; he was youthful in character, and it was evident in the way he thought, the way he spoke and the way he held himself.

"Overall, good. Although, the accident shook me up a lot."

"I heard. Are you feeling alright now?"

"Much better thanks. I'm pretty sure I'll be ok to drive again, but I'm not sure Rupert is ready to have me drive myself around the island." The alcohol was swirling in my system and I attempted to make light of Rupert's response to the accident. "He says it's for my protection, but really, I think he's just concerned for his cars."

Hector paused mid-step, then recovered himself quickly. He did it with such professional prowess, no onlooker would have noticed. "It is for your protection, Viv."

His words floated above me. "Has anyone told you the story about our family dog, Dita?"

I shook my head.

"Dita belonged to all of us, but Rupert was most fond of her. She followed him everywhere, even to school. This one time, a boy a few years older, Clinton, threw a stone at Dita while she waited for Rupert outside the school gates. Rupert saw it happen."

"What did he do?" I muttered, afraid to look around in case my eyes landed on the subject of our conversation as we waltzed past.

"He broke both of Clinton's arms."

I gasped and lost my footing. Hector tightened his grip so I wouldn't stumble over his feet. When we resumed the steps, Hector continued as if Rupert breaking someone's arms was an everyday occurrence. "So, if I know anything about my brother, it's that he will go to the ends of the earth to protect the things he cares about."

I stared at Hector's shoulder, unblinking, as he continued to move me around the dance floor. There were two things wrong with what he'd just said. First, he'd implied that Rupert cared about me, which couldn't be so. And second, that Hector himself was well aware of this fact, which was possibly even worse.

A hand on my shoulder ripped me from my thoughts. "May I cut in?"

The hair on my nape stood tall and Hector's arm slipped from around my waist. "She's all yours."

Rupert's comparatively thicker, more solid arm took the place of Hector's, and his other hand wrapped around my fingers. I didn't dare look up at his face. He pulled me into his body, far closer than Hector had, so that when we moved, it felt like we were one. I pressed my cheek into his chest and felt his heart pounding beneath his crisp shirt.

"Move with me," he said into my hair, then proceeded to lead me with even greater skill than his younger brother had just moments before.

The faster pace made my intoxicated brain whirl. I was feeling pretty drunk. Throwing caution to the wind, or rather sense into the sewer, I opened my mouth. "You and Elspeth make a nice couple."

He stiffened but continued to move us elegantly around the dance floor. "No, we don't."

"Your banquet isn't far away."

"I'm not going to talk about that with you."

"Ah, right. Because I'm not part of the Consortium."

Rupert brought us to a standstill so suddenly my head continued to spin while he held me rigid. "No." His eyes beat down on me like I'd committed a crime. "Because it's none of your business."

I stared up at him. "Why did you want to dance with me?"

He looked over my head before moving me again. "Because I'd prefer that to watching you dance with someone else."

"I thought you liked watching me."

"Fucking yourself with your fingers, yes. Watching some guy leave his dirty fingerprints all over you, no."

My hazy brain tried to keep up. "That 'some guy' was your brother."

"Do you think I care who it was?"

I replied, blithely. "I don't think you have a right to care."

"Do I need to blackmail you again, Vivian?"

My insides smiled and I looked up into intense features. "It depends. What will you have me do?"

His eyes bore into mine. "What would you like me have you do?"

I let him lead me through a spin then returned with a challenging stare to match his own. He already knew I was attracted to him. The jig was, in effect, up. So, after a brief moment of reflection, I decided to have a little fun.

"I would like you to bend me over the bonnet of your Ferrari."

He swallowed, the contours of his cheeks sharpening under the weight of my words. "And?"

I held his gaze as he led me around the room, pressing me into a solid erection. "And I would like you to push my dress up over my hips…" He watched my lips as I wet them, imagining the scene playing out for real. "And pull my thong to one side…"

"Are you wearing stockings?" he asked, his voice dry.

"I'm wearing whatever the fuck you want," I purred, loving his enraptured gaze, his focus solely on me.

His lip curled. "Wrong answer. Tell me what you're wearing."

"Stockings. Suspenders. Stiletto heels."

His Adam's apple bobbed and I was instantly addicted to his reaction.

"I'm soaking wet," I continued, watching his eyes widen. "Just like I was in the library when you made me come for you." It wasn't a total lie. I was brazenly turned on despite waltzing in a room full of at least two hundred people.

He swallowed again. "And?"

"I want your mouth on me, Rupert." I said the words slowly, revelling in his loss of control. "Your mouth and your fingers. I don't just want to scream your name. I want to hear my name, from your mouth, on me."

Suddenly, he pulled us both to a standstill. He glared at me with a look that was loaded with dynamite. "I will have my security take over your protection. All of it."

I cocked my head. "Isn't that what they've been doing?"

"Not all the time, no. I've been doing the night shifts."

My alcohol-addled brain struggled to keep up. "All of them? Every night?"

This time he did lean into me, his hot breath burning my cheek. "Every. Night."

"But… I only saw you that once."

"That was the idea. But Vivian, now I have to not see *you*. I'll do whatever work shit I need to help you with, but beyond that, I need you to stay away from me."

What? I glared up at him. Had he lost his mind? He'd just goaded a load of dirty talk out of me and now he was telling me to keep away? "Why, Rupert?"

His eyes were glassy, his pupils as large and as black as the night sky. His skin had a light sheen of sweat as though he'd just run to get here, and his jaw jutted where he ground his teeth. "Because you just painted a picture that I would give my right fucking arm to have. And I can't."

And with that, his hands released me, his fingers setting fire to my hips, and all I saw was his back walking away from me amidst a sea of slender, muted people still waltzing to the music.

I looked around for Minty, fresh blood soaking my cheeks. Rupert had just abandoned me in the middle of the dance floor and it felt as though every single person in the room was watching, hungrily, for my reaction. Eventually, I spotted her walking back into the ballroom through a doorway I hadn't noticed before. Her hair was scattered about her face in curling tendrils and she was hastily pinning it up with shaking fingers. Something wasn't right. I made a beeline for her and noticed guilt flood her features as she spotted me coming.

"What's happened? Are you ok?"

Her eyes widened while mine dropped to her lips, which were now devoid of makeup. She took my hand and was about to lead me towards the bar when I noticed another figure emerge from the same doorway Minty had. Tall, dark, handsome, two shadowy dimples in his cheeks. Tucking his shirt into his pants and looking about with the smugness of someone who'd just got laid, was Hector. I looked back to Minty and my mouth dropped open.

"It's not what you think—" she rushed out.

"You and H*ector*?" I whispered as she pulled me fiercely away from where the youngest Thorn had stopped to chat to the Barringtons.

"Shh," she hissed, dragging me into a corner. "You can't tell anyone, Viv. Promise me, please. If anyone finds out, Hector and me… we'll both be crucified."

"Don't be—" I began, with a laugh.

Her grip tightened around my arm. "You think whoever tried to run you off the cliff was *joking*?" She let the words settle uneasily. "They wanted you killed. People here get killed. If anyone finds out Hector has been… *involved*… with a common islander, one of us – probably me – will be removed from the equation."

I glared at her, too many uncomfortable truths crashing about in my head like waves in a storm. "How can Hector put you in that position?"

Minty sighed and looked at her feet. "He didn't want to. It just happened. Just the once, and then…" She covered her face with her hands. "Oh God, Viv. We can't stop. We've tried, so many times, but… I love him, and I think he loves me."

I pulled her into my arms and held her close. "It's ok," I whispered. "Things will work out. They have to." *One way or another*, I added, silently.

She pulled back and looked deep into my eyes, her

gratitude searing through my soul. "I hate these families," she said, with a bitter smile. "I hate these fucking rules and the fact they only benefit the incredibly rich. I hate it all."

I nodded, unsure of what to say.

"Do you still want to get the drug? For your sister?"

I nodded, eagerly.

"Ok." She stared at me with steely determination. "Everyone's here, in this room. If you go now, you're less likely to be seen wandering the halls."

My chest filled with adrenalin. I nodded again.

"Go back through that door Hector and I just came through. Go to the end of the corridor and you'll see a small door on the left. It's a passage to the north tower. It's dark but you can't turn the lights on. Follow it right to the end, then turn right and go up the staircase. At the top are three doors. Take the middle one. It's a bedroom. Used to be Dax's. In the far right corner of the room is another door. Through there is where the tablets are kept."

"Are you sure?" I whispered.

"That's where they were six months ago. It's the best I can do," she shrugged and looked up at me, pleading. "They're about to do toasts and speeches. If anyone asks where you are, I'll cover for you."

"What will you say?"

She shook her head. "I'll think of something."

Behind us, the master of ceremonies tapped the side of a crystal flute. Minty's hands clasped my cheeks, turning me to face her. "Go," she hissed.

I nodded once, then straightened and made straight for the door, stone-cold fear stopping me from looking back.

Chapter 24

V ivian

PANIC DROVE me forward as I tried to recall each of Minty's directions. I found the passage and entered the long tunnel of darkness. I felt too light-headed to be nervous about cobwebs, rats or whatever else might be lurking in there. I felt my way along, pressing my hands into the cold stone walls. I held my breath as I pushed open the door at the end and allowed my eyes the beat of a second to adjust before I hitched my dress and ran up the stairs two at a time. The north tower stretched high above my head, peaking into a sharp turret at the top. I was sure if I lingered long enough, bats would plummet towards me like cannonballs.

I reached the top of the stairs and let the hem of my dress fall to the floor. Heaving from the exertion, I looked at the three doors. The middle one stared back at me, daring my fist to turn the doorknob.

IN THE DISTANCE I heard the outbreak of applause echoing around the Great Hall. Blocking it out, I tiptoed to the door and rested my palm on the brass handle. Just as I was about to turn it, I heard the floorboards creak behind me. The next sound was that of my heart plummeting into my stomach. I didn't need to turn around to know who was standing behind me, filling the space with his blackened eyes and imposing form.

"What do you think you're doing in this part of the house, Vivian?"

I paused for a beat at his use of the word 'house' like it was some two-up two-down semi in Croydon. This place was no house. It was a fucking walled city. An empire in itself.

"I'm trying to find…" I stalled while I tried to think of some reasonable-sounding explanation.

"The bathroom?" His cocked brow was audible. I let out a breath of surrender and turned my body towards him, though my face remained turned away. Part in embarrassment, part in irritation. Why the hell did I keep getting caught? It felt as though this entire place – or Rupert himself – was rigged with cameras.

He took two steps towards me. "Why don't we skip all the bullshit and get straight to the truth this time? You won't find any red tops in these corridors, butterfly."

I pinned him with a sharp glare. "I wasn't looking for any."

His own eyes narrowed, like a sheet of black ice. "So, what were you looking for?"

I shrugged and huffed. "Nothing. I wasn't looking for anything in particular, ok? I was just curious."

"Curious?"

"This is practically my home for a year." I forced a sigh. "I deserve to know what's in it."

He took another two steps until he could touch me if he so wanted. "This is *not* your home. It will never be your home. You are a guest, and this part of *my home* is off limits to you and everyone else."

I closed the gap and tilted my chin so I was right beneath the hoods of his eyes. "What don't you want me to see? What are you hiding?"

His throat was directly in front of me. I saw and heard as he swallowed dryly. Just when I thought I had him stumped, his giant hand wrapped around my elbow. Before I knew what was happening, his foot kicked the door I'd been about to open and I was pulled sideways into an opulent suite. I didn't get a chance to take it all in before I was pushed backwards towards the wall. My spine bruised the instant I hit the intricate mouldings but Rupert remained several steps away from me.

"What makes you think I'm hiding something?" he said, with a glint in his eye.

"You assume that simply because I'm curious, I'm snooping. Only someone with something to hide would assume that."

A smile quirked at the corner of his lip. "And you assume that because I'm protective of my home and want to keep some things private, that I'm hiding something."

"You didn't follow me here because you thought I might be snooping," I said, tilting my chin.

He pushed his hands into his suit pants and met my gaze with defiance of his own. "Yes, I did."

"Even though you just said you never wanted to have to see me again?"

He ground his jaw as his chest filled. "Yes."

I shook my head and straightened. "Lies look good on you, Rupert."

His eyes widened in surprise, and I thought I caught a slight glimpse of triumph in them. "Is that an insult?"

"Did it sound like a compliment?"

"Yes, it did." His eyes glided from my face, slowly down over my dress, the curve of my breasts, the round of my hips, to where it bunched on the floor. "Now, take off that dress and say it again."

The shock of his words rippled through me like a heat-wave, landing squarely between my legs. "You can't be serious."

"Don't make me repeat myself," he replied.

"What's it for this time? What dirty deed do you need me to do now?"

He took a step towards me. "I haven't decided yet." His glare pierced the thin satin just below my collarbone. "Take. It. Off."

Heat pooled at my core the longer he stared at me. I took my time easing the gossamer thin straps over my shoulders knowing the second they dropped, the whole slip would fall to a puddle at my feet. When it did, Rupert's eyes followed it to the floor. I watched as he pulled his bottom lip between his teeth then looked at me through heavy lashes as he lazily dragged it out again.

"Lies look good on you, Rupert," I repeated.

He closed his eyes and inhaled deeply. "Christ, butter-fly," he breathed. "You're going to ruin me."

"What do you want me to do?" I asked, batting my lids, eager for his next instruction.

"Fuck yourself with your fingers," he said in a gravelly voice.

"Again?" I pouted. "Can't you think of something more imaginative?"

He backed up against one of the bed's four posters and smiled. "You know I can't touch you," he replied, taking his fingers to his zipper. "But no one said anything about joining you."

My heart crashed against my ribcage and my head swam. I tried to anchor my eyes on his hand but the anticipation of seeing him laid bare, raw, wanting, was too much.

"Touch yourself, Vivian," he whispered from his place against the bed post.

I closed my eyes and did as he asked, slipping two fingers into my already soaked underwear. A long, pent-up gasp left my throat as my fingers found my clit.

"Look at me," he said, his voice hoarse.

I forced my eyes open then had to somehow stop them from popping out of my head at the sight of Rupert, exposed. His cock stood long, thick and tall, protruding from his thick, calloused hand. My fingers stilled and he saw it.

"Is this what you want inside you when I bend you over the hood of my Ferrari?" he asked, in a voice laced with hunger.

I dragged my eyes back to his face. It seemed somehow darker, his eyes contained within the shadow of his deepened brow. I swallowed, almost choking on the dryness that coated my throat.

"I would give anything to slide into you," he confessed, making my stomach wilt. My eyes dropped to his hand and watched it move, commanding his cock with long, slow, firm strokes. "Rub your clit, butterfly."

I gasped, releasing my control. Second by second I relinquished whatever modicum of self-respect I'd surrounded myself with, and I relished it. My fingers stroked over my clit and I jumped with the shock of just how turned on I was.

"That's it, Vivian," Rupert said, glueing his gaze to my core like he wanted to feast on it. The sassy quips retreated from my mouth as I realised with a jolt there was nothing funny about this. We were both desperate, and this was the only way we could scratch the itch. I couldn't do what Minty had done with Hector. I couldn't fall off the edge like that, never to be able to return to safety. This was as far as we could go.

"Come here," I pleaded, my voice husky. "I... I won't touch you. I just want to see you."

He gripped his cock and stood. His pants fell to the floor and he stepped out of them before walking towards me, slowly, still stroking his thick length.

He stopped two feet away from me. "Is this close enough?"

I nodded, my eyes glued to the movement of his hand and the glistening crown as it emerged from beneath his curled fingers. "It's beautiful," I whispered.

A hand plummeted into the wall at the side of my head and I looked up sharply to see Rupert's face inches from mine. "Nothing's as beautiful as you," he murmured.

"I thought you said this island was full of pretty faces," I said, working my fingers around the nub of my clit.

"Pretty, yes," he said, panting slightly. "Beautiful, no."

"What did you see that first night you sat outside the cottage?" I asked him, my voice beginning to break.

"Everything," he said, with a silky smile. "And you know it."

I dipped my fingers into my hot core and moaned, loving every second of his proximity, the view in my peripheral vision of his hand stroking himself more and more vigorously. "I have no idea what you mean," I said, with an innocent half-smile.

"So, you didn't strip in front of your window, or roam around naked with the curtains open, or fondle your breasts as you looked out to sea for my benefit?"

"No," I pouted. "I do it all for me. For the thrill I get knowing you can watch, but you can't touch."

His teeth clashed together and a growl rose up through his throat. "Are you fucking yourself, Vivian?"

"Yes, sir."

He dropped his gaze to my fingers. "Push them in deeper."

I did as he asked.

"Now use your thumb on your clit. Roll it around the outer edge, softly."

As soon as I obeyed, fire ignited across my core and came out through my lips in a heated gasp.

"That's it, butterfly. Now curl your middle finger towards me. Don't look down."

I fixed my eyes on him as I followed his instructions. Everything he asked me to do felt incredible. A small moan escaped my lips. "Caress yourself, butterfly. Gently. Just like I would."

My knees almost buckled as I devoured his sacred words. "I'm so fucking close," I whispered.

His eyes narrowed on me. "So am I."

"I want you to come all over me," I said, surprising myself with words I had never before spoken and a guttural need I had never before felt.

He hesitated, then nodded and I closed my eyes. I realised I wanted it more than anything. To feel his scorching semen coat my breasts, my stomach, my neck...

Suddenly, my throat constricted. My eyelids popped and Rupert's face was less than an inch away from mine. His fingers tightened around my jaw and his hot breath skittered across my face.

"You like it when I do this, don't you, butterfly? When I hold your face in my fingers," he groaned low, sinking his tips into the flesh of my jawline.

I nodded.

"Good. Me too," he breathed. "I love holding you still like this, knowing I could end your life with one squeeze of my hand. I love knowing that you know that too, yet here you are. Trusting me. Not wanting me to stop."

His words began to tip me over the edge. "Rupert..." my voice came out in a strangled whisper. He leaned into me so close I felt the hairs on his lips brush against mine.

"Curl your finger, press down on your clit and come for me, Vivian," he breathed.

I did as he said and the ball of heat uncurled inside my pelvic bone, rolling outwards, peaking at my apex and rocketing up through my stomach. I wanted to fold myself in two but I couldn't force myself forward into Rupert. I was vaguely aware of his hand pumping fiercely, his breaths growing hot and needy. Then he roared, a sound that began in his gut and battered up through his lungs and out into my ear. Then I felt his release hit my stomach in hot, silky threads, lashing at me in decadent ropes. His eyelids opened and in them I saw nothing but black.

He pumped his fist harder and more cum shot out of him landing on my sex. A final growl left his throat and his hand released mine and slammed back against the wall. We both stood still, panting hard, his breath still covering my face like a silken pillow.

I was stunned by the rawness of what we'd just done, and staggered by the unquenched thirst it had left in its wake.

It felt like a full five minutes passed before either of us dared speak. We'd crossed over into a territory so intimate it was painful.

"I'm sorry, butterfly."

My heart stilled at the sadness in his voice.

"That shouldn't have happened. It was a mistake."

A mistake? It was the closest I'd ever felt to anyone. The way he'd looked at me, baring his truth, his vulnerability, letting me live through his climax with him. It softened my soul; bent it to let him in. I shook my head but a pointed glare stopped me.

"Do you hear me? That was the biggest mistake. And I'm asking you… *begging* you… to forget it ever happened."

He released the wall and stepped backwards, reaching down to pick up his suit pants.

I cocked my head to one side and let out an exasperated breath. "It's hard to forget your biggest mistake when it's running down your thigh."

As if I'd just notified him of the evidence he'd left on my body, he pulled on his boxers and stalked quickly to a door, emerging a second later with a small pile of paper hand towels. He came towards me and pressed a towel to my stomach. Slowly, he stroked it around, catching his semen as it coursed down my skin. He gently wiped it from my chest, my hips and the tops of my thighs.

The care he applied was painstaking and his eyes never wandering from the task at hand. I waited for him to finish then pointed to a droplet on the crest of my left nipple. "You missed a bit."

His black eyes darted up to mine. "Think of it as my autograph."

"I'd rather have that on paper."

He held my eyes as he walked to a desk adjacent to the bed, reached for a pen then turned to scrawl his name on a hand towel. Then, he walked back to where I hadn't moved from the wall and gently dabbed my nipple. He folded the towel into quarters.

"What's this?" I arched a brow. "A keepsake?"

He pressed it into my hand and echoed my earlier words from the Great Hall. "It's whatever you want it to be."

Chapter 25

*R*upert

INSTEAD OF THROWING the towel back at me like I'd half expected, she tucked it into her underwear. My signature nestled against her pussy. She would never know the extent to which that seared my skin.

I waited until she'd slipped back into that silk handkerchief of a dress before I resumed my interrogation. "What are you doing in the north tower, Vivian?"

She sank into an armchair by the window and sighed, avoiding my gaze. "I heard Basidiomine was kept in here."

My eyebrow hitched. "In this room?"

"Yes. Behind one of these doors." She gestured to the three doors that I knew led to a bathroom, a walk-in closet and a lounge. Not a secret store of Basidiomine.

"Whoever told you that was mistaken. Look, come with me. I'll show you."

• • • •

I WALKED her through the rooms opening every door and even the safe in the lounge that I knew was empty. The disappointment rolled off her in waves.

We were standing in the bathroom when I turned to her again. "Why do you need it so badly?"

She walked past me back to the main bedroom, sank onto the bed and put her head in her hands. After a few moments, she looked up at me, her eyes brimmed with tears. "My sister," she said, simply.

I braced my shoulders. "You have a sister?"

She sighed. "Yes. I lied about it. I knew your father wouldn't hire me if he knew I have family ties back home."

"That's a damn brave thing to do," I warned.

Her gaze levelled. "I did it for her."

"Why?"

She watched me carefully as if sizing me up. "She has chronic pain. Fibromyalgia. She has episodes that are so bad she knocks herself out so she doesn't have to deal with the pain."

"I'm guessing you wouldn't go to these lengths if you hadn't already tried paracetamol?" I sighed, pushing my hands into my pockets.

"We've tried everything. Over-the-counter painkillers, prescription drugs, marijuana, Chinese herbs, ice packs, heat packs, everything. Nothing has worked."

"Who's looking after her? Your parents?"

She shook her head and dropped her gaze to the floor. "Our mum died four years ago. Dad left long before that. We have some friends, honorary godparents I suppose. They're looking after her. It was their suggestion I try and get some Basidiomine. We've tried everything else."

"You asked me for a sample. Was it for her?"

She nodded, sheepishly.

"I didn't know it was for someone genuinely in need."

Her eyes flicked up to mine, bathing me in a clear blue sky. "There are many people in genuine need, Rupert. And they don't include city boys and politicians."

My teeth ground together before I answered. "I know that. Believe me."

I felt her cool gaze on me as I rubbed my eyes. I had a horrible feeling that what I was about to say would backfire on me, but right at that moment, I didn't care. For some inexplicable reason, I just wanted to make Vivian happy. "I will try and get you some of the tablets."

"You will? Really?" Her whispered reply, filled with disbelief and gratitude, made me hot all over.

"The operative word being 'try', Vivian. The drug is held tight under lock and key and there has to be an exceptional reason for taking it. People pay thousands for a week's supply. I'll need to think of something."

She nodded, tears filling her eyes. "Thank you."

"I can't promise anything, Vivian," I warned. "But I'll try. And I don't need to remind you, not a word of this can be breathed to anyone. You understand?"

She nodded again. More vigorously this time.

"Come on," I said. "We'd better get back. My mother has eyes on me like a damn hawk."

I straightened up and stood over her, holding out my hands. Slowly, she reached up and placed her small palms in mine. I lifted her gently, and brought her into my chest. So, I was touching her. So what? It wasn't sexual. So far, so clear.

My arms wrapped around her shoulders and I felt her

breath hot against my chest, warming me to the bone. Without thinking I raised a hand and stroked her hair. I dipped my lips and spoke into the crown of her head. "I'm sorry for coming all over you."

"I'm not," she whispered. "I loved it." The realisation hit me like a Cat 5 hurricane. I wanted this woman physically, so much that it made my damn balls ache. I wanted so badly to bury myself inside her and fuck away her fears. Give her what her body had told me three times now she wanted. I brushed my lips against her hair, then I closed my eyes, and inhaled as much of her as I could.

"What the fuck rattled your cage?"

When I opened my eyes, Hector was right up in my face. I blinked at him. "What?"

"You were just downright rude to Mother. All she did was ask which shoes you wanted to wear. What's got into you?"

"What do you think?" I snarled.

He folded a hand over my arm and guided me out of the dressing room and into my study. As soon as we were safely closed inside, he let me go and sighed heavily. "What's going on, Rupert? You know you have to go through with this. You've always known. Why are being such an arsehole about it now?"

I ground my teeth and looked over his shoulder towards the window.

"It's not like you didn't know this was coming."

My fists clenched at my sides. "I don't want any of them," I seethed. "Not one."

Hector parted his feet and stood solid in front me, his arms folded. "Does it matter? They're all good girls. Whoever you choose… you'll grow to like them. Probably love them. That's what happens with these things, isn't it?"

I shot him an incredulous glare. "Really? What if there's a chance I might love someone else, huh? What happens then?"

I was genuinely curious, not that I loved Vivian. I couldn't love her. I hardly knew her. And what I did know of her was decidedly infuriating, albeit hot as fuck. But, I was curious. What if I *did* love someone else?

His voice dropped to a whisper. "What?"

I walked past him to the window and braced my hands on the sill, bringing my forehead to the cool glass. I felt Hector come up behind me. "You don't," he said, quietly. "You can't."

He grabbed both my shoulders and turned me to face him. "Nothing would happen," he said, serious eyes looking out from a petrified face. "That's what. You would still be made to marry an island girl. You know that. It's a rule as old as time in this place. And if you refuse, well…"

I repeated Mother's words to him. "I will be removed from the island, from the family and from all beneficiaries to which I am currently entitled."

"There's your answer," he finished. I turned back to the window and looked out at the never-ending gardens, the borders filled with thousands of rose bushes readying themselves to bloom.

"Who is it?" Hector asked, softly.

"No one."

"It's Vivian, isn't it?"

I stilled, then turned my head slowly to face him. "I said, no one."

He scrubbed a hand down his face. "*Damn* Father," he spat.

"Why Father?" I frowned.

"He put her in your office, didn't he? Isn't that where it all started?"

"No, it isn't actually."

"What?" Hector dipped his head. "Then where?"

"I was sitting in the morning room. A maid was pouring my coffee. Vivian walked past on her way to Father's office. I felt her before I saw her. Without even laying eyes on her."

Hector stared at me like I'd gone nuts. I probably had.

"Tell me Hector." I turned to face him. "What it is when you don't even need to see someone? You just have to feel them, to know they're there? You don't need to know what they look like before you realise you connect more with that person than anyone else in your life. What is it Hector?"

He looked at me, dumbfounded.

"Well, come on!" I shouted. "Fucking tell me. Seeing as you think it's going to be so easy to spend the rest of my life with someone I don't give a flying fuck about." I hammered a fist into the wall and stared down at the gardens below.

My eyes squeezed shut when I repeated, "What *is* it?"

Hector sighed and shook his head, as though he'd just got a glimpse of the real Rupert Thorn and it was an image he didn't have the mental capacity to deal with.

"I don't know Rupert." His voice trembled. "I don't know what it is. But, I'm sorry. I'm so sorry."

My head dropped like a heavy weight and I sensed Hector, the only brother I felt close to, turn away.

"Do you feel the same about Minty?"

He stopped at the door, his palm stilled on the handle. "What?"

I turned to face him and sighed. "I'm in no place to judge you, Hector. I know it's been going on for months. Do you love her?"

He ran a hand round the back of his neck and focused on the door before turning a guilty gaze towards me. "I don't know. Maybe."

"Then, I'm sorry too."

He nodded, smiling bitterly. "I'll get off your case, brother."

"Yeah," I replied, feeling a small slither of relief that it was no longer just me affected by this ridiculous law. "Me too."

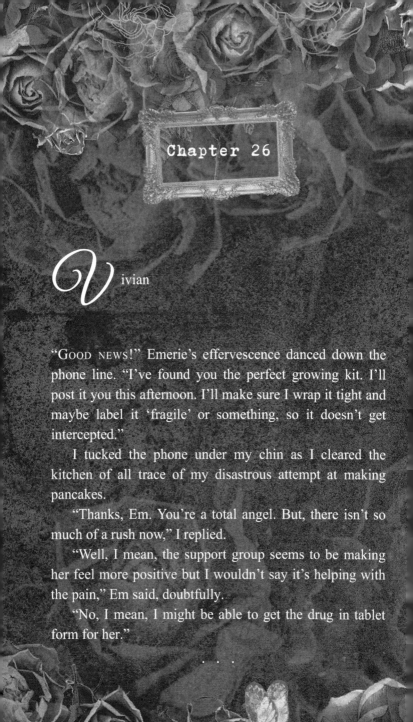

Chapter 26

$\mathcal{V}$ivian

"GOOD NEWS!" Emerie's effervescence danced down the phone line. "I've found you the perfect growing kit. I'll post it you this afternoon. I'll make sure I wrap it tight and maybe label it 'fragile' or something, so it doesn't get intercepted."

I tucked the phone under my chin as I cleared the kitchen of all trace of my disastrous attempt at making pancakes.

"Thanks, Em. You're a total angel. But, there isn't so much of a rush now," I replied.

"Well, I mean, the support group seems to be making her feel more positive but I wouldn't say it's helping with the pain," Em said, doubtfully.

"No, I mean, I might be able to get the drug in tablet form for her."

. . .

"What? How?" She lowered her voice despite being three hundred miles out of earshot of anyone physically standing on the island. "Have you stolen it?"

"No." I almost laughed but that wouldn't have been too hard to imagine. I'd become quite the sticky fingered tour guide in the space of two months. "Rupert says he's going to try and get hold of some for me."

"Rupert who? She started, then I heard her hand clasp over her mouth and the muffled words, "No. Rupert *Thorn*?"

"Yup," I replied, feeling an unwarranted sense of smugness.

"What did you do? Give him massages every morning? Rub his feet? Perform sexual favours?"

"No!" I gasped. "Don't be ridiculous! He's a Thorn! A billionaire! Why on earth would I want to perform sexual favours for him?!"

Emerie fell quiet.

"Em?"

"Hmm, I think the lady doth protest too much," she mused.

Fuck. "Seriously, nothing is going on between me and Rupert."

"Vivi… I didn't ask if anything was going on. I asked – in jest, mind – whether you'd somehow bribed him for the drugs. Now, what aren't you telling me? And remember, I can smell a lie like a fart in a car."

I closed my eyes even though she couldn't see me. "It's complicated," was the best I could do.

"*Everything*'s complicated," she replied. "Spill."

"He's been blackmailing me," I winced. That didn't sound good. "He overheard me, um…" Now, this was embarrassing. "Um… having a little play with myself in a sauna one evening."

I heard a smirk. "Go on."

"He recorded it on his phone."

"He *what*?" she screeched, almost deafening me.

"Yeah, then asked me to do it again so he could film me."

"You… *what*? Are you fucking serious?"

Man, it sounds a lot worse than I remember it.

"Is he hot?"

Now, that was a question I could answer. "Yes. Extremely."

"Oh hell, Viv. Are you in deep?"

"It depends what you mean. If you mean deep shit… probably."

"I'm getting off topic," she hissed, quickly. "Is he still blackmailing you?"

I sighed. "No. That stopped after someone tried to run me off a cliff."

"*What??*" Oh jeez. That slipped. "I think you should come home, Viv," she continued, her voice grave. "We'll figure something else out. It's not worth risking your life for. Who the fuck would try to run you off a cliff?"

In my head I replied, "Rupert's older brother and one of my bosses," but that would have taken us down far more complicated lines of inquiry which I simply didn't have the answers for or mental capacity to deal with.

"Case of mistaken identity," I said.

"Are you ok?" She sounded out of breath.

"I'm fine. But, back to the topic. Rupert hasn't black-mailed me since. If anything, he's become overly protec-tive." *Even though he can't seem to decide whether to avoid me completely, or wrap me in his own personal brand of cotton wool.*

"And he's going to get you the pills?"

"Yes. He's going to try."

"Try?" Em sounded understandably suspicious. "It's his drug, isn't it?"

"Yes, but it's in such high demand even he has to jump through hoops to get it. But, I trust him. I just don't know how long it will take."

"Ok, well, I'm going to send you this growing kit anyway. I went all the way to Kew Gardens and spoke to the gardeners myself. This is the best shizzle, ok? If this doesn't work, nothing will."

I sighed gratefully. "You're a star, you know that?"

"Yes, I do," she clipped. "And you are one slightly fucked up, crazy-ass billionaire fucker if ever I knew one."

"I haven't slept with him," I said, wearily. "He's barely even touched me."

And, as I hung up the phone and looked down at the hand towel on the kitchen counter, his signature hidden in its folds, I lamented the fact it was still so very true.

Chapter 27

*R*upert

I INSISTED on accompanying Vivian to my father's office for her weekly meeting with him and my brother. It wouldn't hurt for them to see me showing more interest in the business and the tours, especially when I had to somehow convince them to let me have this drug. For a sister she lied about having.

She shivered as I rested a hand on the back of her dress and I clenched my jaw against the urge to shove her back against the wall and scrape my teeth down her throat. Since she'd allowed me – asked me – to shoot my cum all over her creamy, perfect skin, I'd found it impossible to get her out of my head and far away from the blood that stiffened my cock whenever I laid eyes on her. The urge to salivate at the feel of her spine beneath my fingers was painfully acute.

. . . .

"Rupert," Father announced, his angular face beaming at my surprise entrance. "To what do we owe this pleasure?"

"I could hazard a guess," Ossian sneered under his breath as I took a seat between him and Vivian.

I patted his arm with faux affection. "I thought you'd be pleased to see me," I grinned.

"Well, your timing is perfect," Father continued, oblivious to Ossian's wariness. "We have to discuss the drinks menu."

"Is something amiss, sir?" Vivian asked, readying her pen adorably to take notes.

"Hmm," Father murmured. "I'm not sure we're getting our guests drunk enough."

I frowned. "Are you sure? We've had to pay extra for dry-cleaning after people have puked all over the premium leather seats of the ferry during their return leg. I'd say they'd probably had enough."

"Yes, perhaps," he mused. "But I want people to wake up with a hangover they'd never otherwise be able to afford and memories so hazy they think they were laced with platinum."

"We've already had great press coverage and incredible testimonials," Vivian said, placing a thick wad of paper clippings on the desk. Despite all manner of technological apparatus on his desk, Father still didn't relish email. "I'm not sure we could make the experience more positive or memorable, or… not."

"Hmm," Father murmured again, steepling his long bony fingers. "Fine. Let me think more about it."

Before he could move on to another topic, a loud knock came at the door. "Yes?" Father barked. Being interrupted in meetings was his biggest peeve. Whoever was at the other side of the door had either balls of steel or some-thing very important to tell us. Something… life or death.

I recognised Wilson before his pathetic limp gave him away. "I… I'm so sorry to interrupt," he stammered, making me feel almost sorry for him.

"Spit it out, lad," Father grumbled.

"We've, um… we've had some news."

Ossian made a circle with his finger to hurry Wilson along. We could both feel Father's patience wearing thin.

"McFadden's dead," he blurted out. Instead of looking questioningly at Ossian and my father, who in my mind would be the number one suspects, my eyes shot to Vivian. She would feel responsible. She would be shattered.

Her hand curled slowly over her heart as she turned her saucepan eyes to Wilson. "What? Archie McFadden?"

"I'm afraid so, ma'am. We just pulled his body out of the water. It was floating out from the south tip." *The Glade*.

In the corner of my eye I saw Ossian's jaw tick.

"Do we know the cause?" I asked, monotone.

"It'll be suicide," Ossian answered, casually. "He suffered from depression pretty badly."

"I certainly didn't get that impression," Vivian gasped, standing up. "When he drove me here the day I arrived, he was so chatty, happy, devoted to his family." She slapped a hand over her mouth and let out a sob that wrenched my heart.

"It's always the quiet ones," he replied, with a menacing tongue.

"Has anyone told his wife?" Father asked, dragging his eyes from Ossian back to Wilson.

"Not yet, sir."

"Fine," Father sighed. "I'll do the honours."

He picked up his phone and I stood to take Vivian out of the room. Father held up a hand. "I'll take it into the gardens," he said. "Something about the sound of birds helps soothe people after a trauma."

I refrained from raising my eyebrows in surprise at his rare show of sensitivity. As soon as he left the room, I turned to Vivian who was still standing on shaky legs, staring into space. "Are you ok?"

She shook her head slowly. "Is he really dead?" Her eyes darted to Wilson who nodded.

"Yes, ma'am. I identified the body myself. It's defi-nitely... dead." A wince passed across his face.

"Well," Ossian said, sitting up straight. "We should probably crack on. I have somewhere to be in fifteen minutes."

Both me and Vivian stared at Ossian in disbelief. He ignored us and jerked his head to the door. "Thanks Wilson," he hissed, dismissing the messenger.

"I'm sorry," Vivian whispered. "I don't think I can focus. I won't be of any help." She looked at me. "Is it ok if I go home? I'm sure after a night's sleep I'll be fine. It's just... it's a shock."

I tried to convey my despair and apology to her through my gaze but she didn't hold my eyes. She could hardly look at me, and that felt like a spear slicing through the wall of my chest. "Of course," I replied, ignoring Ossian's huff. "I'll call you a driver."

WORD GOT around the island fast. Only twenty-four hours later the whole place felt like a walking morgue. I'd tried calling Vivian to check she was ok, but she wouldn't pick up. I toyed with the idea of driving to the cottage myself but figured she might actually need some time. I knew Ossian was behind McFadden's death. It didn't take a genius to figure it out. But he was good at covering his tracks. Despite that, the islanders feared him. Even if evidence wasn't forthcoming, the rumours were, and that's what I think he loved the most. It was the stuff of myth and mystery, the only thing less tangible than unimaginable wealth.

I arrived in the office three hours before that day's tour was due to dock, hoping to catch Vivian before she headed down to the port. I wasn't disappointed. One hour later she strutted into the office with a serene look on her face. She didn't utter a word as she sat at her desk and booted up her computer.

"Morning," I said.

She shot me a thin smile and clenched jaw of silence.

"Are you ok?" I asked again.

"I'm fine," she clipped.

"You don't look fine," I hedged.

"Then don't look."

I inhaled a long breath and let it out slowly, keeping tight tabs on my frustration. She wasn't opening up to me because I was a part of McFadden's demise and she knew it. And I'd made her complicit.

"I had nothing to do with it—" I began.

Her face snapped towards me. "You had everything to do with it. And so did I."

I shook my head, determinedly. "That's not true,

Vivian," I almost pleaded. "You can't think like that. We didn't hold a gun to anyone. We didn't push anyone off a cliff, or whatever it was that happened. It wasn't our fault."

Her eyes narrowed on me. "It was all our fault. If we hadn't meddled in Ossian's business, whatever the hell it is, McFadden would still be alive…"

I let out a bitter laugh. "We don't know that—"

"His children would still have a father," she ground out through shaking lungs. She was so angry. With me. And I deserved every ounce of it.

"I'm sorry, Vivian," I said. "I should never have got you involved."

She smacked a hand on her desk, sending a multitude of pens, sharpeners and other useless bits of office paraphernalia clattering to the floor. "You're damn right, Rupert. You should never have got me involved. I'm sorry I ever went into that sauna. I'm sorry I tried to take those damned mushrooms. I'm sorry I got lumped in this rabbit warren with *you*. I'm sorry I ever met you."

She spun back to her computer and bashed at the keyboard. I watched her for a few minutes feeling the one thing that was never mine slipping further and further away. When I couldn't bear it anymore, I stood and left the room. Before I'd even got as far as the entrance hall, my phone rang. It was the port office mobile, only used in emergencies. What the fuck now?

"Rupert Thorn."

I could hardly hear the person at the other end amid the noise of men shouting loudly and what sounded like buildings crashing to the ground.

"Sir? It's the port. Someone's set it on fire."

My chest thumped. "How bad is it?"

There was a long pause while my heart crept stealthily into my throat.

"It's gone, sir. The whole building just sank."

I hung up and spun around, breaking into a run. We had a tour arriving in less than an hour and we had nowhere to dock the visitors in. The port had just been burned to the ground. My mind raced as my feet sped along the corridors back to the office. Vivian almost fell off her chair when I burst into the room.

"Get your coat, your phone, everything. We're heading to the dock. There's been a fire."

The genuine look of fear and determination that filled her eyes confirmed everything I had already concluded. Vivian had nothing to do with this.

I waited for Vivian to buckle up before I secured my foot to the floor, powering the car down the drive at an ungodly speed. Vivian was already on the phone to her contacts at the port. I could hear the screams and shouts from two feet away. She stared at me wide-eyed as someone relayed the details, then she hung up and stared out of the windscreen.

"A speedboat was seen in the early hours of this morning, about two a.m., sailing away from the port. They think some kind of explosive device was planted below the decking." She faced me with renewed fear in her eyes. "Do you think they wanted to blow up the ferry?"

I shook my head. "That would have led to unnecessary complications for whoever did this. They would have simply wanted to put the tours out of business for a while, give us a bad name."

"Any idea who it might have been?"

I shook my head slowly, thinking. "We have plenty of

enemies, for all kinds of reasons. It could have been any one of them."

"Would it be an islander avenging McFadden's death?"

"Possibly," I said. "But, I doubt an islander would want to ruin their only route off the island for the foreseeable future." I gripped the wheel. "My concern is, what do we do with the boat that's on its way? Do we turn it back around? Put the tours on hold, just as the perpetrator probably hoped?"

Vivian chewed her lip, deep in thought. "There are no other ports on the island."

"No."

"Do we know of any other safe places where the ferry could dock?"

"No. We've only ever used the port. The coastline is rocky. I wouldn't feel confident just bringing the boat in anywhere."

She gasped. "The helicopter! What about the helicopter that brought me here?"

"It isn't big enough. Besides, the boat's already left the mainland."

She chewed her lip again as I steered the car round the winding road to the port. Suddenly, she picked up her phone and pulled up a number that didn't look local.

"Wait," I said, placing my hand over hers and doing my best to ignore the physical thrill that wound through it. "Who are you calling?"

She clasped her own hand over mine and looked at me with soft eyes. "Don't worry. My friend mentioned that some people from her organisation came here recently to explore the coastline. They might have seen something that could be useful."

I glanced at her, doubtful.

"She's my best, best friend," she assured me. "She'll be discreet. I promise. It might help."

I nodded, reluctantly. "Make sure she doesn't breathe a fucking word."

She muttered quietly into her phone, her eyes occasionally flicking sideways at me, then she held her hand over the mouthpiece and turned to me. "She's gone to ask the guy who led the recce. They were out here for three days and they scoured the entire coastline."

She turned back to the phone and listened intently.

"Right. Ok. So, to the south of the port... No? Right the way around?"

I shook my head. "We can't take them anywhere near the Sunken Glade. There's no route up from there."

"Did you hear that?" she asked her friend. "Ok, so the only other option is what? The west? Uh huh. Uh huh. Ok. Thanks Em, you're a lifesaver."

She was about to hang up when her friend spoke again. Whatever she said turned Vivian's face crimson. "No," she hissed. "I'm hanging up now. Love you."

She snapped the cover over her phone and kept her blushing cheeks turned away. "The west side is clear. No rocks, just pebbles. The team saw a road leading up from a small beach so there's access."

"I know it," I replied. "What did she say that got you all flustered?"

She anchored her face to the side window. "Nothing. She said nothing."

I bit back a smile as the flames of the port came into view, and turned the car towards them.

Chapter 28

*V*ivian

"I won't be driving you home tonight," Rupert said as he followed me to the now-full coach-load of guests recently loaded on the west coast of the island, none the wiser at to why there and not a proper port. I thought the entry point felt more rustic, more authentic. Definitely more fitting for an island that nobody ever leaves. "But one of my guys will meet you back here after the tour to take you home."

I smiled. "Ok."

His hand wrapped around my elbow, making me stop. "Thanks for doing this."

"It's ok," I smiled again.

"No, I mean it." His eyes seemed lighter in the reflection of the turquoise sea. "After everything that's happened… I wouldn't have blamed you if you hadn't helped. No port, no tours. You could have taken the opportunity to leave."

A QUICK BREATH escaped my lips. "I don't want to leave." And in those very seconds, as I looked into his eyes, raw and open, I meant it.

"Why?" he whispered.

I took a deep breath and panned my gaze from him to the coach, the deep green hillside, the softly lapping shore. "I like it here. The Isle of Crow is beautiful. It deserves to be seen."

I didn't miss the deflation in his chest that forced my own to clench painfully.

"You know I can't tell you the other reason," I said, softly. "Because that reason can't exist."

He held my eyes as his hand reached out. Hidden against the side of the coach, he laced his fingers through mine and rubbed the back of my hand with his thumb. My eyelids fluttered with the tingle of fire that crept across my skin and his breath stuttered as he watched.

"I'll see you tomorrow," I forced out.

He nodded and slowly dropped my hand, the tips of his fingers trailing fine lines of lava across my palm as they released me.

His gaze followed as I climbed into the coach and sat on the front seat. The doors hissed closed and the driver set off up the winding road, leaving Rupert standing tall and anchored, as we disappeared into the distance.

The second we crested the hill, my phone buzzed. There was no name but I recognised the Glasgow number. It was the journalist who'd given me his card. I swiped open the message and felt my heart plummet to the country road below.

"*Now* do you have news for me?"

It was too soon for anyone else to have known about the fire, but something told me he'd had a birds' eye view.

———

THE AIR WAS CHARGED as I sat opposite Rupert in the library of Blackcap Hall. It was raining outside and the walls of his office had been closing in on both of us. The library was the next logical place to meet to discuss next steps for the tour. Now that the port was out of action, we had to rethink the route.

I handed him a map with my proposed changes and sat in silence as his eyes roamed it. He rubbed his jaw and I noticed, for the first time, day-old stubble covering his cheeks. He released his jaw to run a finger over the route, then stopped and looked up at me. "What's this?"

My eyes followed his finger to the map. "Sunken Glade," I replied, innocently.

"The tour doesn't pass through the Glade. It can go through the woodland from the west and up to the lab, then on to Caspian House." He handed the map back to me. No discussion.

"Why can't we visit Sunken Glade? I've been up to the fence and the only thing beyond it is beautiful countryside. Every tour I've done, the visitors have asked me why that part of the island is off-limits. They're curious about the petrified forest and the other side of the hill. They can see some of it from the sea – they've even shown me photographs they've taken. It's so picturesque."

"It's dangerous," he said, turning to the next item on our agenda.

"Why is it?"

"Landslides."

"In the photos I've seen, there is no evidence of land-slides. At the very least, there must be parts of the Glade that are accessible. I saw trucks heading towards the area only last week. I pointed them out to you."

His head snapped up and a look crossed his face that chilled me to the bone. I'd seen many expressions on the face of Rupert Thorn, but not one of simmering rage.

"There is no access to public vehicles. Only site vehi-cles. It's a working site. It's *dangerous*."

"I never see any trucks in the vicinity of the labs or the surrounding land during the day," I pressed.

He put his papers down on the table with a frustrated grunt. "That's irrelevant, *Vivian*. You are not taking the tour through the Glade. End of."

His total dismissal of what I'd seen and what I'd asked felt like someone was rubbing shards of glass over my arms. I hated being patronised and ignored, more than anything.

I stood abruptly and smoothed down my dress. "You're being unreasonable," I snapped.

His response was bitten back. "I have good reason to be unreasonable."

"Then I need to know what it is. I can't do my job well if I don't have all the information."

"You don't need any more information in order to do your job well."

His stubbornness was infuriating. "It is if I need to explain to visitors why they can't go any further than the woodland. They can't see anything dangerous from the ocean, and with the amount of money they're paying for a ticket, some are starting to demand to know why they can't go there. There *must* be a better reason."

He stood and kicked the table between us. It rocked onto its side with a loud crack, sending our papers across the floor. In a beat, his chest was pressed against mine, his fingers right where I liked them: around my jaw.

"And there is," he growled, abrasively. "You just don't need to know it."

I blinked up at his face. The tension made his contours appear even more chiselled. His nostrils flared as he glared down at me, each rasping breath pushing his chest into mine. I felt a flame ignite deep in my core, spreading heat fast around my body until I began to shake.

"Don't you trust me?" The question left my lips as a whisper.

"Yes. You know I do," he hissed through gritted teeth.

"Then… why won't you tell me what's going on?"

His breath seethed in and out through his clenched jaw. "It's for your own protection."

His closeness was burning me up almost as much as his fingers melted my skin, but we needed to have this conversation. I wrapped a hand around his forearm and pulled his hand away.

"My protection? From what? I've got half a mind to go there myself after dark and see what all the damn fuss is about." I turned my back to him and shook my head.

"What did you say?" he rumbled, menacingly.

At two steps away I was at a safe enough distance to face him again. I planted two hands on my hips and gave him my best pissed-off pout. "I said, I've half a mind to go there myself after dark and see what all the damn fuss is about."

"Don't fuck with me on this," he bit out.

I gasped. "What?"

With a face like thunder, he closed the gap again. "I said, don't fuck with me on this." He combined the last words with the ramming of both his palms against the wall either side of my head, caging me in.

He was so close I could almost taste him. "I will do it," I threatened, wanting to keep him there.

"You know what will happen if you do," he growled.

"That sounds like another threat, Rupert. Are you *trying* to turn me on?"

His nostrils flared and his eyes blackened. "If I was trying to turn you on, butterfly, my mouth would be having this conversation with another part of your body."

I almost collapsed as heat pooled between my legs. I loved that I inspired such intensity in him, but I hated that it could only travel inwards. The fury and the passion could never be unleashed. It would slowly burn us both up. At least, as long as our crisp, charred corpses could rest together, I would die happy. His nostrils flared above me, his eyelashes fluttering from the racing thoughts beneath.

"Don't push me, Vivian." He squeezed his eyes tight and his breath brushed my lips as he spoke. It sent me flying back to the sensation of his orgasm coming to life all over me, and I suddenly wanted more. *Needed* more.

"Or else?" I teased. I waited until he opened his eyes narrowly before I licked my tongue along my top lip and pulled it between my teeth. His gaze darkened, the indigo turning black as night, his furrowed brow pained.

"I don't know what's killing me more," he whispered. "The fucking *need* to kiss you or the pain of not knowing what you taste like."

It almost broke my heart.

"I'm sor—" I began, but in the beat of a second he filled my vision and his hot lips pressed ravenously against my mouth. The hollowness of my chest, my booming heart and the flame in my pelvis collided, and I opened my mouth, letting him storm in. His tongue was aggressive and dominant, swiping across mine with violent need. The more I opened up, the more he leaned in, until I could hardly breathe. I would have chosen death over stopping him.

A pained moan passed from his mouth to mine and I swallowed it, hoping it would be enough to keep him in the moment. I knew that the second he pulled back, this would never happen again. He had too much to lose. And it was all worth more than me.

His palms scraped down the wall. One slipped round my waist, just beneath the fabric of my sweater. The feel of his calloused fingers against my naked back made me levitate. The other threaded up through my hair, tugging me back down like he owned me, and his mouth imprisoned mine in a slow, nasty tongue kiss that made me wet.

He pulled me into his torso, his arms caging me in, and I felt him hard against my pelvic bone. I was so close to passing out. It still seemed laughable that I had done this to him. Impossible.

As though he could read my mind, he shifted slightly, rubbing himself against my stomach. Then it was my turn to moan. It left my throat, untethered and brazen.

Then, he was gone. Six feet away, to be exact. His eyes narrowed and a string of angry curses was spat from his lips.

"I can't do this, Vivian."

I gasped, still trying to catch my breath after that mind-numbing kiss. "What?"

"This…" he gestured to the space between us. "I have to choose a fiancée in two days." He stared at me like I had an answer. When it became clear I had no such thing, his shoulders dropped. "I can't do this."

"I know," I said in a whisper, and even though it was so far from what I really meant, I said, "Neither can I."

I UNLOCKED the door to the cottage and an air of finality seemed to hover over me. That kiss with Rupert told me everything. That he struggled with me being there, with everything I was. I knew that while I was on the island, he wouldn't be able to find peace. As soon as I'd gone, he would be able to get a clear mind, choose a sensible match – someone he could come to love over time. I knew I had to leave.

Even the main reason I'd come to this island didn't seem so compelling now. My sister's health. Of course I wanted to ease her pain, but I couldn't sacrifice my sanity or Rupert's. She needed me to be strong, not lovesick.

I did as I always did and made a beeline for the parlour. When I flicked on the light and looked at the pots below the windowsill, my heart sank again. Still nothing. And I was almost out of the fungus spawn. Even though Rupert had promised to get me the drug, he'd made it clear it would take time, and even then, he couldn't guarantee it. I had to continue with my plan B.

I'd tried compost from the cottage shed, I'd tried soil from the cottage's own garden, I'd tried the blindingly expensive growing kit Emerie had sent me, but, nothing. I had to think of something else.

I walked out of the parlour and turned off the light. As I passed through the kitchen, my eyes landed on the hand towel Rupert had written his name on. So much had happened between then and now, I hadn't actually read it. I sat at the kitchen table and carefully unfolded it. My pulse drummed at the base of my throat. Two words gripped my heart and wrung it dry.

Your Rupert.

I parted my fingers and let the towel float back down to the tabletop, then I sank my face into my hands and cried.

Chapter 29

*R*upert

"Well, don't you look handsome?"

Hector's voice melted round the doorframe like ice cream on a hot summer's day. It was the only comforting thing I was going to get in the next twenty-four hours.

"Anyone can look good in a bespoke Tom Ford suit."

"That isn't true, and you know it." Hector walked around me to the cocktail cabinet. "I need a stiff one. You?"

"Whatever you've got," I said. I honestly didn't care if I walked into that place tonight hammered. It would cost my family their reputation but I felt more reckless than ever before in my life. I simply didn't care.

Hector passed me a triple shot of whiskey with a single ice cube. "Do you remember the first time we attended one of these?"

. . .

I TOOK A LARGE SWIG, relishing the way it burned my throat. Maybe a few more of these and I would have a viable excuse for not speaking to anyone. I nodded. "Teddy Manson. I'd just turned twenty. You must have been seventeen."

"That's right. At the time it seemed like a wet fucking dream. There was Teddy, looking like he'd enjoyed several too many rich meals, his pants about to burst at the seams, cheeks all pink from the champagne. And he was surrounded by all these women, practically salivating over him because they wanted a slice of his family's fortune. They weren't interested in him, and I don't think he cared to be honest. He just saw pussy."

We both stared at the swirling amber in our glasses, avoiding the elephant in the room.

"Any idea who you'll choose?" he ventured, quietly.

"Nope," I shook my head. "None."

"Elspeth Cartwright?"

I snorted. "Father's favourite. That makes me want to deliberately avoid her."

"Elspeth's a good girl," Hector said. "Don't cut off your nose to spite your face."

I filled the space where a response would usually be required with another swig of whiskey.

"What about Sienna St. John?"

I shrugged. My answer remained the same. I didn't want to marry any of them.

"Adele Lamont?"

I gave a hollow laugh. "I wouldn't do that to her."

Hector huffed and walked across to the window. The sun was setting and the sky above had turned the colour of burning leaves. "People are arriving," he said, gazing at the driveway below.

"I'm thrilled to hear that," I replied, deadpan.

"I have duties, I'm afraid. I have to go. Mother wants me to 'warm up' the girls as they arrive. Put them at ease with my charming good looks and witty banter. And that's Caroline Bartholomew getting out of a car. I quite fancy her myself to be honest."

He placed his glass on a mahogany side table and passed me on his way to the door.

"Just pick someone, Rupert. You're going to hate it whatever happens, so my advice is to just do it, then learn to live with it. They're nice girls – you could do a lot worse."

I stared at a spot on the wall the whole time he spoke and remained fixed on it as the door closed. I've already picked someone, I thought. I'm just not allowed to have her.

TEN MINUTES and another triple whiskey later, one of Father's butlers knocked on the door.

"Mr. Thorn, sir, you are expected downstairs at the reception."

This was it. I took a deep, sobering breath, which only served to inhale the whiskey fumes deeper into my lungs. I didn't feel drunk enough. "Thanks," I replied on a tight sigh.

I dropped the glass on the same side table Hector had, although mine landed with a bang, and followed the butler down the corridor. It opened out to the balcony that over-looked the entrance hall. Some guests were hovering, taking glasses of Belle Époque from trays held aloft by highly polished waiters. A few of them glanced upwards, their sightings followed by mutterings of "There he is," and "Here comes the guest of honour." I wanted to spit in their sparkling drinks.

I followed the butler down the stairs and fixed a fake smile to my face, knowing that if I didn't at least look like I was happy to be there, my father would have something to say on the matter. And heaven forbid I risk casting a shadow over the respected Thorn family name. We turned a corner into the reception hall and a hush immediately fell over the two-hundred gathered guests. A few started to clap but I held up a firm hand signalling for them to stop. I didn't particularly want the most heinous night of my life to be accompanied by fucking applause.

I cut through the decadently dressed bodies, nodding politely at the women I knew had been summoned for the sole purpose of potentially becoming my wife. Elspeth, of all the women in my eye line, without a doubt shone the brightest. Her willowy figure was draped in pale grey silk that ran over her curves like a glittering waterfall. Her blonde hair had been contorted into an elaborate pattern of plaits, curls, pins and, by my less-than-expert-eye, not a small amount of pain.

Sienna stood six feet away with her parents, shining in a whole different way. Her waist-length auburn hair had been tamed into a twist that fell over her left shoulder, and complemented by a dark green ball gown adorned with crystals. Adele stepped forward from the centre of the gathering, her black bobbed hair straight and sleek. It matched her dark, feline eyes and shimmering fishtail gown encrusted with black sequins. She looked like a gothic mermaid and part of me wondered whether she'd consciously chosen black to signal her disapproval of this event and the role she had to play in it.

Of all the girls I'd grown up with, Adele was the only one I'd ever been fond of. Sure, I got a lot of female attention but it was rarely, if ever, returned. Adele never fawned over me though, unlike the others. She buried repressed anger, an underlying streak of bitterness. She too had been born into a life she didn't want. I wouldn't choose her because I wouldn't want to play a part in committing her to a life she had dreaded since we first met behind the gymnasium to spoke weed.

We exchanged a look of combined reassurance and dread, and I continued through the parting crowd. Before I reached my father, who'd made a point of saying he would guide me through the evening's proceedings, possibly so I didn't leave his sight and run for the hills, I saw *her*.

I knew she'd been invited, presumably because Mother wanted her to see I was fully off the market. I knew she didn't want to come. But we both knew suspicions would be raised if she didn't. In a single look I devoured her whole. She wore narcissus yellow and stood out like sunshine on a dark day. The satin draped around her collarbone and rested just off the shoulder. It clung to her curves like the skin of a viper and fell to her feet like the gown of a vintage starlet. Her brown unruly hair had been almost tamed for the occasion, the curls tumbling down her back, sleek and purposeful. Her freckled face was almost make-up-free, but for a slick of red across her lips. Her smile was timid and when my eyes dropped to her hands, they were shaking like butterfly wings in the wind. She was the brightest star in the entire room, and the one I would be most burned by if I touched it.

It took the sound of my father clearing his throat to make me realise I'd stopped mid-stride to look at the true vision in the room. It took all my strength to tear my gaze away from her and continue walking towards my parents.

"Darling," Mother purred through a sigh of relief that I'd actually shown up.

I kissed her on both cheeks. "Mother."

"Rupert." Father took my hand and shook it firmly. A waiter arrived instantly with a glass of champagne which I didn't need to be offered twice. I needed this evening to be blurred around the edges. Her eyes felt like summer on my back but I couldn't look around. There was a dagger pointed at my heart and the closer I let myself get to Vivian, the deeper it would cut.

"So, what happens now?" I asked in a bored tone, as guests finally resumed their conversations.

"The fathers are going to formally introduce you to their daughters. You will converse with each of the ten young women for exactly three minutes each, then dinner will be announced."

"Do you have a stopwatch?" I asked.

Either my sarcasm glided over his head or he chose to ignore it. "Angelina does," he clipped, nodding briefly to one of his many assistants standing at a nearby wall. "She will signal to me when your time is up with each."

I sighed heavily. "Well, then. What are we waiting for?"

I spent the next thirty minutes making polite, torturous

small talk with the buffoons my father called friends and their poor, pimped-out daughters. Each of the ten young women were beautiful, well-mannered, and immaculately presented. Some were flirtatious, others defiantly not. Adele and I made a point of discussing money and politics, which made my mother visibly shudder. But none of them could distract me from the presence of *her*.

She stayed out of my eye line, for which I was grateful, but there would be no avoiding her during the banquet. At the final nod from Angelina, my father clicked his fingers and the master of ceremonies announced that dinner would be served in the banquet hall.

It took about ten minutes for every guest to file through the giant doorway, checking for their seating positions around the table. This was where the inhabitants of the island, even the Consortium families, got a cold, hard look at where they stood in the pecking order. The closer one was seated to the host family, the higher up the hierarchy one sat. The Cartwrights sat next to my father and Ossian, the Barringtons next to my mother and Hector. As was traditional, the host's extended family sat further away to allow for this unsubtle display of marriage preference to take place. I caught Aro's eye as I sat at the head of the table. He nodded encouragingly, but I thought I caught a glimpse of pain darken his features.

"I want you to observe them all, Rupert," Father clipped in my ear. "Decorum at the table is a reflection of the way they behave in the home. You want a woman who is in command of her behaviour and her manners. Someone who can participate in intelligent conversation without dominating it." He leaned in until I could feel his sour breath on my cheek. "Someone who knows when to shut up."

I recoiled and darted my eyes to his face. It registered nothing but clarity and determination. My father had never been the most politically correct grown man I knew, and this wasn't the first time I'd heard brazen chauvinism pour from his mouth, but it never got easier to hear.

One first did follow swiftly. My appetite had taken a vacation. The most mouth-watering plates of seafood, meats, salads and cheeses were placed in front of me, but I could barely eat a bite. I noticed Mother glance worriedly at my father when I asked for a triple shot of whiskey.

"Take it easy, Rupert," she said, placing her hand over mine.

"I'm tense," I replied. I was also exhausted from avoiding eye contact with the only person in the room I wanted to look at. When the whiskey arrived, I lifted the tumbler to my lips and stared through the glass at Vivian. Her figure was distorted through the cut crystal but she was still the most beautiful woman in the room. I noticed her cutlery pause halfway to her mouth and she stared back at me. In that moment, my heart beat with hers, loudly, solidly, reaching across the table. When I lowered my glass I took her in with one last glance then looked away.

Seconds later, I heard the scrape of a chair against the marble floor and caught a vision of yellow in the corner of my eye. Looking over, I watched her turn quickly, revealing a delicate expanse of bare skin. I had no idea her dress was backless. One look at that delicate butterfly knocked all the wind out of my chest. My eyes caressed the length of her spine as she straightened, placed a hand on her neighbour's shoulder, then walked away. As she reached the door, she paused, half turning her head, just enough for me to see the tear that spilled down her cheek.

Everything in me wanted to run to her, spin her around and claim her, here, on the fucking floor, in front of everyone.

Instead, I swallowed, dryly, and watched her leave.

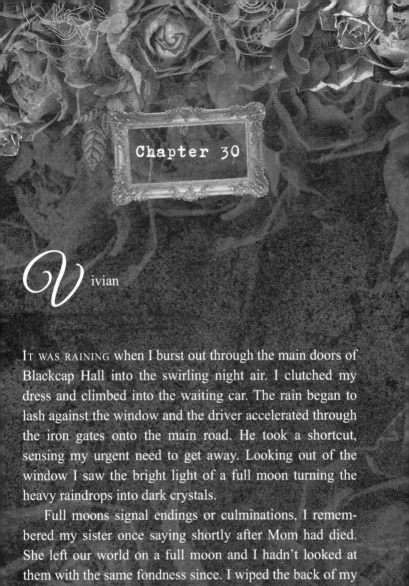

Chapter 30

*V*ivian

I<small>T WAS RAINING</small> when I burst out through the main doors of Blackcap Hall into the swirling night air. I clutched my dress and climbed into the waiting car. The rain began to lash against the window and the driver accelerated through the iron gates onto the main road. He took a shortcut, sensing my urgent need to get away. Looking out of the window I saw the bright light of a full moon turning the heavy raindrops into dark crystals.

Full moons signal endings or culminations, I remembered my sister once saying shortly after Mom had died. She left our world on a full moon and I hadn't looked at them with the same fondness since. I wiped the back of my hand across my cheek, unable to tell what was rain and what was tears.

MY HEART HAD BROKEN in that banquet hall. Something otherworldly existed between me and Rupert and I only saw it clearly for the first time when he gazed at me through cut crystal. It was as if the truth could only be seen through distorting glass, whereas lies could exist unchallenged in the clear light of day. Seeing Rupert surrounded by so many beautiful, perfectly deserving potential brides brought me face-to-face with the finality of us. I would have to sit on the sidelines from now on and watch as preparations were made for a marriage that would last the rest of his life. If the greatest kindness I could pay both of us in that moment was to remove myself from the pomp and pageantry that surrounded it, then remove myself I would.

Watching him entertain, like the gentleman he was, the far more beautiful ladies of the Isle of Crow made me sick to the stomach. Seeing Elspeth's long feline fingers grace his arm, hearing her tinkling laugh light up the room, made me want to curl up in a ball and hibernate for a very long time.

I felt the eyes of the banquet table on me as I left but I didn't care. I knew there would be gossip, but I didn't care. I was on this island for one thing and one thing only. To find a cure for my sister. Rupert or no Rupert. That one thought would have to keep me going. I was contracted to work for the Thorns for another eight months, but if I could get the mushrooms to grow sooner than that, I would find a way to leave. Even if it meant paying my way out of the contract. I would do it. I couldn't stay there anymore. I had to find a way to grow the damn mushrooms, and I would, even if it killed me.

I let myself into the cottage, hung up my coat and

dashed to the parlour with renewed hope. A full moon. Culmination. There had to be some growth, some evidence of my efforts coming to fruition. My heart dropped the second I opened the door. Still nothing. The spawn wouldn't last forever. My time was running out. I had to get my hands on the very soil the Thorns used, and soon.

As I stepped out of the parlour I came face-to-face with my reflection in the hallway mirror. I didn't have the heart to change. The yellow dress – another work of genius by Madame Gallette – was stunning. I would never again get to wear a work of art like this. I would treasure it for the rest of my life. It would always be known to me as the dress I wore when I fell in love with someone I would never be able to have.

I dragged my jewel-encrusted feet into the kitchen and poured myself a glass of wine, then leaned back against the island, sipping the cold liquid in a bid to soothe my burning heart.

I welcomed the sound of the heavy rain lashing against the windows; it helped to drown out my racing thoughts. When a crack of lightning appeared overhead, the room lit up like a spotlight on my pain. The rain had intensified the second I left Blackcap Hall, as though the weather was in perfect step with my mood. The deeper it dawned on me that Rupert and I could never be, the angrier the storm felt. I heard a dull thud against the door and let out a heavy sigh. The overhanging branch from the ancient oak outside must have finally lost hope, like me. When I heard the thud again, I placed the glass down on the counter. If the branch was swinging against the door, it might do damage, and this cottage was too perfect to be marred by a raging storm. One broken thing was enough for tonight.

I reached for my coat, took a torch from inside the hallway cupboard, and made my way to the door. The second I reached it, it banged again, making me jump backwards. I quickly fastened my coat and opened the door a crack. I didn't want to be hit if the branch was swinging heavily. The rain slammed through the gap and I had to blink, but before I had a chance to clear the rain-drops from my eyes, the door swung open, almost knocking me over, and suddenly, Rupert was in the room.

I pushed the door closed against the howling wind and turned to stare at him. "What are you doing here? The banquet isn't supposed to finish for another hour."

His shoulders heaved up and down, and rivers of rain ran down his coat into a puddle forming on the stone floor. He pushed his hood back and dragged a hand through his hair. The front section stayed flicked up as rain drops rolled off his thick, perfect eyebrows. "I had to leave," he replied, dryly. "And you know exactly why I'm here."

"Nothing can happen," I choked, alarmed at how viscerally I felt the truth. "You said so yourself." I gestured between the two of us. "Nothing can exist here."

He stepped forward and gripped my shoulders. "But it does."

I looked up through his damp lashes into the indigo eyes that haunted my dreams, and spoke with quiet, resigned calm. "You have to leave, Rupert."

He stared at me, unblinking, scanning my face for something I wasn't telling him.

"Rupert. Go." My words felt sour and I pressed my hands to his heart as he pushed me back against the wall. Even as I kept him at arm's length, I fisted his shirt so he couldn't leave. "You have to go." I swallowed and took a deep breath. "And I should leave the island."

"No." My arms buckled as he defied their resistance to push his forehead against mine. "Not yet. Don't go. Not yet."

My heart pounded in my ears and a dark voice warned me bleakly. *He isn't yours. He will never be yours.* "The longer I stay, the harder this will be," I said, trying to hold on to some modicum of sense.

"You're meant to be *mine*," he rasped, squeezing his eyes closed. "I should never…"

"Never what?" I gasped, breathless.

"I should never have objected to the tours. I should never have blackmailed you. I should never have kissed you. I should have fucking walked away before I knew who you were."

"What do you mean?" I croaked, all the emotion wrung out of my voice. "Who am I?"

His eyes opened, absorbing me into their black depths. "The one, Vivian," he whispered, hoarsely. "You're the one."

My pulse pumped at the base of my throat, drawing Rupert's eyes to it. He was telling me everything I wanted to hear, everything that deep down, I already knew. And everything my body needed so it could pump every freaking hormone I had around my body at warp speed. He could probably smell it on my breath. My chest physically craved him and so did my thighs, my pelvis, my core. I vibrated with need. I lifted my nose to brush against his. A small, affectionate gesture. It was the closest I could let myself get. A desperate whimper escaped his lips along with words I couldn't make out.

I closed my eyes. "What did you say?"

"Once," he whispered. "Just once."

I pulled back to look him in the eye. "Just once... *what*?"

A rough thumb stroked down my cheek. "Let me make love to you. Let me show you what we could have in another life. Let me give us something to hold on to. I can't carry on without knowing the depths of you. It *hurts* to not know."

The room spun. "We can't, Rupert," I replied, firmly. "This is your *engagement* night. We can't."

"Let me ask you something, butterfly." His eyes roamed my face and I saw so much adoration in them, my knees almost gave way. "Do you love me?"

My jaw dropped but I knew the answer without needing to think. "Yes," I whispered.

Before I could process what I'd just admitted to, his mouth was on mine, devouring me in a hard kiss. I melted into him as his lips caught mine again and again. He threaded his fingers through my hair, holding me still against him while his other hand pushed my coat off my shoulders. Once free, my hands reached up to his face, feeling the strong jaw move with unbridled determination. I was an instant juxtaposition. Drunk on lust and flying high, yet filled with a dread so deep it pinned me to the floor.

I trembled uncontrollably as he shrugged off his coat, flung it to the side and stroked his hands around my middle, pulling me flush against his front. His hard chest rose and fell in measured breaths and his lips devoured me like he couldn't get enough.

His mouth left mine for another brief moment. "Give

me all of you, Vivian," he breathed, and I nodded. We'd come this far and I wanted it too, more than anything. He kept his eyes open as he kissed me again, and lifted me off my feet. I hitched up my dress and curled my legs around his waist, then I looked deep into his eyes as he carried me up the stairs.

Mine was the first room we came to and he lowered me gently to the bed. He nestled between my thighs and sat back on his heels, dragging his gaze down my body.

"You were the most delicious-looking creature in that room, butterfly."

Then he closed his eyes and took a long, slow breath. Opening them again he rose up to his knees and pressed his hands into the bed covers either side of my head. He dipped down and lowered his lips to the corner of my eye. My eyelids fluttered shut and I let myself focus on the sensation of being worshipped by the man I was sure I loved.

He moved across to my other eye, then placed kisses on my brow, the bridge of my nose, the edge of my mouth, the tip of my chin, then his tongue darted out, drawing a hot wet line down my throat to my collar bone. He lifted himself up again and took both hands to the thin straps hooking my dress over my shoulders. Nipping them delicately between his fingers, he trailed the yellow strands down over my arms, so slowly my eyes almost rolled back in my head, until they hung loose at my wrists, exposing my bare breasts. I heaved in a nervous breath. He'd seen me almost naked before, but this was different. It felt as though he was looking right through to my bones.

"If we can only do this once, I want to do it properly," he murmured, closing a searing mouth around my nipple.

The decadent sound of sucking filled the otherwise silent room. My back arched and I gave a brazen moan. He moved his mouth across to my other breast, using his fingers to stroke and knead them gently, making my skin fizz. My back arched again of its own accord the second his lips closed in and I throbbed beneath him. He moved with such care and decadence it made my mouth water. His tongue traced a line down my stomach, then stopped above the lemon silk of my dress. I raised my head to look at him. His eyes were narrowed, his brow lines deep. He looked like he was battling with himself.

"You know that thing you asked me to do?"

I shook my head, my mind blank of everything but what was happening right there, right then.

"You want to hear *your* name, from *my* mouth, on *you*."

I swallowed. Oh God.

His fingers curled over the top of the dress and drew it down softly over my hips. I lifted my bottom, letting him graze the silk along the skin to the top of my thighs, down my legs and over my ankles. I shivered violently despite feeling so hot it was bordering on uncomfortable.

He gently dropped the shimmering fabric to the floor and returned his needy gaze to me. Without another word, he dove down, parted my thighs and pressed his hot mouth to my pussy. I cried out. I'd imagined him there so often but the reality of him lapping at my most tender spot was too much to contain.

He closed his lips around my tightened clit and sucked it like he had my nipple. Then he alternated with laps of his tongue. He groaned like no one was listening, but my body heard it with every sense and I shook with anticipation.

He hooked his arms around my thighs, and pressed them against his head while he licked and sucked. It was too much, too quickly.

Only a minute or two in and my body overrode every sense I had. "Rupert…" I warned.

He picked up the pace and the pressure, curling his tongue into my heat, flicking it across my bud and French kissing my sex like it was my mouth.

I came hard, his name hitting the walls with force. His thick arms held me steady as I writhed under his tongue, my back arching and bucking under his mouth. Then another sensation gripped me as he growled into my flesh. My name rolled off his tongue onto my clit and set off a whole new wave of convulsions. It felt as though the orgasm would never end.

I laid there, hazy, while he shed his jacket and loosened his bow tie. His lips quirked up in a half smile as he unbuttoned his shirt. He gently shook his head again as he watched me come round.

"I could do that for days," he said, then he leaned forward letting the edges of his shirt brush against my beaded nipples. He urged my lips open with his and swiped his tongue across mine. I kissed him back like I was starved, until he sat back on his heels again. His eyes didn't leave mine as he unbuckled his leather belt. "You even *taste* delicious."

"I'm one part chocolate and two parts wine," I sighed. "Of course I taste delicious."

My eyes dropped to his fly as he lowered the zip. He

did it slowly, prolonging the agony at wanting to see all of him. Every inch of flesh and blood.

"I want to fuck that sassy mouth of yours," he said, with not a trace of humour. I swallowed again, assessing him.

I watched his hand emerge, wrapped around a thick and long cock. It was dark, heavily veined and pulsing. I nodded, even though my heart was banging wildly against my rib cage. Rupert leaned forward resting his cock against my thigh and licked his tongue across my lips. "I'll try to be gentle with you, butterfly," he whispered. "But I can't promise anything." Then, he crawled up over me until the head nudged against my jaw. Something primal gripped me and I caught him in my mouth, sucking in the tip.

My name was wrenched from his throat as he braced his arms in the bed, holding himself steady. "*Jesus*," he hissed between clenched teeth. His cock throbbed against my tongue as he gathered himself, then slowly he pushed himself deeper. The head of him hit the back of my throat. I opened it instinctively and let him slide in as deep as I could allow. Then he pulled out slowly, a moan caught in his throat. I tugged his pants and boxers as far as they would reach and stroked my palms across the soft, taut skin of his ass. He groaned above me as I dug my nails in to take control of his thrusts.

I pulled back to lick the length of him from the base to the crown and smiled inwardly at the hiss that left his mouth when I wrapped my lips around him again. His balls slapped against my chin as we picked up the pace and my eyes watered with the rhythmic grazing against the back of my throat. But I couldn't get enough. I pulled back only to wet my lips, then devoured him again, needing to please him and taste him and relish every bit of him. Just this once.

"You take all of me so good, Vivian," he stated, his hips flexing into me. "Too fucking good." He pushed himself upright and looked into my eyes as he thrust smoothly in and out of my mouth. He reached down and threaded his fingers through my hair, caressing it softly while his rock hard cock plundered my throat. It was such an intimate gesture for such a raw and brazen act.

He hissed a curse then pulled out, leaving my mouth bereft. In a second, his lips were back on mine and he kissed me harder and more urgently than before. His hips shifted and I felt him at my entrance. Then his movements slowed, deliberately. "The depths of you," he whispered into my mouth. "I want to feel them."

He reached down and parted my legs then gently pushed a finger into my heat.

I sighed with an overwhelming sense of relief.

Rupert's eyes closed and his jaw ticked. "Make that sound again," he urged, pushing a second finger inside.

I didn't need to force anything or pretend. The gush of relief that escaped my chest was real. I was balled up with need and he was unravelling me, finger by finger.

"Again," he ordered, pushing a third finger into me. My walls closed snug around him and I moaned aloud.

His eyes still closed, he shook his head. I watched the veins in his arm thicken as he held himself above me. "God, Vivian. What are you doing to me?"

What was he talking about? What was *he* doing to *me*?

"Rupert," I gasped. "I'm going to come and I want it to be on you… on your…" I couldn't say the word but his eyes shot open and he stroked my insides, making my teeth grit.

"You will, butterfly. But first, I want to feel you come on my fingertips. I need to feel you come apart from the inside out."

I reached for his wrist. I wanted to hold the arm he brought me to orgasm with. I looked deep into his eyes and fingered his palm as he stroked the inside of me. I traced the top of his thumb as he circled the tip around my clit. I gripped his wrist as he fucked me with a fourth finger, pushing them deep and massaging my walls with exceptional skill. My eyelids fluttered closed in ecstasy.

"I can feel you getting close," he murmured, his rhythm unwavering. "You're tightening around my knuckle. Open your eyes."

I obeyed and, with effort, focused on his face. "Keep them open. I want to see your soul when you come for me, Vivian."

His words pushed me over the edge and a rush of heat made me jerk upwards. My stomach muscles clenched tight, buckling me in two. My vision blurred. He'd found a spot inside me and was lighting it up with his fingertips, and it kept on going. "Eyes on me," he ordered. I focused drunkenly on his dark irises, watching his arm muscles flexing in my peripheral as he continued to massage a relentless orgasm out of me. When it finally released me from its heavenly grip, Rupert's mouth landed on mine again and the head of his cock nudged against my now sopping entrance. "That's the most beautiful thing I've ever seen," he murmured against my tongue.

"What was?" I croaked. He inched inside of me and my eyes rolled back in my head.

"Your soul."

I reached down to pull him deeper but he held himself rigid. "Easy, butterfly. I want to savour this." I felt him swallow. "I need to…"

I silently finished his sentence. *Because we only get to do this once.*

He eased his way to the very edge of me, pausing to breathe. Then he thrust short, sharp and deep, as though trying to reach a place my body was denying him.

"Relax, butterfly," he moaned into my ear. "Let me in."

He remained still as I slowly, consciously, let go, opening up a space I'd never let anyone enter before. He pushed himself into it with an animalistic groan. "*Yes*, Vivian. How does it feel?"

I tried to put into words the sensation but it was inexplicable. "Overwhelming," was all I could manage.

He grabbed a handful of hair and held me still as he softly tongued my mouth. Then, he pushed further into me, further than anyone else had been, further than I thought was humanly possible. I lit up inside and gasped into his mouth.

"There it is," he smiled against my lips. "I've got you."

I marvelled at the satisfied look on his face as he gently rotated his hips. My eyes rolled back into my head. I'd never felt anything like it.

"You're so beautiful," he breathed, kissing the underside of my jaw. My skin was burning with desire and every kiss he placed on me stoked the fire. His movements picked up pace and his strokes lengthened until I could feel every ridge entering me and journeying to my core. The more I relaxed around him, the more it felt as though he'd always been there, that in some sick and twisted way, we'd been made for each other. He moaned into the side of my throat and I ran my hands down his back, kneading the hard muscles beneath his skin.

How can you be so perfect?

"You make me perfect," he whispered, dipping his tongue between my breasts. I froze, realising I must have spoken the words aloud. He felt it and his eyes darted back to mine. "From the very first second I saw you, I've been a different person. You've made me want to do better, and be better. If I'm perfect, it's because of you."

I reached up and tugged my fingers through his hair. "I love you, Rupert," I whispered. "So much it hurts." And right in that moment, I believed it with all my heart.

He rammed his lips onto mine. I felt a tear roll down my cheek, but my eyes were dry. He moved his mouth to my ear. "I keep telling myself it's a good pain," he said, his voice tinged with desperation. "At least if we feel some pain, we know we've lived."

I nodded against his cheek, not wanting to say that if life felt this painful, I didn't want it.

It was only later I realised he never said he loved me back.

Chapter 31

*R*upert

I HELD BACK for as long as I could but the feeling of being inside her made me crazed. I was so deep I knew I was massaging the very depths of her. She was perfectly snug, pulling me in with each thrust. I never wanted it to end.

"You are incredible, Vivian," I said, pressing kisses to her mouth as I moved on top of her. She responded with little gasps that told me she was close. I loved that I knew that. That I knew when my little butterfly was about to come. I'd felt her on my tongue and around my fingers. She was soft and delicious – everything I'd dreamed about. As I nipped her lip between my teeth, she gasped my name. It was game over. The final push.

I fisted her hair tightly so she couldn't move and fastened her ankles behind my back, then I drove into her so hard she cried out in shock. I didn't stop. I was on another plane. *Fuck, fuck, fuck.*

I PUNCTUATED each thrust until my balls tightened and I roared out her name. She tightened around me and gripped her legs to my sides so hard I bruised. I kept thrusting, coaxing her through, until my name fell from her lips softly, as though she had no energy left.

I held her tightly, feeling her breath slow and her heart rate return to normal. I didn't want to let her go. In the end, it was she who broke the spell.

"Rupert… I really need to pee."

I bit back a laugh and reluctantly rolled off her soft body.

When she returned from the bathroom, I was lying on my back, my hands beneath my head.

"So, you saw it, huh?" she asked.

"Saw what?" I asked, lazily.

"My soul." She slid beneath the covers beside me and propped herself up on one arm.

I stared up at the ceiling, enjoying the sensation of her gaze warming the side of my face. "I did."

"What did it look like?"

I took a deep breath and released it slowly. "It's hard to put into words. It wasn't something I saw with my eyes. I sensed it all around me, like a warm halo that felt and smelled like you."

"Smelled like me? Are you saying my soul smells?" I rolled over to face her and frowned. "I'm sorry," she shook her head. "It's just… it's beautiful hearing you talk about my soul. I'm not sure how to handle it."

"What is there to handle? I saw your soul. It felt and smelled like you. It wrapped me in a blanket of light and made me feel as though everything was going to be okay. That nothing else mattered. It felt like it was part of me."

Her face stilled. Only her eyelids moved in a slow blink. "If that's what it was…" she whispered, "then I saw yours too."

We stared at each other for a few long seconds, then I pushed my fingers through the hair at the nape of her neck and brought her onto my mouth. She kissed me back with fevered restlessness and I felt myself go hard instantly.

Reluctantly, I released her with a grunt. "I'm going to fuck you again, Vivian," I warned.

Her eyes danced. "I thought you said we could only do it once."

"One night, Vivian," I growled, pushing her onto her back. "I meant one night."

She tipped her head towards the clock on the wall. The short hand was pointing at the number two. "It's already the next day."

I was all out of patience. "Do you want me to fuck you again or not?" I leaned forward and bit her neck, to which she squealed.

"Yes! Fuck me Rupert. Fuck me until I see stars up there."

"Oh, butterfly," I smiled, brushing my lips across her ear. "If you can still tell which is up, we're not finished."

IT WAS five a.m. when we looked at the clock again. I had never before wanted time to slow down as much as I did in that moment. I knew I would have to leave soon to face whatever music my parents decided to put on to illustrate their disappointment in me.

"Are you ok?" she whispered, pulling my eyes away from the clock.

I nodded and kissed her forehead. "Right now I am. In a couple of hours… maybe not."

"What will happen when you get home?" she asked, softly.

I shook my head. "I don't want to talk about it with you."

Her two small, warm palms at either side of my face drew my eyes to hers. "I know you don't, but we're both in this mess. We may not be able to be together again like this, but I've given you my heart, Rupert. And apparently my soul," she added with a shy smile. "The least we can do is share the burden somehow. What was it you said to me? *Let me in*."

"That was different. I was talking with my cock, butterfly."

She raised both brows. "And I'm talking with my ladyballs, sir."

My jaw opened in shock. "You didn't just call me sir."

She sat up, defiantly. "Yes, I did."

"Fuck me," I hissed, looking up at her. "That makes me want to spank you."

"As much as I think I would *love* that, sir, you have to leave soon, and I need to know what's awaiting you."

I sighed out a heavy boulder of air. How could I be denied this woman? This perfect, funny, sassy, *gorgeous* woman? I must have done something heinously shit in a former life.

"My parents will request a meeting. They'll want to know why I disappeared last night, and why I wasn't in my rooms. And they'll want to know my decision."

She cleared her throat. "And what if you haven't decided?"

That was easy. "They'll decide for me."

She swallowed and considered my response before speaking again. "Who do you think they would choose?"

I squeezed the bridge of my nose to black out the vision of my parents. I didn't want them in this room with Vivian, even if only on the insides of my eyelids. "Elspeth Cartwright."

She held a hand over her mouth, then nodded.

Seeing her wordlessly accept my fate did something to me, and suddenly I saw my future in true, unblemished clarity. And it wasn't with Elspeth. It was with Vivian. I was infused with conviction. With hope. Maybe it was delivering the running order of my morning that made me realise how fucking absurd it all was. Maybe it was the inexplicable connection Vivian and I had created over the past eight hours – and ten weeks. Whatever the reason, it made no sense to me to marry someone like Elspeth just to keep my father happy. So what if they disowned me? I could make my money elsewhere. I could move to London with Vivian, start a new life. What was stopping me?

I sat up and held her face softly. "I'm not going through with it."

She gulped loudly. "What?"

I laughed. A loud, hearty, reckless laugh. "I'm not going to marry any of them. How can I when I want you? Only you?"

"Rupert," she frowned. "What are you saying?"

"I'm saying, my parents can fuck their engagement."

A hand flew back up to her mouth, failing to hide her

shock. "You can't, surely. After the banquet – it must have cost a small fortune... And, what about the Consortium?"

"My parents can afford to hold a banquet every day of the week if they chose to, and everyone else was so drunk they wouldn't have remembered they'd even attended one. And the Consortium can go screw themselves."

She shook her head in disbelief.

"There is the matter of being disowned and disinherited," I added. "Which is a small price to pay for getting to be with someone I actually care about."

"No, Rupert," she pleaded. "Don't leave your family for me. We don't even know what this is—"

"Where've you been for the last eight hours?" I asked, catching her breath in a deep kiss like she needed a reminder.

When she pulled back, her lips were like ripe rosebuds. So plump that if a thorn were to pierce them, they would bleed for days.

I stared at her. "I know what this is," I said, without a trace of doubt. "And if I can't have heaven, I'll settle for raising hell."

"Rupert," she warned, her eyes wide. "People burn in hell."

I caught her lips in another kiss. "Don't worry about me, butterfly. I like it hot."

She sighed out a trembling breath. "At the very least, don't do anything rash. Please Rupert. There are things to think about. My job, my sister, your life... Can you pretend to go along with this engagement until we can come up with a plan?"

I dragged an impatient hand through my hair and let out a low growl. I didn't want to wait. I'd seen my future and I was done with waiting for it to begin. But, she was right. If we were going to do this, we should do it properly.

"Fine."

She sighed with relief. "I still think you're nuts. You have *everything*."

I inhaled her form wrapped around me. "But you are the only thing worth keeping."

———

LEAVING VIVIAN LYING IN BED, the sheets in disarray around her perfect, milky, voluptuous body, her hair fanned out across her pillow, her sex-drained eyes following me out of the door, was enough to make me want to throw the whole engagement out of my third floor bathroom window. But, my butterfly was right. The only way we could make this work without ripping our lives to shreds was if I played along. For a short while, at least.

It was seven a.m. when my driver rolled up to the front door of Blackcap Hall. I nodded to the doorman on my way in. It was probably the first time he'd ever seen me smile. The corridors were still, my footsteps echoing along the wooden floor as I made my way up the stairs to my rooms. I was relieved no one was around. I assumed they were all sleeping off their hangovers, like most days. Once they'd surpassed a certain threshold, there wasn't much else for the rich to do other than drink. Hangovers were par for the course.

I opened the door to my suite and walked inside, finally letting out a long breath. The walls and corridors of Blackcap Hall had always felt oppressive to me, which was why I chose to spend so much time on the mainland. It was only once inside my rooms I felt fully able to breathe. I threw my jacket into a basket for dry-cleaning and walked across the living room. My bed beckoned me through the gap in the door and I needed some sleep before I faced the baying crowds.

"Where the hell have you been?"

A sharp voice from the shadows made every muscle in my body tense and I spun around to face the draped window. Only a thin shard of light revealed the form of a woman sitting in my favourite armchair, her legs and arms crossed, ready to head into battle.

"Good morning, Mother. Why are you in my suite?"

"Why did you leave the banquet?"

I ground my teeth. I knew this was going to happen. "I was free to leave at any time. You told me that yourself."

"It was bad form. Where did you go?"

"I drove around."

"You'd had too much whiskey to drive. Don't tell me you were *that* stupid, on the night of your banquet of all times."

"I had *my driver* drive me around."

"Where to? The roads were deserted. The chief constable confirmed that."

"And he has omnipotent vision, does he?"

"Rupert!" Her voice sharpened further and her lips narrowed into a point. It struck me that Ossian, in a certain light, was the spitting image of Mother. They were far more alike than I'd dared to believe. She stood, fiercely, bracing her hands by her sides. "What are you playing at?"

I shrugged. "I was having my own little bachelor party," I lied. "Just me and Alan, my driver. You know I've never been one for big celebrations."

Her eyes narrowed as if she was trying to work out whether or not to believe me.

"So, did you choose a girl, or not?" she snapped.

"Not," I answered. "Funnily enough, I can't decide between Girl A whom I have no feelings for, and Girl B whom I have no feelings for." I couldn't resist digging the knife in just once.

"Well, then, your father and I did the right thing." A look of smug satisfaction crawled across her pointed features.

"And what 'thing' was that?"

She smiled so sweetly I wanted to boil her up and turn her into toffee. "It's settled, darling. On December fifteenth, you will marry Elspeth Catherine Cartwright. Congratulations."

She slid past me to the door and held it wide as she departed. "I have no doubt you will be very happy together."

Then the door slammed closed, the noise punctuating my hatred for everything my name stood for.

Chapter 32

*R*upert

THE FLOORBOARDS by the window groaned under the weight of my nine-hundredth paced length since Mother had left my rooms. The anger simmering in my bones hadn't abated in the slightest. Any second now, an announcement would appear in the local paper and word would spread across the island like wildfire. Elspeth's parents would be arranging a celebration and we'd have our first official 'date'. I had to get out of this quickly.

A soft knock came at the door and it opened a crack.

"Come in, Aro," I grumbled.

He walked in and let the door close gently behind him. His manner always soothed me and he seemed to know when I needed that.

"How are you holding up, kid?" he asked, joining me at the window. As much as I'd stared at it, the view hadn't changed. It was still bleak and claustrophobic.

. . . .

I HUFFED OUT A SIGH. "NOT GREAT."

"I'm sorry," he said, patting me on the back. "I truly am. But she's a great girl. She'll make you happy, I'm sure."

"I'm not marrying her, Aro."

"What?" I felt his confused gaze pan towards me. "You did choose Elspeth, didn't you?"

"No, Mother did. But it doesn't matter. I'm not marrying her."

He turned away again. "You don't mean that."

"I do," I said, firmly.

"Think of everything you'll lose, Rupert. You wouldn't be so stupid."

I turned to him. "What's stupid is staying here and going through with something I've never wanted, all because other people want me to run a corrupt, greedy business and carry on the supposedly revered Thorn family name. I don't want to be a part of any of it."

Aro took a deep breath and thinned his brow. "I'm going to ask you something, Rupert. And I want you to think carefully about your answer, ok?"

"Ok." I pushed my hands into the pockets of my day-old suit.

"Do you care about the people on this island? The people who've entrusted us – our family especially – with their care and their livelihood for generations? Do you?"

"Of course I do."

"Are you prepared to abandon them when your father deports you to the mainland without a penny to your name, never to be allowed back on this soil again? Do you trust your brother to act in their best interests when you are out of the picture?"

I knew the answer and it physically hurt to admit it. "No. I don't trust him."

Aro walked to the same chair my mother had sat in, sighed heavily and looked up at me. "You've been doing to Ossian exactly what I've been doing to your father."

I frowned. "What do you mean?"

"I know you've been deliberately sabotaging parts of the operation."

My pulse thundered through my temples. "That's not tru—"

He held up a hand. "You don't have to admit or deny it, Rupert. Just know this. I did the same to your father when he set up various shady businesses. He seemed to be drawn to anything grey, anything that meant fast money, whatever the method. It worked. It slowed him down. It made him lose interest quicker. It stopped countless people being exploited and hurt. I can see what you're doing, Rupert, and I want you to know, it's helping. It's making a difference. Even if it doesn't feel like it."

"Didn't you ever speak to Father about it? Wouldn't that have been easier?"

Aro shook his head with a barren laugh. "I tried, once. He just shut me out, did his dirty dealings in secret. Just like Ossian has done with you."

"Has he ever suspected you?" I asked, turning away from the window.

"Yes, he did. That's why I don't do so much anymore."

"Why? What happened?"

"Ossian," Aro spat. "Ossian is what happened."

I steadied my breathing, somehow knowing what Aro was about to say.

"Sinclair used *his* son, to hurt *my* son, to hurt *me*."

My stomach floundered. "The acid attack."

Aro nodded, as though he couldn't say the words aloud.

"My father put Ossian up to that?" I felt sick.

"We'll never know for sure, but Ossian and Dax were friends until that point. That's partly how Ossian lured him into the shed where he kept the chemicals. Dax trusted Oz."

"I can't believe it," I muttered. "I mean, I suspected Ossian might have been involved, but not that Father was in on it too."

"And I know Ossian can be a nasty piece of work, but I can't imagine he would have done that of his own volition."

We remained in silence for a few minutes while I digested the blow.

"So, what are you saying, Aro?"

He looked up at me again. His expression was tired and he seemed to have aged considerably, even since the banquet. "Get married. Stay close. Keep doing what you're doing. It's the only way we can keep the islanders safer for longer."

I glared at him as the bottom fell out of my heart.

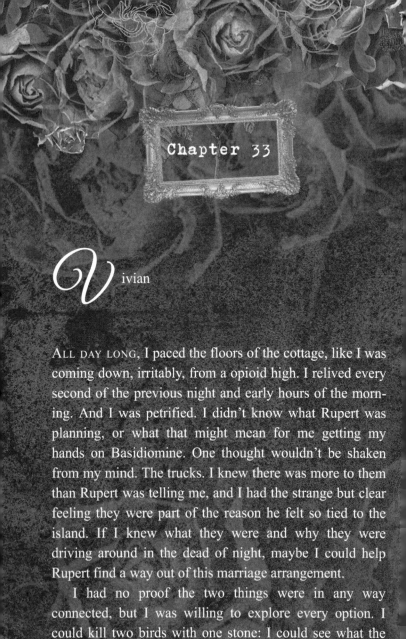

Chapter 33

*V*ivian

ALL DAY LONG, I paced the floors of the cottage, like I was coming down, irritably, from a opioid high. I relived every second of the previous night and early hours of the morning. And I was petrified. I didn't know what Rupert was planning, or what that might mean for me getting my hands on Basidiomine. One thought wouldn't be shaken from my mind. The trucks. I knew there was more to them than Rupert was telling me, and I had the strange but clear feeling they were part of the reason he felt so tied to the island. If I knew what they were and why they were driving around in the dead of night, maybe I could help Rupert find a way out of this marriage arrangement.

I had no proof the two things were in any way connected, but I was willing to explore every option. I could kill two birds with one stone: I could see what the trucks were all about and I could pocket some of the mysteriously nutritious soil while I was there.

. . .

I WOULD HAVE to do it in the dead of night.

I was determined.

I was going to enter the Sunken Glade.

I finally sat at the kitchen counter dressed in black leggings, a hoodie, a beanie hat and a light coat, jigging about like a child with chicken pox, waiting for night to fall. When it did, I threw everything I could possibly need into my pockets – a torch, scissors, plastic bags, a garden trowel – and walked out of the cottage. Given my predicament with cars and Rupert not trusting anyone to try toppling me off a cliff again, I'd borrowed Minty's bicycle. I wasn't a cyclist by any means, but needs must when the devil drives. I left via the back of the cottage so the security guy in the grey Range Rover wouldn't see me, and set off further up the main road, using a head torch to light the blackened surroundings. Using my memory, instinct and the power of smell, I made my way to Thorn Pharmaceuticals, or rather, the edge of the cultivation sets. I had to find answers, and fast, before Rupert did something that landed us both at the opposite side of the ferry crossing.

I CROUCHED behind the hedgerow and watched. I knew there were cameras laid out along the fence but I wasn't completely sure of their movements. I spotted two facing each other but moving slowly. I vaguely recalled Rupert saying they needed to upgrade the security system. I could only hope the cameras didn't have motion sensors.

I watched the cameras swing in opposite directions - one towards me, the other away. They were covering a lot of ground and there wouldn't be much room for error. I timed the movement by counting slowly in my head. There was roughly a forty second period during which neither camera was on the fence itself. It wouldn't leave me much time to scale it unseen but it was better than nothing. My heart pounded harder and harder, and not for the first time in the last hour I questioned what the hell I was doing. But I couldn't not do this.

As the camera to my right began inching back towards the other side, I ran, crouched at the knees to the fence. At this time of night, the moon was directly above, ensuring that any overhanging branches cast a shadow deep enough to conceal me against the fence as the other camera angles itself towards me. I pressed my back to the fence and held my breath as the lens flashed in the reflection of the moon, passing over my form as I hid. This was the exact point I would have to climb, when the cameras were at their widest. I breathed out slowly and waited for the cameras to move through their ninety degrees. As soon as they were back in primed position, I launched myself upwards, grasping onto the wire with both hands and pulling myself up. I had never been sporty, and I rarely worked out, so I had zero upper body strength and I was feeling it now. My forearms and biceps screamed as I pulled myself up. *Eight, nine, ten, eleven.*

My eyes darted from one camera to the other as I continued to dig the toe of my boots into the small holes offered by the wire netting. Fourteen, fifteen. Fuck, I wasn't even near the top; I still had about six feet to go. I reached up to grasp higher still when one of my feet slipped out of its wire cradle. The weight of my body falling dragged the palms of my hands down and my fingers curled painfully around the thin wires. The pain was so acute it felt as though my hands were being sliced in two. I kicked my feet wildly, finally wrenching out a breath of relief when the pressure eased off my fingers. I knew there would be blood. DNA. And I realised I was doing something unutterably stupid. Why hadn't I pressed Rupert on the delay? Why hadn't I tried to befriend Jasper whom I'm sure would have been able to sneak me something? Why had I chosen the most dangerous, perilous route? *Twenty-eight, twenty-nine. Shit.*

With renewed vigour I gripped the wire, dug in my toes and pulled myself up the last six feet. *Thirty-three, thirty-four...* holy crap, I didn't even have time to climb down the other side, and it was an eighteen foot drop. *Thirty-five...* I gripped the bar at the top of the fence and swung my left leg over so that I laid straddling it. I looked over the edge and almost vomited. *Thirty-seven...* One glance up at the camera ahead and I knew my time was up. If I didn't jump now, I'd be caught. I'd lose my job, I'd lose my life here, I'd lose Rupert... Without thinking, I grabbed the bar with both hands, swung my right leg over and let my body swing like a pendulum over the other side of the gate. Then I squeezed my eyes shut and let my hands slide free.

It felt as though I'd been falling for days by the time my legs crumpled beneath me and I landed hard and heavy on the firm soil. I clung to the fence, biting back a squeal from the pain in my hands, knees and ankles. I waited with my breath held tight in my lungs until the cameras orbited through their range. As soon as the coast was clear again I scrambled away from the fence to a hedgerow beyond and concealed myself inside its wooden tendrils. I waited a few seconds to catch my breath and inspect my hands. They looked like thorns had dragged over them leaving a criss-cross formation of bloody scratches in their wake.

For a second or two I savoured the feeling that I was over the other side. Free. No sirens had been triggered, no alarm bells had rung. No one was any the wiser I was on forbidden Thorn land, oh so close to the raw goods the whole of the western world was so interested in.

Now safe, I looked out into the woodland. A tremble ricocheted along my spine as I remembered the last time I entered a woodland alone. I still didn't know who had wrapped a hand around my throat and threatened to end my life on this island before it had even begun.

But I was stronger now, and I had a good reason for being here – a purpose. I felt over the top of my coat pocket reassuring myself the torch was still there should I need it. But I was determined to go as far as I could without any risk of being seen so I kept it snug and secure inside my coat.

Slowly, I ventured forwards, away from the hedge towards the dense tree formation of the woodland. I stepped carefully so as not to make any more of a sound against the fallen twigs and leaves than any other wild animal out at night. After about ten minutes of tiptoeing through shadows, the smell of the agarics hit my nostrils. That was when I knew I was about half a mile from the edge of the cultivation set. Just as I came to within two-hundred yards of the border, a moving light caught my attention. It was heading for the Glade.

I unpacked my binoculars and focused the lenses. For once, the darkness was an advantage and I could spot the moving light easily. There were actually two lights – head-lights – moving towards the area Rupert had been so determined I couldn't let anyone enter. The glow of the headlights suggested they belonged to a truck or lorry, just like the other trucks I saw that Rupert had quickly dismissed. The vehicle disappeared over the horizon and I lowered the binoculars. Almost immediately, another vehicle appeared further behind. *What the fuck?* I raised the binoculars again and focused on another truck, the same size as the first. It too was headed towards the Glade. The only part of the island deemed off limits to anyone, even those who lived here.

An uneasiness gripped me. How did the trucks get there? The Isle of Crow frequently had cargo ships dropping off supplies – the trucks could have travelled on one of those. But more importantly, why wait until the dead of night? What were they doing that they couldn't do in broad daylight? This was it. If I was going to find any answers with which to help Rupert, I had to find out what was going on.

Before I knew it, my feet were crossing into the border of the south cultivation set and taking me around the outer edge towards the Glade. It took less time than I expected because, somehow, I ran. Until I couldn't run anymore because another fence blocked my path. This one wasn't as high as the outer perimeter fence but it was charged. If I touched it, not only would everyone connected to the site be notified of an intruder, but I would suffer an electric shock extreme enough to cause temporary paralysis. I scanned the fence in both directions, looking for some sort of lever, like an overhanging branch or something to get me over it. But the Thorns had everything covered. All tree growth had been cut back by at least twenty yards either side of the fence. Refusing to feel defeated, I walked quietly alongside the fence until I spotted it. A gap wide enough that I might – *just might* – be able to get through without inflicting upon myself a six Kilovolt wake-up call.

I dropped to my knees and placed my hands through the hole and onto the ground at the other side. Then I held my breath and dipped my head. A stray hair brushed the fence and the wire sparked to the side of my face. My heart beat thundered through my chest. I questioned again what the hell I was doing but it was too late now. I had to know what the trucks were for, otherwise, knowing me, I would blurt it out without thinking one day, only for Rupert to ask how I'd come by them in the first place. I had to do it. I couldn't waste any more time. I closed my eyes and pushed off with my feet, crawling through the hole at the bottom of the fence. I had no idea how far through I'd reached, so I just kept going, my held breath burning my lungs. Eventually I stopped, opened my eyes and looked behind. I'd made it through unscathed. The relief was knees-frozen-to-the-floor immense and I hung my head as it washed over me.

I jumped to my feet and ran again, this time along a path through the set. The red tops there were large and plump, closer to cultivation, and the vile smell was so intense I had to pull my jacket around my nose and mouth in an attempt to muffle it. My legs carried me right the way across the set to where the land dropped down towards the sea, to the Glade, where the lorries were headed. I merged into the shadow of a tree and watched the two lorries pull up next to each other. Another moving light to my right notified me a third lorry was also heading that way. I heard voices and instinctively clung closer to the tree trunk. I listened carefully and realised there were people actually *working* here. In the *middle of the night.* A sense of dread started up around my heart. *What's going on Rupert? What aren't you telling me?*

Keeping to the shadows of the trees, I inched my way carefully down the hillside until I came to one more, final, fence. Just as I began to assess it for a way through, I heard a series of clicks. I looked behind me and there it was. The security camera. My heart sank into the earth below as the realisation hit me. I'd been caught. In a matter of minutes I would be thrown off the island. I'd never get to see Minty again. Or Rupert. Or Hector. My throat constricted painfully as a lump lodged itself there. *What have I done? What was I thinking?* And one last thought that rose above the rest. *It's over.*

With nothing left to lose, I ran and threw myself up the side of the fence. It was made of wire, like the first, but wasn't as high, so I scaled it quicker. I didn't even look down as I reached the top; I simply let go. Landing in a crouch, I leapt up and ran towards the trucks. If I was going to be thrown off the island, it had to be for something. I needed to know what the trucks were there for. The smell of the red tops intensified to the point my eyes began to stream.

As I glanced down to wipe them I noticed the ground was bare. There were no more red tops.

So, what was that smell?

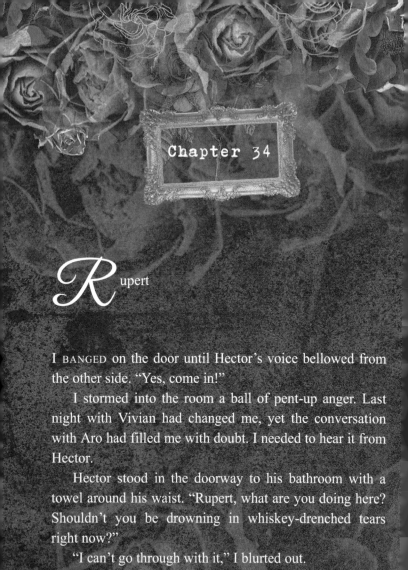

Chapter 34

*R*upert

I BANGED on the door until Hector's voice bellowed from the other side. "Yes, come in!"

I stormed into the room a ball of pent-up anger. Last night with Vivian had changed me, yet the conversation with Aro had filled me with doubt. I needed to hear it from Hector.

Hector stood in the doorway to his bathroom with a towel around his waist. "Rupert, what are you doing here? Shouldn't you be drowning in whiskey-drenched tears right now?"

"I can't go through with it," I blurted out.

"With what?" Hector's tone was one of boredom as he reached for a couple of lowballs in his prohibition-era cabinet. "The requisite post-announcement bender? Ossian's lasted three days. I had my money on you taking it to four."

. . . .

"The engagement!" I yelled. "The marriage. All of it."

A look of confusion crossed his face as he looked up. "Are you drunk right now?"

I needed to get his attention. I stalked across the room, took one of the lowballs from his hand and threw it at the wall. It smashed, raining small diamonds of glass down onto the marble floor.

"Jesus! What the fuck, Rupert?"

"I need you to hear me, Hector. I can't do it. I can't marry Elspeth."

The confusion intensified. "But... your engagement has been announced. You agreed to it. You can't suddenly change your mind."

I snatched the other lowball from his hand and flung that against the wall too. "I didn't agree to it. I didn't agree to anything. I wasn't even fucking *there*."

"Yes, you were. I sat right next to you at dinner."

"And then I left." I glared at him, willing him to remember through the drunken haze that most people had found themselves in by the time the fish course was served.

"How? Why?"

I raised an arm glacially towards his door. "I just walked out." Then I turned back to face him and shook my head. "You know why."

His shoulders fell as though he was finally giving to the inevitability of acknowledging what he already knew. "Vivian."

I grabbed the whiskey bottle he'd been about to pour, popped out the cork and swigged some back.

"She left halfway through dinner. You went after her."

He watched as I continued to swig neat whiskey like it was water. "What happened, Rupert?"

I lowered the bottle, wiped the back of my hand across my mouth and ran my tongue over my teeth.

"You didn't." I detected fear in Hector's voice. "You didn't sleep with her."

I glanced up at him neither confirming nor denying. I was still gauging his reaction.

"On the night of your engagement. Rupert, tell me you didn't."

"I wasn't engaged," I said, in a voice I hardly recognised as my own. "I never made a choice."

"But… then… how?" For the first time, I saw a frown line appear in Hector's young brow, and I hated that I was the reason for it.

"They decided for me, Mother and Father. This morning. Made the decision before I even got home."

"You spent the night with Vivian." Hector glanced at the floor trying to comprehend what I'd done. "When you should have been announcing your engagement."

"Yes." I took another swig of whiskey. "And I don't regret it for one second. I don't want Elspeth, Hector. I don't want any of them. Only Vivian."

He lifted his head finally, his eyes darting between mine. "When did this happen?"

I sighed and passed the bottle back to him. He proceeded to swig back twice what I had. "The very second she arrived at Blackcap Hall. I told you."

"But I thought you'd got over it. We talked about it. You knew then it couldn't happen. But you pursued her anyway?"

"I didn't pursue her." I walked across to one of the dressers and picked up a framed photograph. It was a picture of Mother, Father, Hector, Oz and me. I was six and Hector was two. It was the only picture I'd ever seen of us so young. It was as though no other pictures had been taken before that, which I always thought was strange. But then, supposedly, Mother didn't like the way she looked when she was pregnant. Maybe she didn't like the way she looked soon afterwards either, which would explain why Hector was already two when that picture was taken. I didn't remember seeing her pregnant. I guessed four-year-olds didn't register that kind of thing. I scanned the faces. None of us looked particularly happy.

"It just happened. It wasn't something I could... *stop*."

"Rupert—"

I placed the photo back on the dresser and turned to face my little brother. "It was like this force. It drew me to her, and her to me. We both knew it was wrong, but the force was stronger than either of us. She's the one for me, Hector. Not Elspeth. Not any of the other girls on the island. I won't be happy if I'm not with Vivian."

Hector sighed heavily. "So, what are you going to do?"

"I'm going to talk to Father. Try to convince him to let me out of this stupid arrangement. I've done everything else he's wanted. I got good grades, I run the distillery, I agreed to this stupid tour. What more does he want? My fucking heart on a platter?"

Hector watched me, cagily, then a sudden flash of fear crossed his face.

"Rupert... Think carefully about this. What if he disowns you?"

I shook my head. "He won't."

"But that's always the threat, isn't it? If we don't marry within the island, we'll be disowned."

"They've never done it before. No one from the Consortium families have."

"That's because no one has ever tried."

"Look at Dax," I said. "He wasn't forced to marry someone from the Isle of Crow, was he?"

Hector's gaze softened. "Dax was different, and you know it. No one wanted to marry Dax. Any one of those women at the banquet would have given their right arm to marry you."

"Not everyone," I said, thinly.

"Okay, maybe not Adele, but the rest of them would have. What I'm saying is, you have the fucking world at your feet. A thriving business, a senior role in the premier family, the pick of all the women on this island. They are not going to let you simply sidestep this rule because you're crushing on the tour guide."

I saw red.

The next thing I knew, I was holding Hector by his throat, ramming his body against the same wall I'd thrown his crystal lowballs at. His face was turning a putrid red, his arms and legs flailing aimlessly. I grit my teeth and released him.

"She is not just a fucking *tour guide*," I snarled as he stood, his hands braced on his knees gasping for breath. "And this is anything but a crush."

After a few minutes, Hector straightened, walked back to the cabinet and downed another quarter bottle of whiskey while glaring at me over the top of the bottle.

"I'm not sorry I did that," I warned.

"I know. That's what scares me."

I dragged a hand through my hair. "What else can I do, Hector?"

He waited for me to stop pacing. "Go through with it."

I spun around to face him. Had he not heard anything I'd just said? Had he not felt my fingers digging into his throat as he wheezed through his disbelief that I was downright fucking serious about Vivian? "I'd rather walk away."

"From what?" His tone was even.

"Everything. This family, this island. The lot."

"You're not serious." A thread of panic wove through his voice as he walked around the wingback chairs towards me.

"You know what? I am. I don't need this shit. If this is all it takes for my own parents to disown me, maybe they're not worth sticking around for."

"Rupert, no." Hector placed a hand on my arm, drawing my determined eyes to his pleading ones. "You can't leave the family."

"Why?" I challenged him. *Say it, Hector.*

His eyes widened as if he needed them to say what his words couldn't. "We *need* you. You know we do."

"For what?" I pressed.

Hector breathed hard, the air squeezing and inflating his nostrils. A front for the debate taking place in his mind. The same debate we all had to contend with. Whether or not to say what we were really afraid of, out loud.

"To protect the Isle of Crow."

I narrowed my gaze on him. "From who?"

He ground his jaw, then a wave of relief passed over him as he uttered the word. "Ossian."

I placed my hands on Hector's shoulders, noticing him flinch at the proximity to his throat. "Tell me what you know."

He shook his head, sadly. "I know everything."

I pushed my hands through my hair then scrubbed them down my face. It wasn't just Aro then. Hector understood too.

"That's why you can't walk away, Rupert. Father won't be around forever, not that he's any less corrupt. But when he goes, Ossian will be the ultimate authority on this island. He will run this place. There'll be no stopping him." Hector took one more swig, finishing off the bottle. He placed it down gently and lifted his eyes to mine with a warning. "And he has to be stopped."

"What do you think I've been trying to do the past three years?" I sighed, exasperated.

"And it's helped," Hector replied. "Can you imagine how much further he'd have gone had you not intervened with the deliveries, messed with the schedules, intercepted conversations? You can't stop now."

"I can't do it alone."

Hector brightened instantly. "I'll help you. Ok? I'll do more. I've stayed out of it this long because I didn't want to make it obvious we were trying to mess up the business. But I'll do whatever you need, Rupert. Just stay. Please."

I looked into the face of my younger brother. I had never seen him plead with such raw intensity. It broke my heart to see him need something so badly. It broke my heart that he'd had to grow up in this toxic family too. He was right. I couldn't leave him and I couldn't leave the rest of the island to live with the effects of Ossian's corruption now and long after I'd gone. Because he wouldn't stop. That wasn't Ossian's style.

An unspoken agreement passed through the thick silence between us, only to be pierced by the ring of my phone. I held Hector's eyes, trying not to let Vivian's pass across my lids, then put the phone to my ear.

"Rupert, sir. It's Jasper."

The daytime security guard had been upgraded to the night shifts now McFadden had gone. So him calling me in the middle of night didn't bode well. "What's up?"

"We've got an intruder."

My expression must have changed in that split second because Hector straightened, his muscular arms stiffening. "Where?"

"The south set. Entered from the road."

I glanced out of the window. "That's two miles from the site."

"She ran, sir."

"She?" My eyes shot back to Hector. He nodded to me and made a hasty run for his bedroom to dress.

"Yes, sir. It's hard to see the footage clearly, but it's definitely a woman."

My heart thumped. "Is Ossian there?" He would kill her. No questions asked.

"Yes sir, but… I saw him walking to the labs. I don't believe he is near to any cameras."

Jasper knew what would happen if Ossian found an intruder. It struck me, that's why he was calling me first. So I could get to her before Ossian did.

"Where is she now?"

"She's…" He fell silent, the tension growing thicker with every passing second.

"Jasper?" I said softly.

"She's entering the Glade."

My heart stopped and it took me a second or two to remember where I was. "Keep Ossian occupied," I rasped. "I'll be there in ten minutes."

Chapter 35

*V*ivian

MY EYES WERE GLUED to the scene before me, trying to make sense of what I was seeing.

Behind me, footsteps – *his* footsteps – slowed until they stilled, and the only part of him I could hear was his chest heaving lungfuls of air in and out.

"What is this?" My whisper was almost drowned out by the sound of metal on metal as two giant trucks tipped their beds at an angle. Rupert didn't answer. My eyes dropped from the gleaming white vehicles to the ground. The nutrient-rich soil was exposed without the presence of little umbrella tops glowing brightly, even in the darkness. Below the trucks was an opening in the ground and I still couldn't compute what was about to happen.

When it did, it happened in slow motion. A flap door at the back of each truck dropped outwards and mounds upon mounds of rubble started tumbling out, disappearing into the soft, pregnant earth.

THE SOUND WAS SO DEAFENING I clasped both hands over my ears. I watched as more and more stuff came flooding out of the trucks. In the midst of it all, though it passed in the blink of an eye, I could have sworn I saw a leg. A human leg.

My breath caught in my throat as I began to run towards the edge. Rupert's hand leapt out to grab my arm but I somehow found the strength to yank myself free. I reached the edge of the land and heard voices shouting at me to stand back. And when I looked down, my heart, my chest, my soul thudded to the floor.

Bags of razor blades, syringes, bloody bandages and protective gloves stared back at me. Another load tumbled out of a second truck. Bags filled with what looked like meat plummeted into the ground. As the light of the trucks illuminated the crater I was able to make out actual body parts. Flaps of flesh, clusters of bones, bags of fat. The smell was foul. I gawped at the scene in disbelief until an acidic burn rose up my throat. I turned my back to the trucks and vomited.

"*Vivian...*"

More shouting came from the trucks as they tipped further and even more pieces of human came rushing out into the ground. I stood on shaky legs and turned slowly to face him. I almost choked on his expression. He was as white as a sheet, his indigo eyes wide and blackened against the glow of the toxic waste surrounding us. I cast my eyes to the hand he'd tried to pull me back with. It was shaking.

"It's not what it looks like," he said, his voice trembling.

"It's biomedical waste," I gritted out. "You're burying

body parts. Pieces of people. Dead people. Medical equipment. It's hazardous – *toxic* – waste. And you're burying it here." I shook my head in disbelief. "Why?"

Rupert's jaw ground hard in response and I followed his gaze to the fairy tale toadstools that shone from the fence I had scaled. I swallowed and met his eyes again. "This is how they're grown?"

He answered with the briefest of nods.

"Rotting flesh," I stated.

"All fungus grows on decaying matter," he said, as though that explained everything.

"But this stuff should be incinerated," I cried. "It's potentially infectious…" I stopped, memories from conversations I'd had rushing back to me like an avalanche. "The tuberculosis. This is where it came from…" My heart thundered against my ribcage. "The air that feels so different, so thick… This is why."

He stared at me, knowing I would work it all out whether he owned up to it or not.

"This is what you've been trying to stop? Trying to intercept?"

He strode up to me, stopping at arm's length, before reaching out a hand to touch my face. "Vivian…"

I knocked his hand away, not even feeling the impending bruise blossoming on my wrist. "How?" I hissed at him. "How did you even work out how these things could be grown?" I glanced towards the red tops which before had seemed beautiful, otherworldly, precious. Now, they were ugly, disgusting and downright dangerous.

"We discovered the red tops ten years ago. No one ever came to this part of the island. We started experimenting

with them, like kids do, hoping they were magic mushrooms. Then we discovered this weird ability to focus. A
confidence that wasn't in our character. It happened to all
of us. And the only thing we had in common was the red
tops. When Father and Pops got hold of this information,
they closed off this whole area to investigate. That's where
it all started." He pointed to the west, where the road
brought visitors up to the labs. "They were growing over
an old graveyard."

I panted from the exertion of holding myself together
as the revelation was rolled out before me. "And you
thought you could *expand* that graveyard, illegally, for
your own profit?"

Rupert tried to put his hands on my shoulders but I
shrugged them off with a growl.

"I know what it looks like. But, you have to believe
me, I've been working around the clock to find an alternative method of cultivation. And you know full well I've
been trying to slow the production. I don't want this,
Vivian. Please believe me."

My voice was so low it sounded menacing. "You
started selling Bas three years ago. Are you telling me that
with all the money and influence you people have, you
couldn't find a safe and ethical way to grow this stuff, in
three years?"

His lack of response gave me the answer I needed.

I yanked the hat off my head, flung it to the ground,
and screamed. Venom I didn't know I possessed rose to the
surface, seeking a way out. "*I trusted you!*"

His hands darted out again to grip my shoulders. "You
still can, Vivian. It's still me."

I shook my head, tears filling my eyes, until his face

started to blur. "You lied to me, Rupert. You *lied*. How could you?"

"I'm telling you the truth now. Please, Vivian. Listen to me. I'll tell you everything."

My voice came out low and menacing. "Isn't this everything? What else is there to know?"

"Please, Vivian…" He trailed off because there was nothing more he could say.

Devastation set into my bones. "You used me." I flung an arm uselessly around myself. "All of this. I played a part in it. I found a way to get people here when I could have run, I could left it all behind. But I stayed because people '*deserved to see it.*'"

I threw my arms up. "I was bringing them to a toxic fucking wasteland! But *you*…" I stepped up to him close, so he could feel the anger pouring out of my skin. "You were the real reason I stayed." I shook my head with the humiliation of being taken for a total and utter fool. "You tricked me. You lied to me. You covered all of this up. I thought we actually had something, Rupert, but you've dragged a knife through it all, by duping me into selling your lie. You had no right to do that to me."

I dragged my eyes back to his, the fresh pain of a broken heart pricking them like a needle. Seeing the face I still loved look as broken as I felt sent a rush of sorrow through me, from the crown of my head to the tips of my toes. The heaviness of it pulled me closer to the dead bodies beneath our feet, and I collapsed to the ground. "Oh *God*, Rupert," I choked. "What have you done?"

We remained there in silence, me on my knees, clawing at the polluted earth, him standing rigid, hands covering his face, long after the trucks had been emptied and driven away. The mouth of the hole gaped open, the steam of the sullied earth rising up into the atmosphere, the smell fouler than ever.

My breathing settled into a shallow stutter as my hand curled over my blistered heart. Then the whole of me tensed when Rupert pierced the darkness with a thunderous, high-pitched curse.

Almost immediately, other noises punched the heavy air. Voices. Male voices. Gates banging. Dogs barking. They were coming for us both.

I stood again, amazed my legs still worked. "What's it to be, Rupert?" I asked in a shaky voice. "Now is your chance. Are you going to come with me? Leave all this corruption behind? Like you promised? Or are you going to stay here and continue to commit this evil?"

I glared at him.

"This is it, Rupert. What are you going to do? Are you coming with me? Or are you staying?"

His jaw clenched, his eyes darting from me to the noises behind. Suddenly, the thought of him not coming with me ripped my heart in two. I ran the short distance to him and fisted his jacket. "Rupert, come with me."

His hands reached up into my hair and held it fast as he closed his mouth on mine. I melted into him despite my anger and the sound of angry voices getting closer and louder.

"You promised," I moaned into his mouth, the desperation tangible.

His tongue swept around my mouth, tasting me as if for the very last time. Then, he tugged my head backwards and speared me with dark eyes. "I love you, Vivian."

My heart leaped. He was coming.

"I will always love you."

What?

"But, I have to stay."

I staggered backwards and his hands dropped to his sides. The conviction in his voice told me begging would be pointless, and the footsteps of angry men were frighteningly close.

"No," I whispered.

He squeezed his eyes closed. "I'm sorry."

I didn't wait for him to open them again. I took one last look at the man I loved with all my heart despite everything I had just discovered.

Then, I ran.

To be continued…

ABOUT THE AUTHOR

January James lives in East Sussex with her husband, daughter, crazy sprockapoo, Ralph, and the occasional errant grass snake. Until recently, she inhabited the fast-paced, adrenalin-fuelled workplaces she writes about as a communications professional. Now she spends her days dreaming up new characters and stories and trying her best to avoid indoor soft play.

ALSO BY JANUARY JAMES

Thorn Trilogy

Jagged Thorns

Twisted Vines (Summer 2023)

Severed Roots (Summer 2023)

Scorched Rose: a prequel

(part of the Merciless Desires anthology)

The Imperfect Billionaires series

The Perfect Deceit

The Perfect Betrayal

The Perfect Pretence

Standalones

The Mogul and the Siren

Dirty Diana

Starling Key series

The Brain

The Brawn

The Banker

Made in the USA
Monee, IL
24 June 2023

37174439R00219